"Too li
We have lost   **y."**

He dipped his g

He wasn't quite ^   ted,
but close enough. The Starhawk was dropping now past
the twenty-kilometer mark. The sky above was still
space-dark, the brightest stars—Arcturus, especially—
still gleaming and brilliant, but the cloud decks below
rose thick and towering, their tops sculpted by high-
altitude winds and tinted red and gold by the rising sun.
He'd crossed enough of the planet's face that the local
sun was well above the horizon now, casting long, blue-
purple shadows and hazy shafts of golden light across
the distinctly three-dimensional surface of the cloudscape below.

Gray adjusted his ship's hull-form again, sculpting it
for high-speed aerial flight, absorbing the deep entry
keel and extending the wings farther and deeper into
their forward-canted configuration. Behind him, a
sudden burst of shooting stars marked another cloud of
sand or debris entering atmosphere, a barrage of silent
flick-flick-flicks of light.

He let his AI target on the Marine beacon, bringing
the SG-92's prow left across the horizon, then dipping
down into a plunging dive. He opened his com suite
to the Marine frequency and began sending out an approach vector clearance request.

He hadn't crossed seventy-one AUs and survived a
near-miss by a thermonuke to get shot down by the
damned jarheads.

By Ian Douglas

Star Carrier

EARTH STRIKE

And the Galactic Marines Series

The Inheritance Trilogy

STAR STRIKE
GALACTIC CORPS
SEMPER HUMAN

The Legacy Trilogy

STAR CORPS
BATTLESPACE
STAR MARINES

The Heritage Trilogy

SEMPER MARS
LUNA MARINE
EUROPA STRIKE

EARTH STRIKE

STAR CARRIER

BOOK ONE

IAN DOUGLAS

An Imprint of HarperCollinsPublishers

EOS
An Imprint of HarperCollins*Publishers*
10 East 53rd Street
New York, New York 10022-5299

Copyright © 2010 by William H. Keith, Jr.
Cover art by Gregory Bridges
ISBN 978-0-06-184025-8
www.eosbooks.com

First Eos paperback printing: March 2010

HarperCollins® and Eos® are registered trademarks of HarperCollins Publishers.

Printed in the U.S.A.

10 9 8 7 6 5 4 3 2 1

For Brea,
who has seen me through many, many light years

Author's Note

Readers of the Galactic Marines series may wonder at first why the background for *Earth Strike* seems so different from the universe of Heritage, Legacy, and Inheritance. Where are the Xul, the Builders, the Marine Corps families and traditions extending across two millennia?

There's a simple explanation. *Earth Strike* is the opening volley of a completely new military-SF series, Star Carrier, which explores the lives of Navy combat fighter pilots of the far future. Welcome aboard the Star Carrier *America* as she faces a new and deadly threat to Earth and all of humankind.

I hope you enjoy the cruise!

Ian Douglas
December 2009

Prologue

TC/USNA CVS America
Emergence, Eta Boötean Kuiper Belt
32 light years from Earth
0310 hours, TFT

The sky twisted open in a storm of tortured photons, and the Star Carrier America *dropped through into open space.*

She was . . . enormous, by far the largest mobile construct ever built by humankind, a titanic mushroom shape, the kilometer-long stem shadowed behind the immense, hemispherical cap that was both reaction mass and radiation shielding. Her twin counter-rotating hab rings turned slowly in the shadows. Swarms of probes and recon ships emerged from her launch tubes, minnows streaking out into wan sunlight from the bulk of a whale.

Around her, the other vessels of the *America* Battlegroup emerged from the enforced isolation of metaspace as well, some having bled down to sublight velocities minutes before, others appearing moment by moment as their emitted and reflected light reached *America*'s sensors. Some members of the battlegroup had scattered as far as five AUs from the star carrier in realspace, and would not again rejoin her communications net for as much as forty more minutes.

The ship's pitted and sandblasted forward shield caught the wan glow of a particularly brilliant star—the sun of this system nearly seventy-one astronomical units distant. The data now flooding *America*'s sensors were almost nine and a half hours old.

Within his electronic cocoon on the *America*'s Combat Information Center, the Battlegroup Commander linked in through the ship's neural net, watching the data scroll past his in-head display.

STAR: Eta Boötis

COORDINATES: RA: 13h 54m 41.09s Dec: +18° 23′ 52.5″ D 11.349p

ALTERNATE NAMES: Mufrid, Muphrid, Muphride, Saak, Boötis 8 (Flamsteed)

TYPE: G0 IV

MASS: 1.6 Sol; **RADIUS:** 2.7 Sol; **LUMINOSITY:** 9 Sol

SURFACE TEMPERATURE: ~6100°K

AGE: 2.7 billion years

APPARENT MAGNITUDE (SOL): 2.69; Absolute magnitude: 2.38

DISTANCE FROM SOL: 37 ly

BINARY COMPANION: White dwarf, mean orbit: 1.4 AU; period: 494 d

PLANETARY SYSTEM: 14 planets, including 9 Jovian and sub-Jovian bodies, 5 rocky/terrestrial planets, plus 35 dwarf planets and 183 known satellites, plus numerous planetoids and cometary bodies . . .

Rear Admiral Alexander Koenig was, in particular, interested in the planetary data for just one of the worlds circling that distant gold-hued star: Eta Boötis IV, known formally as Al Haris al Sama, informally as Haris, and more often and disparagingly within the fleet as "Ate a Boot."

"God," he said as he watched the planetary data unfold. "What a mess."

America's AI did not reply, having learned long ago that human statements of surprise or disgust generally did not require a reply.

Eta Boötis IV was not even remotely Earthlike in atmosphere or environment—greenhouse-hot with a deadly, poisonous atmosphere—a wet Venus, someone had called it. What the Arabs had seen in the place when they put down a research station there was anybody's guess.

As the *America*'s computer net built up models of the sensor data, it became clear that the enemy fleet was already there, as expected, orbiting the planet—or, rather, that they'd *been* there when the electromagnetic radiation and neutrinos emitted by them had begun the journey over nine hours ago. It was a good bet that they were there still, circling in on Gorman's Marines. *America*'s delicate sensors could detect the hiss and crack of EMP—the telltale fingerprints of nuclear detonations and particle beam fire—even across the gulf of more than seventy AUs.

"All stations, we have acquired Objective Mike-Red," the fleet commander said. "Launch ready-one fighters."

The *America* had a long reach indeed.

And now she was going to prove it.

Chapter One

VFA-44 Dragonfires
Eta Boötis System
0311 hours, TFT

Lieutenant Trevor Gray watched the numbers dwindle from ten to zero on his IHD, as the Starhawk's AI counted them off. He was in microgravity at the moment, deep within the carrier's hub core, but that would be changing very soon, now.

"Three . . ." the female voice announced, a murmur in his ear, "two . . . one . . . *launch.*"

Acceleration pressed him back into the yielding foam of his seat, a monster hand bearing down on chest and lungs until breathing deeply was nearly impossible. At seven gravities, vision dimmed. . .

. . . then flashed back as the crushing sensation of weight abruptly vanished. It took the Starhawk 2.39 seconds to traverse the two-hundred-meter cat-launch tube, and as it emerged into open space it was traveling at just over 167 meters per second relative to the drifting *America.*

"Blue Omega Seven, clear," he announced.

"Omega Eight, clear," another voice echoed immediately. Lieutenant Katie Tucker, his wing, was somewhere off his starboard side, launched side-by-side with him through the twin launch tubes.

He brought up an aft view in time to see the rapidly receding disk of the *America*'s shield cap dwindling away at over six hundred kilometers per hour. In seconds, the dull, silver-white shield had fallen astern to a bright dot . . . and then even that winked out, vanished among the stars. Icy and remote, those stars gleamed hard and unblinking across night; the other fighters of VFA-44, even the other capital ships of the Confederation fleet, all were lost in dark emptiness.

"Imaging, full view forward."

The view from his SG-92 Starhawk's cockpit was purely digital illusion, of course. At his command, the aft view projected across the curving inner surface of his cockpit vanished, replaced by different stars. One, directly ahead, gleamed with an intense golden brilliance—the local sun, though it was too distant to show a disk.

To port and low, another gold-red star shone almost as brilliantly—twice as bright as Venus at its brightest, seen from Earth. That, Gray knew from his briefings, was the star Arcturus, just three light years away.

Arcturus, however, was not his problem. Not anymore.

And not *yet*.

"Imaging," he said. "Squadron ships."

Green-glowing, diamond-shaped icons appeared on the stellar panorama, above, below, and to the left, each attended by a string of alphanumerics giving ship number and pilot id, and Gray felt just a little less lonely. Eight other Starhawks besides his drifted in the void out there, their AIs nudging them now into a ring ten kilometers across. As the minutes passed, three more strike-fighters moved up from astern, taking their places with the squadron.

The formation was complete.

"Okay, chicks," Commander Marissa Allyn said over the squadron comnet. She was VFA-44's CO, and Flight Leader for this op. "Configure for high-G."

Each of the Starhawks had emerged from the diamagnetic launch tubes in standard flight configuration, a night-black needle shape twenty meters long, with a central bulge housing the pilot and control systems, and the mirror-smooth outer hull in a superconducting state. At Gray's command, his gravfighter began reshaping itself, the complex nano-laminates of its outer structure dissolving and recombining, drive units and weapons and sensors folding up and out and back, everything building up around the central bulge in a blunt and smoothly convoluted egg-shape with a slender spike tail off the narrow end, and with the fat end aligned with the distant, golden gleam of Eta Boötis.

"Blue Omega Leader, Omega Seven," he reported. "Sperm mode engaged. Ready for boost." Gravfighter pilots claimed their craft looked like huge spermatozoa when they were in boost configuration. His Starhawk was now only seven meters long—not counting the field bleed spike astern—and five wide, though it still massed twenty-two tons.

"*America* CIC, this is Alpha Strike Blue Omega One," Allyn said. "Handing off from PriFly. All Blues clear of the ship and formed up. Ready to initiate PL boost."

"Copy, Blue Omega One," a voice replied from *America*'s Combat Information Center. "Primary Flight Control confirms handoff to *America* CIC. You are clear for high-grav boost."

"Acknowledge squadron clear for boost," Allyn said. "Don't forget about us out there, *America*."

"Don't worry, Blue Omega. We'll be on your asses all the way in."

That wasn't quite true, Gray thought. According to the operations plan, the task force would be following, but it would be another eighteen hours, total, before they reached the target planet.

The squadron would be on its own until then.

"Blue Omega Strike, Omega One," Allyn said over the squadron's tac channel. "Engage squadron taclink."

Gray focused a thought, and felt an answering sensation of pressure in the palm of his left hand. The twelve fighter craft were connected now by laser-optic comnet feeds linking their on-board AIs into a single electronic organism.

"And gravitic boost at fifty kay," Allyn continued, "in three . . . two . . . one . . . *punch* it!"

A gravitational singularity opened up immediately ahead of Gray's Starhawk.

He was falling.

In fact, he was accelerating now at fifty thousand gravities, falling toward the artificial singularity projected ahead of his gravfighter, but since the high-G field affected every atom of the Starhawk and of Lieutenant Gray uniformly, he was not reduced to a thin organic smear across the aft surfaces of the cockpit. In fact, he felt nothing whatsoever beyond the usual and somewhat pleasant falling sensation of zero gravity.

Outwardly, there was no indication that within the first ten seconds of engaging the gravitic drive, he was traveling at five hundred kilometers per second relative to the *America*, his speed increasing by half a million meters per second with each passing second. The stars remained steady and unmoving, unwinking in the night.

After one minute he'd be traveling at three thousand kilometers per second, or 1 percent of the speed of light.

And in ten minutes he'd be pushing hard against c itself.

In strike fighter combat, speed is *everything*.

CIC, TC/USNA CVS America
Eta Boötean Kuiper Belt
0312 hours, TFT

Admiral Alexander Koenig watched the slowly growing green sphere of local battlespace, now four light minutes across and still growing. Perhaps half of Battlegroup *America* was accounted for now. The others were out there, but scattered so far by the uncertainties of pinpoint navigation across interstellar distances that the information heralding their emergence from metaspace wouldn't arrive for some time yet.

The *America*'s Combat Information Center, located just aft of the bridge, was large, but had a tightly packed, almost cluttered feel. Located at the carrier's hub, it was designed to function in microgravity. CIC personnel were tucked into workstations that let them link electronically with the ship and with other stations. Curving bulkheads and the shallow dome of the overhead displayed seamless images of the sky surrounding the huge ship, relayed from CCD scanners on the rim of the shield cap forward. The local space display was on the stage at the center of the compartment, just below Koenig's station. By moving his hand within the glowing and insubstantial console projected in front of him, he could rotate the sphere and enlarge a portion of it, checking the ID alphanumerics.

Altogether, some twenty-seven ships made up the task force, including heavy cruisers and a battleship, four destroyers, half a dozen frigates, a small flotilla of supply and repair vessels, and a detachment of eight troop transports, all empty. Of all of those, only nine ships were linked in so far.

Ah! Good. The railgun cruiser *Kinkaid* was visible now, two light minutes abeam, at 184 degrees relative. They would need the *Kinky*'s massive kinetic-kill firepower if this op degenerated into a fleet action . . . and Koenig was certain that it would. And the destroyers *Kaufman* and *Puller* were on-line now as well. They would be vital if—no, *when*—the Turusch va Sh'daar spotted the battlegroup and deployed their heavy fighters to meet it.

That made eleven so far.

A gangly, long-legged shadow swam across the scattering of stars against the overhead dome, backlit by the gold gleam of Eta Boötis. John Quintanilla, the battlegroup's Political Liaison, floated upside-down, from Koenig's perspective, clinging to the back of the admiral's couch.

"Shouldn't we be accelerating or something?" the civilian asked.

"Not until the rest of the battlegroup forms up with us," Koenig replied.

"Your orders from the Senate Military Directorate," Quintanilla said, his voice low, "require you to reach Gorman's force in the shortest time possible. Time is critical! He can't hold out very much longer."

"I am very much aware of that, Mr. Quintanilla."

"Those fighters you launched aren't going to have much of a chance against a Turusch war fleet. Your orders—"

"My *orders*, Mr. Quintanilla," Koenig snapped, "include the requirement to keep my battlegroup intact . . . or as intact as combat allows." Koenig moved his hand, calling up an AI-generated image of the planet nine and a half light hours ahead, outlined in green lines of latitude and longitude. "We will not help General Gorman if we piss away the ships of this battlegroup a few at a time!"

"But—"

"*This* is what's waiting for us in there, Mr. Quintanilla," Koenig said, interrupting. The sphere at the center of the CIC display enlarged sharply, and a number of red pinpoints sprang into sharp relief against the green background. Each red dot was accompanied by alphanumerics showing mass, vector, and probable id.

"Fifty-five vessels that we've been able to detect so far," Koenig told him. "*So far*. There are, no doubt, others on the far side of the planet that we haven't picked up as yet. We will be *seriously* outnumbered in this engagement, sir, and I will not divide my fleet in the face of a superior enemy!"

Most of the enemy ships were in orbit around the planet, but a few were farther out, decelerating as they backed down in their approach vectors. The Turusch had definitely arrived in force.

"You know what is best, of course," Quintanilla said, his face stiff, expressionless. "At least from a *tactical* perspective. My job is simply to remind you of the . . . of the political ramifications of your decisions. General Gorman is an extremely important person in the Senate's estimation. They want him rescued and returned safely."

Koenig made a face. He detested politics, and he detested playing politics with brave men and women. "Ah. And Gorman's Marines?"

"Of course, the more Marines you can pick up, the better."

"I see. And the Mufrids?"

Quintanilla gave him a sharp look. "Certainly, any of the colonists for which you have transport berths can be brought out, especially any with information on Turusch capabilities. But I'll remind you that General Gorman's rescue is your prime consideration."

"I *know* my orders, Mr. Quintanilla," Koenig said, his voice cold. "Now . . . if you'll excuse me . . ."

He moved his hand in his workstation's control field, and the electronic image of Eta Boötis IV vanished again, replaced by the map sphere of space immediately surrounding *America* and her consorts. More ships were popping up on the display's expanding battlespace globe, including the *Ticonderoga* and *The Spirit of Confederation*, the first a heavy cruiser, the second the task force's single line-battleship, with heavy kinetic-kill railguns that could pulverize a planet.

Unfortunately, the Confederation task force could not pulverize the planet ahead, not without killing some five thousand Marines of the 1st Marine Expeditionary Force and the colonists they'd been deployed to protect.

Quintanilla floated above Koenig's workstation for a moment longer, then grunted, pushed himself off from the couch, and drifted toward the CIC entrance behind the command dais.

Located beneath Koenig's station was the section of the CIC known as "the orchestra pit" and, more usually, simply as "the pit." Twelve workstations nestled within the pit, where *America*'s CIC officers stood their watches. One of them, Commander Janis Olmstead, the primary weapons control officer, caught Koenig's eye and arched an eyebrow. "Since when did micromanagement become Navy SOP, sir?" she asked.

"Mind on your links, Weps," Captain Randolph Buchanan's electronic avatar said. He was *America*'s commanding officer, and Koenig's flag captain. Physically, he was on the bridge next door to CIC, but the compartment's electronics projected his image to the command dais next to Koenig's couch.

"Yes, sir. Sorry, sir."

"She's right, you know," Koenig told Buchanan, but he texted the words to Buchanan's screen, rather than speaking them aloud. He would not criticize Buchanan's running of his ship and crew, not publicly. "It's not going to be the Sh'daar that defeat us. Or their client races. It's going to be the damned Confed politics."

Out of the corner of his eye, he saw Buchanan's image scowl as the captain read the words on a screen.

"Agreed, Admiral." The words appeared silently on one of Koenig's screens a moment later. "I have to tell you, sir, I don't like this."

"No," Koenig typed back. "But we play by the rules we're given."

Buchanan seemed to hesitate, and then the avatar looked at Koenig. "How the hell do we fight a galactic empire, Admiral?" he asked aloud.

Damn. Buchanan should have kept the conversation private, exchanging text messagers. Glancing down into the pit, Koenig could see that Olmstead and the others were carefully watching their own link channels and displays, but they'd obviously heard. The conversation would spread throughout the *America* before the end of the next watch.

"I don't believe in 'galactic empires,'" Koenig said. He snorted. "The whole idea is silly, given the size of the galaxy."

"Well, the Sh'daar appear to believe in the concept, Admiral," Buchanan's image said. "And I doubt very much that it matters whether they agree with you on the point or not."

"When the Sh'daar show themselves," Koenig replied carefully, "*if* they show themselves, we'll worry about galactic empires. Right now, our concern is with the Turusch."

It had been ninety-two years since humankind had made contact with the Sh'daar, or, more precisely, since they'd made first contact with the Aglestch va Sh'daar, one of an unknown but very large number of technic alien species within what was somewhat melodramatically called the Sh'daar Galactic Empire. Quite early on, the Aglestch—some humans still referred to them as "Canopians," even though that brilliant, hot F0-class supergiant could not possibly be their home star—had explained that they served the "Galactic Masters," the Sh'daar.

Then, fifty-five years later, an Aglestch delegation had tentacle-delivered a message to Earth, inscribed in English, Spanish, Russian, and transliterated Lingua Galactica, purportedly from the Sh'daar themselves.

They claimed to be the overlords of a galaxy-spanning civilization. After five and a half decades of peaceful trade between the Confederation and the Agletstch Collective, the Sh'daar now stepped in and "suggested," with just a hint of velvet-shrouded-mail fist, that the human Confederation submit to them and take their rightful places as a star-faring species—under the hegemony of the Sh'daar Masters.

And until that happened, humans were forbidden to have any contact whatsoever with the Aglestch.

The problem was, in fifty-five years an active and spirited trade had sprung up between the Aglestch worlds and the nearest star systems colonized by humans. StarTek and Galactic Dynamics, the trading corporations involved, hadn't wanted to give up their lucrative contracts for Agletsch art and basic technical information. A Terran naval task group had been deployed to protect human trade routes in the region, and the Confederation Diplomatic Corps had made overtures to the Aglestch Collective about maintaining trade and diplomatic contact apart from Sh'daar oversight.

The result had been the disastrous Battle of Beta Pictoris, in 2468, the equivalent, in human eyes, of reaching out to shake hands and pulling back a bloody stump.

And for thirty-six years now, the war had continued . . . with a very few minor victories, and with a very great many major defeats. Humankind's principle foes so far had been the Turusch va Sh'daar, a different Sh'daar client species that first had made its appearance thirty years before, at the Battle of Rasalhague. The First Interstellar War, as the news agencies had termed it back home, was not going well.

The infant planetary system of Beta Pic had been just sixty-three light years from Sol, the furthest humans had yet ventured from their homeworld, a microscopic step when compared with the presumed extant of the galaxy-spanning Sh'daar: Rasalhague had been closer still—forty-seven light years.

And Eta Boötis was only thirty-seven light years from Sol. The enemy was closing in, relentless, remorseless.

In 2367, the Terran Confederation had incorporated 214 interstellar colonies and perhaps a thousand research and trade outposts on planets scattered across a volume of space roughly one hundred light years across and perhaps eighty deep, a volume embracing almost eight thousand star systems, the majority of which had never even been visited by humans. And after less than four decades of bitter fighting, Confederation territory had dwindled by perhaps a quarter.

Humans still knew almost nothing about the Sh'daar—so far as was known, no human had ever even seen one—but their brief contact with the Agletsch had suggested that the Sh'daar presence might well encompass several hundred billion stars. Whether you called it a galactic empire or something else, in terms of numbers and resources, it seemed to pose an insurmountable threat.

The sheer impossibility of the Confederation fighting such an overwhelmingly vast and far-flung galactic power had strongly affected human culture and government, deeply dividing both, and affecting the entire Confederation with a kind of social depression, a plummeting morale that was difficult to combat, difficult to shoulder.

And one symptom of plunging morale was the increasing micromanagement out of C^3—Confederation Central Command—on Earth. All military vessels now carried one or more Senate liaisons, like Quintanilla, to make certain the Senate's orders were properly carried out.

If anything, direct Senate oversight of the military had made the morale problem even worse.

And that was why Koenig was concerned about his flag captain speaking his pessimism in front of the bridge personnel.

"We'll know more when we rescue Gorman and his people," Koenig added after a thoughtful pause, stressing the word *when*, rejecting the word *if*. "The scuttlebutt is that his Marines captured some Tush officers. If so, that could give us our first real insight into the enemy psychology since this damned war began."

"Tush" or "Tushie" was military slang for the Turusch . . . one of the cleaner of a number of popular epithets. He saw Olmstead's head come up in surprise at hearing a flag officer use that kind of language.

"Yes, sir," Buchanan said.

"So we play it by the op plan," Koenig added, speaking with a confidence he didn't really feel but which he hoped sounded inspiring. "We go in, kick Trash ass, and pull our people and their prisoners out of there. Then we hightail for Earth and let the damned politicians know that the Galactics *can* be beaten."

He grinned at Buchanan's avatar. He suspected that the Captain had spoken aloud specifically to give Koenig a chance to say something inspiring. A cheap and theatrical trick, but he wasn't going to argue with the psychology. The crew was nervous—they *knew* what they were in for at Eta Boötis—and hearing their admiral's confidence, even an illusion of confidence, was critical.

On the battlespace display, five more ships appeared—the destroyer *Andreyev*, the frigates *Doyle*, *Milton*, and *Wyecoff*, and the troopship *Bristol*.

They would be ready to accelerate for the inner system soon.

VFA-44 Dragonfires
Eta Boötis System
0421 hours, TFT

Lieutenant Gray checked his time readouts, both of them. Time—the time as measured back on board *America*—was, as expected, flashing past at an insane pace, thirteen times faster, in fact, than it was passing for him.

In its high-G sperm-mode configuration, the SG-92 Starhawk's quantum-gravitic projectors focused an artificial curvature of spacetime just ahead of the ship's rounded prow—in effect creating a gravitational singularity that moved ahead of the fighter, pulling it forward at dizzying accelerations.

Accelerating at 50,000 gravities had boosted his Starhawk to near-light velocity in ten minutes. For the next hour, then, he'd been coasting at .997 *c* . . . except that the mathematics of time dilation reduced the time actually experienced on board the hurtling fighter to 0.077402 of that—or exactly four minutes, thirty-eight point six seconds.

Put another way, for every minute experienced by Trevor Gray in his tiny sealed universe of metal and plastic, almost thirteen minutes slipped past in the non-accelerated world outside. Since launching from the *America*, the Blue Omega fighter wing had traveled over a billion kilometers, nearly eight astronomical units, in what seemed like less than ten minutes.

Through the Starhawk's optics, the universe outside looked very strange indeed.

Directly ahead and astern and to either side, there was nothing, a black and aching absence of light. All of the stars of the sky appeared to have been compressed into a frosty ring of light forward by the gravfighter's near-*c* velocity. Even Eta Boötis itself, directly ahead, had been reshaped into a tight, bright circle.

And, despite the expectations of physicists from centuries ago, there was a starbow—a gentle shading of color, blue to deep violet at the leading edge of the starlight ring, and deep reds trailing. Theoretically, the starlight should all have appeared white, since visible light Doppler-shifted into invisibility would be replaced by formerly invisible wavelengths. In practice, though, the light of individual stars was smeared somewhat by the shifting wavelengths, creating the color effect known as the starbow.

Gray could have, had he wished, ordered the gravfighter's AI to display the sky corrected for his speed, but he preferred the soft rainbow hues. Most fighter pilots did.

When the fighter was under acceleration, the sky ahead looked even stranger. Gravitational lensing twisted the light of stars directly ahead into a solid, bright ring around the invisible pseudomass in front of the ship, even when the craft was still moving at nonrelativistic speeds. For now, though, the effect was purely an artifact of the Starhawk's speed—

an illusion similar to what happened when you flew a sky-flitter into a rainstorm, where the rain appeared to sleet back at an angle even when it was in fact falling vertically. In this case, it was photons appearing to sleet backward, creating the impression that the entire sky was crowded into that narrow, glowing ring ahead.

He checked the time again. Two minutes had passed for him, and almost half an hour for the rest of the universe.

He felt . . . lonely.

Technically, his fighter was still laser taclinked with the other eleven Starhawks of Blue Omega Flight, but communication between ships at near-c was difficult due to the severely Dopplered distortions in surrounding spacetime. The other fighters should be exactly matched in course and speed, but their images, too, were smeared into that light ring forward because their light, too, was traveling just three thousandths of a percent faster than Gray's ship. Some low-level bandwidth could be held open over the laser channels for AI coordination, but that was about it. No voice. No vid. No avatars.

Just encircling darkness, Night Absolute, and the Starbow ahead.

The hell of it was, Gray was a loner. With his history, he damned near had to be. By choice he didn't hang out much with the other pilots in the ready room or flight officers' lounge. When he did, there was the inevitable comment about his past, about where he'd come from . . . and then he would throw a punch and end up getting written up by Allyn, and maybe even getting pulled from the flight line.

Better by far to stay clear of the other pilots entirely, and avoid the hassle.

But now, when the laws of physics stepped in like God Almighty to tell him he *couldn't* communicate with the others, he found he missed them. The banter. The radio chatter.

The reassurance that there were, in fact, eleven human souls closer than eight astronomical units away.

He could, of course, have called the avatars of any or all of the others. Copies of their PAs—their Personal Assistants—resided within his fighter's AI memory. He could hold a conversation with any of them and be completely unaware that he was speaking to software, not a living person . . . and he would know that the software would report the conversation with perfect fidelity to the person when the comnet channels opened later on.

But avatars weren't the same. For some it was, but not for Trevor Gray.

Not for a Prim.

He closed his eyes, remembering the last time. He'd been in the lounge of the Worldview, a civilian bar adjacent to the spaceport at the SupraQuito space elevator. He and Rissa Schiff had been sitting in the view blister, just talking, with Earth an unimaginably beautiful and perfect sphere of ocean-blue and mottled cloud-white gleaming against the night. The two had been in civilian clothing, which, as it turned out, had been lucky for him. Lieutenants Jen Collins and Howie Spaas had walked up, loud and uninvited, also in civvies, and both blasted on recs.

"Geez, Schiffie," Collins had said, her voice a nasal sneer. "You hang around with a Prim loser like *this* perv, you're gonna get a bad name." Spaas had snickered.

Gray had stood, his fists clenched, but he'd kept a lid on it. Allyn had lectured him about that the last time he'd gotten into trouble with other squadron officers . . . the need to let the insults slide off. The shipboard therapist she'd sent him to had said the same thing. Other people could hurt him, could get through his shields only if he *let* them.

"Who asked you, bitch?" Gray had said quietly.

"Ooh, I'm afraid," Spaas said, grinning. "Hey, Riss . . . you need to be careful around creeps like this. A fucking Prim monogie. You're *never* gonna get any . . ."

It had been worth it, decking Spaas. It really had. It had been worth having the Shore Patrol show up, worth the off-duty restriction to quarters for a week, worth the extra watches, even worth the searing new asshole the skipper had given him. Commander Allyn could have put him up for court martial, but she'd chosen to give him a good old-fashioned ass-chewing instead.

He still remembered that next morning in her office. "The

Navy appreciates pilots who want to fight, Gray," she'd told him. "But the idea is to fight the Turusch, not your shipmates. You hear me? You have *one more chance*. Blow it and you get busted back to the real Navy."

Prim monogie.

Yeah, it had been worth it.

Chapter Two

CIC, TC/USNA CVS America
Eta Boötean Kuiper Belt
0428 hours, TFT

Admiral Koenig took a final look at the heavens revealed through the encircling viewalls of *America*'s CIC. Eta Boötis gleamed in amber splendor directly ahead. Off to port, red-golden Arcturus shone as well—not as brilliantly as Eta Boötis, but still with twice the brightness of Venus as seen from Earth at its closest.

Someday, we'll make it back there, Koenig thought, gazing for a moment at Arcturus, just three light years distant. He still felt the bitterness of that last, desperate fight at Arcturus Station last year.

That was for later. Right now, it was Mufrid that required his full attention.

Two of the naval transports never had checked in . . . which might mean they'd suffered malfunction or disaster en route from Sol, or, more likely, that they'd emerged from Alcubierre Drive more than 1.3 light hours from the *America*.

It *would* be the transports, he thought—the entire reason for coming to Eta Boötis in the first place. Still, if they'd made it this far, they would follow the task force in. Gray couldn't hold up the mission any longer waiting for them.

Over the course of the past eighty minutes, the task force

had been pulling slowly together, until most occupied a rough sphere half a million kilometers across. All were now electronically connected through the laser-link tacnet, though the most distant vessels would lag fifteen minutes behind in receiving any message from the flagship.

"Captain Buchanan," Koenig said, "you may inform the ship that we are about to get under way."

"Aye, aye, Admiral," Buchanan's voice replied immediately.

It was a formality. All hands had been at maneuvering stations since their arrival in-system. The announcement went out silently, spoken through each person's in-head e-links. "Now hear this, now hear this. All hands, prepare for immediate acceleration under Alcubierre Drive."

"Make to all vessels on the net," Koenig told the ship's AI. "Engage Alcubierre Drive, acceleration five hundred gravities, on my mark . . . and three . . . two . . . one . . . *mark!*"

That *mark* was variable, depending on how long it took for the lasercom command to crawl across emptiness from the *America*. The massive carrier began moving forward first, accompanied by the heavy cruiser *Pauli* and the frigates *Psyché* and *Chengdu*, close abeam. One by one the other vessels began falling into train, the sphere slowly elongating into an egg shape as more and more vessels got the word and engaged their drives.

The principles of the Alcubierre Drive had been laid down by a Mexican physicist in the last years of the twentieth century. It was old tech compared to the artificial singularities employed by modern gravfighters, but it used the same principles. Essentially, drive projectors compressed spacetime ahead of each vessel, and expanded spacetime astern, creating a bubble in the fabric of space that could move forward at any velocity, ignoring the usual constraints imposed by the speed of light because everything within the bubble, imbedded in that patch of spacetime, was motionless compared to the space around it.

Practical considerations—both size and mass—limited Alcubierre acceleration to five hundred gravities. At that rate, *America* would be pushing the speed of light after sixteen hours, thirty-seven minutes.

However, after that length of time they would have traveled almost sixty astronomical units, which meant they wouldn't have time to decelerate in to the target.

Instead, they would accelerate constantly for just over nine hours, at which point they'd be moving at .54 *c*, then reverse their drives and decelerate for the same period.

They would arrive in the vicinity of Eta Boötis IV ten hours after fighter wing Blue Alpha had engaged the enemy.

And until that time, Blue Omega Strike Force would be fighting the enemy alone.

VFA-44 Dragonfires
Eta Boötis System
1015 hours, TFT

For Trevor Gray, half an hour passed. In the universe outside, six and a half hours slipped away, and with them another 7 billion kilometers, or forty-six more astronomical units.

He was just over three quarters of the way to the target.

He wondered how the other eleven pilots of the squadron were doing . . . but shrugged off the question. His AI would alert him if the tenuous data link with another fighter snapped. That hadn't happened yet, so the chances were good that the others all were out there, as bored and, paradoxically, as nervous as he was.

In another eleven subjective minutes, he would begin the deceleration phase of the strike, but that would be handled by his AI. Coordination of the timing within the flight of twelve gravfighters had to be exact, or they would drop down to combat speed scattered all over the sky, rather than in attack formation.

He spent the time studying the world now just two and a half light hours ahead.

His AI had last updated his target data from *America*'s CIC just before the squadron had boosted, which meant that his information about the enemy's strength and dispositions around Eta Boötis were now a full seventeen hours out of date. That was the tricky aspect to near-c deployment; once you boosted to relativistic speeds, you couldn't be exactly sure of what you were getting into until you were nearly there.

His Starhawk's forward sensors, at this speed, were all but useless. Radiation from ships around Eta Boötis IV was strongly distorted both by relativistic effects and by the "dustcatcher," a high-gravity zone maintained ahead of the fighter at near-c even when the ship wasn't accelerating, to trap or deflect dust and gas in the grav-fighter's path. Any information that made it to the fighter's sensors was lost in the light-smeared ring representing the star dead ahead.

According to the most recent electronic intelligence, though, there were fifty-five ships there—almost certainly all Turusch—orbiting Eta Boötis IV or on final approach. And there *was* a way to slightly improve the view.

He moved his hands within the control field. On the mirrored black surface of his Starhawk, three sensor masts detached from the hull and swung out and forward, each two meters long at the start, but unfolding, stretching, and growing to reach a full ten meters from the ship. The receivers at the ends of the masts, spaced equidistant around the fighter, extended far enough out to let them look past the nebulous haze of the dustcatcher. As Gray watched, the inner circle of light on the cockpit display grew sharper and brighter. Incoming radiation was still being distorted by the Starhawk's velocity, of course, but now he could see past the distortion of the singularity, and even take advantage of the dustcatcher's gravitational lensing effect.

Bright flashes silently popped and flared across the display now, however. Extended, the sensor masts were striking random bits of debris—hydrogen atoms, mostly, adrift in the not-quite-perfect vacuum of space and made deadly by the gravfighter's speed. Impact at this speed with something as massive as a meteoric grain of sand could destroy the mast; his AI had to work quickly.

The data came up less than five seconds later, and with a feeling of relief Gray retracted the sensor masts back into the hull, safe behind the blurring distortion of the dustcatcher. The fighter's artificial intelligence had sampled the incoming radiation, sorting through high-energy photons to build a coherent picture of what lay ahead.

Resolution was poor. Only a few ship-sized targets—the most massive—could be separated from the distortion-induced static. The AI did its best to match up the handful of targets it could see now with those that had been visible to *America*'s sensors hours earlier. By combining the *America* data with this fresh, if limited, glimpse, the AI could make a close guess at the orbits of a few of the enemy vessels, and predict where they would be—assuming no changes in orbit—in another 136-plus minutes, objective.

Fifteen targets. Gray had hoped there would be more, but it was something with which to work. Fifteen large starships appeared to be in stable, predictable orbits around the target world, their orbital data precise enough to allow a clear c-shot at them. Of those fifteen, six, the data predicted, would be on the far side of the target planet 136 objective minutes from now, so they were off the targeting list. The remaining nine, however, were fair game.

The actual targeting and munitions launch were handled automatically by the AI-net, requiring only Gray's confirmation for launch. So long as there was no override from Commander Allyn, all eleven Starhawks would be contributing to the PcB, the Pre-engagement c Bombardment.

Release would be at a precisely calculated instant just before deceleration. He checked the time readouts again. Five minutes, twelve seconds subjective to go.

He worked for a time trying to get a clearer look at the objective. The visual image was blurred, grainy, and heavily pixilated, but he could make out the planet, Eta Boötis IV, sectioned off by green lines of longitude and latitude, the shapes of continents roughed in. Fifteen red blips hung in space about the globe, most so close they appeared to be just skimming the globe's surface, and he could see their motions, second to second, as the AI updated their locations.

A white blip on the surface marked the objective—General Gorman's slender beachhead. It was on the side of the planet facing Gray at the moment, the planet's night side, away from the local sun, but in another two hours objective, it would be right on the planet's limb—local dawn.

Additional red blips flicked on, a cloud of them, indistinct and uncertain, centered around and over Gorman's position. Those marked enemy targets for which there was no orbital data and that most likely were actively attacking the Marine perimeter. Or rather, they *had* been 136 minutes ago, when the photons revealing their positions had left Eta Boötis IV. For all Gray knew, the perimeter had collapsed hours ago, and the squadron was about to make a useless demonstration at best, fly into a trap at worst. He shoved the thought aside. They were committed, had *been* committed since boosting clear of the *America*. They would know the worst in another few subjective minutes.

He opened his fighter's library, calling up the ephemeris for Eta Boötis and its planets. He scrolled quickly through the star data, then slowed when he reached the entry for the fourth planet.

PLANET: Eta Boötis IV

NAME: Al Haris al Sama, (Arabic) "Guardian of Heaven"; Haris; Mufrid.

TYPE: Terrestrial/rocky; sulfur/reducing

MEAN ORBITAL RADIUS: 2.95 AU; Orbital period: 4y 2d 1h

INCLINATION: 85.3 ; **ROTATIONAL PERIOD:** 14h 34m 22s

MASS: 1.8 Earth; **EQUATORIAL DIAMETER:** 24,236 km = 1.9 Earth

MEAN PLANETARY DENSITY: 5.372 g/cc = .973 Earth

SURFACE GRAVITY: 1.85 G

SURFACE TEMPERATURE RANGE: ~30°C – 60°C.

SURFACE ATMOSPHERIC PRESSURE: ~1300 mmHg

PERCENTAGE COMPOSITION: CO_2 30.74; SO_2 16.02; SO_3 14.11; NH_4 13.63; OCS 12.19; N_2 5.55; O_2 3.85; CH3 2.7; Ar 0.2; CS_2 variable; others <800 ppm

AGE: 2.7 billion years

BIOLOGY: C, N, H, S_8, O, Se, H_2O, CS_2, OCN; SESSILE PHOTO-LITHOAUTOTROPHS IN REDUCING ATMOSPHERE SYMBIOTIC WITH VARIOUS MOBILE CHEMOORGANOHETEROTROPHS AND CHEMOSYNTHETIC LITHOVORES . . .

Gray broke off reading at that point, shaking his head. The squadron had been briefed on the native life forms on Haris, but he'd bleeped past the recorded lectures. He wouldn't be *on* the planet long enough to worry about any native life forms.

Hell, from what he *had* picked up at the briefing, it was mildly bizarre that there was any life on the rock at all. One point seven billion years ago, the stellar companion of Eta Boötis had burned up its hydrogen fuel stores and entered a red giant phase before collapsing to its current white dwarf state. Planet IV had probably formed farther out than its current orbit within the star's habitable zone, but migrated in closer as friction with the outer layers of the red giant's atmosphere both baked it dry and slowed it down. The current ecosystem could not have even begun evolving until about a billion years ago . . . an impossibly short time by cosmological standards.

Whatever was growing on Haris's surface wasn't going to be very bright. In fact, the chances that it would find humans tasty, or even interesting, were vanishingly remote.

Gray shrugged the news off. He was a fighter pilot, not a ground-pounding grunt. His only view of Harisian biology would be from space, which was perfect, so far as he was concerned.

The subjective minutes ground slowly along, as objective minutes and kilometers streamed past at a breakneck gallop.

"Deceleration in one minute, subjective," the AI's voice announced in Gray's head. "Confirm A-7 strike package release command at deceleration." It was a woman's voice, sultry, attention-commanding.

"Strike package release order confirmed," Gray replied.

Another minute crawled past. Then, "Deceleration with strike package release in five . . . four . . . three . . . two . . . one . . . release. Commence deceleration."

At the precisely calculated release point, a portion of the Starhawk's outer hull turned liquid, flowed open, and exposed a teardrop-shaped missile nestled within. The fighter's AI fired the missile, then triggered the spacetime-twisting immensity of the drive singularity, this time astern, off the Starhawk's spiked tail. At fifty thousand gravities, the Starhawk began slowing; the strike package pod kept accelerating and, from the gravfighter's perspective, flashed forward at five hundred kilometers per second squared, the dustcatcher winking out just long enough for the teardrop to flash past unimpeded, before switching on once more.

Ten seconds later, the gravfighter's velocity had slowed by five thousand kilometers per second. After a minute, he was down to .87 of the speed of light, and his velocity continued to decrease.

Six hundred thousand kilometers ahead, the strike package, still accelerating and moving at better than .997 c, began to deploy.

At this point on the timeline, the Turusch at the planet half an AU up ahead would still be unaware that the Confederation task force had even arrived.

They were in for one hell of a surprise.

Tactician Emphatic Blossom at Dawn
Enforcer Radiant Severing
1241 hours, TFT

Emphatic Blossom at Dawn had been named for a species of hydrogen floater on the homeworld that stunned its prey with an electric charge fired through trailing, gelatinous tentacles . . . emphatic indeed. It was a tactician, and a gurgled suffix on the Turusch sound-pulse translated as "tactician" carried the added meaning of a *deep* tactician . . . very roughly the equivalent of a general or an admiral in the enemy's fleet.

The phrase Emphatic Blossom at Dawn also implied stealth, relentless determination, and a sudden strike at the end, all qualities of mind that had contributed to its being designated a deep tactician.

There was little stealth involved in this operation, however. The enemy was hemmed in on the planet's surface, huddled beneath its enclosing force-bubble as Turusch particle beams and thermonuclear warheads flared and thundered. For nearly thirty *g'nyuu'm* now, the Turusch fleet had been hammering that shield, and it was showing signs of imminent failure.

Victory was simply a matter of time.

"Tactician!" a communicator throbbed from a console-shelf overhead. "Enemy ships, range twelve thousand *lurm'm!*"

The news chilled . . . and excited. Emphatic Blossom had hoped the enemy would deploy its fleet. At that range, it would have taken light nearly five *g'nyuu'm* to reach the fleet's sensors. And *that* meant—

"All vessels!" the Tactician pulsed. "Disengage from the enemy! Power deep! Ships in orbit, change vector *now!*"

Everything depended now on the Turusch hunterforce having the time to change course and speed. The enemy force would have launched their fighters within moments of dropping out of superluminal drive, which meant that those fighters, and any kinetic-kill devices they'd released along the way, would be *just* behind the light-speed wavefront bearing the news of the enemy's arrival.

How fast were the approaching kinetic devices traveling, how close on the heels of light? How far behind them were the enemy fighters? That depended on the enemy's technology—how fast they could accelerate—as well as on how quickly Turusch scanners had detected the enemy fleet in the first place. Five light-*g'nyuu'm* were a *great* depth. Many, many *g'nya* might have passed before Turusch scanners—or even the automated systems they controlled—had noticed the enemy's arrival. How long had they been out there?

Blossom felt the kick of acceleration as the Turusch command hunter *Extirpating Enigma* increased speed, breaking free of synchronous orbit, and with it an answering surge of relief. If the enemy had targeted the *Extirpating Enigma* several *g'nyurm* ago, while still en route, their missiles would miss the command ship now.

Unfortunately, Emphatic Blossom's warning would take time to reach the other ships. Some of them might detect the threat in time and act independently, but independence of action, independence of *thought* were decidedly *not* imperatives in Turusch tactical planning.

But it was vital that the command ship survive any opening kinetic barrage by the enemy. By boosting clear of a predictable orbit, they had—

"Enemy kinetic-kill missile has just passed our tail!" the scanner throbbed. *"Speed—"*

And then the *Languid Depths of Time* exploded in a white-hot glare of vaporizing metal.

In another instant, three other Turusch hunterships exploded, and two dazzlingly brilliant stars appeared against the surface of the planet, expanded, *blossoming.* The claw-transport *Victorious Dream of Harmony* staggered as a portion of its tail vanished in a flare of silent light, the shock setting the massive vessel into an uncontrolled tumble.

Lasered messages began flashing back to the flagship, speaking of projectiles passing through the fleet at speeds just a *mr'uum* less than that of light itself.

The hunters had just become the prey.

VFA-44 Dragonfires
Eta Boötis System
1245 hours, TFT

Gray's Starhawk was still slowing swiftly, still traveling at nearly eighteen thousand kilometers per second—a mere 0.06 *c*, a snail's pace compared to typical high-G transit speeds.

In principle, speed in combat was as important as it had ever been in the long-gone era of aerofighters and atmospheric dogfights in the skies above Earth. However, if your closing velocity was *too* high relative to your opponent, there simply wasn't time to react, even with electronic senses and AI reaction times. The target was there and gone before you could do a thing about it.

The universe had minutes earlier slipped back into its more usual, low-velocity appearance. Eta Boötis, the star, glared dead ahead, smaller than Sol seen from Earth, but a hair brighter. Other stars gleamed in constellations distorted to Earth-born eyes; Arcturus was a golden beacon high and to the left relative to Gray's current attitude.

Haris, the target planet, was a tiny crescent close by the star, 1.8 million kilometers distant, growing larger moment by moment.

At Gray's command, the Starfighter began rearranging itself once again, adopting standard combat configuration—a blade-lean crescent, slender black wings drooping to either side of the thicker central body, the crescent tips stretched forward as if to embrace the enemy. Sleek streamlining wasn't as necessary at these velocities as it was when plowing through near-vacuum at near-c, but there was always the possibility in these sorts of engagements that a fight would drop into planetary atmosphere, and then streamlining was very necessary indeed.

Minutes earlier, as he dropped past .5 c, Gray had released the dustcatcher, sending a microscopic speck of collected dust and hydrogen atoms compressed into a neutron microbody hurtling ahead at half the sped of light. If it, by sheer, random chance, hit an enemy spacecraft as it zipped through the system, so much the better, but there was no way to aim it. Like the vaporized whiffs of any A7 strike packages that had missed their targets, the dust balls released by the infalling fighters would remain interstellar navigation hazards for eons to come.

Data flooded across Gray's navigational and combat displays. As he glanced this across the screen, his in-head display opened windows, showing magnified views.

Expanding spheres of star-hot gas marked the funereal pyres of four Turusch ships, while a fifth tumbled end for end through space, spilling a haze of vaporized armor, internal atmosphere, and sparkling debris in its wake. Patches of bright-glowing turbulence on the planet's night side showed where two A7s had missed orbital targets and struck the planet instead.

So . . . five hits total. Not bad, considering the Kentucky windage involved from sixth tenths of an AU out. That left fifty enemy vessels to deal with . . . correction, fifty-*three*. Three others must have either been masked by the planet when *America* had first scanned the inner system, or had arrived in the objective hours since.

Enemy warships were scattering from the vicinity of the planet, a swarm of nest-kicked hornets. Turusch vessels were characteristically large, bulky, and clumsy-looking, the space-going equivalents of fortresses painted in bold swaths of either green and black or a starker red and black. Even their fighters, painted in green-and-black stripes, had the look of lumpy potatoes, each four to five times the mass of a Confederation Starhawk.

Despite appearances, they were fast and they were deadly. Gray caught one huge capital ship with his eyes and held it as he triggered a weapons lock. The Starhawk's offensive warload consisted of thirty-two VG-10 Krait smart missiles, a StellarDyne Blue Lightning PBP-2 particle beam projector, and, for very close work, a Gatling RFK-90 KK cannon. At long range, smart missiles were always the weapon of choice.

A tone sounded in his ear, indicating that a VG had acquired lock.

"Omega Seven!" he called over the tacnet. "Target lock! Fox One!"

The missile streaked from beneath the embrace of Gray's wings, the heat dump from its miniature gravitic drive gleaming like a tiny sun as it streaked through space.

The other Starhawks were all there, still in the circle formation they'd adopted out in the system's Kuiper Belt. The circle was opening now as the fighters applied lateral thrust and spread themselves apart. Other pilots were calling *Fox One* now, the code-phrase that meant they were firing smart missiles. More missiles flashed into the gulf ahead, tracking and dogging enemy warships, each accelerating at close to one thousand gravities.

His missile and two others were closing with the big green-and-black enemy warship—a Tango-class destroyer, under the standard Confederation nomenclature for enemy ships. The enemy was dumping sand—blasting clouds of tiny, refractive particles into space both to defeat laser targeting systems and to serve as a physical barrier against incoming kinetic-kill or high-velocity warheads.

One missile hit the expanding sand cloud and exploded, a ten-kiloton blast that pulsed in the darkness, but the other two missiles plunged through the hole vaporized in the Turusch ship's defensive barrier, striking its magnetic shielding and detonating like a close pair of bright, savage novae.

Enemy shield technology was a bit better than the Confederation could manage yet. Neither nuke penetrated the envelope of twisted spacetime sheathing the destroyer, but enough of the double blast leaked through to crumple a portion of the warship's aft hull. Atmosphere spilled into space as the ship slewed to one side, staggered by the hit.

Gray was already tracking another Turusch warship, however, a more distant one, a Juliet-class cruiser accelerating hard toward the planet.

"Omega Seven!" he called. "Target lock! Fox One . . . and Fox One!" Two Kraits streaked into darkness.

"Incoming, everyone," Allyn warned. "Jink and pull gee!"

The half of the sky in the direction of planet and sun was filled now with red blips, the icons marking incoming enemy missiles. Turusch anti-ship missile technology was better than human systems, and their warshots packed bigger warheads.

This, Gray thought, is where things get interesting.

Chapter Three

VFA-44 Dragonfires
Eta Boötis System
1251 hours, TFT

Throughout his gravfighter training back at SupraQuito, they'd hammered away at one essential lesson of space-fighter tactics: *always*, when an incoming warhead reached your position, be someplace else.

Gray had been in combat twice before, at Arcturus Station against the Turusch and at Everdawn against the Chinese, and knew the truth of that statement. There was no effective way to jam incoming warheads. The missiles used by both sides were piloted by brilliant if somewhat narrow-minded AIs, using a variety of sensor systems to track and home on an enemy target. No one set of standard countermeasures could blind *all* of an enemy's sensors—heat, radar, mass, gravitometric, X-ray, neutrino, optical.

Nor was it possible to outrun them. Turusch anti-fighter missiles could accelerate faster than a Starhawk, at least for short bursts. They operated on the tactical assumption that if they couldn't kill you outright, they could chase you out of town, forcing you into a straight-run boost out of battlespace to where you no longer posed a threat.

So when enemy missiles were hunting you down, the ancient aphorism about a best defense was decidedly true. You dodged, you weaved, you accelerated . . . but you also struck back.

A swarm of missiles approached from ahead, brilliant red pinpoints projected by the Starhawk's display system against the stars. Gray's AI picked out no fewer than six enemy missiles that, judging by their vectors, were homing in on him.

"Here comes the reception committee," Allyn announced. "Independent maneuvering."

"Copy that, Blue Omega Leader."

He accelerated toward the oncoming missiles, hard, then threw his Starhawk into a low-port turn, as tight as he could manage at this velocity.

Vector changes in space-fighter combat were a lot trickier than for an atmospheric fighter; they were possible at all only because gravitic propulsive systems allowed the fighter to project a deep singularity above, below, or to one side or the other relative to the craft's current attitude. Intense, projected gravity wells whipped the fighter around onto a new vector, bleeding off velocity to throw an extra burst of power to the inertial dampers that, theoretically at least, kept the pilot from being squashed by centripetal acceleration.

Enough gravities seeped through the straining damper field to press Gray back against the yielding nanofoam of his seat; stars blurred past his head.

"Six missiles still locked on and tracking," the AI voice of his Starhawk told him with emotionless persistence. "Time to detonation nine seconds . . . eight . . . seven . . ."

At "three" Gray grav-jinked left, firing passive sand canisters. The enemy missiles were now a few thousand kilometers off his starboard side, using their own gravitics to attempt to match his turn. He kept pushing, kept turning into the oncoming warheads.

Blinding light blossomed from astern and to starboard . . . then again . . . and yet again as three missiles struck sand clouds and detonated. Three down, three to go. He punched up the Starhawk's acceleration to 3,000 gravities, turning again to race toward the planet.

As always happened for Gray in combat, a rushing sense

of speed, of acceleration washed through him, matching, it seemed the acceleration of his fighter.

He might not be able to outrun Trash missiles in a flat-out race, but in most combat situations, outrunning them wasn't necessary. Most missiles held their acceleration down to a tiny fraction of their full capability. If they didn't, they wouldn't be able to match a low-G turn by their target, and they would wildly overshoot. So the remaining missiles on Gray's tail were putting on *just* enough speed to slowly catch up with him.

"Two new missiles now locked on and tracking. Terminal intercept in twenty-four seconds."

And that was the other half of the equation. Standard Turusch tactics were to fire whole swarms of missiles, sending them at him from all directions, until no maneuver he made could possibly jink past them all.

"Three missiles of original salvo still closing. Terminal intercept in eight seconds."

Gray moved his hand through the control field and the Starhawk flipped end-for-end, bringing his particle accelerator to bear. The three closest missiles appeared as a triangle of red blips, the alphanumerics next to each flickering as range and time-to-impact swiftly dwindled.

His eyes held one, and a red square appeared around the blip at the triangle's apex, signifying target lock. He moved his hand and a stream of neutrons turned the missile into an expanding cloud of plasma. He shifted his attention to a second blip, and watched it explode as well.

The third had vanished.

"Ship!" he said. "Confirm destruction of all three missiles!"

"Two anti-fighter missiles confirmed destroyed," the AI's voice said. "Negative confirmation on third missile. Two missiles of second salvo still locked on and closing. Terminal intercept in sixteen seconds. Third salvo fired, locked on and tracking. Terminal intercept in thirty-seven seconds. . . ."

That was the way it worked in modern space-fighter combat . . . with more missiles fired, and more, and *more*.

Worse, from his mission's perspective, the more time he spent trying to dodge incoming missiles, the less able he would be to carry out his primary objective, which was to close with Turusch capital ships and destroy them.

He pulled the Starhawk around until it was again traveling straight for the planet ahead.

"This is Blue Omega Seven," he called. "Request clearance for PCO launch on this vector."

"Omagea Seven, Omega One," Allyn's voice came back. "You are clear for AMSO."

"Firing PCO in three . . . two . . . one . . . *Fox Two*!"

In space-fighter combat, *Fox One* signaled the launch of any of a variety of all-aspect homing missiles, including the Krait. *Fox Two*, on the other hand, signaled a sandcaster launch—Anti-Missile Shield Ordnance, or AMSO. An AS-78 missile streaked from beneath his cockpit, accelerating at two thousand gravities. After five seconds, it was traveling one hundred kilometers per second faster than Gray's Starhawk and, when it detonated, the individual grains of sand—actually sand-grain-sized spherules of matter-compressed lead—were released in an expanding cloud of grains, each traveling with the same velocity and in the same general direction. Sandcaster missiles were dumb weapons as opposed to smart; protocol required requesting clearance for launch, because a grain of sand striking a friendly fighter at several thousand kilometers per second could ruin the day for *two* pilots, him and his unintended target.

Over the tacnet, he could hear other Omega pilots calling *Fox Two* as they slammed sand at the oncoming missiles.

In a few more seconds, the sand cloud had dispersed to the point where it created a physical shield several kilometers across. His initial velocity after his turn-and-burn with the enemy ship-killers had been just over twelve thousand kilometers per second; he increased his speed now by an extra hundred kps, slipping up close and tucking in behind his sand wall and drifting at the same speed.

White light blossomed ahead and to starboard, dazzling even through the stepped-down optical filters of his fighter's sensors.

A second nuclear blast, ahead and below . . . this one close enough that the shell of expanding plasma jolted his ship and sent hard radiation sleeting across the Starhawk's electromagnetic shielding.

Gray decelerated, braking hard. Eta Boötis IV was rapidly swelling to an immense crescent just ahead, as thousands of brilliant stars flickered and flashed against the planet's dark night side—sand grains striking atmosphere at high velocity and vaporizing in an instant. By now, the defensive cloud had either dispersed to ineffectiveness or been swept aside or vaporized by repeated nuclear detonations. But he'd run the gauntlet in close to the planet, and now he was within combat range of the majority of the Turusch fleet.

The near presence of the planet complicated things, but more for the defenders than for the Blue Omega Strike Force. The planet's bulk now blocked the line of sight to a number of the Turusch warships in low orbit, provided the gravitational mass for free course changes, and in this world's case even added an atmosphere that could be used either as a defensive screen or for simple delta-V.

The other fighters of Blue Omega were scattered across the sky now, each operating independently of the others. Gray could hear the cockpit chatter, but had to focus on his immediate situation. His wingman . . . where the hell was his wing?

There she was—Blue Omega Eight, two thousand kilometers aft and to starboard. Katie Tucker was engaging a big Turusch Echo Sierra—an electronic scanner vessel. That, at least, was what Intelligence thought those monsters might be, with their far-flung antennae and hundred-meter sensor dishes.

Confederation tactical doctrine suggested that pilots work together in wings for mutual protection, but standing orders didn't require it. One Starhawk could kill a Turusch capital ship as easily as two, and a single one of those thermonukes they were tossing around could take out a pair of gravfighters if they were too close together.

"This is Blue Seven," he reported. "I'm going to try to get in close to the objective."

Objective meaning the Marine perimeter in Haris, Eta Boötis IV. It took him a moment to orient himself as his AI threw up the curving lines of longitude and latitude on the image of the planet. Haris was tipped at an extreme angle, with an axial tilt of nearly 90 degrees. At this point in its year, Eta Boötis was 30 degrees off the planet's south pole, the Marine perimeter at 22 north.

There it was . . . a green triangle marking the Islamic base and the Marine expeditionary force sent to protect it, just now rotating into the local dawn. Turusch ships swarmed above and around it, or poured fire down from orbit. It was what carrier pilots liked to call "a target-rich environment."

Gray loosed another half dozen missiles, then spotted a special target. Three thousand kilometers ahead, a Turusch fighter transport lumbered just above the planet's cloud-choked atmosphere, fighters beginning to spill from her bays.

"Blue Omega Leader, Blue Seven," he called, bringing the nose of his Starhawk around and accelerating. "I have a Fox Tango dropping Toads. Engaging. . . ."

"I copy, Blue Seven. Blue Five! Blue Four! Get in there and give Blue Seven some backup!"

"Ah, copy, Blue Leader. On our way. . . ."

The Turusch heavy fighters code-named "Toads" by Confed Military Intelligence were big, ugly brutes thirty meters in length and half that thick. Less maneuverable than their Confederation counterparts, they could accelerate faster, and individually, could take a hell of a lot more punishment in combat. As Gray swung onto an attack vector with the transport, the Toads already released had begun boosting into intercept courses.

"Fox One!" Gray shouted over the net as he released a Krait. "And Fox One . . . Fox One . . . Fox One!"

The red-and-black Toad transport was a prime target, easily worth the expenditure of four nuke-tipped Kraits. Confederation fighter pilots steadfastly refused to refer to Fox Tango transports as "carriers." They insisted that the code name Fox Tango, in fact, was short for "Fat Target" rather than the more prosaic "Fighter Transport."

Missiles released, Gray snapped out an artificial singularity to port and rolled left, breaking off the run. The enormous transport was throwing up a cloud of defensive fire—sand, gatling KKs, particle beams, and point-defense HELs.

The Toads already released by the transport were falling into echelon formation as they accelerated toward Gray's fighter. There were five of them, and they were already so close they were beginning to loose missiles at him.

He plunged for atmosphere.

By now he'd bled off most of his velocity, and was dropping toward the planet's night side at a relatively sedate eight hundred kilometers per second. Using full reverse thrust, he slowed still further as his Starhawk's crescent shape flattened and elongated somewhat for atmospheric entry, growing aft stabilizers and a refractory keel. He was moving at nearly thirty kilometers per second, eight kps faster than the planet's escape velocity.

He felt the shudder as his craft sliced through thin atmosphere, and used the aft singularity to slow him further still.

"Alert." The ship's computer voice somehow managed to convey the illusion of sharp emotion. "Shielded anti-ship missile closing from one-eight-zero, azimuth plus zero five! Impact in six . . . five . . ."

The lost missile, coming in from dead astern. There was no time for maneuvering, and no way to outrun the thing with the bulk of Eta Boötis dead ahead. Gray flipped the fighter end-for-end, searching for the telltale red star of the incoming warhead.

There! Twenty kilometers! Lock . . . and *fire*. . .

The warhead detonated in the same instant that he gave the fire command.

Seconds passed before Gray blinked back to full awareness. Motion-streaked stars alternated with blackness spinning past his field of view. "AI!" he cried out. "Situation!"

There was no immediate response. Possibly, events had momentarily overloaded it. He didn't need a ship AI to tell him the situation was bad. He was in a tumble, power and drives were out, and he was falling through thin air toward Eta Boötis's night side at an unknown but fairly high velocity.

Very soon, the Eta Boötean atmosphere would be getting thick enough that the friction would incinerate him.

He was still getting sensor feeds, but life support and other ship's systems were out. IC was down, com was down, attitude control was down.

The SG-92 Starhawk had a robust and highly intelligent SRS, or self-repair system. Advanced nanotech modules allowed broken or burnt-out systems to literally regrow themselves, dissolving into the ship's hull matrix, then reassembling. When he checked the details on the dead life-support system, it told him it was 75 percent repaired, and that number jumped to 80 as he watched it. Power and control systems, too, were moments from being back on-line.

He directed the system to give priority to power and flight control; there was enough air in his personal life support to last for quite a while, and the temperature inside the cockpit was not uncomfortable yet.

The operative word being *yet*. The external temperature was at five hundred Celsius, and rising quickly.

"Blue Omega Flight, this is Blue Seven," he called, not with any real hope of establishing contact. Communications, according to his IHD, were also down, though there was always the possibility that it was his display or even the ship's AI that was faulty rather than his lasercom. There was a set list of things to try in the event of catastrophic multiple-system failure, and attempting to reach the other members of the flight was high among the priorities.

As he expected, however, there was no response. He directed the repair systems to lower the priority of the com network in order to focus more of the available power to power and control.

Abruptly, the dizzying alternation of star streaks with planet night halted, the shock of acceleration jolting him hard. He had partial attitude control now, though the main gravs were still out and only a trickle of power was coming through from the zero-point modules. The fighter shuddered as the keel cut thickening atmosphere, shedding more and more velocity.

He searched the sky display for more missiles, but saw none. That didn't mean they weren't out there, closing on him. The warhead that had just blasted him into an uncontrolled planetary descent had been shielded and smart, using the sensor-blinding flash of a nuclear detonation to drop to a velocity *just* faster than the Starhawk without being seen. It had stalked him then, for long seconds, reappearing on his displays only when it began punching through atmosphere, growing hot and leaving a visible contrail.

Turusch anti-fighter missiles, it seemed, were getting smarter and smarter.

But he was deep in the planet's atmosphere now, and if AFMs were tracking him in, he should be able to spot their ionization contrails. He decided to focus all of his attention on his fighter, and on surviving the next few minutes.

He was close to the dawn terminator, 180 kilometers above the night-black surface of Eta Boötis IV. Daylight was a sharp-edged, red-orange sliver along the curve of the planet, with the intolerably brilliant orange dome of Eta Boötis just beginning to nudge above the horizon. The cloud tops far beneath the Starhawk's keel were glowing a sullen red, casting long shadows across the deeper cloud decks.

And then the ionization cloud enveloped the Starhawk with the roaring intensity of a blast furnace. The fighter shuddered and bucked as Gray took the manual controls, trying to keep the nose high and spreading the keel to better disperse the heat. He wondered how many Turusch ships might be targeting him right now on his heat signature alone . . . then decided that since there was nothing he could do about it, there was no sense in worrying. Plenty of debris, from anti-missile sand grains to the shattered hulks of Turusch warships, were falling across the night face of the planet, and his Starhawk was just one more chunk in the debris field.

With manual control restored, he could hold the Starhawk in an entry glide and adjust its attitude, but the gravs were still out, meaning he was falling like a somewhat aerodynamic brick. In any case, primary gravitics were worse than useless in a planetary atmosphere. A 50,000-G singularity would gulp down molecules of air so quickly it would become star-hot in the process, overload, and explode like a tiny supernova. There were weapons—so-called gravitic cannon—that used the effect, and no fighter pilot wanted one of those detonating right off the nose of his ship.

What he did have were his secondary gravitics, drive units built into the structure of his spacecraft that could generate about ten to twelve gravities, and which allowed the Starhawk to hover. Carefully, Gray began feeding power to his secondaries, adding their drag to the already considerable drag of the atmosphere to further slow his descent.

His power tap, fortunately, was feeding him enough power to drive the secondaries at full pull. Without that, he would have been thoroughly and completely screwed. He brought the nose of his ship higher, rotated his acceleration couch into the optimal position, then engaged the secondaries. Without his ICs, his inertial compensators, the shock slammed him down and back against his seat and would have broken bones had the deceleration not scaled up smoothly, if swiftly, from zero-G to ten. He felt the uncomfortable jab of medfeeds pressed against his neck beneath the angle of his jaw, at his back, and in his groin as they monitored and adjusted his blood pressure, keeping him from blacking out. Even so, his vision narrowed alarmingly, as though he were seeing his surroundings through a black tunnel. His IHD, painting images and words against his visual field, winked out momentarily, replaced by white static. For an age, it seemed, he lay there beneath a crushing weight, scarcely able to breathe, blind and deaf as the Starhawk shuddered and thumped and shook around him.

Then, like a drowning man reaching the surface and gulping down fresh air, Gray struggled from the dark and the smothering pressure. The fireball surrounding him dissipated, and he emerged into open air.

And his flight systems were coming back on-line. He had half power now, more than enough for anything short of generating a fifty-K boost. Weapons were on-line, full sensory input, IC, AI, it was all there. Relief burst through him like the golden morning light on the horizon ahead. Voices crackled and called over his audio circuit, the other members of his squadron.

"Blue Ten! Blue Ten! I have Tango fighters inbound at five-zero, Azimuth minus four-one! . . ."

"Copy, Ten! Breaking right-high!"

"Here's the merge! I'm on him, Snorky!"

"Fox One! Fox One!" Static flared and crackled, and, with it, a brilliant flash from somewhere above and astern. "*Jesus*! Did you see that? . . ."

"Flame one Bravo-Bravo!"

"Blue Omega Leader, this is Blue Seven," Gray called. "Do you copy?"

"Copy, Seven!" The voice was tight and unemotional—probably Allyn's AI avatar rather than the squadron CO herself.

"I got toasted a bit and chewed air down to the deck. Systems are back on-line now, at eighty percent. Moving toward the Mike perimeter."

"We copy that, Blue Seven." That was the real Commander Allyn's voice. "Excellent job, Prim. Get in and offer the Marines whatever help they need, channel four-niner-three Zulu. The rest of us will be in there as soon as we can work through."

Gray felt wildly contrasting emotions, a sharp thrill of pleasure at the atta-boy from his CO, and anger at her use of his detested ready-room handle.

"Rog that," he replied. He dipped his gravfighter's nose and accelerated.

He wasn't quite "down to the deck," as he'd reported, but close enough. The Starhawk was dropping now past the twenty-kilometer mark. The sky above was still space-dark, the brightest stars—Arcturus, especially—still gleaming and brilliant, but the cloud decks below rose thick and towering, their tops sculpted by high-altitude winds and tinted red and gold by the rising sun. He'd crossed enough of the planet's face that the local sun was well above the horizon now, casting long, blue-purple shadows and hazy shafts of golden light across the distinctly three-dimensional surface of the cloudscape below.

Gray adjusted his ship's hull-form again, sculpting it for high-speed aerial flight, absorbing the deep entry keel and extending the wings farther and deeper into their forward-canted configuration. Behind him, a sudden burst of shooting stars marked another cloud of sand or debris entering atmosphere, a barrage of silent *flick-flick-flicks* of light.

He let his AI target on the Marine beacon, bringing the SG-92's prow left across the horizon, then dipping down into a plunging dive. He opened his com suite to the Marine frequency and began sending out an approach vector clearance request.

He hadn't crossed seventy-one AUs and survived a near-miss by a thermonuke to get shot down by the damned jarheads.

MEF HQ
Mike-Red Perimeter
Eta Boötis System
1259 hours, TFT

Major General Eunan Charles Gorman looked up as another incoming gravitic round struck the perimeter shields with piercing thunder. The deck of the headquarters dome rocked with the impact, and both lights and display monitors dimmed and flickered as the screens strained to dissipate the surge of energy grounding out of the sky. It wouldn't be long before the screens overloaded; when that happened, the defense of Mike-Red would come to an abrupt and pyrotechnic end.

The large three-view in the center of the HQ dome currently showed the Marine beachhead—a slender oval five kilometers long and perhaps two wide, sheltered beneath the shimmering hemisphere of an energy shield array six kilometers across. They were well-situated on high, rocky ground, but the terrain offered few advantages at the moment. The enemy was attempting to burn them out, pounding at the shield with nukes and heavy artillery, some fired from space, some fired from emplacements surrounding the beachhead and as far as a hundred kilometers away. All of the ground immediately around the Marine position was charred and lifeless, the sand fused into black, steaming glass. Incoming fire was so heavy the Marines could not lower the screen even for the instant required for a counter-battery reply.

That was the worst of it—having to sit here day after day taking this hammering, unable to shoot back.

"General!" one of the technicians at a sensor console nearby called out. "We have friendlies inbound!"

"Eh? How far? How long?"

"Two thousand kilometers," the tech replied. "At eleven kps, they should be at the perimeter within about three minutes."

"Thank God. It's about time."

Another gravitic round struck, the thunder echoing through the protective shield with a hollow, rumbling boom. A thermonuke struck an instant later, white light enveloping the base, hard, harsh, and glaring.

General Gorman looked at the small man in civilian dress standing beside him. "Well, Jamel. We may have help in time after all."

Jamel Saeed Hamid gave Gorman a sour look. "Too little, too late, I fear. We have lost the planet, either way."

"Maybe. But we'll have our lives."

The Marines on Haris had become aware of the arrival of the Confederation fleet only nineteen minutes earlier, when a tightly beamed X-ray lasercom burst transmission had reached the planet. Minutes later, high-energy detonations in planetary orbit had marked the beginnings of a long-range fighter strike, first as sand clouds and dust balls had swept through local space at near-c, then as SG-92 fighters had entered the battlespace and begun engaging Turusch fleet units.

The arrival was welcome, certainly, but what the Marines on the ground needed more than a fleet action right now was close support, fighters scraping off their bellies on the Haris swamp growth and putting force packages down on Marine-designated targets around the perimeter.

"Bradley!" he snapped, naming his Combat Information

officer. "Punch up a list of targets for the flyboys. Priority on grav cannon, nukes, and heavy PC emplacements."

"Aye, aye, sir!"

Gorman was a Marine, and he would have preferred Marine aviators out there . . . but right now he would take any help he could get, even damned Navy zorchies. If they could take just a little of the pressure off, there was some hope that the Navy transports would make it through, and they could begin the evacuation.

How many transports were there? Enough for everyone in his fast-attenuating command? And the Mufrids too?

Don't even think about that now. . . .

"Looks like a general engagement in local battlespace, sir," Bradley added. The colonel was standing behind two scanner techs, watching a glowing sphere representing nearby space, highlighting planetary schematics and the slow-drifting red and green blips of spacecraft, Turusch and human.

"Who's winning?" Gorman asked.

"Hard to say, sir. The Navy boys hit 'em pretty hard with that first pass, but they're starting to lose people now. Two . . . maybe three fighters have been knocked out."

"Understood."

A handful of gravfighters had no chance at all against a major Turusch battle fleet. The hope was that they would be able to maul that fleet badly enough that the capital ships could take them out when they arrived in another nine or ten hours. Better yet, if the fighters hurt the Tushies badly enough, they might withdraw before the Confederation fleet arrived.

Gorman had been in combat often enough to know that you never counted on things breaking your way like that. If the bad guys cut and run, fantastic.

But the Marines would plan for something less optimistic. They *had* to.

Their survival depended on it.

Chapter Four

Blue Omega Seven
Approaching Mike-Red
Eta Boötis System
1301 hours, TFT

Trevor Gray held his gravfighter snug against the deck, streaking across open water a scant twenty meters up. His velocity now down to eight kps, he was still throwing out a hypersonic shock wave that dragged across the surface of the shallow sea, sending up a vast, white wall of spray stretching out in a knife-straight line for over a hundred kilometers behind him.

The Marine perimeter was five hundred kilometers ahead.

He'd dropped down through the clouds and hugged the deck to avoid Turusch tracking systems, though it was likely they could still see him from orbit. Nothing was dropping on him out of the sky at the moment, however, so just maybe he'd slipped in unnoticed.

The surface was gloomy after the brilliant sunlight above the cloud deck. Haris—Eta Boötis IV—was shrouded in thick clouds, a solid blanket tinted red, orange, and yellow by various sulfur compounds in the atmosphere, and those colors were echoed by the oily sea below. The surface temperature was hot—hotter than the world's distance from its sun would suggest. The cloud deck and airborne sulfur compounds created a greenhouse effect that substantially warmed the planet—not nearly to the extent of Venus back in the Sol system, perhaps, but hot enough to render the place less than desirable as real estate, even if humans could breathe the air. What the hell had the Mufrids seen in the place, anyway?

The temperature outside his hurtling Starhawk, he noted, was 48 degrees Celsius—a swelteringly hot day in the tropics back on Earth, and it was only a short time past local dawn.

Targeting data flowed through his IHD, appearing in windows opening against the periphery of his visual field. God . . . the Marines had listed hundreds of targets out there, far too many for one lone gravfighter.

But he began dragging down targets with his eyes and locking on. He heard the tone indicating a solid lock. "Mike-Red, Blue Omega Seven. I have tone on the first six targets on your list. Request firing clearance."

"Blue Seven, hell yeah! Slam the bastards!"

"Copy. Engaging." He lifted his fighter slightly higher above the water, up to eighty meters, to give himself launch clearance. "Fox Three!"

Six Krait missiles dropped clear of the Starhawk's keel, emerging from exit ports melting open around them in the hull, then accelerated. *Fox Three* was the firing code for targets on the ground, or for extremely large ships or bases in orbit. Once, centuries before in the skies above Earth's oceans, *Fox One* had designated the launch of a short-range heat seeker; *Fox Two*, a radar-guided missile; and *Fox Three*, a particular type of long-range missile called a Phoenix. The terminology had remained the same, though the meanings were different now, applied to much different technologies.

Guided by their onboard AIs, the six Kraits streaked ahead of the Starhawk, their grav drives glowing brilliantly as they plowed through the dense atmosphere. Gray banked left and accelerated slightly; Turusch sensors in orbit would have spotted that launch even if they'd missed his fighter, and they would be trying to target him now.

A blue-white detonation flared at his back, searing a tunnel down through the atmosphere and vaporizing a stadium-sized chunk of seawater. A second blast ignited the sky to his right. He was traveling too fast for the shock waves to catch him, but he cut right and slowed, riding the fast-expanding wave front of the second explosion in order to take advantage of the mushroom cap of superheated steam overhead. Those shots had been from a Turusch orbital particle cannon; each shot ionized air molecules and tended to momentarily block sensors trying to read through the muck.

It might mask him for a precious couple of seconds more.

"Target fifteen on the Red-Mike targeting list ahead, coming into range," his AI announced. His IHD showed the target as a red triangle on the horizon—some kind of Turusch gun emplacement or surface battery. It was already too close for a Krait lock-on; he switched to his PBP, his particle beam projector, or "pee-beep," as it was more popularly known.

At his AI's command, the nose of his fighter melted away half a meter, exposing the projector head. "Fire!"

A beam of blue-white light stabbed ahead of his grav-fighter, intolerably brilliant; a high-energy UV laser burned a vacuum tunnel through the air, followed a microsecond later by the proton beam, directed and focused by a powerful magnetic field. Twenty-some kilometers ahead, a surface crawler, a squat and massive floater nearly one hundred meters long, was struck by a devastating bolt of lightning before it could fire its next gravitic shell. Secondary explosions lit up the sky, visible from the Starhawk's cockpit as Gray broke hard to the left.

His AI began loosing Krait missiles, each locking onto a different target on the Marine list. More energy beams and high-velocity kinetic-kill slugs slammed into the sea a few kilometers astern. Gray increased his speed and began jinking, pulling irregular turns left and right to make it harder on the Turusch gunners some hundreds of kilometers above him. At a thought, a half dozen decoys snapped clear of the Starhawk and streaked in various directions, trailing electronic signatures like an SG-92.

The burnt-orange and deep-red sea a hundred meters beneath him lightened suddenly to pale yellow-orange as he crossed over shallow water, then gave way to land—bare rock and a rolling carpet of orange. Gray was moving too low and too fast to see details, moving too fast to see *anything* beyond a vague brown-and-orange blur.

A map display in his IHD showed blossoming white flashes in a ragged circle around the Marine position. His Kraits were slamming home in rapid succession now, loosing thermonuclear fury across the alien landscape. Turning sharply, the G-forces negated by his inertial compensators, he angled across a narrow arm of the sea toward the Marine position. His missiles were expended now, the last of them flashing off toward the gloom of the west.

"Red-Mike, this is Blue Omega Seven. I'm Echo-Whiskey and coming in toward the perimeter."

"Copy, Blue Seven," a Marine voice said. "We're getting drone evals on the eggs you laid. Good shooting. Looks like you tore the bastards up pretty good. Nice shooting!"

"Almost up to Marine standards," Gray quipped.

"I didn't say you were *that* good, Navy. . . ."

The Turusch particle beam stabbed down out of the cloud deck, a violet-and-blue bolt meters across, scarcely ten meters off Gray's starboard wing. Static shrieked from the electronic interference and blanked out the displays in Gray's head. The shock wave caught him from the side, tumbling him over wildly. His AI intervened with reflexes far faster than a human's, engaging full thrust and pulling up hard before the blast could slam him into the sea.

Then his power system shut down, and with it his weapons, his primary flight controls, and his life support. He had just enough juice in reserve to put full thrust into his secondaries before they, too, failed and he began dropping toward the alien sea. Slowed now, to less than a kilometer per second, he tried to pull his nose up for a wet landing, but then *everything* went dead, leaving him in darkness.

"Eject, eject, eject!" his AI was shouting in his ear before its voice, too, failed. The Starhawk's ejection system was self-contained and separate from other ship systems. He grabbed the D-ring handle on the deck, twisted it to arm the mechanism, and pulled.

The cockpit melted away around him, the nanoflow so quick it was more like an explosion than an opening, the blast of wind shrieking around his helmet. Rocket motors in the base of his couch fired, kicking him clear of the falling spacecraft seconds before it slammed into the surging red waters of the sea.

With his inertial compensators out, the jolt of acceleration rattled his bones and brought with it a stab of terror. Despite both his flight training and numerous experiential downloads, Gray didn't share the seamless relationship with technology enjoyed by the others in his squadron. He *couldn't*. For a long moment as the couch carried him in stomach-wrenching free fall, panic clawed at the back of his mind, and he struggled to control it.

The eject sequence, fortunately, was entirely automated, a precaution in case the pilot was crippled or unconscious. Scant meters above the surface of the sea, braking rockets fired with another jolt, slowing him suddenly, and then Gray splashed down in the shallow, oily water.

Smoke boiled from the sea a kilometer or two away as his Starhawk dissolved, its nano components turning suicidal and melting the rest of the ship so that it wouldn't fall into Turusch hands . . . or whatever they had that passed for hands. Gray wasn't sure. Overhead, orange-red clouds roiled and twisted, dragged along by high winds a few kilometers up.

He struggled to free himself from the chair's embrace. He felt *heavy*, dragged down by the planet's gravity. The water, he was surprised to note, was only about a meter deep. He'd come down perhaps a kilometer from the shoreline—he could see an orange-cloaked land mass toward local north—but the seabed here was extremely shallow—a tidal flat, perhaps. Eta Boötis IV had no moon, but the large sun exerted tidal forces enough, he knew, to raise substantial tides.

Gray tried standing up, leaning against the chair, and nearly fell again. The artificial spin gravity on board the carrier *America* was kept at around half a G—a reasonable compromise for crew members from Earth and those born and raised on Luna, Mars, or Ganymede. The surface gravity on Eta Boötis IV was 1.85 G, almost four times what he was used to. Another low swell passed, hitting him waist-high, and he did fall; the *water* was heavy, with a lot of momentum behind it. He landed on his hands and knees, struggling against the planet's dragging pull.

His e-suit would keep him alive for days. Skin-tight, pressure sealed, and with a plastic helmet almost invisible in its clarity at optical wavelengths, it was colored bright orange to help rescue craft spot him, though on this red-orange world, they would have to rely on other wavelengths to see him. A nanobreather pack was attached to his right hip, with its small bottle of oxygen beneath. The unit would recycle oxygen from CO_2 for days, and in an atmosphere, even a toxic one like this one, could pull oxygen and other gasses from the compounds outside, extending the unit's life, and his, indefinitely.

None of that was likely to help, though, if he couldn't reach friendly forces. He'd been shot down several hundred kilometers south of the Marine base—exactly how far, he wasn't sure. Using his radio might well call down the Turusch equivalent of fire from heaven, so he wasn't anxious to try that. His couch should have sent out a marker code when it touched down, a burst transmission, meaningless— he hoped—to the enemy, but indicating a successful ejection and landing.

The question, however, was whether to stay with the couch or try to reach the marine perimeter. Red-Mike was a *long* hike, but, on the other hand, he was nakedly exposed here on this tidal flat, and there would be clouds of Turusch drones moving through the area very soon, looking for him. And the drones would bring larger, more dangerous visitors.

Better, he decided, to be moving. He could work his way closer to the Marine perimeter, and give friendly forces a better chance of picking him up. If they could find him . . .

He didn't think about how slender those chances might be. Hell, the Marines probably assumed he'd been shot down and killed, and couldn't leave the safety of their protective screens in any case. His squadron was heavily engaged far

above. They would be free to initiate a search only if the Turusch fleet left the area, and the Tushies weren't about to do
that if all they were facing was a handful of gravfighters.

The biggest problem, however, was moving. Gray couldn't
walk in Eta Boötis's gravity, not for very far, at any rate. He
would need some help.

The back of the couch opened up to reveal a compact
emergency locker. Inside were extra bottles of oxygen for
long-term excursions in hard vacuum, an M-64 laser carbine, medical and emergency survival packs, and a spider.

The spider was the size of a flattened football, with four
legs folded up tight. When he activated the unit, the legs
began unfolding, each extending for over a meter from the
central body. Immediately, the unit moved behind him, put
the tips of two legs on his shoulders to steady him, then
began to snuggle in close, the main unit snuggling up against
his spine, each leg adjusting and reconfiguring to conform
exactly to his body. In seconds, it had adhered to his e-suit,
clamped tight at ankles, knees, and hips. There was a vibrating whine of servos, and the unit straightened up, pulling
him upright.

He stood now in knee-deep water, supported by the exo-
skeletal unit, or ESU, and when another heavy wave surged
slowly past, it adjusted with his movement, shifted with his
weight, and kept him upright. He took a sloshing, heavy
step forward, then another. He still felt like he weighed 150
kilos—he *did*, after all—but he could stand without feeling
like his knees were about to buckle, and the spider on his
back fed his servos power enough to help counteract the drag
of gravity. The extensions secured to his arms were flexible
and slack at the moment; if he tried to lift something, however, they would match his movements and contribute with
support and lift of their own. Wearing one of these rigs, a
person could do anything he could do in his normal gravity
field, including running, jumping, and lifting heavy objects.
The word was that with practice he could run a Marathon
and not get winded. They were standard issue to civilian
tourists to Earth from low-G worlds like Mars.

Med kit and survival gear snapped to clamps on the spider,

and the carbine slung over his right shoulder. He wouldn't need the O_2. There was plenty of oxygen in the atmosphere, bound up with carbon dioxide, sulfur dioxide, carbonyl sulfide, and a witch's brew of other gasses, and his suit would have no trouble processing it to keep him alive almost indefinitely. The little unit would handle his food and water requirements as well, so long as he fed it CHON—shorthand for carbon, hydrogen, oxygen, and nitrogen. He needed to add an occasional handful of dirt or organic matter to provide trace elements like phosphorus and iron, necessary for the nanufacture of certain vitamins and amino acids.

There was no emergency survival radio in his survival kit, because, in fact, his e-suit had radio circuitry built into it, both for communication and for tracking. He needed line-of-sight to reach the Marine base directly, but his squadron and a large number of battlespace drones would be above the horizon now, somewhere above those blood-hued, low-hanging clouds.

A direct call to them, however, might generate way too much interest on the part of the Turusch, who would be closely monitoring the electronic environment around the planet, and a stray, coded signal might bring down anything from a KK projectile to a 100-megaton nuke.

His personal e-hancements, computer circuitry nanotechnically grown into the sulci of his brain, had downloaded both the ghost-shadow of his fighter's AI and the position of the Marine base in those last seconds before he'd crashed. As he turned his head, his IHD hardware threw a green triangle up against his visual field, marking a spot on the horizon . . . in *that* direction, toward the beach.

That was where he had to go, then. Taking a last look around, he started wading toward the shore.

CIC, TC/USNA CVS America
35.4 AUs from Eta Boötis
1330 hours, TFT

Admiral Koenig checked the time once again. The fleet had been traveling for 9.4 hours, accelerating constantly at

500 gravities. They were nearing the midpoint now, half-way between the Kuiper Belt space where they'd arrived in-system and their destination. Their speed at the moment was .77 *c*, fast enough that for every three minutes passing in the universe outside, only two minutes passed within the *America*.

It had been an uneventful passage so far, thank God. He was all too aware, however, that by now the gravfighters of VF-44 had reached the planet and were engaging the Turusch fleet.

He checked the time again. The Dragonfires had been mixing it up with the bad guys for forty-five minutes already, an eternity in combat. It was entirely possible that the fighting was over.

If so, twelve brave men and women were dead now—dead, or trapped in crumpled hulks on high-speed, straight-line vectors out of battlespace.

Best not to think about that. . . .

"Admiral?" the voice of Commander Katryn Craig, the CIC Operations officer, said in Koenig's head. "Mr. Quintanilla is requesting permission to enter the CIC."

Koenig sighed. He would rather have given orders that the civilian be kept off the command deck entirely, but he was under orders from Fleet Mars to cooperate with the jackass, and playing the martinet would not smooth the bureaucratic pathway in the least.

Politics. He made a sour face. Sometimes, it seemed as though his job was nothing else but.

"Let him in," Koenig said, grudgingly.

Quintanilla entered from the aft passageway a moment later. "Admiral? I was wondering if you could give me an update."

"We're roughly halfway there," Koenig told him. "Nine hours and some to go."

Quintanilla pulled his way to the display projection at the center of CIC. There, small globes of light glowed in holographic projection, showing the positions of both Eta Boötis A and B, fourteen major planets, the task force's current position just outside the orbit of one of the system's gas giants, and a red haze around the objective. The carrier task force had no way of receiving telemetry from the fighters it had launched nine and a half hours earlier, of course, not while its ships were encased in their Alcubierre bubbles, but if everything had proceeded according to the oplan, the Dragon-fires should have reached the vicinity of Eta Boötis IV some forty-five minutes earlier.

"Does that mean we're going to do a skew-flip, Admiral? To start decelerating?"

"No, sir, it does not. You're thinking of the gravitic drives on the fighters. The Alcubierre Drive works differently . . . an entirely different principle."

"I don't understand."

Koenig wondered if that man had been briefed at all . . . or if he'd been given a technical download that he'd failed to review.

Quintanilla seemed to read Koenig's expression. "Look, I'm here as a political liaison, Admiral. The technology of your space drive is hardly my area of expertise."

Obviously, Koenig thought. "The type of gravitational acceleration we use on the fighters won't work on capital ships," he said, "vessels over about eighty meters in length. With ships as large as the *America*, projecting an artificial singularity pulling fifty-kay gravs or so ahead of the vessel would cause problems—tidal effects would set up deadly shear forces within the ship's hull that would tear her to bits.

"So for larger ships, we use the Alcubierre Drive. It manipulates the fabric of spacetime both forward and astern, essentially causing space to contract ahead and expand behind. The result is an enclosed bubble of spacetime with the ship imbedded inside. The ship is not accelerating relative to the space around it, but that space *is* sliding across the spacetime matrix at accelerations that can reach the speed of light, or better."

"That makes no sense whatsoever."

Koenig grinned. "Welcome to the wonderful world of zero-point field manipulation. It's all pretty contra-intuitive. Free energy out of hard vacuum, artificial singularities, and we can reshape spacetime itself to suit ourselves. No wonder the Sh'daar are nervous about our technology curve."

"Explain something to me, Admiral?" Quintanilla asked. He was floating near the system display, and had been studying it for several moments.

"If I can."

"Why only one squadron? That's . . . what? Twelve spacecraft? But you have six squadrons on board, right?"

Koenig blinked, surprised by the abrupt change of topic. He'd been expecting another physics question.

"Six strike fighter squadrons, yes," Koenig replied, cautious. What was the civilian hammering at? "Plus one reconnaissance squadron, the Sneaky Peaks; an EW squadron; two SAR squadrons; and two utility/logistics squadrons." EW was electronic warfare, specialists in long-range electronic intelligence, or ELINT, and in battlespace command and control. SAR was search and rescue, the tugs that went out after high-velocity hulks, attempting to recover the pilots.

"But you just sent one fighter squadron in, and they have, what? Another nine hours in there before we arrive?"

"Nine hours, twenty-one minutes," Koenig said, checking his IHD time readout.

"So what are the chances for one lone squadron against . . . what? Fifty-five Turusch ships, you said?"

"More than that, Mr. Quintanilla. Fifty-five was just the number we could see from seventy AUs out. And even more might have arrived since."

Quintanilla shrugged, the movement giving him a slight rotation in microgravity. He reached out awkwardly and grabbed the back of Koenig's seat. "Okay, twelve fighters against *over* fifty-five capital ships, then. It seems . . . suicidal."

"I agree."

"Then why—"

"Every man and woman of VF-44 volunteered for this op," Koenig told him. He could have added that Koenig's own contribution to the plan hashed out by Ops had called for *three* squadrons, half of *America*'s strike-fighter compliment. Ultimately, that had been rejected by the Fleet Operations Review Board at Mars Synchorbital. His was still the final responsibility.

"It just seems to me that your plan should have allowed for more fighters in the initial strike."

"It's a little late to start second-guessing the oplan working group's decisions now, isn't it?"

"But you could launch the rest of your strike squadrons now, couldn't you? We're a lot closer to the target. It would take them—"

"No, Mr. Quintanilla. We could not."

"Why not?"

Koenig sighed. Would it serve any purpose whatsoever to educate this . . . civilian? "I just told you how the Alcubierre Drive works, Mr. Quintanilla."

"Eh? What does that have to do with it?"

"As I said, each ship in the fleet is imbedded inside a bubble of warped spacetime, contracting the space ahead, expanding behind. The bubble is moving. Right now *America*'s bubble is moving at about three quarters of the speed of light. But each ship in the task force is imbedded within the spacetime inside its bubble and is relatively motionless compared to its surroundings."

"So? Why can't you just drop out of this bubble and launch more fighters?"

"Because we would drop back into normal space with the velocity we had when we engaged the Alcubierre Drive, out in this system's Kuiper Belt, something less than one kilometer per second. We would then have to begin accelerating all over again. If we started decelerating at the halfway point, our total trip would take twenty-five and a half hours. If we keep accelerating, we'll reach Haris in a total of eighteen and some hours. At that point we'll be zorching along at one-point-oh-eight *c*, just a hair faster than light, but we'll cut the Alcubierre Drive and drop into normal space at a modest one kps."

"I just hope when we do, we'll find those fighter pilots alive."

"War means death, Mr. Quintanilla, the deaths of brave

men and women doing their duty. I don't like it any more than you do, and if I could wave my hand and change the laws of physics, I would."

"But another nine and a half hours . . ."

"Let my people do their jobs, Mr. Quintanilla. There's nothing you can do to change things, one way or the other."

Quintanilla thought about this a moment, then swam for the CIC exit.

The hell of it was, however, that Quintanilla was right about one thing. The oplan *should* have called for more fighters in the first strike. The mission planners on Mars, however, had feared the consequences if *America* didn't have a sufficient defensive capability once she started mixing it up with the Turusch.

Had it been up to Koenig, he would have launched all six fighter squadrons from the Eta Boötis Kuiper Belt, and trusted the destroyer screen to keep the carrier safe.

But, as he'd told the damned civilian, it was too late for second-guessing the mission plan now.

Blue Omega One
VFA-44 Dragonfires
Eta Boötis System
1335 hours, TFT

A nuclear fireball blossomed a hundred kilometers ahead, and Commander Marissa Allyn twisted her gravfighter hard into a tight yaw. A trio of Turusch fighters flashed past her starboard side, bow to stern, particle beams stabbing at her Starhawk. She sent three Kraits after them, then followed that up with the last two Kraits in her armament racks, locking on to an immense Turusch battlespace monitor just emerging from behind the planet.

The sky around her was filled with fire and destruction, with twisting fighters, lumbering capital-ship giants, and tumbling chunks of wreckage. "*Mayday! Mayday!*" sounded over her com link. "This is Blue Eleven . . . two golf-mikes on my tail . . ."

"Blue Eleven! Blue Three! I'm on them! . . ."

Golf-mikes—gravitic missiles—were looping through battlespace, their sensors locking on to any powered target not transmitting a Turusch IFF code. The damned things were next to impossible to shake, and there were so many of them in the battle now that the Confederation pilots were having to concentrate on evading them more and more.

"This is Blue Eleven! Breaking right! Breaking—"

The voice cut off with a raw burst of static. The icon representing Oz Tombaugh, Blue Eleven, on Allyn's tactical display flared and winked out.

Damn . . .

"Omega Strike, this is Blue Omega One!" she called. The squadron's expendables were almost gone, and there was little more serious damage they could do to the Turusch fleet with what was left. "Let's get down on the deck! Make for the planet and home on Mike-Red!"

Eight members of the squadron remained in action, including Allyn.

And they still had more than nine hours to go before the relief forces arrived.

Chapter Five

Blue Omega Seven
Eta Boötis IV
1353 hours, TFT

Trevor Gray slogged across wet, marshy ground, a soft and yielding surface smothered in a vibrantly red-orange tangle of vegetation. It was raining now, with big, heavy drops splattering across the ground cover, which appeared to be stretching and expanding under the pounding.

He'd heard and felt a savage boom behind him some minutes before—probably the Tushies dropping something nasty on the wreckage of his fighter or the abandoned acceleration couch, so he kept moving, trying to put as much distance as possible between himself and a possible area of Turusch interest. Moments before, he'd waded out of the shallow water, stumbling ashore on a beach covered by what looked like stubby, blunt-ended tentacles.

The thickness of the vegetation around him was surprising, though it had taken him a moment to realize that it *was* vegetation. In fact, he still wasn't sure. The stuff was *moving*. Each tentacle was perhaps ten to fifteen centimeters long and as thick as his wrist; the tips were open, the weaving shapes hollow, and they appeared to be filled with small holes, like sponges. Though overall they were orange in color, each, in fact, shaded from deep red at the base to bright yellow at the rim of the opening. Their movements were slow and rhythmic, ripples spreading out from his feet with each step and traveling eight or ten meters in all directions, and quivering in response to the rain. He would have assumed they were animals, except for the fact that they were firmly rooted in the soft ground.

According to the readout from the circuitry woven into his e-suit, the atmosphere was a poisonous mix of carbon dioxide and gaseous sulfur compounds, with smaller amounts of ammonia, nitrogen, methane, and just a whiff of oxygen. The sea he'd just emerged from was water, but with a high percentage of sulfuric acid; the rain, he noted, was almost pure sulfuric acid—H_2SO_4—and it steamed as it splashed across the vegetation. The external temperature was up to 53 degrees Celsius, and climbing rapidly as the local morning grew more advanced.

Gray's e-suit was composed of a finely woven carbon composite that, in theory, at least, would resist anything the local atmosphere could throw at him, including strong acids and high temperatures. He wondered, though, if any material substance could stand up to this kind of acidity for very long. There were, he noticed, quite a few rock outcroppings thrusting above the orange vegetation, all of them soft and rounded, as though smoothed by geological ages of acid rain. Some of the larger outcrops had holes eaten clear through them, and they stood above the quivering orange ground like alien gateways.

Gray's internal circuitry had memory enough for some backup data, but had nowhere near the capacity of his wrecked fighter. There was nothing there, for instance, on the flora and fauna of Eta Boötis IV . . . and he wished now that he'd paid more attention when he'd been scanning through the data files on board the Starhawk.

What the hell was a chemoorganoheterotroph, anyway?

A ripple of motion caught his attention out of the corner of his eye, something dark, quick, and low to the ground. He turned . . . but saw nothing beyond the writhing of those damned orange plants.

The place, he decided, was starting to get on his nerves, and now his imagination was playing tricks on him . . .

Blue Omega One
VFA-44 Dragonfires
Eta Boötis IV
1412 hours, TFT

Commander Marissa Allyn brought her gravfighter into a steep climb as kinetic-kill projectiles, heated white-hot by atmospheric friction, stabbed down out of the sky and struck the sea in white bursts of vapor. Her ship vibrated alarmingly with the maneuver. Despite the advanced polymorphic hull, able to drastically reconfigure its shape according to mission or aerodynamic requirements from moment to moment, the SG-92 Starhawk had not been designed with atmospheric flight in mind. You could maneuver the thing with gravs, or you could use the change of airfoil shape and ailerons to maneuver against the airflow, but it was tough to do *both*.

Turusch fighters relied solely on gravitics for flight, whether in space or in atmosphere; those ugly, potato-shaped lumps were just about as aerodynamic as bricks.

There were three of the damned things on her tail at the moment. A particle beam seared past her head, the dazzling blue-white flash making her flinch. Lasers and charged particle beams normally were invisible in the vacuum of space; only in atmosphere did the beams draw sharp trails of ionization across the sky. In space, her IHD graphics showed the beams, but not with such eye-dazzling intensity.

Blinking, she told her AI to stop down the intensity of the light and kept hauling her Starhawk up and over in a hard, tight loop. The Toads tried to match her climb but were carrying too much velocity. She could see their hulls glow white-hot as they tried dumping excess speed. "Target lock!" she called. "Fox One!"

But that was her last Krait. "This is Blue One!" she called. "I'm dry on VG-10s! Three on my tail! Switching to beams and guns!"

"Copy that, Blue Leader! This is Blue Five! Got you covered!"

Blue Five—Lieutenant Spaas—dropped out of empty sky, trying to get on the one of the Toads' six, the sweet spot directly behind its tail. The Turusch fighter broke left and Spaas followed, trying to get a clear shot.

Allyn's missile twisted around, then arrowed almost straight down, striking the lead Toad and detonating with a savage, eight-kiloton blast that sent a visible shock wave racing out through the air. The outer skin of the Turusch spacecraft peeled away from the tiny, sudden sun . . . and then the entire craft disintegrated in a spray of metallic shreds and tatters as the fireball swelled and engulfed them.

The last Toad boomed through the fireball. Allyn completed her loop, rolling out at the top and entering a vertical dive. Her IHD slid a targeting reticule across the Toad, which was coming up at her from below, head-on. She triggered her particle beam an instant before the enemy could fire, sending a blue-white lance of energy stabbing into and through the Toad's hull. The fighter came apart in glowing fragments; a half second later she plunged through the debris cloud, feeling the tick and rattle of fragments impacting across her fuselage.

"Scratch two Tangos!" Allyn yelled, adrenaline surging through her. Damn, she *never* felt this alive, save when she was turning and burning in combat. She hated that about herself.

"And scratch one!" Spaas added, as another nuclear sun blossomed in the fire-ravaged sky over Haris.

Allyn looked around, orienting herself. The dogfight, or part of it, had drifted down out of space and into Eta Boot's atmosphere. They were over the day side of the planet, perhaps a thousand kilometers north and east of the Marine perimeter. "All Blue Omegas!" she called. "We need to work in closer to Mike-Red!"

Turusch fleet elements were attempting to keep the Dragonfires from engaging enemy positions around the Marine perimeter. The squadron actually had two mission elements—crippling the Turusch fleet as completely as possible before the Confederation carrier task force arrived, and taking some of the pressure off of the Marines. Of the two, the first, arguably, was the most important . . . at least that was what they'd told her in the pre-mission briefing.

Even so, the mission was pointless if the Marine perimeter collapsed before the *America* arrived. The Turusch were doing their best to keep the Dragonfires away from Red-Mike, and the volume of fire directed against the Mariners appeared to be growing more intense.

Fifteen kilometers away, a nuclear fireball consumed Blue Twelve.

If the surviving fighters could tuck in close to the Marines, perhaps the two might be able to support each other.

Blue Omega Seven
Eta Boötis IV
1415 hours, TFT

Gray had to rest.

The spider strapped to his back continued responding perfectly to his movements, adding its considerable strength to his own as he staggered across the alien landscape. The planet's gravity continued dragging at him, however, until his heart was pounding so hard inside his chest he began to fear the possibility of a heart attack.

Theoretically, the med circuitry woven into his e-suit was supposed to monitor his health, and would inform him if he was in any real danger of hurting himself, but he wasn't sure he trusted that technology yet. He stopped and leaned against a smoothly sculpted rock outcropping, breathing hard.

Again, something moved, half glimpsed out of the corner of his eye.

His rapid breathing was fogging the inside of his helmet, and he wasn't sure he'd seen anything at all. Turning, he stared at the patch that had snagged his attention. What the hell was he seeing? . . .

They looked like shadows, each leaf shaped and paper

thin, gray in color, each the size of his hand or a little bigger. They flitted across the orange vegetation as though gliding over it, traveling a meter or two before vanishing again among the weaving tendrils.

Again, Gray wished he'd understood—or paid more attention to—the briefings on the biology of Eta Boötis IV. Even if he'd ignored the canned downloads, Commander Allyn had gone over it lightly in the permission briefing. What he best remembered, however, was her stressing that the star Eta Boötis was only 2.7 billion years old . . . far too young to have planets with anything more highly evolved than primitive bacteria. Gray was no xenobiologist, but those . . . those *things* slipping and gliding over the orange plants, or whatever they were, looked a hell of a lot more advanced than any bacteria he'd ever heard about.

Were they dangerous? He couldn't tell, but it did appear that more and more of them were visible from moment to moment, as though they were following him.

Or might they be some sort of Turusch or Sh'daar biological weapon? Not much was known about their technology, or about whether or not they might utilize organic weapons or sensor probes.

A rumble drifted out of the sky. He looked up, trying to penetrate the low, reddish-gray overcast, and wondered if that was thunder, or if it was the battle somewhere overhead.

Blue Omega One
VFA-44 Dragonfires
Eta Boötis IV
1418 hours, TFT

Commander Marissa Allyn brought her gravfighter into a flat, high-speed trajectory, hurtling low above the surface. The orange ground cover gave way in a flash of speed-blurred motion to bare rock. The surface for fifty kilometers around the Marine perimeter was charred black or, in places, transformed into vast patches of fused glass. Over the past weeks, since the Turusch had brought the Marine base under attack, hundreds of nuclear warheads had detonated against the Marine shields, along with thousands of charged particle beams. The equivalent of miniature suns had burned against that landscape, charring it, in places turning sand to molten glass.

She checked the tactical display for the entire squadron. Three of her pilots were still in space, tangling with Turusch fighters and a Romeo-class cruiser in low orbit. Four were in-atmosphere with her, forming up with her as she arrowed low across fire-scorched desert toward the Marine defenses.

"Mike-Red!" she called over the assigned combat frequency. "This is Blue One! Five Blue Omegas are coming at you down on the deck, bearing three-five-five to zero-one-zero!"

"We've got you on-screen, Blue One," a calm voice replied over her com. "Come on in!"

"Just so you don't think we look like Trash," Allyn replied.

"Or Tushies. I think we can tell the difference."

"Copy! Here we come!"

"Watch out for slugs," the voice told her. "If you can drop some salt on them on the way in, we'd appreciate it."

"Copy, Red-Mike. Five loads of salt on the way."

Ahead, the Marine perimeter screen rose above the horizon, a pale, scarcely visible dome-shaped field highlighted by the sparkle and flash of incoming particle beams and lasers. According to her tactical display, the perimeter was still under attack by Turusch ground crawlers—fifty-meter behemoths code-named "slugs" by Confederation intelligence. Each was similar in appearance to a Toad fighter, but squashed, with a flat bottom that seemed to conform to the ground as it crawled over it. Turrets and blisters on the upper surface housed weapons emplacements, which were keeping up a steady fire against the Marine position. There were a dozen enemy crawlers out there, scattered across the burnt area on all sides of the Marine base.

She extended the sensitivity of her scanners, searching for hot spots—slang for any sources of electromagnetic radiation, including heat and radar. Large patches of scoured-bare rock and glass were radiating fiercely, glowing white-hot and molten in some places, but her computer began cataloguing possible targets out beyond the dead zone, where individual Turusch soldiers or combat machines might be gathering.

One Turusch ship, the Romeo-class cruiser, was almost directly overhead, three hundred kilometers out from the planet. It had been slamming the Marine perimeter with particle beams, but now appeared to be occupied by an attack from two of the Dragonfire fighters.

The five gravfighters all were out of Krait missiles by now, but they still had plenty of KK rounds, as well as power for their particle beam weapons. KK rounds—the letters stood for "kinetic kill"—were lumps of partially compressed matter, each the size of a little finger massing four hundred grams, steel jacketed to give the magnetic fields something to which they could grab hold. Hurled down a gravfighter's central railgun at twenty kps, they released the energy of a fair-sized bomb on impact; the weapon could cycle seven hundred rounds per minute, or nearly twelve per second.

She had to slow sharply, though, to see the targets. Swinging left slightly, she watched the red diamond of the targeting cursor slide over the icon marking a Turusch slug at the very limits of visibility and triggered her cannon. Rapid-fire rounds howled from her craft, as her gravs kicked in to compensate for the savage recoil of that barrage. Ahead, rounds slammed into the Turusch crawler, sending up immense plumes of dust and dirt, then a fireball erupting, then immediately snuffing out in the oxygen-poor atmosphere.

The explosion an instant later flared white almost directly in front of her. She punched through the fireball, the shock wave jolting her fighter. Dropping her right wing, she jinked back to the right, targeting a second crawler, with a third five kilometers further off, on the bleak and fire-scourged horizon. Again, a stream of compressed matter shrieked from her high-velocity railgun.

High-energy particle beams probed and snapped past her head. The mobile fortresses were swinging their weapons to engage this new threat coming out of the north.

Blue Omega Seven
Eta Boötis IV
1429 hours, TFT

Gray felt something slap against the back of his left leg.
He looked down, startled, and saw one of the dark gray leaf
shapes clinging to his calf. He reached down and tore it off;
it peeled away from his e-suit with a ripping sensation, like
it had been clinging to him with suckers, and as he held it
up, it twisted and writhed in his grasp. The underside of the
creature was covered with tiny tube feet, like a starfish of
Earth's oceans, with a central opening like a sucker, ringed
by rough-surfaced bony plates.

He threw the squirming leaf away, shuddering with a
wave of revulsion. The thing reminded him of a terrestrial
leech, but much larger and more active. The tube feet put
him in mind of the far larger tendrils covering the swampy
ground.

Three more of the things hit him in rapid succession, two
on his lower right leg, one on his left hip. He could feel the
rasp of those ventral plates, grinding against the carbon
nanoweave of his suit.

Revulsion turned to gibbering panic. The atmosphere was
toxic, and would kill him in minutes if his suit was breached.
He ripped the creatures off and hurled them away. One, he
saw, landed on its back three meters away, twisted over until
it was upright, and immediately started gliding toward him
once again. Dozens of the creatures were visible now in all
directions, moving toward him with a fascinating delibera-
tion.

He started to unsling his carbine, then thought better of
it. There were too many of the things, and none was bigger
than his open palm and fingers. Shooting them would be like
solving a roach infestation one bug at a time. Five slapped
against his legs and clung there, gnawing at his suit. With a
scream, Gray peeled them off, terror yowling up from the
depths of his mind. There were too many of them, coming
too fast!

He started running.

His spider pumped and throbbed with his movements, giving him better speed than he could have managed on Earth, to say nothing of the Harisian high-grav environment. He stumbled, but he kept running, his boots splashing through shallow ponds and mudflats and the sea of soft-bodies, orange vegetation that weaved and twisted in front of him; and the shadow-creatures followed, hundreds of them now.

He was screaming as he ran.

MEF HQ
Mike-Red Perimeter
Eta Boötis System
1445 hours, TFT

"General?" Major Bradley said. "They're ready to come through the screen."

"Do it," General Gorman said. "Watch for leakers and pop-ups."

"Aye, aye, sir."

The gravfighters of VF-44 had completed three wide sweeps all the way around the Marine perimeter, smashing Turusch slugs and ground positions and even small groups of enemy soldiers wherever they could find them. Up in space, three hundred kilometers overhead, more fighters were slamming missiles against the defensive screens of a large Tush cruiser. For the first time in weeks, the Marine perimeter was not under direct fire, and the terrain surrounding the base was free of enemy forces.

He watched the main tactical display with its glowing icons marking the defensive dome and five incoming fighters. At a prearranged instant, one segment of the defensive screen wavered and vanished.

Energy screens and shields were three-dimensional projections of spacial distortion, an effect based on the projection of gravitational distortion used in space drives. Shields reflected incoming traffic, while screens absorbed and stored the released energy.

While screens were useful in relatively low-energy combat zones, they could be overloaded by nukes, and they weren't good at stopping solid projectiles like missiles or high-energy KK rounds. With shields, incoming beams, missiles, and radiation were twisted through 180 degrees by the sharp and extremely tight curvature of space. Warheads and incoming projectiles were vaporized when they folded back into themselves, beams redirected outward in a spray of defocused energy. Warheads detonating just outside the area of warped space had both radiation and shock wave redirected outward.

As the ground around the outside of the perimeter became molten, however, some heat began leaking through at the shield's base faster than heat-sink dissipaters could cool the ground. When the projectors laid out on the ground along the perimeter began sinking into patches of liquid rock, they failed. The enemy's strategy in a bombardment like the one hammering Mike-Red was to overload the dissipaters and destroy the projectors.

The Marines were using shields *and* screens in an attempt to stay ahead of the bombardment, with banks of portable dissipater units running nonstop in the ongoing fight to keep the ground solid.

It was a fight they were losing.

"Perhaps it would be best to have these spacecraft remain outside the energy barriers," Jamel Hamid said. "The Turusch could use this opportunity to—"

"I *know* what the enemy is capable of," Gorman snapped. "Get the hell out of my way."

He brushed past the civilian for a closer look at the 3-D display. One of the energy-shield facets—number three—winked off just ahead of the oncoming formation of fliers. The Starhawks glided across the perimeter, and the shield came up again behind them, flickered uncertainly, then stabilized. An instant later, a particle beam stabbed down from space. The Romeo had spotted the momentary breach and tried to take advantage of it with a snap shot, but the beam struck the shield and scattered harmlessly outward.

"Shit, that was close," a Marine shield tech at one of the boards said.

"Cut the chatter," Gorman said. "Watch those projectors."

"Aye, aye, sir. Sorry, sir."

One reason the beachhead had been set up on a rocky ridgetop was that molten rock tended to flow downhill, not up into the perimeter and the shield projectors. Repeated shocks against the lower slopes of the ridge, however, were threatening to undermine the perimeter. Gorman had already given orders to set out two replacement projectors, for number five and number six, placing them back a hundred meters as the ground sagged and crumbled beneath the originals.

Eventually, enemy fire would eat away the entire hill.

"Number four is failing," the shield tech reported. "I recommend a reset."

"How long do we have?" Gorman asked.

"Hard to estimate, General. An hour. Maybe two. Depends on how soon they resume the bombardment."

Of course. *Everything* depended on the enemy. That was the hell of it. Gorman hated being trapped like this, stuck in a hole, forced to react to the enemy's initiative, unable even to shoot back, since to do so the Marines had to drop one of the shields, which would mean a torrent of Turusch fire and warheads pouring through the gap.

The respite the Navy zorchies had brought the defenders was the first breather they'd had in weeks, but it wouldn't be long before more Tushie ground units moved into the area and took the perimeter under fire . . . or until more capital ships moved overhead and started pounding the beachhead again with nukes and HE-beams.

"I still don't see why you're letting those fighters come inside the shields," Hamid said. "They can't do any good in here."

"In case you weren't paying attention, *Mister* Hamid," Gorman said, choosing his words carefully, "those pilots have been giving the Turusch one hell of a fight. They're out of missiles, and either out of or running damned thin on other expendables. They need to touch down and get their craft serviced. I imagine the *pilots* need servicing as well."

"Perhaps they should land in shifts, then. . . ."

"Mr. Hamid, I've had just about enough of your second-guessing and carping. Get off my quarterdeck!"

"I remind you, General, that *I* am in command of this colony!"

"And I am in command of the Marine Expeditionary Force. Bradley!"

"Sir!"

"Please escort this civilian off of Marine property. If he shows his face around here again, he is to be placed under guard and confined to his quarters."

"Aye, aye, General!"

"General Gorman!" Hamid said, his face reddening. "I must protest!

"Protest all you damned well please," Gorman replied, shrugging, "just as soon as we get back to Earth!"

"Your anti-Islamic stance has been noted, General! Sheer antitheophilia! This will all go onto my report to my government!"

"Get him out of here, Major Bradley."

"With pleasure, General! C'mon, you."

Hamid started to say something more, seemed to think better of it, then turned and strode toward the CIC command center door. Bradley grinned at Gorman, then followed the man out. Hamid, clearly, was furiously angry, and there would be repercussions later. If there *was* a later. Gorman was willing to face the political fallout if they could just hang on long enough to get his people off this toxic hell-hole.

Gorman watched the civilian go, scowling. That crack about his being antitheophilic had been just plain nasty.

But, of course, the colonists on Haris were Refusers—the descendants of Muslims who'd refused to sign the Covenant of the Dignity of Humankind or accept the enforced rewrite of their Holy Qu'ran. Gorman, too, was a Refuser—at least in spirit. His church had accepted the Covenant, but many of its members had not.

Bastards . . .

The five Navy zorchies were settling in on the landing field now, the fighter icons gathering at the field's north end.

"Carleton!" he growled.

"Yes, sir!"

"Get your ass down there and get Stores moving on those g-fighters," he said. "I want their tubes reloaded and those ships ready to boost, absolutely minimum on the turn-around."

"Aye, aye, sir," his adjutant said, heading for the door.

Hamid had been right in principle, if not in execution. The faster they got those ships reloaded and out on patrol, the better.

Another nine hours before the naval battlegroup arrived.

It was going to be close.

Chapter Six

CIC, TC/USNA CVS America
Eta Boötis IV
2320 hours, TFT

Rear Admiral Koenig walked through the hatch onto the Combat Information Center deck. He'd spent the last six hours trying to sleep, but not even the various electronic soporifics available through the ship's medical resources had helped. He'd finally dozed off with a trickle charge to his sleep center, but he felt far from rested now.

The battlegroup was now deep inside the Eta Boötean solar system, closing on Haris. He checked his internal time readout: twenty-seven minutes, fifteen seconds more.

And then they would know.

Traveling now at just over the speed of light, each ship of the battlegroup now effectively was locked up in its own tight little universe. They couldn't see out, couldn't see the starbow as they'd approached *c*, couldn't even see the light of the local sun growing more brilliant ahead.

"Captain Buchanan," he said softly. The AI monitoring CIC picked up the words and linked him through to Buchanan, on the *America*'s bridge."

"Yes, Admiral."

"How's she riding?"

"Twenty-seven minutes, and we'll know the worst."

"It'll be fine, Rand. There won't be much scattering, not after a short hop like this."

In fact, he'd been surprised at how closely in proximity to one another the ships of the battlegroup had emerged out in the Eta Boötean Kuiper Belt early that morning after the thirty-seven light year passage out from Sol.

"I know, Admiral. I've brought *America* to general quarters. We have all five squadrons set to launch as soon as we bleed down to Drift, one on CAP, four on strike. The keel weapon is charged and ready to fire. Battlespace drones are prepped and programmed, ready for launch."

"Very good."

Cut off from all contact with the other ships of the battlegroup, Koenig had to assume the other ship captains were following the oplan, bringing their crew to quarters and preparing for the coming battle. For the past several months, the battlegroup had been training, shuttling between Sol's Kuiper Belt and Mars. Practicing the maneuvers necessary to break out of Alcubierre Drive in the best possible formations, allowing for both flexibility and strength in combat.

There was no way to anticipate what the tactical situation would be in the inner system, and no way to guess how successful the initial gravfighter strike had been. The battlegroup might emerge to find Blue Omega in command of the battlespace, the Turusch vessels destroyed or having fled.

More likely by far, they would find the Turusch bloodied but fighting mad, ready and waiting for the new arrivals. They wouldn't know until they actually dropped out of metaspace and saw the situation for themselves.

At least that damned Senate liaison had finally taken the hint and was staying out of CIC. That was one particular aggravation he didn't need at the moment.

Koenig had already lied to the Senate Military Directorate about one key aspect of this operation, and he wasn't eager to face Quintanilla's questions.

That particular problem could wait its turn.

Blue Omega Seven
Eta Boötis IV
2335 hours, TFT

Daylight had come and gone with astonishing swiftness, and it was dark now. The optics implanted in Gray's eyes allowed him to see by infrared, but he wasn't used to working in an environment where you saw things by the heat they radiated, smeared and fuzzy and out of focus.

He was exhausted. He'd been running, it seemed, for hours before the weaving tendrils underfoot had thinned out and he'd entered a scorched-bare and rocky desert. Scattered patches of surviving tendrils on the ground glowed with radiant heat, their movements an eerie shifting difficult for the eye to follow. Here, too, patches of bare rock glowed yellow-hot under infrared; he suspected that he might have entered the barren kill zone surrounding the Marine base, where the ground cover had been burned off by the ongoing bombardment by Turusch heavy weapons.

He felt more exposed now, to Turusch scanners and observation drones, which were certain to be lurking about. He would have to move more cautiously here. At least those damned leeches, the gray, swift-gliding leaf shapes, appeared to have vanished once the orange ground cover had given out.

What the hell had those things been? His e-suit was still intact, but he'd had the distinct impression that those things had been scraping away at the outer carbon nanotube weave of the garment. That material was incredibly tough, but Gray wasn't about to trust the integrity of his environmental suit with those things swarming over it, not when a single tear could leave him gasping in high-pressure poison.

Gray staggered to the top of a low, bare-rock outcrop and studied his surroundings. Somewhere to the north, across that empty desert, was the Marine perimeter. He needed to decide now whether to keep walking, or if he should hole up here and start transmitting an emergency distress call.

The only way he was going to get through the Marine shield would be if they sent a SAR—a Search and Rescue mission—out to get him. He had no way to get through the tightly folded space of the shield . . . and though his e-suit would protect him well enough from the radiation, it wouldn't let him weather a nearby burst from a nuclear warhead, or a bolt of charged particles searing down from low orbit.

On the other hand, the moment he started transmitting, he was likely to attract attention from Turusch battlespace probes, or even from enemy spacecraft in orbit.

Shit. Damned if he did, damned if he didn't.

He wondered how long he had before daylight. His implant RAM had a brief listing of planetary stats for Eta Boötis IV—Haris, as the human colonists called it. He knew the planet's rotational period was short—only about fourteen and a half hours. But the planet also had an extreme axial tilt, literally lying on its side as it circled its hot primary once each four years. At the equator, daylight lasted about seven hours throughout that long year, followed by a seven-hour night. At the poles, the sun would disappear for a year at a time, alternating with year-long periods of sunlight, and with everything in between.

What a freaking weird world!

He wasn't sure what the length of the day or night was at this point on the surface. Mike-Red, he knew from his briefings, was at 22 degrees north. He knew that this was late fall or early winter in the northern hemisphere. That suggested that the nights in this region were longer than the days, but he didn't know how long that actually might be.

Not that it particularly mattered. Whether he attracted the attention of a Marine SAR aircraft—or of a Turusch battlecruiser—they'd see him, no matter how dark it was.

The distant thunder of battle had faded away a long time ago. He wasn't quite sure when the landscape had become eerily silent, but it had been before it had gotten dark. Did that mean the battle was over, or merely that there was a temporary lull in the fighting?

If the battle was over, who had won?

He looked up at the darkness overhead—a solid cloud deck masked by darkness. Cloud cover over Haris ran around ninety percent. The skies cleared occasionally, but most of the time they were clouded over. He wished he could see the stars.

Gray sagged to the ground, his shoulder propping him up against a small boulder. God, he was exhausted! His legs, his whole body ached, and the high gravity had his heart pounding, his breath coming in shallow gasps.

How long could he survive out here? Theoretically, the e-suit would keep providing him with air, water, and a nanotech-assembled paste that passed more or less plausibly for food, all cycled from the local atmosphere, handfuls of dirt or organic material poured into a hip pocket, and his own wastes. But even the best machines, he knew all too well, had their limits.

In any case, sooner or later someone would detect him and track him down. The question was whether that someone would be human or . . . or whatever the Turusch were.

He shuddered at the thought. Very little was known about the Turusch, about their culture, their biology, their psychology, even their true shape. They were part of the galaxy-spanning empire of the Sh'daar, and they had a military technology equivalent to—or perhaps a little better than—that of the Confederation of Humankind. The scuttlebutt was that the Marines at Mike-Red had managed to capture a few of the bastards, which was why this mission was supposed to be so damned important.

If the Turusch picked up his come-get-me call, he might be about to see them firsthand.

Not a pleasant thought. But there was nothing else he could do. If he didn't start transmitting, he would either die out here or the Turusch would get him, sooner or later. At least if he was broadcasting on the emergency band, there was a chance the Marines would get to him first. Closing his eyes, he focused his thoughts on three discreet mental code groups, then clicked "transmit" on his IHD. The signal was coded, designed to attract the attention of human equipment and to look like noise to the enemy . . . but no one counted on the Turusch not being able to recognize the signal as artificial, at least.

The fleet ought to be overhead within another few minutes. That, more than anything else, had decided him on whether or not to trigger the distress beacon. If the Turusch were still up there, they shortly would be too busy to notice a single pilot on the ground.

Gray wondered if the Dragonfires were still up, still fighting. Hours ago they must have run dry on expendables, but they would be able to restock at the Marine base. Boss Al would be sending them out on CAP over the base, until the battlegroup arrived. And if one of them happened to swing out *this* way . . .

He caught movement, a flash of short infrared sliding across his peripheral vision. Whirling and dropping flat on the ground, he stared into the darkness. Had a Turusch probe, or even a ground patrol, found him already?

There it was again . . . another flash of movement. With a miserable sinking feeling at the pit of his stomach, he realized he was seeing a mass of those leaf-shaped gliders, hundreds of them radiating in the infrared and moving straight toward him through the night.

Gray jerked his laser carbine off his shoulder. The weapon had no stock and, in any case, his helmet would keep him from aiming it by eye. A touch to a pressure plate, however, switched on a targeting reticule in his IHD, a small red circle marking what the weapon's muzzle was pointed at. A second touch brought up the power, and a reedy tone in his earphone told him the weapon was ready to fire.

But there were so many of the things! They moved a few at a time, giving the impression of a huge, flat, glowing amoeba creeping over the ground by extending pseudopods ahead of the main body.

He moved the weapon awkwardly until the targeting reticule was centered on the central mass of creatures, and fired. Infrared vision picked up the flash of the beam as it heated air molecules along its path, though it was invisible at optical wavelengths. The glowing mob of organisms shifted and parted, momentarily becoming two smaller masses with a hot spot between them . . . but they kept flowing forward,

merging and blending until they were a single mass once
more.

He fired again . . . and then again.

"I'm not on the fucking menu!" he screamed, and then
he was triggering burst after burst of laser fire, the shots
becoming wilder and wilder as the gliders started flowing
up the sides of the outcrop. . . .

CIC, TC/USNA CVS America
Approaching Eta Boötis IV
2347 hours, TFT

"Time to normal space transition," *America*'s AI said, "in
twenty-five seconds."

Koenig leaned back in his couch on its raised platform
in the middle of CIC, letting his gaze shift from station to
station. The men and women in the pit all leaned back, their
virtual instrumentation hovering in front of them, glowing
in the muted lighting of the compartment. The tac display
showed *America*'s calculated position relative to both Ea
Boötis and Eta Boötis IV; they would be emerging above
Eta Boötis's night side, between twenty and fifty thousand
kilometers out.

But calculating precisely where a starship would emerge
from the bubble of the Alcubierre Drive always entailed far
more guesswork than navigators or ship captains generally
cared to think about. There was even a chance—an infini-
tesimally small one—that one of the battlegroup's ships
would slam into the planet while still moving faster than
light. The ship itself, of course, cocooned in its bubble of
spacetime, wouldn't be involved in the collision directly.
Only the leading edge of warped space enclosing it would
actually intersect with the planet. But that intersection could
disrupt the planetary crust, and the ship would be dumped
into the middle of the chaos that ensued.

The ship would almost certainly be destroyed, and the
disruption to the planet's crust might finish off the Marines
where the Turusch bombardment had failed.

Koenig wondered if the Turusch ever used the Alcubierre Effect to destroy planets . . . and if the battlegroup would find Eta Boötis IV still intact when they broke out of warp.

They would know in another few seconds. . . .

Those seconds dwindled away, and precisely on schedule *America*'s AI triggered a warpfield collapse.

Light, twisted into a circular rainbow by spacetime shear effect, exploded outward as the field evaporated. *America*'s true velocity relative to the space around it was only a few meters per second, and as the spacetime bubble opened, her effective velocity dropped from just over *c* to almost nothing in a literal flash of tortured photons. To an observer outside, space seemed to open, a circular starbow unfolded from within, and the ship emerged with stately grace into normal space.

From inside the ship, the stars, for just an instant, assumed the characteristic starbow encircling the vessel forward, then shifted back into more familiar patterns.

Eta Boötis glowed hot and yellow orange almost directly ahead, with its fourth planet a slender, silver-yellow crescent bowed away from the star just beside the glare. A readout on his virtual display showed they'd emerged 38,000 kilometers out from the planet's night side—bang on-target. On the tactical display above the pit, red points of light began winking on in rapid-fire succession, starting close to the green-lit globe marking the planet and extending farther and farther out as *America*'s sensor suites picked up EM returns and emissions from other ships near the planet. The ship's AI identified the signals as quickly as they came in, then plotted positions and vectors on the display.

A solitary blue light winked on against the planet's night side. The Marine perimeter, at least, was still intact.

Koenig breathed a sigh of relief when he saw that. The mission had not been launched in vain after all.

All of the lights marking spacecraft, however, were red— enemy ships. None were blue. Either the fighter strike had been wiped out in the attack hours before, they'd been disabled and drifted clear of battlespace, or they were down on the planet's surface.

Other lights were coming on now—yellow ones—indicating unidentified targets. Most of those would be disabled ships—hulks, critically damaged vessels, or even large chunks of debris. The Dragonfires, Koenig noted, had made a definite impression on the Turusch; there could be no doubt about that.

And even as he watched, the first pair of blue fighters emerged from *America*'s twin launch tubes at nearly 170 meters per second. The first pair was followed by a second, and then a third. VFA-49, the Star Tigers, began arrowing into the heart of the Turusch fleet.

At the same time, other fighters were emerging from the drop tubes circling *America*'s spine. As the carrier rotated on its axis, creating spin gravity for her crew, centripetal force flung the fighters of VFA-42, the Nighthawks, clear of the shadow of *America*'s forward shield and into space with a relatively sedate velocity of five meters per second.

In seconds, a cloud of gravfighters began to encircle the carrier, moving outward.

"We're counting thirty-four active Turusch capital ships," Commander Craig told him. "Eight more appear to be heavily damaged, but still have active power sources." She hesitated. "Lots of fighters . . . but we're not picking up any friendlies."

"Very well," Koenig said. "Captain Buchanan? You may accelerate and engage as soon as all of our fighters are clear."

"Aye, aye, sir."

If the initial numbers were to be believed, the Dragonfires had destroyed at least thirteen Turusch warships, and damaged eight more, a *very* respectable showing for just twelve gravfighters. Data tags alongside the slowly drifting red icons in the display showed that several of the remaining enemy vessels were damaged as well.

That gave the *America* battlegroup a decent chance against the survivors of the Turusch fleet, chances better than even, at any rate. A lot would depend on how prepared the enemy was for the Confederation fleet's arrival.

He'd not expected to see any Dragonfires in the battlespace, not after nine hours. He just hoped that most of them had been able to win through to the Marine perimeter on the planet.

Blue Omega One
VFA-44 Dragonfires
Battlespace Eta Boötis IV
2352 hours, TFT

"All Blue Omegas are in position and ready for boost," Commander Allyn said. "We'll take our count from you."

"Copy that, Blue One," the voice of a Marine in MEF HQ Operations Control replied. "The shield is coming down in five . . . four . . . three . . . two . . . one . . . *mark!*"

The five gravfighters were already airborne, configured for atmospheric flight and floating vertical, their noses aimed at the night sky just south of the zenith. As the shield section flicked off, the fighters began accelerating, a slight ripple preceding them as artificial singularities winked into place. Within seconds, they were shrieking skyward. A thick cloud of vapor engulfed each as it lanced toward heaven, stretching out behind and forming a cone shape as the Starhawks went supersonic, then vanishing as they went hypersonic seconds later. Behind and below, the Marine shields switched back on and the base lights vanished.

"Hey Skipper?" Tucker, Blue Eight, called. "I'm getting an EDS here. AI says it's Prim!"

Allyn glanced at her virtual com suite display, saw the wink of a contact light, with bearing and range. So Prim had survived! Or, at least, the emergency distress beacon built into his e-suit was still functioning, which wasn't necessarily the same thing.

"Got it," she said, patching the signal through back to MED HQ.

"Shouldn't I go back down and try to find him?"

Katie Tucker was Prim's wing. Of course she wanted to cover her partner. "Negative, Tuck," she replied. "The Marines'll take care of him." *If they can*, she added to herself, but she didn't speak the thought aloud.

"Yeah, we got other Tushies to fry," Blue Five put in. "Let's *do* it!"

On Allyn's tactical display, six Turusch capital ships and a score of fighters were picked out by red icons above Eta Boötis IV. All were under acceleration, and appeared to be outbound from the planet's night side. She extended the range on her display, and the blue icons of the emerging carrier battlegroup winked on.

The five surviving Blue Omega fighters had pulled several two-ship patrols in the time since they'd arrived at Mike-Red, aimed mostly at keeping the Turusch at a respectful distance. The bombardment of the Marine perimeter had all but stopped. With Blue Omega's arrival, the enemy had known that the battlegroup would be on the way, and they'd obviously been preparing for its arrival, the Marines on-planet now a far lower priority than the approaching Confederation fleet.

The overall tactical situation offered the handful of Starhawks on the surface of Eta Boötis IV a rare opportunity. With the *America* battlegroup emerging from metaspace off the planet's dark side, the Turusch fleet was swinging about and accelerating to meet it . . . and in the process turning their backs on Allyn and the remnants of her squadron.

White light blossomed, startling and stark against the night. The Tushies hadn't entirely forgotten the base, or the fighters hidden there. "Everyone okay?" she called as the crackle of EM static faded.

"Blue Eight, okay!"

"Blue Five, still here."

"Blue Six. Got a little crisp there for a sec, but okay."

"Blue Three. Rog."

The black bulk of Eta Boötis's night side dropped away as the five Blue Omegas streaked out of the turbulent atmosphere.

"Okay, children," Allyn told the others. "Let's put them where they count!"

"Sur*prise*, you freaking Tush bastards!" Lieutenant Tucker called over the tac channel. "Omega Eight, target lock! And *Fox One*!"

Allyn was already targeting a Sierra-class cruiser, eight thousand kilometers ahead. "Omega One! Target lock! Fox One!"

The Krait slid off the rail and through the momentary puckered opening in the Starhawk's smoothly shifting surface and vanished into the distance. Seconds later, it detonated against the Sierra's screens with a swelling, nuclear fireball . . . but Allyn was already breaking right and high, targeting another enemy vessel.

Then the Tush fighters were closing on them from three directions, swinging around and back to engage the sudden pop-up strike from the planet's surface. The five Confederation fighters went into the merge accelerating hard, engaging the fighters with particle beams and KK cannon, saving the heavy-hitting Kraits for capital ship targets.

For the next several seconds, the combat was a confused blur of fast-moving ships, black space, and fireballs. Twice, Allyn's Starhawk AI intervened to throw the ship one way or the other to avoid hurtling pieces of white-hot debris. She saw her CPG beam spear through an oncoming Toad just ahead, and then the sky lit up with an eye-searing explosion, pelting her outer hull with high-velocity bits of shrapnel. Warning tones sounded in her ear as gravitic missiles locked on and accelerated toward her. Sand canisters thumped into the void, blocking the enemy thrusts.

Ahead, two massive battlefleets engaged. . . .

CIC, TC/USNA CVS America
Battlespace Eta Boötis IV
2354 hours, TFT

"Main spinal mount!" Captain Buchanan called from the bridge, "*Fire!*"

On the tactical display, a beam of white light snapped out from the icon of the *America*, connecting the carrier momentarily with an Alpha-class Turusch line battleship—a small asteroid ten times the length of the carrier and bristling with weapon mounts. Its pitted outer surface was pocked and splotched in places by white-hot craters where Confederation weapons had already and repeatedly struck home.

Screens and displays within CIC showed the unfolding fleet action from dozens of different perspectives, the scenes relayed to the battlegroup flag by sensor drones scattered across the battlespace. *America*'s spinal mount PBP fired a proton beam invisible to the eye or to drone cameras, but it impacted the Turusch shields at energies of up to 1.15 TeV.

Most of that kinetic energy was splashed aside by bent-space shields or electromagnetic screens, but enough leaked through to melt shield projectors set into the asteroid warship's surface.

And when enough shield projectors were knocked out, the target became vulnerable. . . .

At this point, Koenig's role was more that of observer than of military commander. He could suggest strategy and coordination with the other ships of the battlegroup, but Buchanan was captain of the *America*, the one fighting the ship.

In fact, he thought with a touch of bemusement, the engagement already had become far too big, too fast, and too spread out for any human mind to grasp it, much less control what was happening. *America*'s AI was running tracking and targeting, firing the weapons, maintaining screens and shields.

All twenty-six of the other Confederation ships in the battlegroup had emerged from Alcubierre Drive and were accelerating now, swiftly building up to combat velocities. The railgun cruiser *Kinkaid* had fallen into position one hundred kilometers abeam of the *America*, and was joining her considerable firepower to that of *America*'s main gun. The *Kinky* pounded at the asteroid warship, now just eighteen thousand kilometers ahead, with kinetic-kill slugs accelerated at five hundred gravities down its kilometer-long superconductor rail.

"Admiral!" Hughes, the CIC tac evaluator, called out, excited. "We're picking up fighters. *Our* fighters, coming up from the planet behind the Trash fleet!"

"How many?" he snapped.

There was an agonizing pause. "Five. *Just* five. But . . ."

"Synch their data inks with ours," Koenig said, interrupting. "Coordinate their attacks with ours."

"Aye, aye, sir."

There'd be time to count the losses later . . . and to mourn them. Right now, the god of battles had offered the Confederation fleet a singular opportunity, and he was going to take the fullest possible advantage of it.

Chapter Seven

26 September 2404

Tactician Emphatic Blossom at Dawn
Enforcer Radiant Severing
0004 hours, TFT

Emphatic Blossom at Dawn, like all of the Turusch, was of three minds.

Literally. The Mind Above, as the Turusch thought of it, was the more primitive, the more atavistic, the original consciousness set that had arisen on the Turusch homeworld perhaps three million of their orbital periods in the past. The Mind Here was thought of as a cascade of higher-level consciousness from the Mind Above, more refined, sharper, faster, and more concerned with the song of intellect.

And the Mind Below was more recent still, an artifact of both Turusch and Sh'daar technology, a merging of Minds Here into a single, more-or-less unified instrumentality.

For Emphatic Blossom, the Mind Above, a shrill demand almost beyond reason, screamed, *"Kill!"* The Mind Here, analyzing the data coming through the artificial awareness of the Enforcer *Radiant Severing*, echoed the demand to kill, modifying it with sensory data and intelligence flowing through its linkages with the ship. *"Kill,"* yes, but with an awareness that the Turusch fleet was now caught between two separate and rapidly closing tentacles of enemy force, that the fleet was caught in a crossfire that seriously hampered its maneuverability and limited its tactical options. There was a distinct possibility of gaining an important advantage if the enemy carrier vessel could be crippled or destroyed.

But the Mind Below carried a different message entirely.

"There are strategic considerations that take precedence beyond the tactical," Blossom's Mind Below was saying. *"The Sh'daar Seed requires that we withdraw."*

"Threat!" cried the Mind Above. *"Kill!"*

"The prime orders have not yet been fulfilled," replied the Mind Here. *"Enemy ground forces remain on the objective world, as do the nonmilitary components. These should be eliminated before we withdraw."*

"The ground forces will soon be withdrawn. This is the judgment of the Sh'daar Seed. The prime orders will be fulfilled."

"Threat!" cried the Mind Above. *"Kill!"*

"But we can yet inflict severe damage on the enemy," the Mind Here insisted. *"Our sensors have identified no fewer than twelve major vessels in the alien fleet massing greater than twenty-eight thousand g'ri, including their fighter carrier. Destruction of those vessels would seriously weaken the enemy's ability to mount a counteroffensive against Turusch fleet elements and bases within the sector.*

"And the Sh'daar Seed, as ever, circulates plans within plans. When the enemy reaches the Bright One, all of the enemy ships shall be destroyed, and their homeworld left defenseless."

"Threat!" cried the Mind Above. *"Kill!"*

The Turusch tactician considered the matter further, then agreed, Mind Below and Mind Here slipping into harmony. It *had* to, since the Sh'daar Seed's suggestions took precedence even over the judgment of a tactician.

Still, it would be extremely difficult for the Turusch fleet to extricate itself without suffering further significant damage. The enemy carrier and several other vessels were concentrating their fire on the *Radiant Severing*, and other vessels of the fleet were being pounded by enemy fighters.

Emphatic Blossom at Dawn could not directly refuse the Seed's suggestion—such a choice was literally and physically impossible—but it did have a great deal of latitude in how it carried out the Seed's suggestions.

The heart of the enemy's offensive capability was their carrier. Destroying that vessel would be the key to extracting the Turusch battle fleet from this pocket.

CIC, TC/USNA CVS America
Eta Boötis IV
0007 hours, TFT

The last of the fighters—SG-92 Starhawks and the older SG-55 War Eagles—were away, VFA-36, the Death Rattlers, flying Combat Air Patrol around the *America*, the rest lancing at high-G into the Turusch battle fleet. Kiloton nuclear pulses flashed in the distance as warheads blossomed with white fury, reduced to twinkling pinpoints by the distance.

"Three Golf-Mikes inbound," a CIC technician reported, her voice calm. "Intercept course, detonation in thirty seconds."

"Countermeasures deployed," another voice said.

"Escort *Farragut* moving to intercept," Craig reported.

Koenig watched the battle developing. The enemy had more ships than the Confederation battlegroup, and a slight technological lead in such areas as gravitics, shields, and beam weaponry, but they'd been bloodied by the fighter strike earlier and were acting in an uncoordinated, almost sluggish manner.

The large vessel ahead—an asteroid, it appeared, partially hollowed out, given massive gravitic drives and mounted with weapons—was probably the enemy command ship. With more and more of the battlegroup's weaponry concentrating on that one giant ship, it was possible that they were having trouble coordinating their fleet.

Gravitic shields blocked radio waves and lasercom beams. Typically, ships coordinated with one another in combat by flickering one section of their shields off and on while trans-

mitting tightly packaged comm bursts precisely timed with
the shield openings. Pile on enough firepower to keep the
enemy's shields up, and you kept him from communicating
with other ships as well.

The Turusch fleet was attempting to rush the *America* . . .
the largest vessel in the Confederation fleet. *That's what I
would do*, Koenig told himself. As more and more beams
and missiles slammed against the Turusch command vessel's shields, the enemy's fleet organization became looser,
less coherent.

But the enemy ships kept moving forward, sending waves
of nuke-tipped missiles and Toad fighters out ahead of the
lumbering capital ships.

Even disorganized, that swarm of Turusch ships would be
able to overwhelm *America*'s defenses in fairly short order.

Koenig looked around, momentarily expecting Quintanilla to be there watching, criticizing. The operational
orders issued by the Senate Military Directorate while the
battlefleet was still gathering off Mars—several hundred
megabytes' worth of detailed instructions—had been *very*
explicit. Koenig was not to risk the star carrier *America*. She
was one of only six ships of her class, and the Military Directorate wanted to minimize the chances of her being lost
or badly damaged. Those orders had directed Koenig, *if the
tactical situation warranted it*, to take the *America* no closer
than fifty AUs to Eta Boötis IV, and to direct the battle from
there. At all costs, the *America* was to avoid direct ship-to-
ship combat.

Sheer nonsense, of course, the appraisal of armchair
admirals and politicians considering the possible course
of a naval engagement from the comfort and security of
their offices and conference rooms thirty-seven light years
away. You could not direct a battle from four hundred light
minutes away, not when the situation was over six and a
half hours old by the time you received a status update
transmission from the rest of the fleet, and with six and
a half hours more before your orders crawled back to the
fleet. Even worse, Koenig would actually have had to split
his small fleet to ensure that *America* had combat sup-

port. If the Turusch detected *America*, caught her traveling alone, they could launch a long-range fighter strike or
send a small detachment of warships to attack the lurking
carrier.

Unsupported, the carrier wouldn't have a chance in ten of
survival.

And so Koenig had deliberately violated his orders. The
phrase "if the tactical situation warranted" was his loophole,
his way out. So far as Koenig was concerned, the tactical
situation did *not* warrant either splitting his fleet or trying
to run the show from over six light hours away. The phrase
was, in fact, a cover-your-ass clause for the politicians; if
America and her battlefleet were destroyed or suffered serious damage, the admirals and the Directorate senators could
shrug and say, "Well, it wasn't *our* fault. Koenig disobeyed
orders."

Pretty standard stuff. If the Confederation won and the
Marines were successfully evacuated, the breach of orders
would be quietly ignored. Otherwise . . .

Three hundred kilometers ahead, the escort *Farragut* had
changed course, moving across *America*'s path to help shield
the carrier from oncoming missile volleys. Two Turusch
missiles struck the escort's shields, the twin, silent flashes
minute but dazzling on the CIC display screens.

But Confederation fire was hammering home among the
Turusch ships as well. The *Kinkaid* continued to slam high-
velocity kinetic-kill projectiles into the suspected enemy
command-control ship. *America* was cycling her spinal
mount weapon as quickly as possible—firing about once
each fifteen seconds—targeting the same Turusch asteroid
ship. If they could just keep up the pressure, if they could
keep the enemy command ship's shields up . . .

"*Farragut* reports heavy damage," Hughes reported.
"She's falling out of the fight."

Koenig turned in his seat to check one of the monitors
relaying visuals from a battlespace drone out ahead of the
carrier. *Farragut* was a missile escort, small and fast with
a bundle of twenty-four mamba launch tubes tunneling
through the center of her forward shield cap, massing 2200

tons and carrying a crew of 190 men and 15 officers. The ugly little missile boats were designed to dash in close, loose a swarm of high-yield smart missiles in the merge with the enemy formation, and accelerate clear under high-G boost. On the display, the *Farragut* was barely making way, her drive fields dead; he could actually *see* her on the screen, which meant her gravitic shields were down or intermittent only, and a portion of her aft drive structure was a tangled mass of wreckage, glowing white-hot and trailing a stream of half-molten debris like streaming sparks in the night. Another·missile struck the craft, the flash lighting up the display, a dazzling, single pulse of light, and as the glare faded, the *Farragut* reappeared, her drive section gone, the forward stem and shield cap tumbling end-over-end. Radiation scanners aboard the drone were pegging the readouts in CIC off the scale.

There was no sign of escape pods evacuating the hulk. Two hundred five men and women . . .

The missile boat's skipper, Maria Hernandez, had been *America*'s Operations officer until she'd been promoted to captain and given command of the *Farragut*.

She'd also been a friend.

"Controller," Koenig said.

"Yes, sir." The controller was Commander Vincent Reigh, and he was responsible for directing all fighters and other secondary spacecraft operating in *America*'s battlespace— the voice who directed the fighters to their targets and who passed new orders to the fighter squadrons as the combat situation changed.

"Have all fighters concentrate on target . . ." He paused to read the code group off the tac display. "Target Charlie-Papa One." Charlie because it was the probable enemy command ship, Papa for a planetoid converted into a warship, and One because it was the most massive vessel so far spotted within the enemy fleet.

"All fighters to target Charlie-Papa One, aye, aye, Admiral."

Right now, most of *America*'s fighters had merged with the enemy fleet and passed through to the other side. There, they would decelerate, reform, and begin accelerating back through the enemy fleet, joining the five fighters coming out from Eta Boötis's night side.

Silent detonations continued to pulse and strobe throughout the Turusch fleet, but more and more were concentrating on the enemy command vessel. So damned little was known about Turisch combat psychology, even after the disasters at Arcturus Station and Everdawn. If the carrier group could decapitate the enemy by taking out that Charlie-Papa . . . would that be enough to send the rest of them running?

White light filled heaven outside *America*'s shields, and the combat display broke up momentarily in static. "What's our Trapper?"

"Transmission percentage at sixty-one percent, Admiral."

As the Confederation fleet attempted to interfere with the enemy command vessel's ability to transmit orders to other Turusch vessels, the Turusch were attempting to do the same, blasting away at *America*'s shields to force them to stay up, blocking radio and lasercom signals to the other battlegroup ships. Transmission percentage—"Trapper"—was a measure of the clarity of ship-to-ship communications during combat. The harder the enemy hammered at *America*'s shields, the harder it would be to transmit orders to the rest of the battlegroup, or receive tactical updates and requests. Sixty-one percent was actually pretty good. It meant *America*'s shields were open and signals were getting through almost two thirds of the time.

But that was changing quickly as the two fleets moved toward the merge. . . .

SAR Red-Delta
90 km south of Red-Mike HQ
Eta Boötis IV
0015 hours, TFT

"There! To the left!"
"God be praised! I see him."
The UT-84 battlefield hopper, a stubby, blunt-nosed tri-wing, canted sharply to port and descended. Its outer hull

nanoflage shifted to reflect the murky night, the utility craft's gravs howling as they bit through the thick atmosphere. Powerful spotlights stabbed down through the gloom, centering on a lone figure struggling atop a low rock outcropping. The guy appeared to be nearly smothered beneath a shifting, oozing mass of darkness.

"Shit! What *are* those things?"

"We call them shadow swarmers. His e-suit *should* protect him, God willing, if they've not been swarming him for too long. . . ."

Lieutenant Charles Ostend gave his passenger a sidelong glance, then shook his head. God willing? Muhammad Baqr was okay as collies went, but he shared the religious passion of all of the other Mufrids. The God-shouting fundy colonists on this miserable rock were utterly beyond his comprehension with their conviction that *everything*, including their very survival, depended solely upon God's will.

Hell, why anyone would voluntarily choose to live in such a place in the first place was a question Ostend and his buddies in the 4th SAR/Recon Group had discussed endlessly in after-hours bull sessions ever since the Marines had landed and set up the perimeter. That had been . . . what? Five weeks ago? He checked his internal calendar. Yeah. Thirty-seven days. *Earth* days, not the crazy-short daylight cycles they had here.

Shadow swarmers? He'd not heard the term before, but it made as much sense as anything else on Ate a Boot. They'd homed in on a military distress transmission—a rescue beacon in a downed flier's e-suit. They'd found him . . . but the guy was almost smothered by a mass of dark gray, leaf-shaped things. Ostend had the impression of millions of cockroaches, each bigger than a man's outstretched hand and fingers.

He shuddered as he brought the SAR hopper's nose high and gentled toward bare rock. He hated roaches, had an almost phobic fear of the things, and he didn't want to think about what was going through that downed pilot's mind right now.

The guy *was* alive, at least. Ostend could see arms and

legs weakly thrashing about as he tried to pull, scrape, or kick the verminous creatures off of him.

"Okay," Ostend said, uncertain. "How do we get to him?"

"We pull him inside," Baqr told him. "The local life forms cannot tolerate high concentrations of oxygen."

"Hey, Doc!" he called over the craft's intercom. "We've got him in sight! But there's a bit of a complication!"

"Doc" was a Navy corpsman, HMC Anthony McMillan, riding on the hopper's cargo deck aft.

"What complication, Lieutenant?" McMillan replied.

"He's covered with local crawlies. We need to pull him out of there. Mohammed says the oxygen in our air mix'll kill them."

"We'll get him," McMillan said. "Just get us there."

The hopper's two angled ventral wings folded up and rotated back out of the way as landing skids extended, and the craft gentled down ten meters from the writhing mass of swarmers. The port-side cargo-bay door irised open, and two men in Marine utility e-suits and armor jumped out, jogging toward the downed man, the spiders strapped to their backs flexing and working against the planet's gravity. As they moved through the spotlight beams ahead of the hopper, exaggerated shadows shifted and flickered through dust-illumined shafts of light.

Ostend and Baqr watched from the hopper's cockpit, keeping the external lights centered on the writhing figure atop the low rock outcrop. One of the corpsmen began pulling swarmers off the man's suit, peeling them off by the fistful and flinging them away into the darkness. The other was plugging something into the pilot's helmet.

"What are those swarmer things doing to him, anyway?" Ostend asked.

"Trying to eat him, of course," Baqr said with a shrug. "Or, rather, trying to eat his e-suit. They must have become sensitized to the carbon in his e-suit."

"They eat carbon?"

Baqr gave him a mild look. "So do you and I. The life on Eta Boötis is carbon-based, as is the life on Earth. And carbon-based life requires sources of carbon for growth and metabolism. Most of the mobile life forms here get the carbon from carbonaceous mineral deposits—they are lithovores. The sessile forms get it from the carbon dioxide in the atmosphere—lithoautotrophs."

"So, just like plants and animals on Earth."

"Only by very rough analogy. The mobile forms, the swarmers, are more like Earth's plants, actually, getting what they need from the soil. Very *active* plants. They can be so here, with the abundance of energy available on this world."

Mohammed Baqr, Ostend knew, was a xenobiologist, one of the senior scientists in the Mufrid colony on Haris, so he must know what he was talking about. It sounded crazy, though— *plants* moving and swarming like hungry piranhas.

"Can they get through his suit?"

"Eventually. Swarmers possess grinding plates within their ventral orifices, very hard, like organic diamond. The carbon nanoweave fiber of our e-suits is extremely tough, but eventually the grinding will wear through, yes. We've lost several of our people to the swarms."

The two corpsmen were unfolding a collapsible stretcher and were strapping the pilot onto it. Swarmers continued to flit through the shadows, circling, moving closer.

"Those things *can't* be plants."

"The analogy is inexact," Baqr told him. "Remember, this is an alien world, with an alien biosphere. We use words like "plant" and "animal" because these are the only words we have, and they come with meanings shaped by our experiences on Earth. The reality is . . . different. *Much* different."

"Yeah, but look at them! Those things are tracking our people!"

"Technically, the individual swarmers all are part of a single organism. It . . . disperses itself across hundreds of square kilometers in order to locate widely scattered deposits of accessible minerals. When one . . . leaf finds a source of easily ingested carbon, we believe it communicates with the others through low-frequency sound waves transmitted through this dense atmosphere. And they begin to swarm. More and more of them, drawn from farther and farther away."

"So we're dealing with walking, meat-eating trees," Ostend said.

"Ah . . . no. The swarmers are not plants, really."

"Then they're animals that *act* like plants . . . except they eat meat and move?"

"They are neither plants nor animals," Baqr said, a touch of exasperation edging his voice, "not in the sense you mean."

Ostend was about to reply to that, but he saw that the two corpsmen were approaching the hopper, carrying the stretcher between them. So far as he was concerned, the Marines would be getting off of this rock soon and he wouldn't have to worry about swarmers, whatever the hell they truly were, ever again.

"How's the patient?" he called over the comm net.

"Alive, Lieutenant," was McMillan's response. "But that's about all. Cargo deck hatch is closed and sealed."

"Here's some fresh air, then," Ostend said, passing his hand through a virtual control. "Don't try breathing it yet, though." Pure nitrogen began flowing into the pressure-tight cargo deck, forcing out the native atmosphere—nitrogen because the higher oxygen content of a terrestrial atmosphere might react unpleasantly with the methane and other compounds in the Haris gas mix. He brought the cargo deck pressure up to two and a half atmospheres, then began bleeding off the overpressure and adjusting the gas mix to Earth standard.

By that time, the hopper had lifted from that desolate, scorched-rock plain and was streaking north, back toward the Marine perimeter.

To Ostend's way of thinking, in fact, they couldn't leave Haris soon enough. The collie they'd assigned as his friendly native guide could have the place *and* its weird biology.

Blue Omega One
VFA-44 Dragonfires
Battlespace Eta Boötis IV
0022 hours, TFT

"Form on me, Blue Omegas," Allyn called. "Staggered right echelon. Make it *count*!"

The Dragonfires, what was left of them, were well into the merge, hurtling through the rear zone of the Turusch fleet. Enemy vessels were pinging her Starhawk's sensors from every side now. A brilliant flash close aboard marked the detonation of an enemy nuke striking a sandfield.

She knew she was rewriting the book on gravfighter tactics. The question was whether she'd be around later to autograph copies.

Five ships, the tattered remnant of Blue Omega, had continued to close with the Turusch battlefleet. Moments before, dozens of Starhawk fighters—the other strike squadrons off the *America*—had merged with the enemy ships dead ahead, then passed through, leaving a trail of silent, blossoming explosions in their wake. Decelerating swiftly, the other Starhawks had swarmed past the oncoming Blue Omega fighters, heading back toward the planet, slowed to a halt, then begun accelerating back the other way, slowly coming up behind the five Dragonfires.

Blue Omega continued to accelerate, approaching the enemy fleet from behind, well in the lead of the rest of *America*'s gravfighters.

She was angling toward one Turusch ship in particular, a gigantic target identifiable only by its enormous mass. The thing was almost certainly a PC—a planetoid converted to a command ship, with a mass registering in the billions of tons and a shield signature five kilometers long. Allyn couldn't see the ship itself. It was still a long way off, almost two thousand kilometers, and its shields were so hard-driven by Confederation fire right now that they were almost constantly up, rendering the flying mountain all but invisible. As she neared it, though, she could see the strobing pulse and flash of Confederation warheads detonating against those shields, a steady, flickering, coruscating volley as incoming beams, nuclear warheads, and KK projectiles were twisted back by the Turusch gravitic shields in raw sprays of radiation.

And the Blue Omegas were dropping straight into the heart of that pyrotechnic hell.

Allyn checked course, velocity, and rate of closure once again. The idea was to skim past as close to the enemy shields as possible without becoming part of that ongoing cascade of radiation and debris. She also checked for incoming mail; occasional point-defense beams snapped out from enemy ships as they passed, probing, slashing, but most of the Turusch warships were fully occupied with the oncoming carrier battlegroup ahead and had no ordnance to spare for fighters. Enemy fighters, mercifully, were not much in evidence. They appeared to be deploying toward the Confederation battlegroup.

In any combat, there is one precious opportunity, one instant where a small bit of leverage can shift mountains and transform the shape of battle. Marissa Allyn believed she had her hand on that lever now, if the Dragonfires could slip in close.

Gravfighter tactical doctrine focused on combat at mid- to long range. Fighters approaching an enemy warship closer than about fifty kilometers were easy targets for point-defense beam weapons, high-velocity KK autocannon and railguns, even sandcasters. But Allyn thought she saw an opportunity here, an opportunity made possible by the fact that the Turusch command control vessel had its shields full up. There would be no point-defense weapons so long as that was true.

Minutes passed, as the five Starhawks moved into echelon formation, a staggered line with Allyn's fighter in the lead. The last few hundred kilometers flashed past as the Turusch vessel loomed huge in her sensors, visible only as a black mass of grav-twisted space.

A Starhawk's weaponry could not penetrate those shields . . . but there would be shield projectors along the vessel's surface, a grid of wave guides and projectors that threw up the fields of sharply warped space. There were points, carefully screened and camouflaged, where those wave guides were exposed to space. Each would have multiple backups and overlapping defensive fields, but if the Dragonfires could smash through even one line of wave guides, one section, at least, of the enemy ship's gravitic shields would fail.

And with that failure, the enemy would be open to the full and devastating power of the Confederation fleet.

Fifty kilometers . . . forty . . . thirty . . .

"Enemy vessel is within effective range of particle beams and Gatling weaponry," her AI announced.

"Target wave guides amidships, lock, and fire," she said, the verbal order backed by a mental command uplinked through to her fighter's AI.

Particle beams, invisible in the vacuum of space, sparked and flared against the Turusch ship's primary shields. All five Dragonfires were firing now, their AIs coordinating the attack to hammer at one slender join between two shield-plane segments. Incoming mail—fire from the Confederation battlegroup—continued to hammer at the asteroid ship's shields, a glaring cascade of raw energy.

Ten kilometers. The black target and the flaring impacts together filled space ahead. The mass of both Gatling KK projectiles and the protons in her particle beam carried considerable thrust, and she felt the jolt of deceleration. No problem. She wanted to decelerate to give her weapons the maximum possible hang time above the target. A corrective boost . . . and then she switched off the forward-projected singularity to give her weapons a clear field of fire.

She moved her hands through the virtual control field, and the SG-92 and the Starhawk braked, then pivoted sharply, its nose swinging to align with the swift-growing mass of the Turusch asteroid command vessel. Moving sideways now, continuing to pivot to keep the enemy ship directly off the fighter's nose and continuing to fire, the Starhawk slid past the Turusch monster's shields scarcely a kilometer away, passing the target with a relative velocity of less than two kilometers per second.

The close passage was far too fast-moving for merely human reflexes. Allyn's fighter AI controlled the target acquisition, lock, and firing, but she was riding the software through her internal link, providing a measure of human control behind the lightning-swift reflexes of the AI computer. Through that link, she could feel the flow of quantum-based fuzzy logic, the sparkle of equations and angle-of-attack, the bright clarity of computer-enhanced sensory input.

For a brief instant, the asteroid filled her forward field of view, a vast, dark blur rendered almost invisible by its tightly closed gravitic shielding. Her AI continued, with superhuman speed, to focus on a single, thread-thin line of a target. Gatling projectiles slammed across the enemy's shields to either side . . . and then, with startling suddenness, the shield collapsed, revealing a backup shield just beyond. The AI shifted aim slightly and began hammering at a second, reserve wave guide . . . and then at a third when the second shield collapsed as well.

How many reserves were there? Something the size of an asteroid could carry a *lot* of layered wave guides, with only the outer two functioning at any given instant. So little was known about Turusch combat doctrine and the engineering details of their warships. All the Dragonfires could do was continue to hammer at any targets that presented themselves to the fast-shifting perspective of the passing fighters.

The actual close passage lasted perhaps two and a half seconds; it felt like *much* longer. Subjective time slowed for a pilot linked in with her tactical computer in a way that had nothing to do with the time dilation of relativistic travel, and everything to do with the sheer volume of information flooding through her neural pathways.

Her Starhawk had just passed the Turusch ship, was traveling tail-forward now as its nose continued to pivot on the enemy, when a final wave guide vaporized and a last-rank gravitic shield failed.

"Soft target!" she yelled over the comm link, as she triggered the last two of her Krait missiles. For the briefest of instants, she could see a gray and powdery landscape pocked by immense craters, the towers of communications and sensor arrays, the dull-silver domes of weapons turrets and gun positions.

Blue Five was too close to the enemy shields.

"Blue Five!" she yelled over the comm. "Change vector!"

Then white light engulfed her forward sensory inputs, filling her universe with raw, star-hot fury. The blast wave—a shell of hot plasma racing out from the surface of the Turusch asteroid ship at tens of kilometers per second—struck her vessel *hard*, smashing her to one side and putting her into a helplessly out-of-control tumble.

More blast waves followed, a succession of them as the other Dragonfires hammered at the opening with nuke-tipped missiles, and then as incoming warheads from the fleet found the suddenly revealed weakness.

But Allyn had lost consciousness with the first savage impact.

Chapter Eight

Tactician Emphatic Blossom at Dawn
Enforcer Radiant Severing
0032 hours, TFT

Tactician Blossom felt the rumble of successive nuclear strikes pulsing against the rock shell of the *Radiant Severing*. Turusch physiology was extremely sensitive to both air- and ground-borne vibrations and the shudders were painful—the equivalent of blasting a shrill noise into a human's ear.

The gravitic shields were failing, the enemy's nuclear munitions getting through.

In point of fact, the *Radiant Severing*'s command centers were buried deep within the mass of nickel-iron that formed the huge vessel's body. The enemy fleet could pound them for *g'nyuu'm* on end and not reach the ship's deepest recesses.

But the shields would begin to fall one after another now, as each failure uncovered another line of shield wave guides exposed on the planetoid's surface. Eventually, all surface structures would be reduced to radioactive debris; the *Severing* would be blind and deaf with its sensor arrays vaporized, helpless with its weapons destroyed, trapped immobile with its drive projectors inoperative.

"*Kill!*" its higher self screamed, but the middle self overrode the instinct-laden surge of raw emotion.

"Swing to new heading," it ordered the *Severing*'s helm control, adding a string of coordinates. "Accelerate to deepest reach. Pass orders for the rest of the fleet to fall back and cover."

"The enemy may pursue," Blossom's tactical coordinator, its second-in-command, told it. "Our power reserves are low, the damage to our shields severe."

"They will not pursue," Blossom replied, the statement arising jointly from both its low and middle minds. "The enemy is focused on protecting, perhaps recovering its colony on the planet surface. When we return with reinforcements, we will find the enemy long gone."

The system *would* soon be within Turusch tentacle-grasp, of that Emphatic Blossom was certain. The tragedy was that they'd not been able to cripple the enemy fleet as planned . . . most particularly that their fighters had not been able to win through to the enemy fighter carrier and destroy it. Such a blow might well have wrecked the enemy's offensive capabilities in this sector for *g'nyi'nyeh* to come.

But if the enemy force was still more or less intact, so too was the Turusch battlefleet. The *Radiant Severing* was not in contact with the other ships. One of the shields had collapsed. The nuclear fury unleashed within the next few seconds against the planetoid's surface had vaporized lasercom projectors and radio antennae. But as the command vessel withdrew, the other Turusch ships would fall back to protect it.

"Accelerating," the tactical coordinator announced.

Blossom's higher self writhed in an agony of angry frustration.

Marine Sick Bay
Eta Boötis IV
0056 hours, TFT

Gray came fully awake with a rush of panic. *Get them off me!. . .*

But the "they" were gone. He was floating in air, face up,

staring up at the glow panels overhead, heart pounding as fragments of memory clawed at his mind. The scream rising in his throat choked off short. He tried to sit up, and failed.

His eyes opened and he looked up into a metallic nightmare. A robot had emerged from a cabinet in the wall and was hovering above him, all metal and plastic and huge, cold lenses for eyes. The remaining panic induced by the local fauna transferred itself to something more immediate—the looming presence of the medical robot. He screamed, tried to lash out against the thing, but his hands were trapped.

"Whoa. Take it easy there, zorchie," a voice said.

Blinking, he tried to focus on his surroundings. He was in a small, metal-walled compartment, floating above some sort of grav bed. An older man in Marine combat utilities stood nearby, watching, his arms folded. A younger man, also in utilities, sat at a nearby workstation.

Abruptly, the robot folded itself back into its cabinet.

"What . . . happened? . . ."

"You got picked up in the desert by a SAR," the standing man told him. "You remember anything, son?"

There were memories, yes, but they were broken and chaotic. He remembered running through a barren, night-cloaked landscape, remembered the flickering movements at the corners of his eyes, the gathering shadows following his trail.

He remembered sensations of drowning as the shadows covered him, gnawing at his environmental suit, the terror, the rising panic. He remembered peeling them away by the handful, as more attached themselves to him . . . and more . . . and more. . .

"Those . . . things . . ."

"Shadow swarmers. The SAR crew said if they'd been ten minutes later, they'd have breached your suit."

Gray allowed himself a long, shuddering breath. *Safe* . . .

"Thank you," he said.

"Hey, don't mention it, zorchie." The man grinned. "You people have been up there saving our sorry asses. It's the least we could do in return!"

The fact that the man had called him *zorchie*—Marine

slang for a gravfighter pilot—suggested that he was an officer. An enlisted Marine, Gray thought, would never have called a naval officer zorchie to his face.

He heard a subdued click, and his hands and arms were free. Gently, he drifted down until his back was against a firm, foam-padded surface.

"Doing our job . . . sir," he said. "I'm Lieutenant Trevor Gray, VFA-44, the Dragonfires."

"We know," the man said, as Gray tried to sit up again and, this time, succeeded. "We downloaded your ID when you came in. I'm General Gorman. Welcome aboard."

And the man was gone. He didn't *leave*; his image flickered and winked out, and Gray realized that the base CO had just paid him a visit via holo projection.

"Does your general always holo-down to chitchat with Navy pilots in sick bay?" Gray asked, looking around.

The man at the console turned and grinned at him. "Not usually, sir. But we've all been praying so damned hard to the God of Battles to send us some help, maybe the old man just wanted to come down in person—or in holo, anyway—to see if you were for real."

"Any word on what's happening up there?"

"You think they tell *us* anything? Last I heard, the bombardment of the perimeter had stopped, and that's about all I care about right now." He extended a hand. "I'm Bob Richards, by the way. HM1."

Gray touched palms with Richards, and the circuitry imbedded in the other man's hand lit up Gray's in-head display. According to the data cascade, HM1 Richards was a Navy hospital corpsman assigned to the FMF, 1st Marine Expeditionary Force, as part of the attached medical unit. Interesting. He'd been born and raised in the Orlando Arcology, which meant he was from the Periphery back home. As always, Gray waited for the reaction—the faint frown, the loss of interest—as the other person saw *his* personal data.

For once, there was no visible negative reaction. "So you're from the Periph!" Richards said, brightening. "Manhattan?"

"What's left of it. You're from Orlando, I see."

"Yup. High above millions of hectares of prime sea-bottom real estate. Your handle, 'Prim.' What's that?"

Gray made a face. "Short for Primitive."

"Don't like machines, huh?"

Gray glanced back at the sealed cabinet. "No."

"You'll get used to it. That was just Medro."

"Medro?"

"Medical robot. He doesn't talk much, but he's great at taking vitals."

"So long as he doesn't indulge in taking vital organs."

Richards laughed, then got a faraway look in his eyes for a moment. "You're married? We can let your partner know you're okay."

"No," Gray said. The memory burned, and he turned his head away. "Old, old data."

"You need to update your ID, then."

"Yeah. I suppose."

If he could ever figure out *how*. He'd received the neural-net implants in his brain while he'd been in officer-recruit training, at the same time they'd grown the circuitry in the palms of his hands. Tam had been alive then, still, when he'd filled out the data that would be stored in his personal RAM, to be exchanged with others with the touching of the circuitry in the palms of their hands. He'd never figured out, though, how to change stored data—something the other men and women on board the *America* seemed to have known from childhood.

And he was too proud—and angry—to ask.

A chime sounded, and Richards said, "Come!"

Another man in combat utilities entered. The rank pips on his wear-stained jacket identified him as a Marine lieutenant. "How's the patient?"

"Doing well, sir," Richards replied.

"Outstanding." The man offered his hand. Again, data flowed across linked circuitry, appearing in a window within Gray's mind. *Marine Lieutenant Charles Lawrence Ostend . . . "Ostie" . . . 4th SAR/Recon Group . . . 1st Marine Expeditionary Force. . .*

"You're the guy who pulled me out of . . . that place," Gray said, his eyes widening.

"Guilty as charged."

"Then I think I owe you a drink. Thank you."

"Damned straight you do." He grinned at Richards. "You get all the bugs off of this guy? I don't like bugs. . . ."

"He's clean." Richards shrugged. "It's not like it's a problem. The local florauna can't tolerate our atmosphere anyway."

"'Florauna'?" Gray asked. He'd not heard the term before.

"Ate a Boot's native biology. It has characteristics of both flora *and* fauna, but isn't either one, really."

Ostend made a face. "Damned cockroaches, if you ask me."

"*Not* cockroaches," Richards said patiently. "*Not* insects. Not even *animals*. Something different. *Alien*."

"Yeah, yeah, whatever." Ostend waved aside the distinction. He slapped Gray on the shoulder. "The important thing, zorchie, is that you're okay. Right?"

"Yeah . . ."

Gray wasn't sure he liked the man's casual familiarity. Within the curious discrepancy among ranks that had evolved out of the long history of Earth's various military services, a Navy lieutenant outranked a Marine lieutenant. Gray was actually the equivalent of a Marine captain, one grade above a Marine lieutenant. Richards should have been calling him *sir*.

On the other hand, Gray had never cared much for the stuffy, pseudo-aristocratic demeanor of the fraternity of naval officers—one of the oldest of the old-boy networks. It was that fraternity—and sorority—that had closed ranks against the poor kid from the Manhattan Ruins and made his life hell for the past three years. *Officers and gentlemen* was the phrase they used, but it included conceited clots like Lieutenant Howie Spaas and arrogant hypocrites like Lieutenant Jen Collins. So far as Gray was concerned, they could *all* go to hell, with their "sirs" and "ma'ams" and formal military etiquette and protocol.

Ostend's informality, Gray decided, made him uncomfortable because it was so out of place, so unexpected. It certainly was better than the usual formality.

As unexpected as General Gorman's holographic visit a few moments before.

"Any word on the battle yet?" he asked the other officer.

"Confused," Ostend replied. "I've been hearing reports come down the line from CIC, but who's winning is anybody's guess. Want my best guess?"

"Sure."

"We're kicking their alien ass. The bombardment stopped about the time the carrier battlegroup arrived, and it hasn't picked up again. That either means we have the bastards on the run, or . . ."

"Or?"

"Or the Tushies are mopping up what's left, and don't really care about us down here at the bottom of our gravity well anymore."

"Cute, Lieutenant," Richards said. "Real morale-building."

"Hey! Any time! Catch you guys later." Ostend left.

"So . . . can I go yet?" Gray asked the corpsman. "I kind of want to find out what's happening with my unit, you know?"

"Mmm . . . not just yet, sir. We have you scheduled for a psych set."

"Psych." His eyes narrowed. "I'm not crazy, damn it."

"No, but you've been through severe emotional trauma. Dr. Wilkinson wants to put you through a stress series . . . and he wants to link you in with Old Liss."

"Old Liss? What the hell is an 'Old Liss'?"

"Psy-Cee BA. Psychiatric computer, for battlefield application. We call her Liss for Lisa, the first of her kind."

"A computer? I don't want . . ."

"I'm afraid what you want, Lieutenant, isn't a very high priority right now. Don't worry, though. It won't hurt a bit."

But Gray had had run-ins with psych computers before.

And he was not at all eager to do it again.

Recovery Craft Blue-Sierra
SAR 161 Lifelines
Battlespace Eta Boötis IV
0104 hours, TFT

Although the news hadn't yet reached all of the Marines and naval personnel on the surface of the planet, the Battle of Eta Boötis IV was, in fact, over.

Or, to be precise, the *active* part of the battle was over. The Turusch fleet, what was left of it, was under high acceleration, already close to light speed and still grav-boosting into the Void. The Confederation carrier group had entered planetary orbit, with fighter patrols orbiting in shells farther and farther out, ready in case the enemy tried to pull a reverse and launch a surprise counterstrike. There was also the possibility that not all of the Turusch warships had in fact left. A lurker or two might remain, powered down and apparently dead, waiting for an opportunity to draw easy blood.

But with the probable withdrawal of the Turusch fleet, the battlespace cleanup had begun.

SAR Recovery Craft Blue-Sierra boosted at a modest two thousand gravities, her forward singularity capturing the light of the system's white dwarf just ahead and twisting it into billowing sheets and streamers of radiance. The ship was a four-thousand-ton converted tug, an ugly beetle shape with outsized grapplers trailing astern, like the legs and antennae of some highly improbable insect.

Search and Rescue operations had been an important part of the military procedure, all the way back to the pre-spaceflight days of the twentieth century. In the days of wet-Navy aircraft catapulting from the decks of seagoing carriers, the destruction of a fighter meant either a dead aviator or one lost in an immensity of ocean or rugged terrain.

In space, though, the problem became a lot more complex. Countless things could go wrong with a gravfighter, through equipment failure or through enemy action, but the usual outcome saw the fighter with power off and drive singularities down, tumbling helplessly through space with the same vector it had been on when its systems shut down. If the pilot survived whatever had caused the situation failure in the first place, he or she was in for a long and uncomfortable ride . . . and an ultimately fatal one if somebody couldn't come get them.

SAR Recovery Craft Blue-Sierra was an old in-orbit work-boat, originally a UTW-90 Brandt-class space-dock tug used for maneuvering large pieces of hull into position. Converted with the addition of singularity projectors fore and aft, it now had the acceleration necessary for locating a tumbling fighter, grappling with it, and bringing it back to the carrier or a repair/service vessel or facility. At the helm was Lieutenant Commander Jessica LeMay.

And she was worried.

"PriFly," she called, addressing *America*'s Primary Flight Control, "this is SAR Blue-Sierra. I have a target at twelve hundred kay-em . . . closing . . . but I can't get a visual. I'm losing signal in the dwarf."

The dwarf was Eta Boötis B, the brighter star's white-dwarf companion. A star with the mass of Sol, collapsed into a sphere the size of the Earth, a white dwarf this young—less than two billion years old—was still hot, with a surface temperature exceeding 20,000 degrees Celsius. A dim, faint point of light compared with the orange glare of the sub-giant Eta Boötis A, the dwarf gleamed with a harsh, arc-brilliant glare, still no bigger than a bright star, just ahead.

The white dwarf orbited Eta Boötis A at a distance of 1.4 astronomical units, with a period of about one and a third years. Eta Boötis IV was more than twice that distance out; the dwarf companion never came closer to Haris than one and a half AU. Apparently that wasn't close enough to seriously disturb its orbit.

But LeMay had spotted a disabled gravfighter tumbling clear of battlespace at high velocity, moving along a vector that would take it quite close to Eta Boötis B, close enough that the dwarf's gravitational pull would snag it within the next hour and pull it down. Radiation from the dwarf, however, was interfering with her optics, making the approach difficult.

At radar wavelengths, she still had a sharp return. Focusing on radar, she locked onto the target and followed. Slowly, LeMay's tug closed with the disabled fighter, using the utility vehicle's powerful singularity to match velocity, then flipping end-for-end to bring its array of mechanical grapplers around to face the target. Using small thrusters, the ungainly vessel nudged closer, arms unfolding, then closing over the Starhawk.

The fighter's tumble slammed it against a grapple, threatening to put LeMay into a spin as well, but she jockeyed the maneuvering thrusters with an expert touch, countering the rotational energy and slowing the other vessel's roll. Another touch on the thrusters, and pitch and yaw were corrected as well; the tug outmassed the fighter nearly five to one, and so could absorb some of the kinetic energy of the tumble without falling out of control.

Got it. Grapples snapped home with a firm authority.

LeMay peered past the other ship on her main display. That damned white dwarf was close enough now to show a tiny disk, swiftly growing larger.

It was time to get the hell out of Dodge, as ancient tradition said.

With the prow of her vessel now aimed away from the dwarf and back toward distant Eta Boötis IV, she switched on the singularity projector, holding her breath as she did so because on a one-way work-boat like this one, there were no backups. The drive kicked in, however, and with a shuddering groan heard by conduction through the hull as the Starhawk's mass stressed the grappling arms, she began decelerating at ten thousand gravities.

Anxious moments passed as the white dwarf glowing dead astern slowed in its apparent growth . . . then, blessedly, it began shrinking, dwindling to a bright star . . . and then to a dim one.

It would take fifteen minutes at this acceleration to make it back to the fleet.

Meanwhile, she engaged another grapple, an arm that

unfolded, then extended a meter-long sliver, like a bright needle.

The needle was sheathed in programmed nanoceramic identical to the active nano that made up the Starhawk's outer hull. As the needle touched the hull, it merged, passing smoothly through the gravfighter's outer shell with seamless precision and without releasing internal atmosphere to the vacuum of space. Guided by the tug's AI, which had an expert knowledge of a Starhawk's internal layout, the probe slipped in deeper until it emerged within the pilot's cockpit. Threads laced out, searching . . . connecting . . . joining. Several merged with the pilot's e-suit, linking in with the medical and life support monitoring functions. Energy flowed through power connectors, as banks of lights switched on.

"Okay, PriFly," LeMay said. "Pilot is alive but unconscious. Life support was down but has been reinstated. I'm transmitting telemetry from the Starhawk to sick bay now."

"Blue-Sierra," a new voice said in LeMay's head, "this is *America* sick bay comm center. We have your telemetry. We're taking over teleoperational control of the patient."

"Copy, sick bay."

Each gravfighter possessed an onboard suite of medical support systems and robotics, but when the Starhawk's power had been knocked out, the med systems had gone down as well. At this moment, on board the crippled fighter, medical robots would be probing the pilot, checking for injury, begin to take steps to stabilize his or her condition.

Idly, LeMay checked the pilot's id, coming through now on her own display. Well, well. Commander Marissa Allyn—CO of the Dragonfires. And it looked like she was going to be okay.

That was good. A *lot* of Dragonfires had been killed in the action a few hours ago. They were still assembling the butcher's bill, still looking for dead gravfighters with live pilots adrift in battlespace or beyond. But it didn't look good; the squadron had almost certainly suffered over 50 percent casualties in the action.

And some of the survivors would be in a bad way.

She boosted her gravitational acceleration just a tad, pushing to get her recovery back to the ship just a few minutes sooner than otherwise.

CIC, TC/USNA CVS America
Haris Orbit, Eta Boötis System
0125 hours, TFT

"Holo transmission coming through," the CIC comm officer reported. "It's General Gorman, sir."

"Patch him through."

The Marine general faded into solidity on the CIC deck, a few meters in front of Koenig's couch. Koenig rose to greet him. The gesture was unnecessary. A Marine major general was exactly equivalent to a Navy rear admiral, and neither had precedence of rank. But formal protocol required a polite reception even of a holographic transmission, and, besides that, Koenig wanted to acknowledge the heroism of the Marines' stand here over the past weeks.

"Admiral Koenig?" the image said. "I'm Eunan Gorman."

"Welcome aboard, General," Koenig replied.

"And welcome to Ate a Boot. I've been briefed. Sounds like you went through a meat grinder up there."

"Four ships destroyed, General, seven seriously damaged. But the battlegroup is intact and ready for action if the Tush come back. We can begin the evacuation at once."

"How many transports do you have? What capacity?"

"Eight troopships, General. Converted Conestoga-class. Enough for your Marines, General. Not for the colony."

"We have just under five thousand Marines here, Admiral. We're willing to double up to get the civilians out."

Koenig sighed. He'd been dreading this. "How many civilians?"

"Approximately fifteen thousand here inside this perimeter, General. Another twenty, maybe twenty-two thousand at three other settlements on the planet."

"I'm afraid they'll have to take their chances, General. We have enough room for your people . . . maybe a few thousand locals if we really pack them in. But not *all* of them."

Gorman's image seemed to sag a bit. "I expected that, of course."

Koenig pulled down a window in his head, linking through to a calculation function and spreadsheets listing the ships and compliments within the battlegroup.

"Hang on . . . okay. The Conestogas are rated at eight hundred men each. That gives us a surplus of fourteen hundred, more or less. If we ditch all of your heavy equipment—"

"That was already a given, Admiral."

"If we ditch the heavy equipment and your Marines don't mind being *real* friendly, we can pack in another four or five thousand people. We can also double up on the other ships as well . . . pack civilians into crew's quarters, mattresses in passageways, on the mess decks, inside pressurized cargo bays . . . call it another thousand . . . *maybe* two."

"That won't be enough."

"Damn it, General, I doubt that our whole Navy has the transport capacity for almost forty thousand civilians, all in one go. We have room for seven thousand civilians. At that, feeding them and handling the sanitation requirements for that many people is going to be a nightmare."

"You *know* what will happen if the Turusch return, once we're gone."

"No, General, I don't. And I doubt that anyone else in the Confederation knows either. The Turusch and their Sh'daar overlords are still very much unknown quantities."

"They killed the researchers at Arcturus. So far as we know, they murdered every last one."

"Again, General, we don't know. Not for sure."

But Gorman was almost certainly right. The last transmission from Arcturus last year had been . . . chaos. Heavily armored Turusch soldiery breaking into the domes, burning down the civilian technicians and scientists . . .

"The perimeter is secure, Admiral," Gorman said. "Start sending down the transports. The shields will be open for you."

"The first shuttles will be down in thirty minutes, General. Uh . . . how about security?"

There was a good chance that there would be panic, once

the Marines started leaving and the civilians saw that they were being left behind.

"We'll take care of that," Gorman snapped. "Gorman out."

And the image winked off.

Koenig stared at the empty spot on the deck for another moment. This was *not* going to be easy.

Chapter Nine

26 September 2404

MEF HQ
Mike-Red Perimeter
Eta Boötis System
1612 hours, TFT

Major General Gorman stood on the HQ elevated walk and looked up. For the first time in weeks, the shields were fully down and he could see the landscape directly, with his own eyes, rather than through electronic feeds. With a scream, four Marine Rattlesnake fighters passed nearby, boosting clear from the landing field and accelerating hard, their passage drawing thin lines of vapor in their wakes as their drive singularities shocked the thick air.

The Rattlesnakes were distinctly old tech—distinctive and non-variable delta shapes that seemed downright primitive in comparison to the more modern Navy Starhawks and Nightmare strike fighters. A single squadron of Marine Rattlesnakes was attached to I MEF for close air support, but sending them out during the siege would have been tantamount to murder. Rattlesnakes simply couldn't stand up to Turusch military technology in an open fight. Their Marine pilots called them rattletraps, a reflection of their technological inadequacy.

But they served now to help secure the perimeter against infiltrators and small enemy ground units that might try to take advantage of the lowered shields as the Navy transports were coming down.

It was past the middle of the daylight hours at this latitude and time of year, the short day already half over. A low, churning overcast blocked the sky, moving swiftly with a stiff westerly wind.

Gorman was struck by the gray, bleak desolation surrounding the base, a plain stretching off to the horizon in every direction, scorched-bare rock intermingled with circular craters with black-glass bottoms. When the Marines had landed and set up Red Mike five weeks ago, the land surrounding the low plateau had been shrouded in orange growth, and there'd been a city—the largest Mufrid colony, right *there* . . . a few kilometers to the west.

Nothing remained now but rock and glass. From up here, he could even see places where the rock had run liquid, bubbled, then frozen in mid-boil. There was a high background rad count now, though the EM screens were keeping most of the hard stuff out. In the darkness, parts of that landscape now glowed with an eerie, pale blue light.

The capacity for technic intelligence to devastate a world was shocking, nightmarish.

Another flight of gravfighters howled through the thick air, following the Rattlers. These were Navy Starhawks, their black outer hulls shifting and morphing as they passed, preparing to transition from atmospheric flight to space. A kilometer from the Marine perimeter, they brought their noses up, then accelerated almost vertically, punching through the orange-red overcast. A moment later, four mingled sonic booms echoed and rumbled across the plain.

The Turusch did indeed appear to have given up the fight and fled with the arrival of the carrier battlegroup, but Gorman was under no illusions about their eventual, inevitable return.

The Confed force's immediate problem was not the Turusch . . . but another problem somewhat closer to home.

A transport shuttle lifted from the landing area at the center of the Marine base, huge, its black skin shifting as it absorbed landing legs and other shore-side protuberances, streamlining itself for the flight to orbit. Navigation lights strobed at its blunt prow, its sides, top, and bottom. A Choctaw Type UC-154 shuttle, it carried nearly two hundred Marines on board. A second Choctaw remained on the landing field, cargo-bay ramps lowered at bow and sides as long columns of Marines, like black ants at this distance, filed on board.

The first Choctaw was accompanied by four Nightshade grav-assault gunships, reduced to black toy minnows dwarfed by the eighty-meter-long shuttle. There was no thunderclap this time; the shuttle and its escorts would reach orbit at a more sedate pace.

"General Gorman?"

He didn't turn at the voice. "Yes, Mr. Hamid."

Jamel Saeed Hamid joined him on the walkway. "You wanted to see me?"

"I wanted to discuss the . . . situation."

"I don't see that there is anything to discuss, General."

"I've been going over the numbers with Admiral Koenig, the CO of the Confederation battlegroup. We estimate that we could take on board between six and seven thousand additional people. They would be packed in with our crews, stacked up like cordwood. Water and food will be rationed. The nanorecyclers will be pushed to their limits. But we *can* make room for them."

"I suspect that most of us will choose to remain here, General."

"God, why? The Turusch will be back. You know that."

"And there is nothing for us back on Earth, or on any of the other colonies."

"The Turusch will almost certainly kill you," Gorman said, blunt, hard. "They are not known for their religious sensibilities."

"Then, if it be God's will, we will die. That has been our choice from the beginning, you understand."

"No, sir. I do *not* understand."

Hamid sighed. "The White Covenant? We will not sign that . . . that document. It is an affront against God."

"Earthstar has said nothing about you signing the Covenant, Mr. Hamid. I'm sure there's room for negotiation."

"What you *mean* is that we will go back into the camps until we either sign or they find another . . . solution." He sounded bitter.

On the landing field, the second Choctaw was buttoning up, the ramps pulling in, the openings slowly irising shut. Four more Nightshade gunships hovered overhead, waiting for the shuttle to lift off.

"There are . . . an infinity of worlds out here, Mr. Hamid," Gorman said quietly. "You'll be able to find another world, found a new colony."

"*Not* an infinity. Many, perhaps. But still a finite number . . . and it's a number made considerably more finite by the *Shaitans*."

"You know what I mean, damn it. You may be back in the camps for a time, sure, but there's plenty of new real estate available, and a lot of it is a damned sight better than *this*!" He waved his arm, taking in the desolate, flame-barren landscape, the poisonous and sulfur-laden cloud deck, the full orange light and heat.

"You do not understand."

"Try me! *Make* me understand!"

"That is not easy." Hamid thought for a moment. "We— the colonists of Haris—are called *Mufrideen*. Do you know why?"

"Of course. Mufrid is one of the names for this star, for Eta Boötis. Arabic, like the name for this planet, Al Haris al Sama. Your people were great astronomers back twelve, fifteen hundred years ago or so. Most named stars in Earth's sky have Arabic names."

"But we do not apply the name to our sun. Only to our-selves. The word *mufrid* means "alone." Solitary. Within our religion, it has the special meaning of one who undertakes the *hajj* alone."

"Hajj. That's the Muslims' pilgrimage to Mecca?"

Hamid nodded. "One of the five sacred pillars of Islam. And the one, of course, that we have been forbidden by your Confederation to observe."

Your Confederation. Gorman started to respond, then

thought better of it. Before 1 MEF's deployment, representatives from the Confederation Bureau of Religious Affairs had briefed him on the Haris colonists, and he'd been warned that emotions among the colonists continued to be harsh and bitter.

The Eta Boötean colonists were the ragtag end of a long-time and seemingly unsolvable problem, one going back to the Islamic Wars of the twenty-first century and, arguably, even further back in history than that, to the Crusades and Jihads of the Middle Ages. With the end of the Islamic Wars, the newly formed Confederation had presented the world with the White Covenant, a document of basic human rights that included strong prohibitions of certain religious practices and activities. In short, *all* adherents of *all* religions had the right to believe what they wished so long as that belief did not harm others. Proselytizing, missionary work, and conversion by force or by threat all were proscribed as violations of basic human rights and dignity.

By the end of the twenty-first century, the Muslim nation-states of the world lay in ruins, their armies destroyed, their populations starving. Most Islamic leaders signed the White Covenant, if only to allow the beginning of relief efforts and food shipments.

Millions of Muslims, however, point-blank refused to accept the White Covenant's terms, seeing them as a direct denial of God's holy word. Numerous groups sprang up among the survivors, especially within the many relocation camps across Africa and the Middle East, calling themselves *Rafaddeen*, "Refusers," because their leaders continued to refuse to sign the document.

That had been more than three centuries ago, and the Rafaddeen continued to be a thorn in the side of the Confederation. Most had chosen to remain in relocation camps that had eventually grown into small, self-contained and self-governing cities, each under the watchful eye of Confederation peaceforcers. Tens of thousands had moved off-world, to orbital cities and to extrasolar colonies, where they would not be a threat to the *Pax Confoederata*.

Another Choctaw drifted down out of the orange overcast,

accompanied by its gunship escort. Landing legs grew from its flat belly, splaying wide as it settled onto the landing field, cargo doors dilating, ramps extending. The next load of Marines was already lined up in ranks at the edge of the field, ready to embark. At this rate, the evacuation would be complete well within the eight hours allotted for the operation.

"Muslims weren't the only ones who didn't like the Covenant," Gorman said at last. "Most of my family were Baptists." He didn't add that he, personally, was a Covenant Reformed Baptist, and would no more preach the Gospel to someone who didn't want to hear it than he would denounce the Corps.

"The Covenant was a gun aimed at Islam!" Hamid snapped back. "Not at American evangelicals! Not at Zionists!"

"It applied to *all* religions. All cultures. All belief systems. It had to, to be fair."

"It denied the commandments of Allah to bring light to the unenlightened! It was not *fair*. It was blasphemy!"

"I am not going to stand here and argue bad theology with you, Mr. Hamid," Gorman said. The capacity for members of various fundamentalist and extremist sects for clinging to battles, grudges, and wrongs done hundreds, even thousands of years ago was astonishing to him. "Seven thousand of your people can get off this rock *if* they want to."

"I will . . . make the announcement," Hamid said, his words and his manner stiff. "I imagine, though, that most of us will stay."

"That's your call. I recommend that that you let women and children have what space on the transports we can find."

"The male children, certainly," Hamid said. He sounded thoughtful.

The statement chilled Gorman. Traditional Islam—in particular the extremist sects, the Rafaddeen who'd rejected the White Covenant—still often valued men more than women, boys more than girls, an artifact of certain ancient tribal cultures more than of the Qu'ran itself. That, as much as the suicide bombers and the tactical nukes, had been a major part of the extremist Muslim doctrine that had led to so much bloodshed in the mid- and late twenty-first century. Most modern Islamic states back on Earth had embraced full equality of the sexes, but out here . . .

"*All* of your children," Gorman said, putting iron into his voice. "Girls too. And the women as well. To care for them."

To the Rafadeen, childcare was women's work. Perhaps he could use that bit of sixth-century logic to force the issue.

Hamid gave Gorman a hard look. "You needn't moralize at us. Our faith has served us well for over seventeen centuries, despite your Western preaching and your Crusades."

Gorman took a step closer, towering above the smaller man. "*All* of the children, *and* the women," he said. "As well as any men who want to go. My Marines *will* enforce this, Mr. Hamid. At gunpoint, if they have to."

Hamid's expression clouded, as though he was going to argue. Then he shrugged, backed down. "It scarcely matters. Allah has judged, and found us lacking."

On the landing field, more columns of Marines were filing on board the open shuttle. He would need to talk with Simmons, the MEF's executive officer, to make sure he stayed on top of a phased and orderly withdrawal. The trick, Gorman thought, was going to be keeping enough Marines behind, on the ground, to oversee the evacuation of six or seven thousand colonists, to make sure that the women and children were evacuated first, to prevent the men, however dedicated they might be to staying now, from panicking and attempting to rush the shuttles . . . then pull those last Marines out without triggering a deadly riot.

And all of that was assuming the Turusch stayed out of the picture.

Gorman watched the shuttle lift off, to be replaced by another dropping from the orange-yellow sky.

He saw a group of locals gathered off to one side, near the enlisted mess hall. They weren't doing anything in particular; they were simply . . . watching, silent, anonymous in their e-suits.

If Gorman remembered accurately, fifteen thousand locals had made it inside the Marine perimeter from the nearby colonial capital of Jahuar when the Turusch first appeared overhead weeks ago, roughly a third of them women and children. The refugees had been crowded in with the Marines ever since, occupying supply warehouses turned into huge open dormitories. There'd been no incidents, fortunately. The biggest problem the Marines had faced had been simply getting their work done with so many civilians in the way.

If that mob down there turned on the dwindling number of remaining Marines, they could end up being just as deadly as the Turusch.

MEF HQ
Marine Sick Bay
Eta Boötis IV
1720 hours, TFT

For Gray, it was as though he were deep within the folds of a lucid dream.

He *knew* he was dreaming, but the reality of the scene was startlingly crisp and real, like being inside a VR threevee. There was nothing automatic or canned about it. He could *choose* to turn his head, looking north, toward the skeletal towers of Central Manhattan looming against the night. Or he could turn and look south, to the submerged and tumbled-down ruins of the ancient financial district projecting above the surf, the warning lights and buoys winking in the dark.

He was standing on a rooftop above something that had once been called East 32nd Street, just north of the drowned section of the old city. He could hear the gentle susurration of the surf fifty meters below.

A UT-84 utility hopper, with Periphery Authority markings showing in blue and white light against all three black wings, hovered overhead, eerily silent, faintly illuminated by the sky-glow of the New City, twenty kilometers to the northeast. Then a shaft of dazzling light speared down from the aircraft's belly and he could not see anything at all. "Halt!" a sharp, neutrally inflected voice called, amplified and immense. "Stay where you are, in the open, your hands clearly visible! Authority peaceforcers will be there momentarily!"

The scene was a virtual reality, a near-perfect replay of events that had occurred five years earlier.

In fact, there were software programs available commercially that acted exactly like this—fed directly into the brain through a marginal AI. You closed your eyes . . . and could go anywhere, see anything, engage in any sport, have sex with any celebrity, and have it all be just like being there.

"What are you feeling right now?" a woman's voice said in his mind. It was, he knew, the voice of Dr. Anna George, a psytherapist with the 1st MEF. She was linked into the program with him, seeing everything he was seeing, experiencing his memories, and his decisions.

"I'm not sure," he admitted. He spoke aloud, the voice sounding distant, somewhere off in his mind, somewhere behind the silently hovering hopper, the ruins of the old city. "Fear, I guess."

"What are you afraid of?"

"*Them*. The peaceforcers."

"But you know they're there to help you."

"No. I *don't*. They've always been the enemy!"

"Who has been the enemy, Lieutenant?"

"The Authority. The peaceforcers. Watching us. Hassling us. Telling us what to do, what not to do. They call us *squatties*. Squatters and primitives. And ferals. To them, we're not people. We're just . . . pests. Problems to be *dealt with*."

"But they got help for your wife."

"And they turned her against me. She's not my wife anymore."

"You sound . . . bitter."

"Am I?" He laughed. "Just because they swept me up, wrecked my life, turned my life-partner against me? Why the hell should I be *bitter*?"

"This will go a lot easier, Lieutenant, a lot *faster*, if you let go of the sarcasm."

"So you keep telling me."

"The hopper has you spotted on top of that building. What will you do now?"

"I don't know. Do you mean what do I want to do now? Or what I did *then*?"

"Either one. This program lets you explore *all* possibilities. What happened. What *might* have happened. Good choices. Bad choices. It's all up to you."

In his dream, he looked away from the glare overhead, looked at the broom at his feet.

It wasn't literally a broom, of course, but a Mitsubishi-Rockwell gravcycle. Three meters long and gleaming dull silver, it was mostly a straight, lightweight keel, with compact grav-impeller blocks front and back, braces for his feet, a long, narrow saddle for his torso, and a small virtual control suite. In street slang they were called gimps, pogo sticks, or brooms, and they were hard to come by on the Periphery. He'd found his eight years earlier in an abandoned, burned-out shop up in Old Harlem, somehow overlooked in a storage room for a century and a half, still in its manufactory-sealed packaging.

Okay. His choice? Well, he remembered what he *had* done that night.

The peaceforcers probably had weapons on him—stunners and a tangleweb, if nothing more. He had to do this fast. . . .

He dropped to his belly, landing on the saddle full length, his legs stretched out behind, his feet slipping into the foot-brace stirrups, his hands grasping the handles to either side of the control suite. Gripping hard with hands and knees, he rolled hard to the left, throwing himself and the broom out of that hard, tightly focused circle of illumination, off the roof of the building, and into the darkness below.

For a giddy moment he was in free fall, the sudden blast of air triggering his helmet safety protocols and snapping down the visor. He felt the brush of something insubstantial across his leg . . . and then the sensation was gone, a near-miss by the hopper's tangleweb projector.

"Citizen Gray, this is the Periphery Authority. Land your vehicle at once."

But he'd already twisted on the handles, engaged the cycle's grav-field, and brought the pogo around, pointing toward the southwest, out over the encroaching sea. Both feet moved, pointing his toes back and down, and the impellers caught with a sudden surge of acceleration.

"Where do you think you're going, Lieutenant?" George's voice asked. It wasn't judgmental, not condemning. It was simply . . . curious.

"Anywhere," he replied. "Nowhere. Away from *them*."

He took the broom down to the deck, skimming now a scant meter and a half above the waters rolling between the steel and concrete cliffs of ruined skyscrapers to either side. Late in the twenty-first century, rising sea levels and the final insult of Hurricane Cynthia had battered through the Verrazano-Narrows Dam and sent the waters of the Atlantic Ocean surging past the Narrows into Upper New York Bay and across the lower half of Manhattan. The total mean rise in sea level across the island and nearby Brooklyn, Staten Island, and New Jersey had been over twelve meters—nearly forty feet. For decades after, there'd been plans to rebuild, even plans to transform lower Manhattan into an enormous artificial island rising above the intruding sea . . . but somehow the money had never been there. Eventually, the New City had arisen to the northeast, in the heights of Riverdale, Yonkers, and the Bronx.

Within a century, water damage, subsidence, erosion, and lack of maintenance had begun to bring the towering skyline of Old Manhattan's downtown section down. Many of the buildings now were eerie mounds covered by kudzu, porcelain-berry, oriental bittersweet, and other ground cover that transformed them into steep-sided, fuzzy green islands. In places, skeletal towers still emerged from the water or from piles of vegetation-choked rubble. Elsewhere, some of the older stone buildings, as opposed to those of mere steel and concrete, stood still like solitary monoliths, monuments to the long-vanished city, windows long ago blown out, stone surfaces partly covered by vines and moss, slowly crumbling.

Those buildings and mounds lay just ahead of Gray now,

a tangled maze of obstacles above the water. The broom's radar and infrared optics were feeding images to his helmet display, highlighting the dangers—the cliffs, the walls, the mounds—in red, the safe passages between in green. He swerved left, then angled right, ducking past the tangled mounds of Soho Island and on toward the crumbling ruins of the old TriBeCa Tower.

Behind him, the hovering utility hopper dropped its nose and darted forward in pursuit. The Authority aircraft was highly maneuverable, more maneuverable, even, than the broom, and certainly faster. Gray held the advantage, though, because he knew Manhattan, *all* of it.

He nudged the broom even closer to the water; the slip-stream of his passage roiled the surface behind him in a rooster tail of spray even though he wasn't touching the water itself. He hurtled along the Broadway Canyon, pushing close to Mach 1, then braking sharply and swerving right up the Franklin Gap. Directly ahead, the TriBeCa Tower loomed vast against the darkness. Once a self-contained city in its own right, one of several arcologies to arise from central Manhattan during the mid-twenty-first century, it shrugged up into the sky nearly half a kilometer, mushroom-shaped, dome-topped, the vertical sides crenellated and textured by balconies, landing pads, overlooks, and walkways.

Accelerating again, he passed underneath the building's massive overhang, deftly avoiding the outstretched claws of severed piping reaching from places where the concrete had fallen away and exposed the rotting and corroded infrastructure. He was home free now. The bastards couldn't follow him under here.

And home was just up ahead.

He wasn't going to go home, though. That was what he'd done wrong originally. There were peaceforcer officers waiting for him there . . . though how the hell they'd known where one anonymous squatter was living within all of this labyrinthine wreckage he didn't know.

No . . . of *course* he knew. He hadn't thought about it before, but he saw it now. Angela had told them.

But he wasn't going to the suite of former apartments and shops that he called home. Slowing again, he scanned the surface of the overhang meters above his head, then spotted the place where, about a century ago, a hundred-meter chunk of reinforced concrete had dropped away, exposing a large and ragged hole in the floor of the tower's amphitheater. Pulling back on the handgrips, he angled up and through the hole, emerging within a dark warren of passageways and rooms.

Slowing just enough to navigate those twisting hallways and corridors, he moved through the tower's inner ruin, working his way higher, working back toward the north. There was a cluster of elevator shafts over there on the north side, empty now, with water below and empty sky above, where a part of the dome had collapsed. He would be able to rise through a shaft to a spot right at the surface of the main dome, a place where he could look for the pursuing Authority ship.

If the coast was clear, he could hightail it across the Hudson and the drowned expanse of Hoboken, and into the wilds of Jersey City Island.

"*Halt*, Citizen Gray!"

The voice, the sudden human shadow looming in front of him, brought him rearing back. His broom skidded out from beneath him and clattered along the wall, out of control. He hit the floor of the passageway, bounced, and rolled.

"*That's not fair!*" he screamed. "*That's not the way it happened!*"

But the Authority troops were already slapping the restraints on his wrists.

Chapter Ten

MEF HQ
Marine Sick Bay
Eta Boötis IV
1732 hours, TFT

"Why do you think it wasn't fair?" Dr. George asked him.

"You're rigging the program," he protested. "Making it so I can't win!"

"Life isn't fair, Lieutenant."

"The bastards were waiting for me at my place," he said. "So I didn't go there. You had one of them just pop up in a corridor."

"How would it have been different if you'd gotten away?"

"I'd have gotten across the river to New Jersey. Or I would've gotten down to Battery or over to Chintown. I have . . . I *had* friends there. . . ."

"But Angela had given them your ID. They'd have caught up with you, sooner or later."

"Yeah, but *why*? There must be thousands of squatters in the Ruins! Why bother with me?"

"Because you'd impressed them, of course."

He snorted. "That stupid test? The three-D navigation thing? That wasn't until later."

"You seem to have attracted their attention early on."

"All we wanted was to be left alone. . . ."

"According to the records, it was you who approached the Authority. When your . . . when Angela had her stroke."

"Yeah . . ."

That, of course, had been where it all had started going wrong.

They were called primitives. And they *were*, in a way, men and women with almost nothing in the way of a technical infrastructure or implants, picking out a precarious living in the Manhattan Ruins and Norport and Sunken Miami and Old London and a hundred other coastal cities half-swallowed by the encroaching oceans, the polar ice caps having melted away three centuries before.

Gray had been born in the Ruins, a part of the TriBeCa Tower community. His discovery of the gravcycle in an uptown shop had let him "be the man"—Prim slang for proving himself—at his coming-of-age by bringing in a load of food and food-nano from New Rochelle. Life within the ruins was only possible if you belonged to a "family" . . . meaning one of the hundreds of territorial gangs. Each mound-island had its own family, and while many cooperated with the others, a few lived by preying on weaker families. That gravcycle had seen the TriBeCa Family through a couple of tough wars and innumerable raids.

The Periphery Authority was a department of the Confederal Police charged with maintaining the law in the Ruins—an all but impossible task, when you thought about it. The inhabitants of the Periphery didn't recognize Confederal control; they didn't fight the Auths, usually, but they tended to fade back deeper into the warrens and labyrinths of the Ruins, and to have nothing whatsoever to do with the Confeds.

But when Angela had suffered a stroke that paralyzed her right arm and badly weakened her right leg, Gray had gone nearly mad with worry. With very little in the way of modern medical technology within the Periphery—few medicines, no nanomeds at all, no docbots or diagnostic software or, indeed, any Net access at all—Gray had taken his broom and flown north to Morningside Heights, the southernmost tip of the New City. A doctor at the Columbia Arcology had agreed to see her, though with no insurance and no cred-implants, of course, neither he nor his wife could pay for treatment. Gray had agreed to talk with someone with the Confederal Social Authority in order to get treatment for Angela.

He still remembered the snickers, the sidelong looks. A Prim, dressed in rags, pleading for help from the Confeds. And for a *wife*, of all things. In the Ruins, among the families, people tended to pair off, to form tight pair-bonds rather than the more typical looser social and sexual associations. Monogies, they were called, and if that Peripheral lifestyle wasn't illegal, on the Mainland it was still widely believed to be possessive, dysfunctional, and just a bit dirty.

The soshies had taken him in and asked a lot of questions. They'd hooked him up to brain scans and thought monitors, and seemed fascinated by the fact that he could fly a broom without a direct neural interface. "That shouldn't even be possible!" one caseworker had told him. "Have you ever thought of getting an implant?"

"Oh, sure," he'd told her. "Absolutely! Just as soon as my insurance comes through!"

They claimed later he'd agreed to join the military, but he hadn't. Well, not *really*, though he might have tried to give an impression of interest in the idea, just so they'd help Angela. Or maybe they'd taken his sarcasm as agreement. It was always tough to tell with the Authorities. They were a damned humorless bunch.

Join the military? *Hell*, no! All he knew was scavenging and Ruinrunning. He could barely read and write, and if the Authorities claimed that the squatters out in the Periphery were still Earth Confederation citizens, Gray and a few million other Prim squatters didn't see it that way at all. They were free. The only law was what they themselves laid down and enforced. They didn't receive any of the Authority's protection, medical or financial services, education, clothing, Net access, entertainment, or food. They didn't have Confed-recognized jobs or welfare status and they didn't pay taxes. So how could anyone claim that they were *citizens*?

But then a Navy lieutenant commander had shown up in

his black-and-golds and told him he was there to administer the Confederation oath. He'd bolted then, bolted and run. He'd found his broom where he'd parked it, on a landing balcony high above Harlem Bay, and launched himself into the night.

He'd been pursued by a hopper, but he'd eluded them.

They'd been waiting for him in the TriBeCa Tower apartments he'd shared with Angela.

The worst part of it all, the most awful revelation that had transformed his recruit training into a living nightmare, had been the discovery that Angela had . . . changed. They'd healed her. They'd grown class-three implants within the sulci of her brain, regrown sections of her organic nervous system, given her palm implants and an ID, even given her training as a compositer, whatever the hell that was, and assigned her to a job up in Haworth. The last he'd heard, she was living with some guy named Fred in an extended community.

She no longer loved Gray, and no longer wanted to see him.

The medtechs he'd talked to later had told him that that happened with strokes sometimes. Old neural pathways holding information on relationships, on emotional responses could be burned out by the neuron storm, lost even beyond the ability of neural prostheses to recapture them.

Gray wondered, though, how much was stroke and how much was reprogramming. *Reconditioning.* When they'd wired her to their machines and downloaded reading and writing, Cloud-Net skills and language training, social norms and Mainland mores, had they also told her what to believe? Who to love? *How* to love?

The last time he'd been able to talk with Angela, he'd asked if that had been what had happened. The simple question had made her angry, unreasonably so, he thought. "*Damn* you, Trev! Don't you think I can think for myself?" she'd demanded.

Maybe she could. But . . . that hadn't been Angela he'd been talking to. She was *different* now, and not just in her attitude or her use of language.

He'd known then that Angela, *his* Angela, was dead.

"You're crying," Dr. George said. She handed him a tissue and he accepted it, dragging it across his wet cheeks until the material evaporated and took the moisture with it as a microparticle aerosol. "We seem to have touched something."

"Fuck you," he said, but without much feeling. He felt dead inside, utterly wrung out and empty. "We're done. *I'm* done. Get the hell out of my head. . . ."

Hangar Deck
TC/USNA CVS America
Haris Orbit, Eta Boötis System
1740 hours, TFT

Commander Marissa Allyn stood on the walkway overlooking the star carrier's main hangar deck, a vast and cavernous compartment three stories tall and over 150 meters long, a noisy, banging, bustling nexus of activity as returning fighters trapped on the recovery deck above and were brought down through the mergedeck barriers and into the pressurized interior of the ship.

The last of the Dragonfires had recovered back on board the *America* hours ago. Allyn had been brought back much later as a tow, rather ignominiously hauled in by the Search and Rescue tug. She'd been unconscious through most of the process, but she'd begun to come out of it as the tug hauled her into the turkey bay . . . carrier slang for one of the utility bay entrances.

They'd whisked her off to *America*'s sick bay facilities, where she'd been stripped and deconned, probed by robotic diagnosticians, and shot full of more nanomed healer 'bots. They'd put her on light duty and discharged her just twenty minutes ago; she'd come down here to find out how many of the Dragonfires had actually made it back safely. The numbers hadn't been posted yet in PriFly, weren't available on AmericaNet, and the pilots themselves were off the radar— presumably up in God's country going through the debrief.

Which was where she would be going soon as well, once

they called for her. In the meantime, she could talk to some of the crew chiefs or recovery deck personnel to get the "straight eye," meaning rumors, gossip, or shipboard intelligence that generally was more accurate than the official word of God.

She'd been proceeding along the elevated walkway toward the recovery officer's suite when a new arrival on the deck below had captured her full attention.

Flashing red lights and a hooter had cleared one particular part of the busy hangar deck—surrounding an elevator column extending all the way from deck to overhead, an area marked off by painted stripes, no-go warnings, and holographic barriers. The elevator began to descend, and the black nanoseal of the deck hatch in the overhead began to bulge downward, taking on the curving shape of the lower surfaces of a returning shuttle. The arrival was unusual for two reasons. First off, shuttles, like the SAR tug, normally recovered through a utility docking bay, not the main hangar deck. Troops and other personnel, in particular, generally came aboard in either a troop bay or at the quarterdeck receiving facility forward.

And second, there were a hell of a lot of Marines down there, falling into a broad semicircle facing the shuttle's starboard side.

Slowly, the shape continued to drop, the shuttle still coated by black nanometal that looked and acted like a viscous liquid, clinging tightly to the shuttle's surface to keep separate the open-space hard vacuum of the recovery deck above and the Earth-normal atmosphere of the pressurized hangar deck. As the shuttle continued to drop, the nanoseal let go, parting along the ventral surface, oozing up the ship's sides like tar, merging above the shuttle's back, then returning to a flat, black rectangle in the overhead. Free now, the shuttle continued to descend until the elevator column had vanished entirely into the deck beneath the splayed landing legs, and the shuttle rested at hangar-deck level. A portion of the starboard fuselage irised open as a ramp extended to the deck beyond the solidifying nanometal pool, and the waiting Marines came sharply alert, weapons at the ready.

This, Allyn thought, must be the shuttle bringing up the Turusch prisoners she'd heard about in the pre-mission briefing. She leaned over against the railing, trying for a better look. There were plenty of rumors about Turusch biology and about their body shape, but nothing that had ever been confirmed.

Aglestch physiognomy was well known, of course. Humans had met them just less than a century before. They were spidery, hairy things that were not spiders at all—the only external skeleton they had on their sausage-shaped bodies sheathed their two-meter legs—and they lived in an oxidizing atmosphere not very different from Earth's, so humans could meet them face-to . . . sense-organ cluster. The Turusch, however, were mysteries. There were rumors, conflicting and confusing, of things like dinosaurs, like whales, like sea slugs, but the things had never been visually recorded. Eye-witness reports at Arcturus Station and at Everdawn had mentioned their heavy combat armor, carballoy mecha the size of small trucks.

This just might be the moment when the mystery was finally ended, the reality revealed.

Humans, Marines in combat armor, were coming down the ramp now. One, an officer, conferred for a moment with the officer in charge of the section waiting on the Hangar Deck.

And then the first Turusch drifted into view.

Allyn felt a stab of disappointment. The thing was wearing what presumably was the alien equivalent of an e-suit, a three-meter-long cylinder floating on grav-lifters. The tank was rounded front and back, and there was nothing like windows or a canopy through which she could glimpse the creature inside.

An armored Marine combat walker stalked down the ramp beside it, a protective measure, no doubt. If that floating tube suddenly started smashing into bystanders or equipment, a single megajoule pulse from the walker's main gun would puncture the Tushie's protective shell and it would choke on oxygen. That, of course, was why the creature was in the e-suit; she'd heard speculation that the things lived in a reducing atmosphere, though she didn't know what the gas mix was. Oxygen would be a deadly poison to them.

A second floater tank appeared, emerging onto the ramp, closely escorted by another Marine walker.

So . . . this seemed to confirm the scuttlebutt that said the Tushies were completely nonhuman, that they couldn't even breathe a standard gas mix. That meant that humans and Tushies weren't fighting over the same real estate . . . unless, of course, they breathed the witch's brew of sulfur compounds that made up the Harisian atmosphere. According to Naval Intelligence, though, the Tushies were the front-line forces for the mysterious Sh'daar, fighting at their orders. Even less was known about the Sh'daar than was known about the Turusch.

The ring of armored Marines in front of the shuttle parted to let the floater tanks pass through, then fell into columns behind them. The cylinders and their escorts vanished into a side passageway a moment later.

Scuttlebutt had it that the Marines on Haris had gone through a lot to capture those two prisoners. Not only that, rumor insisted that the *America* battlegroup had been deployed to make sure those prisoners were returned to human space; recovering them, apparently, had a far higher priority than rescuing the civilians trapped on Haris. That sucked, but she knew how the military mind worked. You had to know the enemy before you could fight him. Who'd said that . . . Sun Tse? She thought so.

"Commander Allyn," a voice said in her head. "We're ready for your debrief."

"Very well," she said. "On my way."

She would have to see if anyone on the debrief team could tell her more about her squadron . . . or about *America*'s new and alien passengers.

MEF HQ
Marine Sick Bay
Eta Boötis IV
1745 hours, TFT

"We're not done with this, Lieutenant," Dr. George told him. Gray scowled. "Yes we are. *Sir.*"

She shrugged. "You'll be kept on limited duty until you complete the therapy to my satisfaction, or to the satisfaction of a medical review board. That means you're off the flight line."

She'd switched off the electronic feed to his internal circuitry, banishing the vivid lucid dreams of Manhattan. Gray was on a recliner in Anna George's office, which had the relaxed air of a wood-paneled library. That would not be real wood on the bulkheads, of course. The entire base had been nanogrown from local raw materials five weeks ago.

But there was no practical way to tell the difference.

"There is *nothing* wrong with me! I . . . I freaked a bit when those things were crawling on me down there on the planet. But I'm okay now."

"Lieutenant Gray, I've entered a provisional diagnosis in your record of PTED. That's post-traumatic embitterment disorder, and it is potentially serious. It has little or nothing to do with what happened to you outside the perimeter yesterday, and everything to do with the events that led you to enlist in the Navy."

"Okay, I'm carrying a grudge, if that's what you mean, sure. I was tricked into the service, my whole life was taken away from me, I lost my wife, why shouldn't I be bitter?"

"Good question. My question for you is . . . who do you blame? The Periphery Authority? The med staff at Columbia Towers? The Navy? Society in general?"

He didn't answer.

"I suggest that you begin digging inside yourself for some answers. You had a responsibility in what happened as well."

"I was not responsible for Angela's stroke!"

"No. Certainly not. But you'd chosen to live on the Periphery, without healthcare, without a socially sanctioned means of support. You then chose to try to bargain with the Authority, to help your wife."

"What would *you* have done?" The words, nearly, were a sneer.

"That's not the question. You and I are completely different people, with different backgrounds, different experiences, different . . . programming. You made certain decisions. Some were good. Some were not as good. You need to figure out why you did what you did, why you made the choices that you made . . . and then you need to see where you go from where you are right now."

"What does any of this have to do with me being on the flight line?" he demanded. "I've been doing my job. My *duty*."

George leaned back in her seat, and appeared to be thinking about it. "Of course you have. No one is saying otherwise. But . . . do you understand the sort of responsibility with which you've been entrusted? What's the typical warload on your Starhawk, when you go out on patrol? I think they used to call it a force package?"

He shrugged. "Depends on the mission parameters. Usually it's anything between twenty-four and thirty-two Krait smart missiles. And we generally carry a PBP and a KK Gatling."

"How big a punch on a Krait?"

"Again, it depends. We usually carry a mix, five to fifteen kilotons. More or less for special operations, special mission requirements."

"So what happens if you get mad someday and fire off a fifteen-kiloton nuclear warhead while you're still inside one of *America*'s launch tubes, or maybe on the flight deck?"

"That would never happen!" He was angry at the mere supposition.

"Why not?"

"Well, there are interlocks to prevent that from happening, a munitions release inside the ship or an accidental warhead arming, for one thing. For another . . . well, damn it, if you don't trust me with those things, why the hell did you turn me into a pilot?"

He'd actually wondered that for a long time. When he'd been taken into custody by the Peripheral Authority, he'd been handed over to the Department of Education for a series of skills downloads and aptitude testing. He'd scored high—"off the scale," according to one of the soshtechs—in three-dimensional visualization, navigation, and conceptualization, plus lightning-quick reaction times and low fear thresholds. They'd fast-tracked him from an uneducated Periphery vagrant to pre-flight training level with downloads in spaceflight engineering, basic astronautics, and military history in six months of download hell. They'd followed that with a year of basic Navy OCS at the Academy, then flight training in California and on Mars.

The government had spent something like two thirds of a million creds to raise him from squatter to fighter pilot. And they didn't *trust* him?

"It's not about *trust*, Lieutenant. It's about your emotional stability, about whether or not you're going to have a bad day someday, maybe get pissed off at someone else in the squadron, and in an emotional moment you make a bad decision." He started to protest, and she gave him a hard look. "It *has* happened before, hasn't it?"

"You mean when I decked Howiedoin' at SupraQuito? That was handled NJP."

" 'Non-judicial punishment.' I know. It's in your record."

"So I did my time. Got scolded by the Old Woman, restricted to quarters, and lost a month's pay."

"But it was a bad decision on your part, wasn't it?"

"The bastard had it coming."

"And you're getting angry and defensive right now, just talking about it. Am I right?"

He was about to tell George to shut up and get out of his face, then realized she was trying to provoke him, trying to prod an emotional reaction out of him. "Don't tell me what I'm supposed to feel," he said quietly. "My mind is still my own. So are my feelings."

"Up to a point, Lieutenant. Up to a certain, and limited, point. What I'm trying to establish is that you boost down those launch tubes almost every day with more firepower at your fingertips than has been expended in all of the wars fought by Humankind since World War I. The jihadist nukes that took out the city centers of Paris, Chicago, and Washington were in the ten- to twelve-kiloton range. The one that got Tel Aviv was a little more, twenty kilotons or so. Your commanding officers—and the Confederation government—need to know that you *are* stable, competent, and reliable. Naval space aviation requires cool reasoning, a clean organic-cyber network connection, and emotions that are under control. No hotshots. No show-offs. And no one who's going to go off half-cocked when someone calls him a name, like *Prim* or *monogie*."

Fresh anger flared for an instant. His fists clenched. "Okay!" He forced his fists to relax, then said, more quietly, "Okay. Look, if I'm a risk, a threat to the Navy, kick me out! Send me back to the Periphery!"

"Is that what you really want?"

The reply stopped him cold.

The Authority might have been swinging its mass around when it brought him in, but the truth was that Trevor Gray had really started growing when he joined the Navy. Hell, you could romanticize the free life of the Periphery . . . but what "free life" *really* meant was constant raids by other clans and families, near-starvation in the winter if you didn't have a big enough stock of nano for food, clothing, and clean water, and a short, brutish life span that generally ended with a gang fight, with an accident, or with disease and exposure, all without the healthcare to see you through.

He missed his friends, the others in his TriBeCa Tower family. But in exchange, he'd received an education, social standing, implants, and a purpose . . . not bad for a filthy gutter kid from the Manhattan Ruins.

"It's not about what I want," he insisted, though the words sounded uncertain even to him. "Why even bring me in in the first place? I wasn't bothering anyone out in the Ruins."

"The Confederation is dedicated to bringing the benefits of technic civilization to all of its citizens," she told him.

"Bull. They wanted someone who could fly Starhawks. If they don't want me to fly, they can send me back to where they found me."

"It's not that easy, Lieutenant, and you know it. You—" She broke off in mid-sentence, listening.

"What is it?" Gray asked. She appeared to be receiving a base announcement of some sort. Gray's in-head circuitry was attuned to the naval Net on board the *America*, not the Marine version in use here.

"It's time for us to evacuate, Lieutenant," she told him. "They're ordering us topside, right now, to the transports."

"So where does that leave me?"

"I'm recommending continued therapy, Lieutenant. With me, or with therapy teams on the *America*, or back at Mars, it doesn't matter. But you're going to need to break that PTED cycle before you launch in a Starhawk again."

And he was dismissed. A Marine escort led him to the shuttle, and he never saw Anna George again.

He did know, however, that he was going to spend a lot of time thinking about just what it was he wanted out of the Navy, and about what the Navy wanted back from him.

Chapter Eleven

MEF HQ
Landing Pad
Eta Boötis IV
1807 hours, TFT

"This way, Lieutenant," said the escort, a young Marine corporal. The name showing high on the right chest of his combat armor was *Anderson*. "This Choctaw is slated for the *America*. You'll be able to rejoin your squadron there."

Gray looked out past a sea of thronging people, civilians, most of them. The large majority were women, most of them veiled inside their clear helmets, many completely anonymous beneath the traditional burqas draped over lightweight e-suits. There were lots of children as well, the youngest in survival bubbles, older ones clinging to mothers or older siblings, the oldest trying to look stolid and brave.

"All of these people are going to the *America* too?"

"These are, yes, sir. They've been sending them up by the shuttle-full for hours now. I hear they're packing them into every ship in the battlegroup."

Gray looked at a nearby child of perhaps three, squalling inside her e-suit's bubble helmet as her mother held her, bouncing her up and down. The inside of the bubble was nearly opaque with moisture from the screaming, though

Gray could still make out the child's red and contorted face. "It's going to be an interesting trip home."

"Yes, *sir*," the corporal agreed with considerable feeling.

Not all of the people boarding the shuttle were women and children, however. There were a few men sprinkled in among them. One, a couple of meters away, wore a black e-suit with a green-and-yellow patch of the Mufrid Defense Militia, a local group that worked as military auxiliaries in support of the Marines.

Gray found the fact that so many women were wearing burqas over their e-suits interesting. Only the most conservative and traditional of Islamic women still wore the things, which were supposed to conceal the woman's shape and keep her from offending—or tempting—male believers. Individual cultures tended to determine for themselves what was properly modest and what was not, and the women of those Islamic states on Earth that had accepted the White Covenant tended not to wear veils or similar heavily concealing garb. The Haris colonists, though, appeared to have reverted to form-hiding drapery, even when the woman was wearing a head-to-toe environmental skinsuit and bubble helmet that could not in any way be described as *sexy*.

"How many are there?"

"God knows, sir. Six or seven thousand, I heard. They're even bringing them in from the other Mufrid colonies out there."

Gray had heard that there were five other outposts on Haris besides the main colony-research station called Jauhar, or Jewel, and that two of those outposts had been incinerated by the Turusch during the past few weeks. Three, however, had not been attacked, and the Navy was trying to get as many women and children out of those surviving bases as possible.

As Gray and his escort started across the field, falling in with the women and children, he heard a low and menacing rumble from the civilians on the perimeter. They'd completely ringed in the landing field, and were blocked from approaching the grounded Choctaw shuttle by a painfully thin line of armored Marines. This crowd, most of them men, had been silent at first, but they were becoming more agitated now. One man was standing on a balcony overlooking the landing field and the mob, shouting something incomprehensible.

"What's he saying?" Gray asked.

"Beats the hell out of me, sir," the corporal replied. He looked nervous, staring across the crowd and fingering the stock of his laser rifle.

"He is saying," said the male civilian with the MDM patch on his shoulder, "that this is blasphemy in the eyes of God and the Prophet, may his name be forever blessed . . . and that those who return to Earth and to Earth's oppression . . ." The man broke off the translation, listening, then shook his head inside his bubble helmet. "I don't think you really want to hear this, sir."

"Maybe we should hear," Gray said. He was measuring the distance they still had to cross to reach the waiting Choctaw, wondering what the chances were that he would make it on board with this pass, or if he would have to wait for the next ride out.

"He is saying that it is God's will that we all stay and face the aliens, that . . . that *Shaitan* waits to devour us all on Earth. . . ."

"God help us," the corporal muttered.

The civilian looked at Gray, and extended a gloved hand. "I am Sergeant Muhammad Baqr," he said. "Militia, attached to the Marine 4th SAR/Recon."

"A pleasure. I'm—"

"Lieutenant Gray, I know. I was part of the hopper team that pulled you out of that tangle of shadow swarmers last night."

"Thank you."

"Don't mention it."

Abruptly, four Marines appeared on the shuttle ramp ahead. One was holding up his hand, his helmet moving slowly back and forth. There was no more room on that Choctaw, and he was stopping the queue.

Screams and cries arose from the waiting civilians, and the men outside the perimeter began shouting and shaking

their fists. The Marines began backing the civilians away
from the ramp, gesturing for them to get back.

"I don't like the looks of this," Gray said.

"Very bad," Baqr agreed. *"Very* bad . . ."

The ramp pulled back inside the Choctaw, and the hopper
began to rise, a spooling whine coming from its power plant,
navigation lights winking, broad, flat wings unfolding. A
stone, hurled from the mob outside the perimeter, struck the
glossy black hull and bounced off, as a ripple in the nano-
sheathing spread out from the point of impact. Another rock
followed, and missed.

The mob surged forward.

"Back!" a Marine on the perimeter line shouted. "Get
back!"

But the mob began breaking through. One of the Marines
fired, the laser a bright flash, and then people in the mob
were screaming and cursing. More rocks flew, most of them
hitting the civilians still lined up at the landing pad.

The roar of the mob was deafening as they shouted in
unison, *"Allahu akbar!"*

God is great.

VFA-44 Squadron Ready Room
TC/USNA CVS America
Haris Orbit, Eta Boötis System
1825 hours, TFT

Commander Allyn was still in debrief when the word
came up from the planet that a riot had broken out, that at
least a thousand Marines and several thousand civilians still
waiting to be evacuated were being attacked by a rampaging
mob.

"Commander," the voice of Admiral Koenig said inside
her head, "are you and your people ready for another mission?"

She started to say, "I don't know," which was the truth.
After arriving at the debriefing, she'd learned that the four
other members of her squadron all had recovered on board

the *America* after the fight with the Turusch fleet, but she didn't know if their Starhawks had been refitted and re-armed, didn't know if they were flight ready, didn't know if her squadron, what was left of it, was flight ready. They'd been through a hell of a lot, and they'd lost six people—she'd heard that Lieutenant Gray had crash-landed safely and been picked up by a Marine SAR. Suffering a casualty rate of 50 percent would definitely have a bad effect on the squadron's combat efficiency.

But Koenig would know all of that.

"Just give us the word, sir," she said. "I'll need to check the readiness status on our Starhawks. And *I* need a new ship." Her Starhawk had been pretty thoroughly savaged by that last detonation off the Turusch planetoid ship; that she had survived at all was nothing less than miraculous.

"We have plenty in reserve," Koenig told her. "What we need are *pilots*. The rest of the squadrons are either on deep patrol, on CAP, or they've been nursemaiding transports up and down from the planet for the past eight hours. Your people are as close to fresh as I've got."

"Yes, sir."

"I want you down on the deck, over the Marine perimeter," Koenig told her. "See if you can discourage those rioters."

Allyn blinked. "You want us to *strafe* them, Admiral?" There were rules about things like that. Firing on civil-ians . . . and the people you were supposed to be protecting in the first place at that.

"I'd rather you didn't," Koenig replied. "But do what looks best to you."

"Sir, why gravfighters? What about the Nightshades?"

"Every one I have is busy escorting Choctaws right now, Commander. Besides, their railguns are not exactly surgical weapons. I want you in there, exercising a bit more in the way of finesse."

Allyn had never received a more unpleasant set of orders. "Aye, aye, sir."

"Are *you* ready for a mission, Commander?" Koenig asked. He sounded concerned. "What's your med status?"

"I'm good to go, Admiral." Another small lie, a lie of omission. When she'd gone down to sick bay a few hours ago, they'd ended up putting her on light duty, with the promise of another checkup in twenty-four hours before she could be returned to flight-ready status. Koenig could have called up the records and seen that for himself, but hadn't. Just maybe she'd slipped through an administrative crack.

"Thank you, Commander," Koenig said. "Take it easy down there."

Which left her wondering if he had read the sick bay report, and was letting her choose to lead her people down anyway. "Aye, aye, sir."

She opened her eyes and looked at the three officers who'd been taking her report. "I've just received new orders," she told them. "I need to go."

"We heard, Commander Allyn," Commander Costigan, head of the battlegroup's intelligence department, said. "I think we're finished here. Good luck!"

"Finesse, sir," Lieutenant Commander Hargrave, from *America*'s tactical department, added with a shake of the head. "I don't envy you this one, Commander."

Twenty minutes later she was on the Number Three launch bay access. Tallman, her crew chief, handed her an e-suit helmet and grinned at her. "Brand new Starhawk for you, Commander," he said. "Try to take better care of this one, okay? I have to *sign* for these things when you lose 'em!"

"No promises, Chief," she said, setting the helmet in place and letting the seal fuse with her suit.

"Luck, Skipper."

"Thanks."

A vertical access shaft took her down one deck at a half-G acceleration, her impact at the bottom cushioned by a modified tangleweb field. Swiftly, she killed the TW-field and closed the hull over her cockpit, the nanomaterial turning liquid and flowing like black water to seal the outer hull shut.

Finesse, the Admiral had told her. If Nightshade railguns were indiscriminate, what the hell did he think a ten-kiloton Krait was? Or a KK Gatling burst?

"Flight designation Dragon," the voice of Primary Flight

Control said in her head. "Dragon One, comm check. Do you copy?"

"Dragon One, I copy. Systems on line. Ready to boost."

"Dragon Two," Lieutenant Howard Spaas said. "Ready."

"Dragon Three," Lieutenant Jen Collins added. "Let's go!"

"Dragon Four," Lieutenant Katie Tucker said. "Ready for launch!"

"Dragon Five," Lieutenant Gene Sandoval said. "Good to go."

Five Starhawks . . . with the exception of Prim, down on the planet somewhere, all that was left of the Dragonfires.

"We show all Dragons on-line, at full power, boards green and ready for launch," PriFly said. "Droplaunch coming up in twenty-seven seconds."

There were three ways to get fighters off of a modern star carrier. Most dramatic, of course, was to fire them out at high-G boost along one of the long twin launch tubes extending up the carrier's spine and all the way through the huge, water-filled shield cap forward. They could also be simply flown off the launch deck like a Choctaw or any of the other auxiliary spacecraft carried on board the *America*.

But the third method—the primary means of launching fighters until the development of high-G boost tubes forty years earlier—took advantage of the fact that the carrier's hab modules were rotating about the ship's long axis, completing one circuit every twenty-eight seconds to create an artificial, out-is-down spin gravity of half a G—about five meters per second per second.

With a jolt, Allyn's Starhawk dropped through a sudden, yawning hatch beneath its keel in the launch deck, coming to rest in a small, steel-walled compartment. The hatch overhead slid shut, and she could hear the air in the small chamber bleeding off as the seconds ticked away. The actual launch had to wait until the drop chamber's outer hatch was properly aligned, to give the fighters the correct vector.

With the compartment in hard vacuum, the lower hatch, the hatch in the launch deck's outer shell, slid silently open. The fighter rotated in its hanger, facing nose down and out. On

Allyn's in-head display, from her forward optics, she could see stars drifting across the narrow rectangle of her view ahead . . . a bright orange star—Arcturus, she thought—and a thick scattering of other, less brilliant but diamond-hard pinpoints of light.

And then a piece of the slender orange-and-white crescent of Haris swept into view, as the last few seconds trickled away.

" . . . and *four*," the launch control officer in PriFly announced. "And *three* . . . and *two* . . . and *one* . . . and *launch*!"

And abruptly, Allyn was in free fall, her fighter sliding off the magnetic grapples and falling out through the open hatch below. As soon as she was clear of the carrier, she switched on her forward singularity, spooling it up to five hundred gravities as she fell away from the *America*, moving more and more swiftly.

The other four Starhawks fell with her, in picture-perfect formation.

In moments, they were slicing through the tenuous upper levels of the planet's atmosphere.

MEF HQ
Main Mess Hall
Eta Boötis IV
1852 hours, TFT

For the past forty minutes, Gray, Corporal Anderson, and Mohammed Baqr had been squeezed back into one of the buildings that encircled the base landing pad, filling the base mess hall and several adjacent compartments. The high steel double door leading out onto the landing strip had been sealed shut.

They could see outside on the deck-to-overhead viewall, however. The short local day had just ended, and beneath the sullen and overcast sky, the Marine base had been swiftly plunged into darkness relieved only by the glare from external spotlights on the buildings and from a few glowglobes adrift in the still air. The mob had surged out onto the landing field and was out there still, packed in shoulder to shoulder, some with laser weapons seized from a militia arms locker. During the retreat into the mess hall, shots fired by several of the Marines had kept them back, kept them cautious, but their chants and shouts, muffled at first by their suits, were growing louder, more agitated.

They'd been chanting *Allahu akbar* more or less nonstop since the riot had begun. Now, though, they'd taken up a new cry. *"Death! Death to the great Shaitan! Death!"*

Gray couldn't tell if by *Shaitan* they meant the Turusch, the Confed military personnel remaining in the base, or the Confederation itself.

Baqr shrugged when Gray asked him about it. "I doubt that *they* know."

"Why aren't you out there with them?" Gray asked.

Baqr made a sour face. "Not all Muslims are fanatics, Lieutenant," he said. He sounded offended. "Not all are jihadists . . . or terrorists . . . or suicide bombers. And not all try to get their own way through juvenile demonstrations like this one."

"My apologies," Gray said. "They seem to be putting up a pretty solid front now, though."

Baqr sighed. "They're scared. And for most of them, the only comfort they have when they're afraid is their religion, submission to God, and knowing where you fit into God's plan. If they think you're trying to take that away from them, that you're threatening their belief, somehow, they can get . . . agitated."

"Are *you* afraid?" Corporal Anderson asked.

"Hell, yeah! Right now I don't know what scares me most . . . the Turusch, the thought of being left behind on this toxic rock, or *them*." He jerked a thumb at the rioters outside. "But damn it, I swore an oath before God to serve with the colonial militia and to support the Confederation. So . . . here I am."

Gray clapped him on his shoulder. "And we're glad you are." He caught movement in the sky and leaned forward, peering up at the viewwall. "Shit. What's that?"

It was only a shadow for a moment, but then it broke through the overcast, another Choctaw shuttle slowly drifting out of the sky, its belly gleaming in the lights from the base.

The mob had seen the shuttle as well. Several lasers fired, the beams invisible, but the flash where they hit brilliant in the darkness.

And then the Starhawks appeared, dropping down out of the clouds. And Gray and several hundred Marines nearby started cheering.

Dragon One
Above MEF Perimeter
Eta Boötis IV
1855 hours, TFT

Commander Allyn glanced down, her gravfighter's optics projecting a view of the Marine base into her in-head display that shifted as she moved her head. She could see the lights, could see the crowd filling the landing field two hundred meters below her keel, thousands of upturned and angry faces.

Starhawks could hover on gravs, but they were awkward at it. She'd been considering at first bringing her craft all the way down to just above the landing field, using the Starhawk itself as an intimidating show of force to force the crowd to disperse.

But the gravitational singularities her Starhawk used to maneuver were dangerous in close proximity to unshielded humans. They would be radiating X-rays and soft gamma as they sucked down molecules of this thick atmosphere, and a careless move at too close a distance might suck down a few dozen rioters as well. She might as well open up on the crowd with her Gatling cannon.

"Hey, Skipper," Spaas called. "I've got a bead on the guy stirring up the crowd down there. How's about we pop him?"

Her tracking system highlighted the target as Spaas

pointed him out electronically. She engaged the optical zoom for a closer look, saw a bearded man in a gold-colored e-suit standing on a balcony overlooking the landing field. He had a couple of assistants or bodyguards in black suits behind him, and he was gesticulating angrily, screaming something at the mob.

It *was* tempting . . . but she wasn't going to open fire on the crowd unless she absolutely saw no other way.

And there might be another option. "Negative, Dragon Two," she said. She shifted to the general combat frequency. "Choctaw One-two-five," she called, addressing the shuttle hovering overhead. "This is Dragon One, do you copy?"

"Dragon One. Choctaw One-two-five. I copy."

"Recommend you go plus-zee at least three thousand meters, over."

"God, Dragon One. What are you going to do?"

"It's called finesse, One-two-five. Just stay out of our way for a moment." Shifting frequencies again, she called to the other Dragonfires. "Okay, Dragons. Stay on me!"

She nudged the virtual controls, sending her Starhawk forward, flattening the ship out into a knife-edged and elongated disc, extending back-swept wings, reshaping her airfoils to bank steeply to the left. One by one, the other four Starhawks dropped into her wake and followed. The Choctaw shuttle, after a moment's hesitation, began gaining altitude once more, slipping back up into the sheltering murk of the cloud deck.

Accelerating quickly now, Allyn swung wide out across the barren desert surrounding the Marine base, hurtling through the night. Her forward singularity glowed white-hot just ahead, an intense, arc-brilliant pinpoint radiating furiously as it chewed through atmosphere, dragging the Starhawk along in its wake.

As she turned, she showed her Starhawk's AI what she had in mind, felt the shifting, inner harmonics as her brain and the computer running the Starhawk worked together, crunching equations and unfolding an optimal flight path in her mind. She studied a computer-generated model of the Marine base, rotating it, judging the clifflike loom of the taller buildings, the openings in between. It was going to be tight. . . .

The Choctaw was hovering well out of the way now, three kilometers above the base. She leveled off into straight flight, hurtling across the invisible surface of the desert at an altitude of scarcely eighty meters, accelerating *hard*.

She went hypersonic.

How fast sound travels depends on the density of the medium through which it is moving. On Earth, at sea level and at a temperature of 20 degrees Celsius, sound travels at 343 meters per second; in water, a much denser medium than air, the speed of sound is around 1500 meters per second.

The gas mix that constituted the atmosphere of Eta Boötis IV was 1.7 times denser than air at Earth's surface, and the molecules of that atmosphere—predominantly carbon dioxide, sulfur dioxide, sulfur trioxide, ammonia, and carbonyl sulfide—all were larger, heavier molecules than the primary constituents of Earth's atmosphere, O_2 and N_2.

At the surface of Eta Boötis, the speed of sound was very nearly 700 meters per second—about 2500 kilometers per hour. As Allyn boosted her Starhawk's acceleration, she was flashing across the desert at nearly 4 kilometers per second, better than Mach 5 for these conditions. Her Starhawk's computer gently increased her altitude slightly, compensating for the height of the ridgetop on which the Marine base was situated.

Twenty kilometers out—five seconds' flight time—she fired her PBP-2.

MEF HQ
Main Mess Hall
Eta Boötis IV
1854 hours, TFT

Gray and the others had felt a sudden letdown, a surge of disappointment and even anger as first the Choctaw had lifted itself back up into the clouds, and then as the five Starhawk fighters had streaked off into the night. "The bastards are *leaving* us!" one Marine had screamed. "The fucking Navy zorchie bastards are *leaving* us!"

Outside, the crowd was jubilant, shouting and laughing and jumping up and down. Some were firing their lasers uselessly into the sky, in celebration or in an empty gesture of defiance, or both.

Gray had spotted something, though. As the line of black Starhawks had begun slipping away out of the glare of the lights below, he'd noticed that they were flattening out, and that they were growing black, swept-back wings. If those fighters had given up, if they were boosting for space and a return to the carrier, they would have adopted a more rounded, teardrop shape. Wings, however, meant they were planning on maneuvering in the atmosphere, probably at low altitude.

And he thought he knew what they were going to do.

"They're not leaving, everybody!" he yelled, boosting the volume on his e-suit speakers to make sure he got everyone's attention. "Everyone get down! Marines . . . stand ready to move out and secure the landing field!"

He bellowed the orders, putting all of the authority and power he could into the words. Across the room, he caught a Marine major staring at him. A major outranked a Navy lieutenant by one pay grade, the equivalent of a Navy lieutenant commander, and, in any case, a stranded Navy pilot normally had no business giving orders to Marines.

"*Do* it!" the major barked. "You! You! You! And you! Over by this door!"

And then the sky outside lit up with lightning.

Gray recognized the signature flash of a heavy particle beam. Navy Starhawks mounted StellarDyne Blue Lightning PBP-2 particle beam projectors which could project a bolt of protons with a yield of around a gigajoule in one tenth of a second. The total energy was about one thousandth that of a typical natural lightning bolt, but at close range, the pulse lit up the sky as the air ionized along a straight-line path.

An instant later, the first Starhawk zorched overhead, traveling so low, so fast, that Gray was aware of a flicker of motion but nothing more.

The sonic boom that followed shook the walls of the mess hall, deafening and shrill. It was followed a moment later by a second . . . a third . . . a fourth . . . a fifth, the hypersonic booms coming in a rapid succession of deafening, high-pitched thunderclaps. Outside, the rioters appeared to crumble in a mass, dropping to their knees or full-length on the ferocrete landing pad, bringing gloved hands up against their helmets as they instinctively tried to cover their ears.

When the Marines and the civilian women and children had fallen back to the mess hall, they'd come in through a large doorway blocked by a nanoseal, the same black, liquid substance used to prevent pressure loss on *America*'s hangar deck when spacecraft were brought in from the vacuum outside. As the mob had surged after them, a Marine had switched on the seal freeze, turning the suspended nanoparticles into a rigid structure, a barrier stronger than plasteel.

Now, the seal freeze was released, and the first four Marines charged outside, weapons at the ready, followed closer by more Marines, and a scattering of Mufrid militia.

"Come on," Gray said to Corporal Anderson. "Let's get out there!"

It took several minutes to elbow through the panicked, milling crowd, but Gray made it to the nanoseal lock and stepped through, pushing against the liquid's yielding resistance and out onto the landing field. The rioting mob had been effectively neutralized, reduced to stunned and disoriented individuals as the Marines began to shove and push unresisting rioters back off the field. He looked up at the balcony overlooking the field nearby, and saw more Marines grabbing the agitator and hauling him back into the building.

All of the floating glowglobes had been swept away by the shock waves, and many of the remaining lights mounted on the buildings had been shattered. The few lighting panels that remained cast eerie, pitch-black shadows across the field, lending a nightmare aura to the scene.

"Get the field clear!" the Marine major was shouting. "Get it the hell *clear*!"

Overhead, the Choctaw had reappeared, running lights pulsing, the black, UC-154 shuttle slowly drifting down for a landing.

Chapter Twelve

CIC, TC/USNA CVS America
Haris Orbit, Eta Boötis System
1945 hours, TFT

With the exception of the Dragonfires, the last of the fighters were recovering on board the carrier, drifting in toward the aft end of the landing deck stretched out along the ship's spine, killing their grav singularities at the last moment possible, then hitting the tangleweb field to kill the last of their forward velocity. As each Starhawk came to a halt, robotic arms snagged the ship and dragged it forward, out of the way of the next incoming ship, then swung it up into nanosealed ports in the deck above, lifting it up into the hangar deck.

The battlegroup was preparing to accelerate, each individual ship slowly swinging around until its broad, hemispherical forward shield faced a nondescript patch of relatively empty sky midway between the beacons of Canopus and Rigel. Earth's sun lay there, somewhere in the emptiness. At thirty-seven light years' distance, Sol was just barely too dim to be seen with the naked eye. On every ship in the fleet, however, the sun's location was marked by a bright green circle.

Home . . .

Admiral Koenig sat at his CIC workstation, reports from all twenty-four ships of the carrier battlegroup flooding through the *America*'s communications suite.

All things considered, the battlegroup had come through in superb shape, much better than he'd hoped. The *Farragut* and the destroyer *Carter* both had been destroyed; three more ships had suffered serious damage in the battle, and one of those, the frigate *Abramson*, had been so badly shot up that her crew was now being transferred to other vessels, including the *America*. With Mufrid refugees already packed into every available ship, crammed onto mess decks and into passageways and storage bays, it was going to be a tight fit getting everyone on board.

It had been the fighters, Koenig knew, who'd tipped the balance, who'd made the lopsided victory possible. Turusch ships heavily outgunned and out-teched equivalent Confederation vessels, and tended to be much tougher, much more powerful than human ships . . . especially when you found yourself up against converted asteroids like that command ship.

"Admiral?" Commander Reigh called from the Controller's workstation. "The Conestogas and their escorts report readiness for acceleration. They're requesting clearance."

"Very well. They are clear for boost."

"Captain Vanderkamp has acknowledged."

On the tac display, the eight converted Conestoga troopships and four escorting destroyers began to move, falling toward a distant, invisible Sol at one hundred gravities. Captain Vanderkamp, on the destroyer *Symmons*, would command the detachment, would get them safely back to Sol.

"Clear the auxiliaries for boost," Koenig ordered.

"Order acknowledged, Admiral."

Five more vessels—fleet auxiliaries: three supply vessels and two repair tenders—began accelerating as well, falling away from the fast-dwindling battlegroup.

Koenig's greatest concern at this point was that the Turusch would counterattack, would hit the battlegroup with its fighter screen on board the carrier. With that in mind, he was sending the troopship and unarmed auxilliaries on ahead, with the remaining seven ships—the *America*, the *Spirit of Confederation*, and five others—holding position as the last of the fighters and shuttles recovered on board.

At this moment, the last of the Marines on the surface of Eta Boötis IV were on their way up from the planet, escorted by the five remaining Dragonfires. The surviving gravfighters from VFA-44 had succeeded in scattering the rioters in the Marine compound down on the planet's surface, had escorted several more shuttles back up to the fleet, and now were seeing to the last of the evacuees.

The eleven gravfighters of VFA-51, the Black Lightnings, were still out there as well. Hours before, he'd sent them out on deep perimeter patrol, following the retreating enemy ships a full thirty light minutes out. If the Turusch did turn around and launch a counterstrike, the Black Lightnings would be *America*'s early warning net. They were returning now, but would not be back on board the carrier for another forty minutes.

"Admiral!" It was Commander Johanna Hughes, the tac evaluator. "Urgent from VFA-51! Enemy fighters inbound at near-*c*!"

Shit. The nightmare scenario.

"How many?"

"Unknown, sir. He says 'a hell of a lot . . . at least fifty.' "

Koenig studied the tactical display. The enemy had retreated in *that* direction—roughly toward the star Epsilon Boötis . . . not that that star would necessarily have been their actual destination. He'd sent the Black Lightnings out line along the same path to watch for just this eventuality. Eleven Starhawk gravfighters against fifty Toads. Not good odds. Not good at *all*.

But the real urgency of the situation lay in the fact that the enemy fighters were coming in just behind the lasercommed message warning of their approach. The battlegroup's rear guard might have mere seconds before the Turusch were among them.

"Make to all ships," Koenig said. "Maneuvering, Code One. Initiate hivel-A defenses *now*!"

"Aye, aye, sir."

Hivel-A was milspeak for high-velocity assault. Defenses included launching clouds of sand, firming up defensive shields, but most of all, *moving*. If there were laser bolts coming in at the speed of light, or plasma beam or other weapons skimming in just behind the light barrier, the best defense of all was to not be there when they arrived.

"Copy the tacsit to everyone within range," Koenig added. He was thinking of the last Choctaw shuttle coming up from the surface, and the gravfighters and Nightshades escorting it. They needed to know what they were boosting into.

Slowly, ponderously, the remaining seven ships of the carrier battlegroup began to move.

Dragon One
Above Eta Boötis IV
1945 hours, TFT

Her Starhawk punched through the last cloud deck and Commander Allyn emerged into the clear, vast emptiness of the planet's upper atmosphere, with stars gleaming down at her with hard and untwinkling brilliance. A moment later, the local sun exploded into view on the horizon, wiping out the stars, illuminating a scimitar's edge of cloud cover dividing planetary night from space.

As the atmosphere rapidly thinned, she reshaped her Starhawk into its needle configuration. The other four fighters of VFA-44 were already doing the same, dragging straight-line contrails behind them as their drive singularities chewed through what was left of the air. The Choctaw, fat and bulbous, didn't have a variable geometry hull, and began lagging behind. Allyn ordered the squadron to slow their ascent, matching their velocity to the transport shuttle. The four Nightshade gunships followed close in the Choctaw's wake, like angular black insects pursuing an ungainly blue-painted cow.

"We are receiving an urgent tactical update from the fleet," her AI told her, the voice a whisper in her mind. "Details follow. . . ."

She watched the incoming data scroll through an open window in her consciousness. "Toads!" Allyn snapped as the data flooding through from the *America* registered. "Hivel-A, fifty-plus Toads."

"Where?" Tucker demanded. "I don't—"

White light blossomed on the night side of the planet directly astern, a searing illumination of the clouds that momentarily blocked out the glare of the bright-rising star. Her sensors picked up the wake of a high-G impactor that had just seared down out of the sky, passing the Confederation fighters and shuttle perhaps eighty kilometers abeam.

"What the—" Lieutenant Collins called over the squadron frequency.

Seconds later, two distinct shock waves struck, first from the ground thirty kilometers below, then a lesser one from the impactor's more distant atmospheric wake, twin sledgehammer blows against her fighter's hull. Had the air been any thicker, had they been any closer to the ground, any deeper inside Eta Boötis IV's thick atmosphere, the shock waves, she knew, would have swatted them all from the sky.

The former Marine base had just been obliterated.

The knowledge stunned her. They'd lifted clear of the base landing pad scant minutes earlier as the rioting mobs had closed in on the loaded shuttle once again. There'd been no point in orchestrating another high-Mach passage over the base. The civilians who'd wanted to get out were getting out; the others had already made their choice.

But it was startling to see how swiftly the consequences of that choice had arrived—as a ten-kilo inert kinetic impactor traveling at just below the speed of light had slammed into the base and released thousands of megatons of energy in a single dazzling flash. As she scanned the planet, she saw a second flash, far up the curve of the northern horizon, and realized that a second impactor had just struck the Mufrid outpost at Kurban.

A third flash . . . that was probably Amal . . . and a fourth, more distant still, Lilistizkar.

The Marine base and the last three inhabited colony domes, all . . . all *gone.*

The suddenness, the sheer savagery of the attack was almost too much to grasp.

She shifted her scan forward, to the carrier battlegroup. Only seven ships remained in planetary orbit; the others had boosted moments before, were already accelerating hard out-system. Those seven, she saw with considerable relief, all were accelerating, breaking orbit, turning in toward the planet to use Haris's gravity to their advantage.

The Turusch, of course, would have had precise targeting information for the planet, could accurately strike the colony outposts from light seconds out. Ships, however, could leave their predictable orbits and not be there when the beams or hivel projectiles arrived.

Collins' scanner picked up numerous faint straight-line trails of ionization ahead, the traces of near-c impactors flashing through dust and stray molecules of atmosphere just ahead of where the fleet had been orbiting scant moments before.

The Confederation had tried exactly the same tactics against the Turusch fleet earlier, with considerably greater success. It appeared that the enemy had missed all seven human warships.

But the thought of what was happening on the planet astern still burned. *Why?. . .*

It made no sense. The Turusch had bombarded the Marine perimeter for over a week; at any time they could have accelerated a rock big enough to vaporize a continent, but they hadn't. They'd been trying to capture the place, not obliterate it.

That strategy, evidently, had changed. The Turusch had just annihilated all human outposts remaining on the planet, killing some tens of thousands of civilians.

Why?

She shook the thought aside. Strategists, xenopsychologists, and admirals could worry about that later. Her problem now was the knowledge that there would be high-G fighters coming in immediately behind the near-c kinetic impactors.

There!

The Toads were coming in hot, decelerating hard in order

to engage ship-to-ship. Among them were Confederation Starhawks—the gravfighters of Sandy Jorgenson's Black Lightnings, following the leading wave of Toads in, trying to burn them down.

The battleship *Spirit of Confederation* opened up with her long-range fusion cannon, and a constellation of oncoming Turusch fighters smeared into tiny, brilliant novae. And then the enemy fighters were sweeping into the battlegroup like avenging angels of death.

CIC, TC/USNA CVS America
Haris Space, Eta Boötis System
1947 hours, TFT

"Enemy fighters at two-three-zero plus five-one, engaging!" Johanna Hughes announced.

Koenig watched the unfolding action on the tactical display—green icons representing Confederation vessels, red the enemy, with a vast, ghosted gray sphere showing the position of Eta Boötis IV.

More hivel impactors, launched at closer ranges, might still be out there, coming fast. If the carrier squadron could maneuver around behind the planet, use the planet as a shield, they might be able to delay acceleration long enough to take the remaining fighters on board.

That was the true hell of the tacsit. Right now, there were sixteen gravfighters out there, plus four Nightshade close-support gunships and one last, lumbering shuttle packed with civilians and Marines. If *America* boosted for *c*, the gravfighters, with their high accelerations, could catch up—assuming the Toads let them—but the shuttle and the gunships would be left behind.

And even the fighters were at risk. Trapping on board a carrier under acceleration was *not* for the fainthearted, nor was there a promise of success.

But the seven capital ships were vulnerable if they stayed put. They might hold the Toad fighters at bay for a time, but Koenig was willing to bet that Turusch capital ships were out there, lots of them, still undetected and burning in tight on the fighters' wakes. If the squadron didn't start boosting for *c*, they would be trapped here, pinned against the planet and annihilated one by one.

A gravfighter—one of the Lightnings—had burned out a Toad, but now two more Toads had dropped onto his tail. He listened to the voices of the cockpit chatter, relayed back to *America*'s CIC by the cloud of battlespace drones serving as comm relays and unmanned intel platforms.

"Lightning, Lightning Five! I got two on my tail!"

"Five, One! Break left, break left!"

"Copy One, breaking left! . . . they're still—"

One of the green pinpoints in the tac display winked out. A tight formation of Turusch fighters were closing on the knot of Starhawks, slashing at them with beam weapons.

"Comm! Make to the *Spirit*," Koenig ordered. "Break up those Toad clusters! Get them off our people!"

"Aye, sir."

The *Spirit of Confederation* had the most accurate of long-range weapons in the formation, with railguns and fusion beams that could pop something as small as a fighter at a range of over one light second.

Of course, she still needed a good idea of where the target would be one second after firing—that was the single major limiting factor in space combat. But so long as the target held course and speed—or a constant rate of acceleration—for more than a second, her targeting computers gave her uncanny accuracy.

Another of the Black Lightnings vanished in a white flare of incandescence.

"Make to all fighters," Koenig told the communications officer. "Break off and rejoin the battlegroup. Prepare for underway trap."

"Aye, aye, sir!"

He looked into the tac display again. Five fighters, a shuttle, and four gunships still coming up from the surface . . . and ten gravfighters of the Black Lightnings tangled in a fur ball with the Trash. Damn. They needed to get that transport aboard. The display readout showed 214 people packed on board—God! They must be sitting in one another's laps! UC-154s were rated for about 180 at most.

He juggled with the possibility of launching another fighter squadron, then decided against it. More fighters might help the long odds against those Toads, but the rest of the Turusch fleet would be along very shortly, of that he was certain. He already stood to loose seventeen good gravfighter pilots out there. He didn't want the number to rise to twenty-nine.

If the capital ships could hold off that swarm of incoming Toads with their point-defense weapons, maybe they could bring the fighters and the shuttle on board as well.

But it was going to be damned tight.

Dragon One
Above Eta Boötis IV
1948 hours, TFT

Allyn heard the orders come down from *America*'s CIC— *rendevous with the carrier. Prepare for underway trap.*

But she saw a tactical opportunity.

As the fighters continued to climb up out of Eta Boötis IV's gravity well, she saw that the enemy fighters, closing with *America* and her escorts, would be passing almost directly above the five hard-boosting Dragonfires. Better yet, the planet's surface directly astern, directly below them, was a flaring, savage glare of white in the middle of a broader swath of red-orange light. Above the light, a fast-swelling, red-lit mushroom cloud was spreading out rapidly above the apocalypse of lava and erupting volcanoes marking the vast, molten crater vaporized by the near-*c* impactor.

There was enough heat and light glaring from that scar, she thought, to mask the fighters from enemy sensors, from some of them, at least. The Starhawks might be tagged by radar—though their hull configuration was already shifting to stealth mode to hide them. And the Toad pilots wouldn't be watching the eruptions on the planet. They would be focused on *America* and the other capital ships ahead.

The Choctaw shuttle and the four gunships were already

angling off in another direction, racing for the distant star carrier.

"Dragonfires!" she called. "Stick close! We're going to give those bastards one hell of a surprise!"

CIC, TC/USNA CVS America
Haris Space, Eta Boötis System
1948 hours, TFT

"Dragonfires have acknowledged, sir," the comm officer announced.

"Then what the hell are they doing?" Koenig asked. The shuttle and its Nightshade escort was breaking for the carrier, but the five fighters were maintaining their course, straight-line from the planet's surface into space.

"Analyses of their vector suggests they're performing a pop-up, sir," Hughes told him.

A pop-up—an ambush by fighters lurking within the atmosphere of a planet, then "popping up" out of the atmosphere to attack. Usually, the relative positions within a local gravity well dictated that the force farther from the planet held the gravitational advantage. Even with drive singularities, it took a lot of energy to fight up out of the bottom of a planetary well. But in some cases, surprise could outweigh the disadvantages, especially if the enemy wasn't paying attention.

And this time, the enemy appeared to be completely focused on the carrier battlegroup. The question was whether five gravfighters could make any difference at all in a scrap against ten times their number.

"God help them," he murmured.

Dragon One
Haris Space, Eta Boötis System
1949 hours, TFT

Allyn cut her drive singularity as she flashed into the path of the oncoming Turusch fighter swarm, targeting the nearest Toad and cutting loose with her RFK-90 KK Gatling at a range of less than ten thousand kilometers. Her AI pivoted her ship as she moved, twisting it to keep the Gatling aligned with the enemy fighter. A stream of magnetic-ceramic-jacketed slugs of depleted uranium, each massing half a kilo, snapped out with a cyclic rate of twelve per second.

With a launch tube five meters long and an acceleration of three hundred gravities, those slugs were traveling at 175 meters per second when they left the Starhawk's prow. The impact of that stream carried the punch of a fair-sized tactical nuke; the Toad's shields went down as the hull opened up with a zipper effect, ripping out its guts and sending molten chunks of debris tumbling through space.

"Dragon One, scratch one!" she cried over the com link.

The other Dragonfires were scoring as well. Lieutenant Tucker was using her PBP-2 in short, controlled bursts, flipping her Starhawk this way and that, acquiring targets, locking on, firing. Collins and Spaas were tucked in close together with a separation of only a few hundred kilometers, their battle AIs linked as they concentrated their fire, one using KK slugs, the other particle-beam bursts to maximize their combined effect. Sandoval was firing his Kraits . . . serious overkill for a Toad, but the results were dramatic enough as white nuclear blossoms swelled and faded against black space, silent and devastating.

"Sandoval!" Allyn called. "Save the Kraits for the big boys! You'll need 'em later!"

"Is there gonna be a later?" he shot back, but he switched to his KK Gatling.

The sudden appearance of the five new Starhawks appeared to have thrown the Toad formation off balance. Intertwined with the Black Lightnings, they'd been focusing their attention, it had seemed, on closing with the remnant of the carrier battlegroup. Now, however, they were faltering, breaking sharply, accelerating in different directions, trying to put distance between themselves and their tormentors.

Turusch fighters were designed to put down heavy fire on capital ships, and they tended to work best at distances of from five to fifty thousand kilometers from their targets—medium range in space combat. They were not as maneuverable as Starhawks, and weren't good dogfighters.

Starhawks, on the other hand, were designed for close-in knife fights, getting in to within a thousand kilometers or less of the target, outmaneuvering it, and taking it down with concentrated KK and PBP fire. If they could get close enough to a Toad, they enjoyed a considerable advantage ship-to-ship . . . but at medium range the Toads' advantage in heavy weaponry could be devastating.

Sandoval twisted in toward a Toad already exchanging fire with one of the Black Lightnings. The Lightning was pacing the Turusch fighter, working to drop squarely onto its tail at a range of less than a hundred kilometers.

At the last moment, the Toad spun end-for-end, hammering at the Black Lightning, which rolled to port, using its drive singularity to jink randomly back and forth, making itself a difficult target. Sandoval was farther out, almost three thousand kilometers, and at that range the Turusch particle beams had bloomed, becoming far wider, far more likely to hit, than when they were fired close-in.

The beam caught his Starhawk aft, slashing through shields, vaporizing critical portions of the gravfighter's projection bootstrappers.

Fighters under drive fell toward an artificial gravitational singularity projected in the desired direction of acceleration; *bootstrapper* was the slang term for the electronics that continually refocused the singularity ahead of the ship from picosecond to picosecond. With the bootstrapper disabled and the singularity still powered, Sandoval's Starhawk fell into its own drive field, its nose crumpling as the fighter began whipping around the pinpoint singularity in a high-velocity blur. In another instant, about a quarter of the fighter was consumed, smashed down into subatomic debris at the singularity's event horizon. The rest sprayed into surrounding space, most of the mass transformed into a blinding flash of energy.

The remaining four members of the Dragonfires continued the attack.

Squadron Ready Room
TC/USNA CVS America
Haris Space, Eta Boötis System
1950 hours, TFT

To the uninitiated, the squadron ready room looked like a place for Dragonfire personnel on board the carrier to relax between missions, a lounge with comfortable recliners, indirect lighting, and soft-padded decks. In fact, it was the nerve center for the pilots of VFA-44, the place where they were briefed before each mission, where they debriefed with the carrier's combat intelligence officer afterward, and where they waited out the hours of a ready alert, waiting for the order to strap on their fighters.

The overhead, vaulted like a planetarium dome, could be set to project maps or combat plots. At the moment, it was set to display an exterior view of space as relayed back by hundreds of drone surveillance modules scattered through battlespace. Lieutenant Gray was alone in the compartment, stretched out on a recliner and watching the battle unfold.

It was a strange and unsettling feeling to be here, knowing that the rest of his squadron—what was left of it—was *out there*, facing the oncoming enemy in a desperate bid to save the heart of the battlegroup.

Gray had not yet been signed off for flight-ready status. He felt . . . alone. Alone and helpless. He saw Sandoval's gravfighter hit, saw its spectacular end. *Flashpoint*, the phenomenon was called in the milspeak slang of fighter pilots, when a gravfighter and its pilot were both devoured by its own drive singularity.

The Toad Sandoval had been stalking exploded as the Black Lightning pilot savaged it from point-blank range with KK fire.

The sky projected across the ready room dome was sliding smoothly now from one side to the other as the *America* continued to accelerate. The black bulk of Haris, the planet, shifted with it, blotting out the sun with an artificial sunset. The battlegroup, Gray knew, must be trying to swing around behind the planet, using its bulk as a shield.

He wondered if the fighters still rough-and-tumbling it with the Toads out there would be able to trap.

The Draghonfires' chatter was coming through over the ready room's link from CIC, faint voices, adrenaline-shrill with excitement and fear.

"This is Dragon Two! Dragon Two! Got one on my tail!

"Hold on, Two, I'm on him!

"Shit! I'm hit! I'm hit!"

"On him, Two! On my mark, break high and right! Ready . . . mark!"

Another Toad exploded in white silence. But Dragon Two had been hit, his telemetry showing serious damage to his ship.

Gray's fists clenched at his sides.

Back on Earth, back in the Manhattan Ruins, you survived by watching out for the others in your extended clan, watching their backs. It was a psychology that translated easily to the military culture, and particularly to the men and women of your own gravfighter squadron. With few exceptions, he hated the others in VFA-44. Sandoval was a stuck-up prig. Spaas, especially, and his partner Collins, were always there riding him about his being a prim, telling him he wasn't good enough to be a part of their elite.

But they were still a part of his new clan. *Family.*

And they were dying out there, all of them, and there wasn't a damned thing he could do about it.

Chapter Thirteen

CIC, TC/USNA CVS America
Haris Orbit, Eta Boötis System
2015 hours, TFT

"Captain Buchanan?" Koenig said. "Bring those fighters aboard!"

"Aye, aye, sir."

Under savage, close assault by the Confederation Starhawks, supported by the deadly and accurate batteries on the *Spirit of Confederation*, the *Kinkaid*, and the other vessels of the shrunken battlegroup, the Turusch fighters, what was left of them, had broken off the attack. *America*, after swinging behind the planet, had aligned with distant Sol but not yet begun accelerating.

The Choctaw shuttle and its Nightshade escorts were rendezvousing with the *America* now, gliding in from astern, aligning their approach vector with the opening at the aft end of the rotating Number Two docking bay. At the last possible moment, they gave a final, brief burst of acceleration before killing their drive singularities and drifting dead-stick into the swinging maw of the docking bay, entering a tangleweb field that slowed them abruptly for the final fifty meters of their approach.

"CIC, PriFly," sounded in Koenig's head. "The shuttle is aboard."

"Thank you, PriFly. I saw."

He had a screen at his CIC station set as a repeater off of PriFly's main board. He'd watched the *Choctaw* enter the gaping opening, could see the gunships coming in through the entrance now, in staggered formation to match the docking bay's rotation, one after the other. Nightshades were essentially large, two-man fighters, but slower and less maneuverable than Starhawks or War Eagles, with a maximum acceleration of only twelve Gs. That made them good for chewing up ground targets and serving as close-support for the infantry, but not of much use in a gravfighter fur ball.

Koenig turned his attention to the fighters—four from VFA-44 and eight from VFA-51. They were eighty thousand kilometers astern of the *America* now, but catching up fast.

"Admiral?" Buchanan's voice said in his head. "Permission to begin accelerating the *America*."

"Granted," Koenig told him. The slow movers were safely on board now. The fighters easily had the acceleration necessary to match velocities with a capital ship. The sooner the last seven capital ships of the battlegroup were pushing *c*, the better. Koenig still expected Turusch warships to be coming in on the tails of those fighters; they could appear on feeds from the more remote battlespace drones at any moment.

On the tactical display, the ships of the battlegroup began moving faster, as data readouts showed the vector change. The fighters were already going all out, the distance between them and *America* dwindling rapidly.

Come on, he thought, the words fierce. *Get your butts in here. . . .*

Dragon One
Eta Boötis IV
2020 hours, TFT

"Okay, chicks," Allyn said. "Final correction is coming up. Lose the dust balls."

At her command, each pilot switched off his or her forward singularity and decelerated, sending the atom-sized collections of dust and debris hurtling into the void. The maneuver was vital; those submicroscopic specks could wreak untold havoc with *America*'s internal spaces if they struck the carrier.

They hadn't been in flight for long, and the dust masses were so minute they likely would have caused no damage. On the other hand, they were traveling slowly enough that the specks might not pass all the way through the carrier. They could become imbedded in her hull, where they would continue to feed and grow.

There were horror stories still told in the service from the earliest days of gravitic engineering, of ships infested with neutron-sized black holes, of ships and their crews dying slowly.

One by one, the fighters dropped into staggered approach vectors.

"Howie!" she called. "What's your sit?"

"Doing okay, Skipper." He sounded scared. Medical telemetry showed his heart rate, breathing, and blood pressure all significantly elevated. "VG is out. So are half my thrusters and some of my sensors. AI off-line. It's gonna be a dead catch."

"Stay with us," she told him. "We're almost home."

Spaas's Starhawk was badly mangled, still flying, but only just. That Toad particle beam had grazed his starboard side, killing both his variable geometry controls, his "VG," and it had knocked out half of his control thrusters and some critical instrumentation, including his onboard computer. "Dead catch" meant he was going to hit the tangleweb as a dead chunk of metal, with no way of fine-tuning the last second of the approach.

His setup for trap would have to be bang-on perfect.

If *America* wasn't in the middle of getting the hell out of Dodge, the likeliest scenario would have been to have Spaas match course and velocity with the carrier, then punch out, allowing SAR tugs from the *America* to come out and pick him up and recover the inert fighter. But they didn't have the luxury of time now, and having the *America* maintain a steady velocity on a constant course for more than a few minutes would invite a barrage of hivel KK rounds that could reduce the carrier to half-molten fragments in seconds.

So they had to do it the hard way—with Spaas landing his crippled Starhawk on *America*'s rotating deck.

Howard Spaas wasn't the best Starhawk driver Allyn had ever known, but he was good. He could be arrogant and elitist at times—he made a game of picking on the nuggets, the new pilots in the squadron—and he'd been written up more than once for disciplinary problems.

But he was part of the Dragonfire's tight-knit family, and she didn't want to lose him.

"Dragon One, Dragon Three." That was Collins.

Here it comes. "Go ahead, Three."

"Request permission to ride Dragon Two in."

Collins wanted to make the trap side-by-side with Spaas. With her ship coming in just off Spaas's forward quarter, he could check his alignment and vector by eye, and not have to rely so much on possibly malfunctioning sensors. Experienced pilots sometimes rode in with nuggets, or with other pilots experiencing instrumentation or thruster problems.

"Negative, Two." Allyn switched to a private channel, so Spaas wouldn't hear. "Damn it, Collie-dog, I don't want to lose *both* of you if this goes bad."

"Acknowledged." Collins' voice was tight, the word bitten off and hard.

Allyn switched back to the squadron channel. "Final turn, people. Let's do it by the book."

The *America* was still invisibly distant, some eight thousand kilometers up ahead. Their dustcatchers jettisoned, the fighters used brief applications of their singularities to align themselves precisely with the ship, then switched them off. The carrier was traveling directly away from them at ten kilometers per second, accelerating at fifty gravities, which increased its velocity by half a kilometer per second every second. The fighters were coming in faster, but slowing; by the time they were a hundred kilometers off *America*'s tail, they would be moving just three hundred meters per second faster than the carrier.

"VFA-44, you are cleared for trap. Landing Bay Two."

"Dragon One. Copy."

"Switch to AI approach," she said.

"Confirmed," her computer said. "AI in control of final approach."

When everything was working right, the computer network between fighter and carrier did a much better job of nudging the ship into the aft opening of a rotating landing bay.

The AI triggered a five hundred grav singularity aft, braking her sharply, just as the *America* appeared ahead, rapidly swelling in apparent size. The singularity snapped off when she was moving just three hundred meters per second relative to the *America*.

The carrier looked so damned tiny, a hard-edged toy almost lost among stars and empty night.

And then the carrier's aft end swelled to fill half the sky and she was into her trap.

Moments before, the carrier had switched off her own grav drive, simplifying the complex ballet balancing velocity and distance. Though conventions like up and down and above and below didn't exist in free fall, the fighter's attitude on final suggested that she was skimming in just beneath the vessel's huge, aft quantum tap power module, the dark, silver-gray metal of the hull blurring past just above her head. Ahead, Landing Bay Two slowly swung in from the right.

The carrier's hab modules were stacked around *America*'s spine, like layers in a cake, bent into a disk nestled in behind the mushroom-cap shield. The modules were in constant rotation, creating a steady out-is-down artificial gravity. A rotation of 2.11 turns per minute created the feeling of half a G at the outer rim, one hundred meters from the ship's spine. A point on the outside rim was moving at twenty-two meters per second, or nearly fifty miles per hour.

The carrier *could* stop the module rotation, but that created chaos on board, as every crew member, every tool or coffee cup or personal item not fastened down drifted away, weightless. And there was an easier solution.

The landing bay was at the bottom of the stack, closest

to the ship's spine. The rotation of 2.11 turns per minute with a radius of just thirty meters created an apparent gravity of just .15 G—a shade less than the surface gravity of Earth's moon—but it meant that the turning landing bay was moving at less than seven meters per second.

At the last instant, the AI fired the fighter's starboard-side thrusters, giving Allyn's Starhawk a sideways kick to its vector of seven meters per second. For just an instant, the broad landing bay opening appeared to freeze motionless ahead . . . and then Allyn flashed past the lines of acquisition lights and into the opening.

Where gravitational acceleration or deceleration acted uniformly on both fighter and pilot, making maneuvers feel like free fall, this was altogether different. The tangleweb field invisibly enmeshed the incoming fighter and dragged it down from a relative 300 meters per second to a relative velocity of zero in the space of three hundred fifty meters.

The Starhawk came to rest, and Allyn sagged back against her seat, her vision slowly swimming back to normal after the brutal seven-G decel. Magnetic grapnels unfolded from the overhead, moving her forward and out of the way of the next incoming Starhawk, thirty seconds behind her. They moved her to one of a dozen deck hatches covered over by the liquid-looking black of an atmospheric nanoseal, lowering her smoothly through the clinging seal and into the air and light of the fighter recovery deck. The grapnels deposited her atop an elevator column and released; the column began sinking into the deck, lowering her to the fifty-meter radius level. As she descended, the hab's spin gravity steadily rose from fifteen hundredths of a G to a more respectable one-quarter gravity.

By the time the elevator column sank into the deck and the cockpit of her fighter melted open around her, Tucker had already trapped and was beginning her descent to the recovery deck, while Collins was in the last ten seconds of her approach.

And Spaas was inbound on final, thirty seconds behind her.

Allyn climbed out of the cockpit and down to the deck,

her knees unsteady after seven Gs. "Welcome home, Commander!" a crew chief told her. She nodded and walked aft, unsealing her bubble helmet and tucking it beneath her arm.

An enormous repeater viewall filled much of the aft bulkhead of the recovery deck, large enough to be seen from any part of the cavernous compartment. It showed a camera view looking aft from inside the landing bay, the wide entrance curving upward slightly in a gentle smile, the aft end of the carrier extending back into space from overhead, the stars beyond gently swinging in a slow circle around the carrier's vanishing point as the hab module continued to rotate. Numbers at the top left of the screen, in green, showed Collins' approach velocity—282 mps. A second number counted down the seconds to trap: six . . . five . . . four . . .

And then Collins' gravfighter was *there*, appearing out of the night as if by magic, hurtling through the landing deck's maw and slowing abruptly as it entered the compartment's tangleweb field. The fighter vanished off the side of the screen almost immediately, but a green light winked on above the viewall, signaling a successful trap.

Thirty seconds more to Spaas' arrival.

She could hear the voice of *America*'s LSO-AI, a machine intelligence tasked with coordinating incoming fighters with the moving landing deck. LSO was an ancient term going back to the era of seaborne aircraft carriers four centuries before—an acronym for landing signals officer. The job was no longer held by humans; machines were *far* faster and more precise. Since the LSO-AI was actually handling the incoming gravfighter's controls, the voice was for the benefit of human observers.

"Vector left . . . vector left . . . stabilize . . . vector left . . ."

The "vector left" was the LSO attempting to fire the fighter's starboard thrusters, to match its incoming vector with the seven-meter-per-second rotation of the landing bay. The numerals on the screen were red, showing an approach velocity of 348 mps, too fast, too fast, as the countdown dwindled from seven . . . to six . . .

"Gravfighter outside safe approach parameters," the LSO

announced, the voice cold and unemotional. The green light above the opening flashed red.

Allyn's heart was pounding. *Oh, God, no . . .*

"Abort," the LSO voice continued, impassive, "abort . . . abort . . ."

Spaas' Starhawk appeared, but too far to the left, much too far to the left, and coming in too fast. His ship was dead; he *couldn't* abort, couldn't fire a ventral singularity to warp his course into a vector that would miss the rotating landing bay and the underside of *America*'s huge cap beyond.

The incoming fighter *almost* made it. . . .

Spaas' gravfighter clipped the trailing edge of the entranceway. Sparks erupted, and then the Starhawk's starboard side disintegrated in peeling, fragmenting metal. The port side flipped into an out-of-control tumble, vanishing off the right side of the screen. The light above the bay flashed red.

Allyn could feel the ship crews around her sag as Spaas died—no one could have survived such a crash. They sagged, they turned away. She heard someone nearby mutter, "*Shit . . .*"

Allyn said nothing. Gripping her helmet tightly, she turned away and started walking toward the recovery deck elevators.

She had a report to file, a debriefing to endure.

She felt exhausted and bruised, and every step dragged at her like death.

Squadron Ready Room
TC/USNA CVS America
Outbound, Eta Boötis System
2022 hours, TFT

Gray stared at the ready room repeater screen, unable to tear his eyes away. It was one thing when a squadron mate bought it in a clean, silent flash of light out in space, quite another when you watched them zorch in for a trap and miss the sweet spot by a matter of scant meters.

He didn't like Spaas. In fact, he'd detested the guy—an arrogant bully, a womanizer, as much the elitist hypocrite as his partner, Collins.

He'd still been family.

Numb, Gray ran through the members of the Dragonfires, startled to realize that where twelve had launched from the *America* out in the local Kuiper Belt early yesterday morning, only four, counting himself, were left. Sixty-six percent casualties was devastating for any military unit; when the unit was as small as a squadron to begin with, with members practically living in one another's pockets, the sense of family was keener still . . . even when you couldn't stand the bastards.

He wondered if the Dragonfires would be disbanded, the survivors sent as replacements to other squadrons.

The hell with it, He found he didn't care right now one way or another, didn't care about *anything*.

But an audio alarm caught his attention, and he switched the display screen to tactical.

God. *That* was all they needed now. The Turusch battlefleet was emerging from behind Eta Boötis, swinging past the planet and accelerating toward the retreating carrier battlegroup. The rest of the Black Lightnings were still trapping in Bays One and Three, and it would be several more minutes before *America* could resume acceleration.

Things were about to get damned tight.

CIC, TC/USNA CVS America
Outbound, Eta Boötis System
2023 hours, TFT

"Lead elements of the enemy fleet now at eighty-two thousand kilometers, Admiral," Hughes reported, her voice as matter-of-fact, as coldly professional as any AI's.

"How long until the last of the fighters gets aboard?" Koenig demanded.

"Two more coming in at Bay One, three at Bay Two. Make it one minute twenty."

Koening considered this. Over a minute until the *America* could accelerate. How close would the enemy fleet get?

Given their known acceleration capabilities, it looked like the battlegroup would be able to escape . . . just. The enemy might pursue them out of the system, but a running stern chase was pretty futile, especially when the fleeing vessels would be jigging and changing acceleration routes from moment to moment in order to throw off the enemy's targeting computers.

"Comm! Make to *Spirit of Confederation*," he said. "Have them lay down a barrage astern. See if they can discourage those Trash jokers."

"Aye, aye, sir."

The view of the stars projected on the CIC viewwalls darkened, returned, darkened again.

"Enemy has opened fire, Admiral," Hughes pointed out. "KK projectiles and particle beams."

"Right. Any damage?"

"Shields are holding, Admiral." A pause. "Cruiser *Montreal* reports damage to targeting sensors and primary fire control."

In the tactical display, the green icon representing the *Spirit of Confederation* was slowly turning, rotating ninety degrees until she was traveling sideways, her port broadside facing the enemy.

As on board the *America*, *Confederation*'s primary weapon ran along much of her kilometer-length and pierced her broad shield cap forward, a large-bore railgun that could accelerate one-ton kinetic-kill rounds to speeds of hundreds of kilometers per second. That was not her only weapon, however. Like an eighteenth-century ship of the line, she possessed an impressive broadside, turret-mounted weapons that could fire in every direction except directly forward, where they were effectively blocked by the shield cap. By rotating ninety degrees along her line of flight, the *Spirit of Confederation* brought about two thirds of her broadside weapons to bear. With the enemy now just half a light second astern, the battleship began hammering away, pouring immense volumes of fire into the narrow corridor just ahead of the Turusch vessels.

Koenig turned his attention back to the last of the fighters still coming aboard.

"*Come on, people*," he murmured, half aloud. "*Come on! . . .*"

Tactician Emphatic Blossom at Dawn
Enforcer Radiant Severing
2023 hours, TFT

Tactician Emphatic Blossom watched the combat display, an emotion roughly equivalent to human anger beating behind its optical organs. A tentacle tip coiled and uncoiled reflexively, nervously. If it didn't know better, if it had not felt the reassurance and calm emanating from the Mind Below, it would have had to assume that the Sh'daar didn't trust it, didn't trust the Turusch.

Abyssal whirlwinds! Emphatic Blossom at Dawn was a trained and experienced master tactician! It knew combat, knew how to lead an enemy into a trap, knew how to spring an ambush, knew how to hammer at the foe until nothing in the kill zone was left alive! The Sh'daar Seed's orders of the past *g'nyuu'm* simply made no tactical sense whatsoever.

The Turusch fleet had been badly mangled by the enemy fighter attack, true . . . and there'd been a very real possibility that the *Radiant Severing* itself would be destroyed. That, however, was a part of combat, a part of war. Emphatic Blossom and every Turusch warrior on board the *Severing* was ready to sacrifice its life if that sacrifice would bring a decisive victory.

But no! The Seed had ordered, had *demanded* that the Turusch battle fleet abandon its prey, break orbit and withdraw toward deep space. And Emphatic Blossom had obeyed . . . as it must. The orders were from its own Mind Below, as inescapable, as relentless as Blossom's own decisions.

And so the Turusch battle fleet had withdrawn, accelerating close to the speed of light, fleeing the battle.

And then the Sh'daar Seed had spoken again, giving new, and contradictory, orders. The Turusch fleet would turn around and return to the embattled planet, would launch fighters to go in ahead of the fleet and cause as much damage as possible, with the main body of the fleet arriving soon after.

Projectiles and particle beams would be fired into the region, timed to arrive just before the fighters appeared. And every enemy outpost on the target world would be deliberately obliterated, targeted by high-velocity masses aimed with mathematical precision at the locations of the alien surface outposts.

And that didn't make sense to the Turusch tactician either. The Turusch had spent twelves of *g'nyuu'm* bombarding the principle enemy base and two others . . . but the intent had been to capture the humans, not kill them. Why change the point of the battle *now*?

The Sh'daar Seed, of course, knew what it was doing. Emphatic Blossom *had* to believe that, or its very existence, its role as master tactician, its very understanding of the cosmos all would be called into question.

But Blossom could not guess what their purpose was now, nor could it understand its role in the battle in these circumstances. As *Radiant Severing* and the other Turusch ships decelerated into the volume of space surrounding the target planet, sensors showed that the enemy fleet had already withdrawn, as Emphatic Blossom had more than half expected. On the planetary surface, seething, yellow seas of molten rock steamed beneath continent-sized hurricanes where the alien colonies had been.

An entire world rendered lifeless, useless to anyone. *Why?. . .*

Radiant Severing shuddered, the rock hull ringing with an impact against the defensive shields. One of the two largest of the enemy vessels had positioned itself at the rear of the human fleet, and was bombarding the Turusch battle fleet as it retreated.

"*Threat!*" Blossom's Mind Above could be unpleasantly predictable. "*Kill!*"

"We can destroy that human vessel," the Mind Here added. "We should . . . *remind* the humans of the risk they take in defying the Seed."

The Mind Below seemed to consider this, weighing the options with a computer's calculating efficiency. "Agreed. But do not pursue the enemy. The survivors should take the report of their defeat back to their homeworld."

"*Deploy all fighter fists!*" The Mind Here commanded, its emotion as raw and as primitive as that of Mind Above. "Concentrate the full offensive fire of all vessels on *that* target!

Some thirty capital ships of the Turusch fleet adjusted their positions, then began firing at the distant enemy. Particle beams, fusion bolts, high-energy lasers, and kinetic-kill projectiles sleeted through emptiness.

And they began to find their target.

CIC, TC/USNA CVS America
Outbound, Eta Boötis System
2025 hours, TFT

"The *Spirit of Confederation* reports she is taking very heavy fire, Admiral," Hughes told him. "Damage to aft shields, damage to primary broadside weapons, damage to two of the three hab modules. Fire control is down."

Koenig was watching the *Confederation*'s struggle on a secondary tactical display, which was relaying the camera view from a battle drone pacing the retreating ships. Straight-edged patches of blackness kept popping on and off along the battleship's length, responding to incoming fire. One set of aft shields was flickering on and off alarmingly, threatening complete failure. Several sections of her long, thin hull had been wrecked by energies leaking through the shields. The damage was severe, but she continued to fire back.

White light pulsed, dazzlingly bright, as an incoming Turusch missile detonated in a sand cloud a hundred kilometers away.

"Comm," Koenig ordered. "Patch me through to the *Confederation*'s CO."

"Aye, aye, sir."

A moment later, the image of Captain Paul Radniak appeared within the holodisplay field beside Koenig's work-station. His face was worn, his uniform disheveled. Smoke wreathed through the image, which kept flickering on and off with sharp bursts of static as the battleship's shields rose and fell, and as electromagnetic pulses from particle-beam hits and detonating nukes interfered with the signal.

"Yes, Admiral?"

"You've done what you can, Paul," Koenig told him. "It looks like the bastards aren't going to follow us."

Radniak's eyes flicked away as he checked a readout out-side the range of the holo's pick-up. "It looks like they're sending fighters after us, Admiral."

"Fighters we can handle. I recommend you ass-end it out of there."

The *Spirit of Confederation* was taking a hellacious pounding. Koenig was suggesting that Radniak rotate his ship another ninety degrees, so that the vessel's stern was pointing in the direction she was moving, and her broad, water-filled forward shield cap was pointed at the enemy. By "ass-ending it out of there," Radniak would be able to pro-tect his ship from further incoming fire as the *Confedera-tion* continued to accelerate out-system. Without the water shield, the crew might be subjected to dangerous doses of radiation as the *Confederation* approached c, but that was preferable to losing the entire vessel when her quantum power tap lost balance and detonated.

Radniak's image shuddered, winked off, then came back up, rippling with static. "I think you're right, Ad—" And Radniak was gone.

In the drone-relayed image nearby, white eruptions of light ate their way up the *Spirit of Confederation*'s spine, ripping out massive chunks of debris. One of her hab mod-ules detached and flung itself outward, tumbling end over end as centripetal force sent it hurtling into space. The aft end appeared to be crumpling, folding in on itself. The black holes in the power center were loose, devouring the ship's aft quarter in multi-ton bites.

The final explosion sent large chunks spraying along the ship's direction of travel. The largest was the shield cap, tumbling end over end, leaving glittering and intertwining trails of ice crystals from a dozen ruptures in its wake. The intolerably brilliant core of the final explosion faded slowly in a flare of cooling plasma.

"Make to the other ships in our detachment," Koenig said quietly. "Go to maximum acceleration."

Two thousand officers and crew, plus God alone knew how many Marines and Mufrid refugees—gone.

God help them, he thought. *God help us all.* . . .

Chapter Fourteen

Koenig's Office
TC/USNA CVS America
Inbound, Sol System
0940 hours, TFT

"Dr. Wilkerson, Dr. George, and Dr. Brandt are all ready to link in, Admiral."

Koenig looked up. Lieutenant Commander Nahan Cleary was his personal aide, which meant he often served as admiral's secretary as frequently as Koenig's secretarial AI. "Very well. I'll take it here."

He switched off the report he was currently writing and reclined his seat back. His office was fairly luxurious as military quarters went, more luxurious than he cared for, actually. There was a small lounge area over by the door, but he generally preferred to stay at his desk.

It was just as well he hadn't gotten too used to the place. He couldn't imagine that they would let him hold on to it much longer.

He brought up the link codes in his mind, letting the circuitry in the office connect with his in-head display. A window seemed to open and he stepped through . . . entering the carrier's main med-research center. Earnest Brandt, the center's senior medical officer, was already there. The virtual images of Dr. Anna George and Dr. Phillip Wilkerson winked on a moment later. Wilkerson was the head of

America's neuropsytherapy department, while George was a psytherapist on loan from the 1st Marine Expeditionary Force, and both had considerable experience with nonhuman psychology.

"Welcome to RC Central, Admiral," Wilkerson's virtual image said. "Thanks for linking in."

"Does this mean you've gotten something, Doctor?" Koenig asked. "Something useful?"

Wilkerson shrugged, his lined face momentarily twisting in an expression of frustration. "That, sir, you'll have to decide for yourself. We *have* established communications."

"You know, sir," Dr. George said, "it took over five years to establish basic communications with the Aglestch a century ago."

"Yes," Koenig replied, "and what we learned was LG. I thought you were using that with these . . . people."

LG—*Lingua Galactica*—was an artificial language learned from the alien Aglestch. Evidently, it wasn't one of that race's native languages, but it was the way they communicated with the Sh'daar, their galactic masters. Koenig had assumed that the Turusch would know LG as well.

"We did, Admiral," Wilkerson replied. "But it's not that simple."

"It never is."

Wilkerson took a deep breath. "The Aglestch speak using phonemes generated through vibrating vocal cords like we do . . . except of course that they use air expressed from their first and second stomachs instead of from lungs or air sacs. The Turusch speak, we think, by modulating a humming or thrumming sound generated by vibrating diaphragms set within the dorsal carapace."

"Meaning they don't use words," Koenig guessed.

"Exactly. Variations in pitch and tone, and the shifting harmonies created by four separate diaphragms, convey the information. Even the name 'Turusch' comes from the Agletsch. We don't know what they call themselves."

Brandt chuckled. "Maybe something like . . ." and he hummed the opening bar of a popular song, "We Were Strangers."

"In four-part harmony," Dr. George added.

"In any case," Dr. Brandt said, "we *did* use LG as a basis—without it I expect it would have taken another five years or more to break the Turusch language *and* figure out how to speak it. We do appear to have established communication. At least . . . we've gotten *some* meaningful syntax out of them. But an awful lot of what they have to say doesn't make much sense."

"There's also the xenopsych angle to consider, Admiral," Dr. George told him. "I've been working with these two since we picked them up, and that was a couple of weeks ago. We don't have a lot of leads on how they think."

Koenig nodded. He knew how difficult it was to learn, not just another language, but a language spoken by a being with a completely nonhuman physiology *and* a completely alien psychology. One species—the primitive Glo of Epsilon Eridani II—appeared to communicate with one another by changing patterns of light and color on their black, oily torsos, using luminous chromatophores like the squid of Earth. The Glo had been known for almost two centuries now, and the experts still didn't know if they were really talking . . . or if they even were intelligent enough to have anything to talk about. There was simply no comprehensible common ground from which to begin either a linguistic or a psychological understanding.

"I wasn't expecting miracles, people," Koenig told the three. "Let me have a look."

"Yes, sir," Wilkerson said. "Um . . . brace yourself. This can be unsettling."   •

"We'll be projecting into NTE robots," Brandt added.

Koenig felt an inner shift, a momentary dizziness, and then he was someplace else, a ship's compartment with blank, white-painted walls and one transplas wall. There were a number of machines in the compartment attached by universal joints and articulated metallic arms to the low overhead. Koenig's own point of view now seemed to be residing within one of those devices, a white sphere supported on the end of a slender, jointed arm.

Non-terrestrial environmental robots—NTEs, or Noters—

had been in wide use for almost three centuries, exploring places as hostile as the surface of Venus, the ice ridges of Europa, and the bottom of the Marianas Trench. The earliest versions had relayed photographs and telemetry from Mars and from Earth's moon; later models had let human consciousness piggyback within their circuitry.

Readouts at the bottom of his visual field showed data on atmosphere, pressure, temperature, and other factors. It was as hot, Koenig noted, as boiling water, and the lighting in the room was sizzling with ultraviolet.

The Turusch were there, both of them, mottled black and dark brown, and gleaming wet in the harsh light. It was difficult to judge distance within this new body without practice, but they seemed to be about four meters away. If so, they were each half again longer than a human was tall and half a meter thick. The body might be described as sluglike, at least where the bare, mucus-wet skin was exposed, but large patches of its body were covered by what looked like sections of shell or carapace—large and irregular on the blunt end, and segmented like the scales of a snake along the belly, leaving most of the rest of the body nakedly exposed. Half-meter tentacles, black, whip-thin, and in constantly writhing motion, sprouted at seemingly random points from everywhere on the body except the armored parts.

One end was pointed. The other end, Koenig decided, must be the head, rounded and sheathed in three close-fitting sections of carapace, and showing recesses for at least two dozen eyes or other sense organs arranged in three lines running back from the blunt end. If those *were* eyes, they were deeply recessed and small, like tiny black marbles. Koenig wondered if that meant the Turusch were from a planet orbiting a star hotter and brighter than Sol. The ultraviolet baking the compartment seemed to validate the idea.

He saw nothing that resembled a mouth. He did see the diaphragms used for speech, however, two set on either side of the head carapace, which took up nearly a quarter of the creature's length.

"So," Koenig said. "Cephalopod? Reptile? Sea cucumber?"

"None of the above, Admiral," Brandt said. "Remember . . . any resemblance to *anything* we know from Earth is superficial . . . either a matter of parallel evolution, or pure coincidence."

"Right. My mistake." He felt clumsy. He knew that aliens were never easily categorized. But faced with the truly alien, the human mind always sought points of similarity, easy starting places, something recognizable.

"At this point," Wilkerson pointed out, "we're not even sure about whether to call these things animal, vegetable, or mineral. They're carbon-based, we know, but they appear to manufacture at least part of their metabolic energy with a chlorophyll analogue in the skin pigmentation. Dr. George figured that much out from skin samples she took on Haris."

Koenig looked at the young woman with new respect. "You actually went in and got a *skin sample* from one of those things?"

"We used robots, Admiral," she replied. "Still, they seemed pretty passive. They might have known we were simply trying to find out about their physical needs."

Koenig nodded. He wondered what *his* reaction would have been if he'd been captured by a pack of these slimy, tentacled slugs, and they—or their machines—had come after him with a sampling probe or scalpel.

How intelligent were they, really?

"Their biochemistries appear to be driven by both carbon and silicon," Wilkerson continued. "They also use a lot of sulfur chemistry."

"What kind of environment?" Koenig asked.

"Hot," Wilkerson replied. "We think their homeworld is a less-extreme version of Venus. Carbon dioxide atmosphere with traces of sulfur, sulfur dioxide, water vapor, and droplets of sulfuric acid. Temperature in the one-hundred-degree Celsius range. Not our kind of place at all."

"Sounds like Eta Boötis Four," Koenig said, thoughtful. He was wondering if the Turusch had attacked the place not because they were working for the Sh'daar, but because they wanted the place for themselves.

"Only superficially," Wilkerson said. "Eta Boötis is colder, has less CO_2, more sulfur compounds, a *lot* more oxygen and ammonia, and not as much carbonyl sulfide. We think the Turusch homeworld has a much lower surface gravity, too—less than one G."

Koenig scowled. "Then we're back to square one in understanding why they attacked us."

"They appear to be the right-hand . . . ah . . . right-*tentacle* representatives of the Sh'daar," Brandt said. "I thought that was understood from the beginning."

"So far as these things are concerned, *nothing* is understood," Koenig said. "Remember, we've never even seen a Sh'daar . . . and this is our very first look at the Turusch. For all we know, the Sh'daar could just be some sort of Turusch ruling caste, and not a different species at all."

"Go ahead and ask them," Wilkerson suggested.

"How?"

"The language software is running. Just use *this* to access it." Wilkerson passed a mental icon to Koenig. He mind-clicked it. "Who are you?" he asked, deciding to stick with the basics, at least to begin.

Two alien heads whipped around, facing the white robotic sphere. Damn . . . these things might look like giant slugs, but they were *quick*. Koenig could hear a kind of humming or buzzing as the robot spoke. A moment later, the aliens answered with the same pulsing buzz . . . but they answered together, and the audio translation came out unintelligible as two computer-generated voices spoke at the same time.

Fortunately, a text version of both replies printed itself out in a side window in his in-head display.

"This one was Falling Droplet, of the Third Hierarchy," one said, while the other replied, "Speak we now with the Mind Here or the Mind Below?"

Koenig read the answers, and blinked, puzzled. "I don't understand," he said without using the translation software. He was addressing the other humans.

"Don't feel bad, sir," Wilkerson said. "No matter how clear your question, the answer always feels fuzzy . . . like you're missing something."

"Can we separate them? Question them singly?"

"We tried that on Haris, Admiral," George said. "They went into a mope, and appeared to be wasting away. And they wouldn't answer *anything*. Our working theory is that they have some kind of gestalt going, a hive mind, maybe. If they're alone, they don't function as well. They might even die. Like worker ants."

"I . . . see." This was getting more and more complicated. He mindclicked the translate icon again. "Why do you work for the Sh'daar?"

"The Sh'daar reject your transcendence and accept you if it is only you," one said, while the other said, "The Seed encompasses and arises from the Mind Below. How would it be otherwise?"

"What do you mean, they reject our transcendence? What is that?"

"Your species approaches the point of transcendence," one said.

"Transcendence is the ultimate evil that has been banished," said the other.

This was going nowhere. "Are your needs being looked after?" he asked them. "Are your nutritional needs being met?"

"We require the Seed," said one. "We are the Seed," said the other.

"Not exactly helpful, are they?" Koenig asked the others.

"Actually, they seem to be very cooperative," George told him. "We just don't have enough background yet to make sense of their answers."

"They mentioned something . . . what? Mind Below?"

"Mind Here, Mind Below," Brandt said. "We've also heard them reference something called 'Mind Above.'"

"Might that be like the human subconscious?"

"Since we're not even sure we can define what the *human* subconscious is," Wilkerson told him, "I'd say it's a bit early to speculate about that."

"Point."

Both of the Turusch were thrashing about now, and he heard the buzzing once again. This time, he could understand the computer-generated audio, because the two were in perfect synch. *"Threat!"* they said in unison. *"Kill!"*

Abruptly, shockingly, the heads of both Turusch split open, the tripartite armored covering separating in thirds and yawning wide. Instead of a mouth or teeth, however, Koenig saw that the openings were blocked with dark-pink tissue, glistening and moist. Something like a slender harpoon, black and a meter long, was stabbing out from the center of the tissue mass, however, together with a shorter but wider fleshy tube growing from beside the harpoon's base.

If it was a mouth, it was like no mouth Koenig had ever seen or heard of.

The humans withdrew into the virtual recreation of the outer research lab, not because they were in danger—the NTE robots were pretty much invulnerable—but because conversation had become impossible.

"So that's the enemy, eh?" Koenig said, shaking his head. "How'd we get them?"

"We recovered one of their Toad fighters," George explained. "It crashed near the perimeter, and we sent a SAR and a weapons squad out to pick it up."

"So you don't think they were trying to surrender deliberately . . . or infiltrate our lines, or anything like that."

"No, sir," George told him. "It certainly didn't look deliberate, anyway. General Gorman was wondering the same thing. He was wondering if they were berserkers. Suicide troops."

Until their psychology was better understood, every move the two made, everything they said, was going to be the subject of long and careful analyses.

"My orders," Koenig told them, "are to get them both to Port Phobos. The xeno department there will want full reports from all of you."

"Yes, sir."

"And . . . I'd appreciate it if you would keep me in the loop, let me know if anything else happens with our . . . guests, or if you learn anything new."

"Absolutely, Admiral."

The Senate Military Directorate, he knew, was extremely anxious to have these two aliens safely secured and under Directorate supervision. They were already assembling a high-powered xeno contact team to keep working on the language, the culture, and the psychology, in hopes of *finally* learning something useful about humankind's interstellar enemies.

"Admiral?" Nahan Cleary's familiar voice spoke in his head. "I'm sorry to interrupt, but the Political Liaison wants to talk to you. He says it's *most* urgent."

Koenig sighed. Since ordering Quintanilla off the CIC deck, he'd been trying to handle the man more tactfully. Diplomacy and tact, however, did not seem to be helping matters.

"Very well. Have him wait in my office. I'll be back in a moment."

"Aye, aye, sir."

He looked at the icon-images of the three psychs. "We're twenty hours from Deimos," he told them. "You have that long to get them ready for transport again."

He ended the in-head conversation and pulled back out of the virtual research lab, opening his eyes to see Cleary and Quintanilla standing in front of his office desk.

"Excuse the wait, Mr. Quintanilla," he said. "I was checking on our two special passengers."

"They are safe?"

"Seem to be. It's tough to tell when they're screaming 'kill' at you."

"That's something, at any rate," Quintanilla said, frowning. "It at least partly makes up for your mishandling of the battle at Eta Boötis."

"Mr. Cleary . . . out," Koenig said.

"Yes, sir."

When the aide had left, Koenig stood up behind the desk. "I will thank you *not* to criticize me in front of my subordinates, sir." His voice was hard, sharp-edged. "My decisions at Eta Boötis will be judged by a court of inquiry once we're back at Mars, *not* by you."

"Had you accelerated in toward the target planet sooner,"

Quintanilla pointed out, "we could have retrieved Gorman's Marines more quickly. There's also the matter of delaying your withdrawal in order to take on board all of those refugees. That, I remind you, was not part of your original—"

"This is not a topic for discussion, Mr. Quintanilla. Now *back off*!"

"Your failure to cooperate with a duly appointed representative of the Senate Military Directorate is noted."

"Note whatever the hell you want, Quintanilla. Get out of my office."

Quintanilla scowled, but withdrew.

"God save us from political micromanagement," Koenig said, staring at the door after it irised shut behind him. Throwing the bastard out made Koenig feel a little better; whatever he thought of political liaisons like Quintanilla, he had to agree that the battle in Haris space had not gone as well as it might have. They'd carried out their orders—gotten in and out, picking up the MEF and their prisoners along the way, but they'd lost too many ships doing it . . . *especially* the *Spirit of the Confederation*. Battleships were expensive, both in money and in the huge crews they carried, and there would be wolf packs both in the Senate military and budgetary directorates and within the senior military leadership who would be howling for blood. Assigning blame and finding scapegoats both were time-honored traditions for the brass and for politicians alike.

Koenig had made the decisions.

It was his head that would roll.

Flight Officers' Head
TC/USNA CVS America
Inbound, Sol System
1027 hours, TFT

Gray stepped naked out of the shower and nearly collided with Jen Collins. "Well, well," she said, her voice acid. "Look here, boys. Our Prim coward."

There was no sexual segregation on board Navy ships;

men and women both used the same shower heads and shared sleeping quarters, a reflection of rapidly shifting societal mores over the past several centuries within the mainstream culture.

"What's your problem, Collins?" he said.

"*You*, Prim. My problem is *you*."

Gray had managed to avoid the woman since his return to the *America*. He'd been on limited duty and non-flight status throughout most of the long trip back from Eta Boötis, and staying in one of the ship's officers' quarters forward; he'd come back to his old quarters in the flight officers' hab section just this morning, after being placed back on full duty.

He still wasn't on active flight status, of course, not with Anna George's diagnosis of PTED in his health record. He was still undecided as to whether he wanted to seek further treatment, or to say the hell with all of it and resign his commission.

Collins had shown up, he thought, right on schedule, with three of her buddies in tow. "Look," he said, stepping past them and into the drying stall. He raised his voice to be heard above the blasts of hot air cutting in from above and below. "I'm sorry about Spaas. I know you two were close—"

"You don't know *shit*, Gray! Where the hell did you duck off to during the first battle over Haris, huh?"

"I imagine you've seen my report by now," he replied. "I got separated, went down on the deck. Our orders were to provide support for the jarheads. So I did."

"Yeah, while the rest of us were getting our asses shot off in hard vacuum! Pretty damned convenient if you ask me!"

"I seem to remember getting my own ass shot off, Collins," he replied. Dry, he stepped out of the stall and the blast of air cut off. They followed him as he walked to his locker and began getting dressed.

"Well, just so you know, Prim, some of us put together a petition for Allyn and the CAG. You're going before a BOI and get busted off the flight line, hell, bust you out of the *Navy* if we have our say! You'll be lucky to find a job as a civilian!"

He glanced at Collins, then at the two men and one woman

with her. All three of the others were support personnel with the squadron—Mackey, with Intelligence; Dole, from Personnel; and Carstin, who was with the squadron's requisitions department. None were flight officers.

"You guys are signing this petition?" he asked. "I didn't see any of *you* out there."

"In case you hadn't noticed, Prim," Lieutenant Lars Mackey growled, "besides you there're only three flight officers with the Dragonfires left! And I don't think you count! Not if you were hiding out down on the planet, like the lieutenant here says."

"We lost some good friends at Haris," CWO Tammy Carstin added. "*Sir.*"

Gray stared at her for a moment, until she broke eye contact, looking down. Everybody in the squadron knew she'd had a thing going with Gene Sandoval. Hell, half the female members of the squadron had something going with Gene Sandoval. He started to tell her that Sandoval had been his friend as well . . . then decided not to bring it up. "We all lost friends," he told her.

"And that makes it *okay*?" Lieutenant j.g. Kenny Dole demanded. "'We all lost friends.' That makes it fucking *okay*?"

"No, it doesn't," Gray snapped back, angry now. "But *I* didn't kill them and *I* didn't get them killed! For your information Commander Allyn *ordered* me to go down and help the Marines!"

"*After* you'd already ducked down to the deck and left the rest of us, including your wingmate, facing the entire damned Turusch fleet!" Collins was yelling now, her face unpleasantly contorted and red.

"You *do* manage to put the worst possible spin on events," Gray told her. "Why don't we just let the Board of Inquiry sort it out?"

Collins stepped closer. She was shorter than he was, and had to look up to look into his face, but her glare carried the mass of someone much bigger. "You're a coward, Gray. And a fucking technophobic primitive. They should have left you in the Manhattan swamps where they found you, a fuck-

ing squattie fighting over scraps with the other maladjies!
You don't belong here. You're not officer material. You're
not even *Navy* material. Do yourself and the rest of us a
big favor and resign your commission now. Because if you
don't, you're going to go up against that Board of Inquiry
and you're going to be disgraced and broken, and sent back
to the Ruins with your tail between your legs!"

She turned and stormed off then, the others following.

Gray shrugged and kept getting dressed.

Why, he wondered, *was* he staying? It wasn't like he owed
the Navy anything, and not a shipboard day went past that he
didn't wish he was still a squattie in the Ruins. Collins was
right. He didn't fit in, and never had. He didn't *want* to fit in,
when it came to that.

For three centuries now, the Navy had tended to recruit
its people from the educated and tech-proficient classes,
first from the old United States, and later with the larger
and farther-flung Earth Confederation. *Tech-proficient* generally meant cerebral neural implants and direct interface
capabilities within the general citizenry, since most jobs
required direct links with computers and access to the VR
facilities of the Net. The Confederation was, arguably, the
most technically advanced and capable of Earth's splintered
social groupings, though the Chinese Hegemony ran a very
close second. Even the mildly technophobic Islamic Theocracy had its own starships, though they felt that mindlinks
were somehow contrary to the will of Allah.

And if the average star sailor was pro-tech and linked in,
the officers were more so. They had to be, since managing
a starship—to say nothing of an entire squadron or fleet—
depended on being able to link in with numerous AIs as well
as other officers, simply to understand a tactical situation
and coordinate all of it according to something like a coherent plan.

And here he was, a squattie from the drowned Manhattan Ruins. Where most kids got their first implants at age
three, before starting school, he'd received his first cerebral implant at the age of twenty-five. That had been when
he'd completed his initial indoctrination, just before being

shipped off to OCS. Officer candidates needed the direct link just to handle the volumes of data they were expected to learn in school. Direct linkages were even more necessary once you hit flight school, and had to learn how to handle a fighter directly, mind-to-AI mind.

Gray still hated the whole idea of having an implant, of having a tiny AI daemon in his skull, watching everything he did, recording, intruding. There were protocols for shutting the thing off when you wanted privacy . . . but the mere act of shutting down was recorded and could be questioned later.

Besides, *how the hell did you know if the thing really switched off when you told it to go away?*

A lifetime of growing up in the Ruins, where the Authority was always hassling, always probing into people's private affairs, had left him both suspicious and skeptical. How could you trust any claim that *they* made?

He finished dressing—a gray utility jumpsuit. The word was that the squadron would not be on the flight line, not with only four flight officers remaining. With no place that he *had* to be officially, he'd decided to head up to the ship's observation area to watch the arrival and docking at Mars orbit. That wouldn't be for hours yet, though, and he wondered what he was going to do in the meantime.

Besides, of course, trying to avoid Collins and her friends.

Yeah, resigning his commission, if they'd let him, might be the best idea after all. He decided to check in with the Personnel Office—*America*'s PO, not with that young idiot Dole—and have an exploratory chat with them.

He'd been strong-armed by the Authority to join the Navy.

Maybe he'd finally proven to himself that his joining the service simply hadn't been a very bright idea.

Chapter Fifteen

CIC, TC/USNA CVS America
Approaching Phobos Space Elevator, Sol System
0850 hours, TFT

Koenig watched, expressionless, as *America* maneuvered gently toward Phobos. Mars filled a quarter of the sky, half in light, half in darkness. The dark side showed isolated gleams of city-dome lights; the illuminated half was dazzlingly bright, a hemisphere of broad ocher swaths of desert, the dark brown crinkles of rugged highlands and heavily cratered terrain, and, here and there, the blue gleam of newborn seas, surrounded by strips of burgeoning green.

The premier naval base of the Earth Confederation was constructed in areosynchronous orbit, seventeen thousand kilometers above the Martian surface. At that altitude, it took precisely twenty-four hours, thirty-seven minutes—the duration of one Martian rotation—for a satellite to circle the planet once, so that it appeared to remain in the same spot in the sky. One hundred twenty years earlier, the former inner moon of Mars, Phobos, orbiting at just under ten thousand kilometers from the surface, had been nanotechnically disassembled, its billions of tons of carbon woven into a buckytube-weave tether connecting the summit of Pavonis Mons on the Martian equator with the outer moon, Deimos, which served now as a counterweight to keep the elevator

cable pulled taut. There were three Martian space elevators now, spaced at roughly equidistant intervals around
the planet's equator—at Pavonis Mons, at the northwestern
rim of Schiaparelli Crater, and in the rugged highlands once
known to the earthbound astronomers of the nineteenth and
twentieth centuries as Aethiopis.

The three space elevators were now the heart of the ongoing Martian terraforming project, serving as conduits for
the millions of tons of nanoformer microbots being shipped
down to the surface to break oxygen out of the rusty rocks
and nitrogen from regolithic nitrates, and for *trillions* of tons
of nitrogen scooped from the murky atmosphere of Titan, or
mined on cold and distant Triton, out at the solar system's
rim. As the atmosphere thickened, the temperature slowly
rose. One day—in perhaps another century or so—men
would walk the surface of Mars beside liquid water seas,
without e-suits.

But the original elevator, the one rising above an extinct
shield volcano known as Pavonis Mons, was also the location of the extensive orbital facilities known, in honor of the
vanished moon, as Phobos Station. The base, most of it, was
located at the areosynchronous orbital point. It included the
headquarters for the Martian terraforming effort, a large research station with extensive xenobiological facilities, numerous orbital manufactories, and the Earth Confederation
military base properly known as Mars Synchorbital . . . and
informally, humorously, and inevitably known as Phobia.

The docking facilities were independent of the elevator-
tethered portion of the base, trailing along in synchronous
orbit a few kilometers behind. The *Kinkaid*, the *Symmons*,
the *Puller*, and a half dozen other ships of the carrier battle
group were already snugged into the docks. *America* was
so large that she had an orbital dock facility all to herself, a
mass of girders, struts, and braces extending out from two
counter-rotating hab modules as bulky as small O'Neil cylinders.

A second dock facility, just as large and as massive, just
as complex, waited empty a kilometer off. The *Spirit of the
Confederation* would not be returning to her home port.

Koenig glanced at the *Spirit*'s berth, then looked away. If the politicians had their way, this would be his last time in command of anything larger than an orbital shuttle, but he was past caring at this point. Well . . . *almost* past.

In point of fact, he was certain that he'd made all the right calls, given all the right orders, made all of the best decisions in the scrap at Eta Boötis, and he was as certain as he could be that the other officers in the Board of Inquiry would agree with him. The problems started when you brought civilian politicians into the mix . . . men and women with their own agendas, their own prejudices, and more interest in how they appeared to their voters than in the realities of military command.

God alone knew what the politicians would do.

America was closer now to the docking facility, which was slowly growing larger alongside, backlit by the brilliance of the sunlight gleaming off of the ocher Martian deserts. This close to the orbiting structures, ships could not use their grav drives without the danger of warping support struts or damaging delicate structures designed for microgravity environments. The ship had to rely on water thrusters to adjust attitude and gently nudge the behemoth into the dock's gantry, assisted by a flotilla of dockyard tugs.

He could hear the ship's captain giving orders over the com net. Just a bit too much velocity now would ruin Buchanan's whole day.

ECN, the Confederation news service, was showing a live report on the battlegroup's arrival. One display in CIC had been tuned to the broadcast, which now showed *America* herself broadside and slowly approaching the camera's position—presumably somewhere on board the docking facility ahead.

A banner across the bottom proclaimed "Disaster at Eta Boötis: the battlegroup returns."

So they were calling the battle a disaster, were they?

Koenig was a student of military history; in his job, you *had* to be. What, he wondered, would the media's response have been to the evacuation of Dunkirk on the French coast of the English Channel, a little over four and a half centuries ago? A fleet of 900 British naval vessels, transports, fishing boats, freighters, and anything else that would float, practically, had managed to pull almost 340,000 British and French troops off the beach and carry them to safety after they'd been cut off and pinned against the sea by the advancing German *Blitzkrieg*. Those troops had lost most of their weapons and heavy equipment, but they'd lived, to form the nucleus of an army that would return one day to liberate a conquered Europe.

Had Dunkirk been a defeat or an incredible victory?

It depended on your point of view, of course. History was rarely as clean, neat, and orderly as the historical downloads suggested, especially in light of the ancient dictum that the victors wrote the histories. Politicians rarely could afford to take the long view. What they and their constituents were interested in was now . . . especially when blame needed to be assigned, and scapegoats found.

Koenig had already reviewed the events at Eta Boötis and his orders with the AI that would be representing him at the Inquiry. The likeliest outcome, he'd been told, was public censure and a private promotion sideways within the Navy—assignment to a desk job, possibly here at Phobia, possibly with the Joint Chiefs or the Military Directorate . . . unless, of course, he opted to retire.

Sacrificing his career had much the same flavor, for Koenig, as it might for a disgraced Roman general throwing himself on his own sword. He wasn't going to go quietly and conveniently; he wasn't about to "fade away," as an American general named MacArthur, broken in a political battle of wills with his commander-in-chief, had once so eloquently phrased it.

One step at a time. First he would face the Board of Inquiry. Then it would be time to face the political fallout of his decisions.

The problem, which he was trying hard not to look at just now, was that he would be running afoul of political considerations at the Board as well. In the Navy, every promotion above the rank of commander required patronage, well-placed friends, and politics, and the politics became thicker the higher up the totem pole you went. Admirals owed favors, had favorites lower in the chain of command they wished to help, or had their eyes on political positions or a seat on a corporate board once they retired from the military. That was how the game was played, how it had *been* played for centuries.

Koenig would rather have played with a Turusch battle-fleet any day.

Sick Bay Psych Department
TC/USNA CVS America
Mars Synchorbit, Sol System
0910 hours, TFT

The carrier's passageways were crowded with refugees . . . even more so now than during the past three weeks of the journey in from Eta Boötis. Mufrids who'd been camping in rec areas, mess halls, cargo bays, and storage compartments were emerging now to strand in narrow passageways, their meager belongings in small suitcases, bags, and parcels, waiting for the order to debark. Gray wondered if the refugees were as eager to get off the carrier as *America*'s crew was to be rid of them.

Gray squeezed past a seemingly endless line of bearded men in turbans and *kufiyyat*, past women veiled in *khimar* or *jilbab*. It was slow going, and his passage provoked angry mutters and dark glances from the men.

God, the ship *stank* . . . three claustrophobic weeks of the accumulating smells of cooking, vomit, urine, feces, and un-washed bodies, the stench of too many people in too small a space, with limited toilet facilities and showerheads.

Gray finally reached sick bay, ducking past the line of ci-vilians waiting to get in and provoking more angry looks. The psych department was just down another passageway to the left.

A reception bot accepted his ID off his palm implant and sent him straight through to Dr. Fifer.

"Well, good morning, Lieutenant," Fifer said, looking

up from his workstation. "Not out watching the docking? I think everyone else on the ship is."

"No room, sir," Gray replied, seating himself in the link-equipped recliner opposite the desk. "The ship's lounges and rec areas are all still off-limits." That had been necessary to provide the large number of Mufrid women on board with an acceptable degree of privacy. He shook his head. "Damn, I thought the Mufrids would be happy to be here. If they'd stayed on Eta Boötis, they'd all be dead now."

"Oh, I imagine they'll be grateful enough once they get out of these confining circumstances. Right now they feel trapped, stifled. And they resent us and what they perceive as our ungodly attitudes. I understand a couple of large transports are here to take them the rest of the way to Earth."

"And good riddance to them."

"You don't like them?"

Gray frowned. Commander Leonard Fifer had a way of turning everything into a discussion of what you felt, what you liked or disliked, what you thought. "I don't mind *them*. I'm glad we were able to help them. But I'll be glad to have our ship back when they're gone."

"As will we all, Lieutenant." He chuckled. "I was wondering, though, if you didn't sympathize with our Mufrid guests on some level?"

"Why? I'm not Muslim."

"Religion has nothing to do with the question. But it occurs to me that they feel like outsiders on the *America*. Marginalized. Out of place. Like you."

Gray had been coming here for sessions with Dr. Fifer every few shipboard days since he'd returned to the *America* at Eta Boötis. He would have preferred to keep working with Dr. George, but she was assigned to the Marines, not the carrier. He'd heard she was working over in the research labs now, in any case, trying to make sense of the two aliens captured on Eta Boötis IV.

Fifer tended to make him uncomfortable. Of course, he knew that these sessions were *supposed* to make him uncomfortable. They *had* to be so, if they were going to help him dig down through the crap and find the roots of what

George had called PTED—post-traumatic embitterment disorder.

And fixing that was a prerequisite to his going back on flight status.

Since yesterday, though, he'd been toying with the idea of never going back to flying, of resigning his commission. He'd swung by the Personnel Office yesterday afternoon to see what his options might be.

Unfortunately, he couldn't just turn in his uniform and walk away. Part of the agreement he'd signed obligated him to ten years of active Confederation military service, if only to pay the government back for the creds they'd invested in his training and his implants. He'd joined the Navy in 2401, but two years had been spent in recruit training, OCS, and flight school. Back in the old days, all of his schooling download time and training would have counted as active duty, but according to the Personnel Office he'd only entered active duty early last year—just in time for Arcturus Station and Everdawn—and he still had more than eight years to serve.

Whether that was as an officer or an enlisted man was up to him. He *could* resign his commission and become a fleet sailor . . . though he might have to sign on for more active duty time. Sailors weren't as valuable in terms of creds and training as were pilots.

The news had put a definite bump in Gray's career path. Flight officers had status, and a certain amount of privilege. They even had *respect*, assuming they weren't a poor squattie kid from the Manhattan Ruins.

He hadn't made up his mind yet. That was part of what he wanted to talk to the therapist about today. But if he *had* to stay in the Navy, being a pilot was definitely the way to go. At least when he strapped on a Starhawk, he could boost for cold, hard vacuum and be *free*, at least for a few hours, free from the constraints of shipboard life, the prejudice of his squadron mates, the rigidity of the rules and regs. Oh, he still faced prejudice and regulations when he was on a mission, sure, but it was different "Outside," surrounded by stars and a beckoning cosmos. You had your orders, your mission to complete . . . but you also got to make decisions, even at times to interpret how best to carry out the mission, a singular freedom and feeling of power that he missed as a relatively junior officer on board a large warship with five thousand other officers and men crowded into its habs.

He realized Fifer was still waiting for a response to his statement about Gray's feeling marginalized, something the two of them had discussed a number of times during the past three weeks.

"I don't know if I would call it feeling marginalized, sir," he said. "It *is* good when I feel like I'm a part of something bigger, something important. Like being a member of the TriBeCa Family back home."

"And how often do you feel that way, Lieutenant?"

He thought about this. "Not all that often, I guess. The other people in the squadron tend not to let me forget who I am . . . where I came from."

"Understandable," Fifer said. "Navy pilots tend to form a tight little circle, like a fraternity. Anyone not in the circle is an outsider, an unknown quantity. You get in only when you prove yourself."

"I've *been* proving myself," Gray insisted. "For a year now!"

"It can take longer than that, Lieutenant. And sometimes it can take forever."

"So what am I supposed to do?"

Fifer gave a gentle shrug. "You have several paths open to you, as we've discussed already. You can resign your commission and become an enlisted man. You can simply turn in your wings, become a non-flight officer. Or you can fold yourself in, hunker down, and ride it out where you are."

Or I can go back to the Ruins, Gray thought. *The hell with the Navy, with the government, with all of it. . . .*

"That is certainly one option," Fifer told him, "but I can't recommend it. You would be found. You would be brought back. You would face a court martial for desertion, and you would either serve time in a military prison or you would be reconditioned."

Gray started. He hadn't spoken out loud about deserting. "You're reading my thoughts!"

"Your personal daemon is linked in with the AI coordinating this session," Fifer told him. "It can pick up surface thoughts, at least, yes. How else do you think I monitor your free-form regressions?"

Gray was trembling, though whether from fear, anger, or some other long-repressed emotion, he couldn't tell. He was beginning to realize that what he resented most about the Navy was the constant high-tech monitoring, the fact that even when he wasn't linked in, there were machines and AIs in the Net-Cloud that could follow where he was going, watch where he went, listen in on his conversations, even hear what he was thinking.

"I noticed a peculiar, extremely sharp spike in the intensity of your emotions just now," Fifer told him. "Can you tell me about what you're feeling?"

"There's a lot of stuff," Gray admitted. "I don't like the constant snooping, the feeling that AIs and Authority monitors are always looking over my shoulder, watching what I do. And . . ."

"And what?"

"I'm afraid."

"Afraid of what? The monitoring?"

"No. I don't like it, but I'm not *afraid* of it."

"What then?"

Gray was trying to put it into words, but found he could not.

"I'm . . . not sure."

"That's okay. I'll tell you what. I'm going to say some words and phrases, list them. Things I mentioned a moment ago, when you had that emotional spike. Just listen to each phrase, think about it. Tell me what you feel."

Gray was sweating now. "Okay . . ."

" 'One option.' "

Gray felt nothing, and shrugged.

" 'You would be found.' "

He felt a quiver of emotional discomfort, but he shook his head.

" 'You would be brought back.' "

"No."

" 'You would face a court martial.' "

Again, he shook his head, but his heart was pounding now. Damn, he *hated* this kind of probing.

" 'You would serve time in prison.' "

"No."

" 'You would be reconditioned.' "

"*Damn* it, Doctor!" Gray was shouting now. "What does any of this have to do with—"

"It's okay, Lieutenant. Just relax. Deep breath . . ."

Gray's heart was pounding in his chest. He wanted to leave, wanted to *run*. . . .

"You see, Trevor, as I told you at the beginning of these sessions, we're recording everything as we proceed with the session. I can call up any part of our conversation, read it on my in-head display. And we can match each phrase with your emotional output. I notice an *extremely* strong response on your part to the idea of reconditioning. Is that true?"

"You can also tell when I'm lying," Gray said, the words close to a snarl.

"Yes, but that's beside the point."

"I don't like the idea of . . . of reconditioning. No."

"And what is it that bothers you about it?"

"What is it that—" Gray broke off his reply. "Having my brains scrambled, my memories stolen . . . shouldn't that bother anybody?"

"There are a lot of public misconceptions about the neural reconfiguration, Lieutenant. It's not what you think."

"No? Then explain that to my wife."

Gray didn't *know* that the docbots at the Columbia Arcology had planted new memories in Angela's brain. The medtechs hadn't told him much of anything. But he'd known that the Angela he'd spoken to after her stroke treatment had *not* been the Angela he'd married. Oh, she'd looked the same, had the same body, the same face . . . but when she'd looked at him she'd been . . . different. The love he'd always seen in her eyes was gone, and her conversation seemed . . . distant. As though she were speaking to a stranger.

The Angela he'd married never would have turned him away, never would have told him she never wanted to see him again.

Fifer had a faraway look on his face as he reviewed records he was calling up within his mind. "Angela Gray," he said. "I see. A serious stroke. Partial paralysis."

"And she changed," Gray said. The words were hard. Bitter. "She changed toward me."

"That can happen. A stroke can destroy established neural pathways. Those that control movement in muscles. And also those that govern memory, recognition, even attitude and belief."

"They told me they had to *adjust* her," Gray said.

"Adjustment isn't the same as neural reconfiguration," Fifer told him. "It's not reconditioning."

"No? It made Angela different. It changed her."

Fifer sighed. "Without direct access to Columbia Arcology's medcenter, I can't really say this for sure, but I suspect that what changed her was the delay in getting her to competent treatment. It says here it was almost twenty-four hours before you got her to a medcenter."

"It took that long to get them to look at her."

"Yes, well . . . there *were* social considerations."

"Yeah. To them I was a damned filthy primitive, a squattie, with a *wife*, of all obscene things."

"That might have been part of it. So was the lack of med insurance, though. That's how you came to join the Navy, isn't it?"

"Yes."

Fifer nodded. "Lieutenant . . . I think we may have identified a key focus of your embitterment disorder."

"Oh, really?" Gray's tone was biting and sarcastic. "Do you think. Maybe? Damn it, of *course* I'm bitter about what happened!"

"And I don't blame you. What happened had a serious, a terrible impact on your life. But you *don't* have to let what happened at the Columbia Arcology control you, control your thoughts and actions, for the rest of your life.

"As with everything else in life, Lieutenant Gray, you have a choice—to be done to, or to *do*. And we're here to determine which it's going to be."

CIC, TC/USNA CVS America
Mars Synchorbit, Sol System
0916 hours, TFT

Koenig felt the faint shudder as *America* finally nestled into the docking facility gantry, the boarding tubes nestling against the access hatchways in the zero-G sections of her spine. Magnetic clamps locked and nanoseals formed impenetrable, airtight connections. Buchanan had already passed orders that the first off the ship would be the Mufrid passengers. The transports that would take them to Earth were already moving toward *America*'s berth.

They were home.

He could hear the steady stream of orders from the bridge as some of the ship's systems were shut down. The hab modules would continue their rotation for a time, providing artificial gravity, at least until the Mufrids were off. And wasn't that going to be fun . . . herding more than a thousand people down to the zero-G regions of the ship and floating them out through the boarding tubes? *America*'s Marine contingent and the Master-at-Arms Division were going to be busy for the next several hours, keeping the civilians moving, keeping them from panicking and thrashing about and possibly hurting themselves. Ship's crew would be responsible for cleaning up after those who got sick in the passageways, though at least they would have robotic help in that unpleasant task. The ship's quartermaster's department was already deploying cleanerbots to the ship's zero-gravity hab areas.

With *America* back in spacedock, Admiral Koenig now was technically off duty. Other ships in the carrier battle-group were still arriving—though a few had been redirected to Earth Synchorbital—but they were now under the individual commands of their respective commanding officers, no longer maneuvering or fighting as a fleet. Now, he thought, might be a good time to go back to his quarters and try to catch some sleep. He'd been awake through much of the inbound passage from Sol's Kuiper Belt, and dead tired. He already knew he would have to appear in person before a review board of the Senate Military Directorate early tomorrow, ship's time . . . and likely face a Board of Inquiry shortly after that.

It might be his last appearance before his peers as a flag-rank officer, and he wanted to be sharp for that meeting.

"I have an incoming communication from Dr. Brandt," his personal AI informed him. "It is flagged 'urgent.'"

"Put it through."

"Admiral Koenig? Brandt, down in med-research!"

"Yes, Doctor. What can I—"

"We've got a problem here! The Turusch are killing each other!"

"Damn it! Separate them!"

"It's . . . too late for that. You might want to link down here and see for yourself."

"Stand by. I'm coming down."

He connected directly with the NTE robots hanging from the ship's overhead in the compartment holding the two Turusch. The two aliens appeared locked in a deadly embrace, heads split wide open, the harpoons and feeding tubes within imbedded in each other's bodies. Several medtecs in red e-suits were there, trying to separate the two, but the aliens continued to thrash about weakly, pushing the humans away with flailing black tentacles. A pair of white Noters suspended from the overhead were trying to help, but were knocked away with ease.

Shit! "Get them apart!" he barked.

"We're *trying*, Admiral!" Brandt said. "Those rigid spears are like injection needles. They squirt digestive juice—sulfuric acid—into whatever they're eating. Then they suck up the soup through those soft tubes."

"They're *eating* each other?"

"That's about the size of it, Admiral."

Moments later, the humans and robots together managed to get a firm grip on both of the alien combatants and drag them apart. Acid dripped from the harpoons as they slipped free, steaming on the deck.

But by then both of the aliens were dead.

Chapter Sixteen

Senate Military Directorate Chambers
Phobos Space Elevator, Sol System
1010 hours, TFT

The preliminary Board of Inquiry was relatively relaxed and laid-back, a session designed simply to explore Koenig's actions at Eta Boötis, and to determine whether any formal charges even needed to be made. The meeting was held virtually, since two of the board members—Admiral Jason Barry and Vice Admiral Michael Noranaga—were linking in from elsewhere. Barry currently was at Noctis Labyrinthus, on the Martian surface. Noranaga was a selkie who at the moment was swimming somewhere within one of Earth's oceans; the current twenty-minute time delay between Earth and Mars meant that he would be represented on the Board of Inquiry by his avatar, uploaded from Quito Synchorbital to Phobia by electronic transfer several days before.

Koenig had already checked the flag officer listings for circum-Mars space, and found that no fewer than thirty-seven admirals were present within easy realtime link distances; why Noranaga was on the board, rather than someone closer at hand, was a mystery. Koenig's best guess was that the genetically enhanced admiral—who held dual flag rank in both the Human Confederation Star Navy and in the surface navy of the North American Confederal Union—had pulled some strings in Columbus, DC. He held considerable authority in C^3—the Confederation Central Command—and might have a political reason for taking part in Koenig's hearing.

The third member of the board was an old friend of Koenig's, Rear Admiral Karyn Mendelson, with whom he'd served back when she'd commanded the *Lexington*. She'd been waiting for him in the meeting chamber, offering him a recliner with the link pad already open and waiting.

"You don't look so hot, Alex," she told him as he walked in. "Are you that worried about this morning?"

"Not about the board, no," he told her. "We have another problem. I'll fill you all in once we get started."

She shrugged. "Suit yourself. Shall we go in?"

He nodded. "Let's get this over with."

He sat in the recliner, placing the network of gold and silver threads visible on the palm of his hand against the link pad. Immediately, he was in a different room, a virtual construct, facing Mendelson, Noranaga, and Barry across a broad, heavy table.

"Very well," Barry said without other preamble. As the senior officer present, he would serve as the board's voice. "These proceedings, an official Board of Inquiry into the command decisions of Rear Admiral Alexander Koenig at the Battle of Eta Boötis, 25 September, 2404, are now open. Admiral Koenig . . . do you have legal representation?"

He tapped his head. "Legal AI."

There were still human lawyers, but most legal matters were handled by highly specialized artificial intelligences. Koenig's was resident within his cerebral hardware. At this level of inquiry, fact-finding more than anything else, legal representation probably wasn't necessary, but it was good to have one linked in just in case things went further, to a full-fledged court martial.

"Will your legal AI be fully on-line, or in observer mode only?"

"Observer mode, sir."

"So noted. And do you have a statement for the board, Admiral Koenig?"

"Not a formal statement, sir, no . . . but I do have information that has a bearing on these proceedings. You should be aware of it before this goes any further."

"And what is the information?"

"Carrier battlegroup *America* was operating under two principle mission orders—to retrieve General Gorman's Marine Expeditionary Force from the surface of Haris, Eta Boötis IV, and to retrieve two alien POWs, a couple of Turusch fighter pilots shot down during the ongoing fighting on Haris before we got there. While the two missions were given equal weight in my operational orders, I was told verbally by Vice Admiral Menendez that it was *imperative* that I bring the aliens safely back to Mars, that that mission should be my primary concern. In his words, 'If you don't get the Trash back to Mars, everything Gorman's grunts have gone through will be for nothing.' "

"Was this statement on or off the record?" Noranaga's avatar asked. The virtual image looked fully human in the simulation, right down to the details of the man's naval dress uniform. The reality, Koenig knew, was quite different.

"Off the record, Admiral. It was unofficial. What I need to tell the board, however, is that the two aliens are dead. That part of the mission was a failure."

"Dead?" Mendelson said. "How?"

"I have the recordings here."

He opened a new window in the virtual room. The four stood as silent and unseen observers in the compartment in *America*'s research lab, watching as the Turusch speared and murdered each other, as the medtechs and robots attempted to separate them.

Afterward, back in the meeting chamber, Noranaga shook his head. "Suicide, obviously."

"We don't know enough about the species, about their psychology or their physiology, to know that for sure, Admiral," Mendelson said. "They might have been . . . hungry. Just that."

"So hungry they couldn't help trying to eat each other?" Barry said. "That doesn't seem likely."

"The research department told me they get at least some of their nutritional needs from light," Koenig said, "through a process in their skins similar to photosynthesis. Their report suggests that the Turusch can go a *long* time without food."

"They're plants?" Noranaga asked.

"Words like 'plant' and 'animal' don't have much meaning when it comes to the truly alien, Admiral," Koenig replied. He was still getting used to that truth himself.

"It's not even that alien, Admiral Noranaga," Mendelson put in. "There are one-celled creatures on Earth—*Euglena*—that move and act like animals, but they use chlorophyll to manufacture food in addition to what it can catch."

There remained, Koenig knew, an ongoing debate among biological scientists about how to divvy up the world of life. One popular scheme called for plants, animals, and four other "kingdoms," including fungi and the protista—which included the genus *Euglena* that Mendelson had mentioned. More recent attempts to describe and group life forms discovered on other worlds than Earth during the past 350 years had so far succeeded only in bogging the entire process down in a morass of conflicting classification schemes.

None of which helped describe what the hell the Turusch were, or how they thought.

"We *do* have additional information on the Turusch, however," Koenig went on, "and possibly about the Sh'daar as well. Brandt and George were questioning them shortly before they . . . died."

Again, a new window opened above the virtual conference table. This time, the two aliens slumped side by side on the deck, apparently watching the robot camera hanging from above. Date and time stamps showed the session as having taken place just over twenty-six hours earlier, an hour before the aliens had killed each other.

Dr. George's voice could be heard in the background. "But why are you attacking us?"

Again, the two spoke together, their buzzing speech creating peculiarly ringing harmonics as running translations appeared at the bottom of the window.

"We do not attack you," said one.

"The Seed attacks to save you," said the other.

"And just what is the Seed saving us from?" George asked.

"The Seed saves you from yourselves and poor choice," said one.

"Too swiftly you grow and lose your balance," said the other.

"I don't understand," George said. "How are we a threat to ourselves?"

"Transcendence looms near."

"Transcendence blossoms."

"Transcendence destroys."

"Transcendence abandons."

"Transcendence of what? Help us understand. *What* is transcending?"

Both Turusch writhed for a moment. Though it was impossible to read anything like emotion in the two, their movements seemed to project frustration, perhaps anger.

"You transcend into darkness," one said, its tentacles lashing.

"You change, change, change," insisted the other.

Abruptly, both turned away from the robot, buzzing at each other.

"Why isn't there a translation of what they're saying now?" Mendelson asked.

"The xenopsych people think they're speaking their own language there," Koenig told her. "Keep in mind that our translations of their speech are based on an artificial language—LG—which we learned from the Spiders. We don't have a clue as to how to break the original Turusch language."

The recording ended, and Koenig again faced the members of the preliminary board across the empty table.

"Transcendence," Admiral Barry said. "That seems to be an ongoing theme with these creatures."

"Yes, sir. In particular, we think they're talking about the GRIN Singularity."

Since the twentieth century—some would say earlier—human technology had been advancing in exponential leaps, each advance in science spawning new advances in dizzying and fast-accelerating profusion. It wasn't just the technology that had been growing; it was the *pace* of that growth, the ever-increasing speed of technological innovation and development. Just five centuries ago, humans had made their first successful heavier-than-air flight in a fabric-and-spruce glider powered by a gasoline engine, a voyage lasting all of twelve seconds and covering 120 feet. Thirty years later, aviator Wiley Post flew a Lockheed Vega monoplane around the world, the first man to do so solo, making eleven stops along the way and logging the total time in the air at 115 hours, 36 minutes.

And thirty years after that, humans were riding rockets into low Earth orbit, circling the globe in ninety minutes, and were just six short years from walking on the Moon.

In the late twentieth century, a science fiction writer, math professor, and computer scientist named Vernor Vinge had pointed out that if the rate of technological change was graphed against time, the slope representing that change was fast approaching a vertical line—what he called the "technological singularity" in an essay written in 1993. Human life and civilization, he'd pointed out, would very quickly become unrecognizable, assuming that humans weren't replaced entirely by their technological offspring within the next few decades.

Other writers of the era had pointed out that there were four principle drivers of this exponential increase in high-tech wizardry: genetics, robotics, infotechnology, and nanotechnology, hence the acronym "GRIN." The GRIN Singularity became a catchphrase for the next four centuries of human technological progress.

"GRIN wasn't quite the apotheosis people thought it would be," Noranaga pointed out.

"That's kind of a strange statement coming from a guy who breathes with gills and can outswim a dolphin," Barry pointed out.

"He's right, though," Mendelson said. "The way the pace of things was picking up in the twenty-first century, it looked like humans would become super-sentient god-machines before the twenty-second. The surprise is that we didn't."

"Well," Koenig said, "we did kind of get distracted along the way."

As Mendelson had pointed out, the only surprising thing about any of this was that the rate of increase hadn't already rocketed into the singularity sometime in the late twenty-first century. Various factors were to blame—the Islamic Wars, two nasty wars with the Chinese Hegemony culminating in an asteroid strike in the Atlantic, the ongoing struggle with Earth's fast-changing climate and the loss of most of Earth's coastal cities, the collapse of the global currency and the subsequent World Depression. The Blood Death of the early twenty-second century had brought about startling advances in nanomedicine . . . but it had also killed one and a half billion people and brought about a major collapse of civilization in Southern Asia and Africa.

Those challenges and others had helped spur technological advances, certainly, but at the same time they'd slowed social change, redirected human creativity and innovation into less productive avenues, and siphoned off trillions of creds that otherwise would have financed both technological and social change. Human technological advance, it seemed, came more in fits and starts than in sweeping asymptotic curves.

Admiral Barry shrugged. "There *are* those who still claim that the exponential increase in technological growth can't be sustained indefinitely, that the rate of growth has actually been slowing over the past three centuries. They say that eventually, things will level off onto a mathematically stable plateau."

While Koenig was aware of the arguments—he *had* to be, to keep track of the rapid-fire advances in military technology—he had no opinion one way or the other. Technology simply *was*; you lived with it, grew up with it, depended upon it to integrate with the modern world. From virtual conferences such as this one to interfacing with the NTE robots in *America*'s research facility to Noranaga's genetic prostheses to the nanufacture techniques used to construct Phobia, GRIN technologies were a part of each and every aspect of modern life.

Of course, the big question was what the technological singularity actually meant. *How* would life become unrecognizable? Modern commentators frequently used the word *transcendence*, without explaining what that might mean. The suggestion was that Humankind would turn into something else. But what?

"I wonder, though," Koenig said, "if what the Sh'daar are worried about is the technological transcendence of humanity. If we *did* become half-machine, half-god hybrids, we might pose a threat to them."

"Maybe," Mendelson said. She didn't sound convinced. "But if we had truly godlike technologies, why would we want to fight or conquer anyone?"

"Well, we have one clue staring us right in the face," Koenig said. "From what we learned through the Agletsch, the Sh'daar have been around for a long time. If anyone should be technological supermen—superbeings, rather—it would be them, right?"

Barry nodded. "Our best information on the Sh'daar suggests that they began moving out into interstellar space from their home planet sometime during the late Ordovician . . . say four hundred fifty million years ago. That's a *long* time."

"Most xenosophontologists think we don't understand Agletsch dating systems," Noranaga pointed out. "A sentient species that exists for almost half a billion years? It's not possible."

"Bullshit, Admiral," Mendelson said. "We don't know yet what's possible and what's not. It they reached a point of perfect stability . . . either no growth or very little, with control over their own genome so they didn't evolve into something else, why not?"

"The point is," Koenig said, "a race that's been around for half a billion years or so ought to be so far beyond us that there's no way we could fight them, no more than clams could stop people from building an arcology on their beach."

"True," Mendelson said. "Even if they're only a half *million* years ahead of us technologically, they'd be like gods from our vantage point, and their technology would look like magic. We wouldn't stand a chance."

"Well, we haven't been fighting the Sh'daar directly,"

Noranaga said. "All we've seen are their front men . . . the Agletsch and the Turusch."

"And why even bother with the likes of *them*," Mendelson said, "if the Sh'daar could just wave whatever it is they use for hands and make us vanish? *Poof!* Problem solved."

"We can't really speculate about their reasoning," Admiral Barry said. "It is, after all, *alien.*"

"But that reasoning is still rooted in the real world," Koenig said. "At least . . . in the real world as they perceive it. If we can understand that reasoning, we might have a chance to come to an agreement with them. To *understand* them."

"All of which is for the xenosoph people to figure out," Barry said, leaning back in his virtual chair. "While interesting, speculation about alien motivations is not germane to this Board of Inquiry. Admiral Koenig, did you have a particular reason for bringing all of this to our attention?"

"Only insofar as it might have a bearing on this hearing," Koenig replied. "Unofficially, at least, my battlegroup's primary orders were to go to Eta Boötis and retrieve those Turusch prisoners, bring them back to Mars. *That* part of the mission, at least, failed. That fact could have a bearing on these proceedings."

"Hm." Barry gave the faint shadow of a smile. "And what does your legal AI have to say about this?"

"It advised me to say nothing about the Turusch killing each other, that I should focus on the fact that we did get the aliens and Gorman's Marines, *plus* several thousand civilians who otherwise would have been killed, back to human space."

"You don't believe in listening to legal counsel?"

"Only when I believe that counsel is the right thing to do. Sir."

"I see. Well . . . I declare this hearing into the conduct of Rear Admiral Alexander Koenig during the recent operational deployment of the *America* battlegroup open. Let's begin by reviewing the operational orders for Carrier Battlegroup *America* from the time when they were issued . . . beginning on 6 September, 2404 . . ."

Intrasystem High-G Transport Kelvin
Approaching SupraQuito
Earth Synchorbit, Sol System
1610 hours, TFT

Lieutenant Gray watched the Earth swelling to blue-white glory just ahead. Within his passenger pod nestled inside the stubby IHG transport, the feed from external optical pick-ups had rendered the craft itself invisible. It seemed to Gray that he was leaning back in his recliner, completely open to empty space, surrounded by a panoply of stars, the sun brilliant off to one side, and Earth and Earth's moon as an unlikely and mismatched pair before him.

Ten hours had passed since he'd boarded the Interplanetary Direct transport back at Phobia. Accelerating at one hundred gravities, the *Kelvin* had reached a midpoint velocity of .06 *c*, almost nineteen thousand kilometers per second, then flipped its drive singularity astern to decelerate for the rest of the flight to its destination.

The trip back to Earth was Fifer's idea . . . an opportunity, the psych officer had told him, to take another look at his roots. In particular, Fifer wanted Gray to see if he still fit in with the tribes of the Manhattan Ruins. He'd boarded the shuttle at 0800 hours that morning, signing out at *America*'s quarterdeck and boarding the *Kelvin* at her embarkation dock with fifteen enlisted members of *America*'s crew heading for Earth on liberty. He'd chatted with one of them, an armaments tech, second class, while waiting to board the *Kelvin*. Usually, enlisted liberty was short—from twelve to forty-eight hours—but twenty hours of travel time between Mars and Earth cut into that time sharply. The tech told him that she'd been granted a seventy-two, as had the others going to Earth. Scuttlebutt had it that *America* would be redeploying to Earth Synchorbital within the next day or two; if that happened, she'd rejoin the ship there—and get an extra ten hours visiting her parents in Columbus, DC.

As an officer, Gray didn't need to worry about liberty. He'd simply signed out after receiving permission from the CAG office to go Earthside for seventy-two hours. Plenty of time to do what he needed to do in Manhattan and get back to the ship, whether she was still at Mars or docked at SupraQuito.

He found himself thinking about Rissa Schiff, the cute ensign from the avionics department he'd met last time he'd been at SupraQuito. He'd found her fun and engaging, had been wondering about taking things further with her . . . at least until Collins and Spaas had busted up the party. The pairing probably wouldn't have worked; he was still looking for something permanent in a relationship. Schiffie had been looking for fun—one night or many, but nothing lasting.

God, he missed Angela.

The moon appeared to be slowly drifting off to one side, turning from nearly full to a crescent as the *Kelvin* slipped past it and into circumlunar space. The lights of cities appeared scattered across those parts of the moon in darkness, tight clusters marking the cities at Crisium, Tranquility, Apennine Vista, Tsiolkovsky, and the others, all woven together by a slender webwork of glowing threads marking the surface gravtubes.

Earth grew larger, the rate of growth slowing with *Kelvin*'s continuing deceleration. Eventually, Gray could make out what appeared to be strings of minute stars drawn out in slender arcs around the planet. After three centuries, Earth Synchorbital had become the preferred location for the vast majority of the planet's off-world manufactories, power production, shipyards, and orbital habitats. Several million people lived in orbit now, the number growing daily. Like Mars, Earth was served by three space elevators—one at Quito, one on the northern slope of Mt. Kenya, and one on the island of Pulau Lingga, on the southern edge of the Port Singapore megalopolis. The habs and orbital factories at Synchorbital didn't extend all the way around the planet yet; it would be centuries more before Earth had a genuine system of rings 36,000 kilometers above its equator. Even so, it was remarkable to see how the hand of man had so touched the world of his birth and that world's moon that evidence of his technology could be seen from this far out in the Void.

Still decelerating, the *Kelvin* continued to close with the nexus of gleaming habs and solar panels at SupraQuito. Gray could see the elevator itself now, a gossamer-thin strand of light stretched taut between a mountaintop in Ecuador and a small planetoid anchor twenty thousand kilometers above synchronous orbit. The *Kelvin*'s launch from Phobia had been timed to arrive at SupraQuito precisely as the receiving facility orbited into position. The *Kelvin*'s onboard AI made a rapid series of final corrections using the drive singularity astern, then switched off the drive and drifted into the tangleweb field at less than a hundred meters per second. Gray felt the surge of deceleration, startling after ten and a half hours of zero-G under gravitic drive.

His travel pod melted away around him as an AI voice thanked him for choosing Interplanetary Direct for his travel needs. Eighty creds had been deducted from his account on board the *America* to pay for the flight.

The receiving bay was in microgravity, of course. Robots hovered nearby, waiting to assist passengers unused to moving in zero-G, but Gray grabbed a handrail and pulled himself along with more or less practiced ease. The local hab section would be rotating, like the crew modules on board *America*, but he needed to enter it at the hub and ride an elevator out and down to the main deck. Hauling himself hand over hand, he followed glowing arrows projected on the bulkhead toward customs. His baggage—a single small satchel—would be forwarded directly down to Quito.

The local time, he noted, was 1125 hours—five hours off of shipboard time, which was set to GMT. And Quito was in the same global time zone as Manhattan.

He would be there, he thought, by late that afternoon.

Solar Kuiper Belt
5.5 light hours from Earth
1830 hours, TFT

High Guard Watch Station 8734 was tiny—a spherical object the size of a woman's fist—and most of its mass consisted of foam insulation against the ambient 50-degree Kelvin temperatures so far from a wan and distant sun. It was one of some hundreds of thousands of AI detector probes scattered across the surface of an immense sphere, with a radius of five and a half light hours, centered on Sol.

The automated High Guard Watch had begun late in the twenty-first century, as the first automated probes were placed in solar orbit roughly at the mean distance of Pluto. Tiny onboard cameras and mass detectors the size of BBs kept a constant watch on the surrounding sky, recording mass and movement, the data spreading across large networks of the probes for correlation and tracking. The idea had been to spot comets or asteroids falling in out of the Kuiper Belt, objects that in future epochs might threaten Earth or Earth's solar colonies. The sooner such objects were detected, the easier it would be to nudge them into new orbits that would never threaten human habitats.

Later, they were programmed for another task—watching for the flash of photons released by starships as they dropped out of Alcubierre Drive. They served as a navigational net, tracking incoming and outgoing ships by their photon release.

And since the Sh'daar Ultimatum, in 2367, they'd watched for the arrival of alien ships that might pose a threat to humankind.

The network was stretched painfully thin. Even half a million probes are few and far between when they're scattered over the surface of a sphere eleven light hours across. The nearest probe to 8734's current position was 3683, now thirty light seconds distant, twenty times the distance between Earth and Earth's moon.

A burst of high-energy photons captured 8734's electronic attention. Twin cameras focused on the disturbance, estimating the distance at nearly one light hour out, deeper into the Kuiper Belt; probe 3683 recorded the flash twelve seconds later, allowing a more perfect triangulation and target lock. The arriving ship was large—enormous, in fact, a small planetoid converted into a starship of alien configuration.

The closest human presence was a Navy listening post on Triton, a moon of Neptune, now 2.9 light hours distant. High Guard Probe 8734 duly transmitted its data and continued to monitor the movement of the intruder vessel . . . as around it more and more new targets began to flash into realspace existence.

Chapter Seventeen

Triton Naval Listening Post, Sol System
2125 hours, TFT

Hostile warships were arriving at the outskirts of Earth's solar system, but it took precious time to get word of the event to Mars. Two hours, fifty-five minutes passed before data arrived at Triton from the first probe to detect the incoming fleet, and the data were already an hour old even before the transmission had begun.

Things tend to happen slowly at the thin, cold edge of the solar system.

Lieutenant Charles Kennedy was the commanding officer of the Navy's Triton listening post, a tiny base housing twelve Navy personnel, a handful of civilian researchers and base technicians, and a modest AI named Sparks. A few kilometers distant, mobile mining platforms the size of battleships crept across the frozen landscape, extracting nitrogen from the surface, pressurizing it, bottling it, and magnetically launching it into the long trajectory sunward for use in the Martian terraforming project.

Kennedy sipped his coffee and decided yet again that his all-too-brief evening with Admiral Brewer's daughter had not been worth it. Being assigned to this frozen ice ball in the solar system's boondocks was about as close to terminal as his career could come. He'd been here for three months now, and could look forward to another nine months of utter boredom and frigid vistas in the wan light of a sun thirty astronomical units distant.

"Class One alert," Sparky announced without preamble. "Data incoming. Our remote Kuiper probes are detecting the emergence of starships almost four light hours out."

Kennedy choked on his coffee, his feet swinging off the console and hitting the deck with a slap. Surface gravity on Triton was just under two tenths of a G, and the droplets of hot spilled liquid cascaded across his face and uniform in slow motion.

"Shit!" Then the pain of coffee scalding his chin registered. *"Ow!"* Mopping at his face, he set the cup down. "Where, damn it?"

A chart opened in his mind, showing the relative positions in three dimensions of Neptune and Triton, the distant sun, and the incoming ships. Data were coming in now from a total of four unmanned probes at the forty-AU shell, highlighted as blinking white pinpoints, some ten astronomical units beyond the orbit of Neptune. The intruders were beyond that shell, off to one side and 10 degrees above the ecliptic, some twenty-two astronomical units away from Triton, forty-five AUs from Sol.

As Kennedy studied the data, he realized that a better question would have been *when*. Those blips, obviously, were starships emerging from the enemy's equivalent of Alcubierre Drive, detected by the pulses of photons released by their emergence into normal space. They would have been moving in the hour since their detection . . . and would have moved further still in the three subsequent hours as the alert was transmitted down to Triton. Those ships could be almost *anywhere* now . . . including bearing down on Triton at just under the speed of light.

"How many?" he asked the AI.

"We are picking up multiple emergence events," Sparky continued. "Fifteen vessels of various masses and configurations so far."

"Can you identify the configurations?"

There was the briefest of pauses as data was correlated

and confirmed. "Affirmative. Configurations match those of several known Turusch warships."

Trash ships! *Here!* "Launch ready courier. *Now!*"

One hundred kilometers above the methane-ice plains of Triton, an orbital laser-communications antenna shifted slightly, taking aim at an unseen point among the stars just to one side of the brightest of those stars—Mars, its light lost in the glare of Sol. Sparky would continue transmitting updates to that data for as long as possible.

"Give me positions on the nearest naval vessels," he said.

"One High Guard destroyer is at fifty-five light minutes' range," Sparky told him. "USNA *Gallagher*."

"Send out a general fleet alert," Kennedy said. His primary orders—getting the warning back to the inner system as quickly as possible—had been accomplished. Beyond that, he could warn any naval vessels in the general vicinity of Neptune . . . and not much else.

The listening post was not armed.

Kennedy watched the incoming blips and decided that, just maybe, boredom wasn't such a bad thing after all.

Minutes later, a false dawn illuminated the ice plains of Triton as the lasercom antenna vanished in a near-*c* impact.

Lieutenant Kennedy and his tiny command died fifteen seconds later, as a city-sized chunk of Triton's surface vaporized, and the naval listening post and most of the human structures located on the frozen worldlet were transformed into superheated plasma expanding silently into space.

Columbia Arcology
Morningside Heights
New City, USNA
1630 hours, local time

"You want to go *where*?"

Trevor Gray drew himself up straighter. He was wearing his Navy dress black uniform, and hoped it was suitably impressive to the local civilian Authority.

"I'm . . . visiting friends in the Ruins," he told the disbe-lieving peaceforcer captain. "That's not illegal, is it?"

"Illegal?" The man scratched his bald head behind one extravagant ear. He'd taken on a genetic prosthesis that had let him grow pointed elfin ears and golden eyes with the slit pupils of a cat. The overall effect, together with the man's hairless scalp, gave him a faintly demonic look. "Not that I know of, no. But why in hell would *anyone* want to go down there? Much less a naval officer!"

Gray wondered what the man would say if he told him he'd been a denizen of the Ruins just five years before. That fact, he decided, would not help his case.

"Let's just say I have business there. With some friends in the TriBeCa Tower."

"What friends?"

Gray smiled. "Would their names really mean anything to you?"

"No." He grinned. "No they wouldn't. To tell the truth, we don't have the faintest idea *what's* going on in there. And we don't want to, either. As long as the squatties stay out in the Ruins, as long as they don't cross the line and come up here, bothering decent folks here in the meg"—he shrugged— "then they can *have* the place, so far as I'm concerned."

Which was the attitude Gray had long since come to expect of the Authority. Of course, the idea of one side not bothering the other only applied to the squatties staying out of the New City megalopolis. There were the hassles and the raids by Authority personnel, the periodic attempts to clear out sections of the Ruins—why, Gray had never been sure. Simple abuse of power, a flexing of Authority muscles just because they had the power to use them? Or a misguided at-tempt to help people who didn't want to be helped?

It didn't matter. The "decent folks" didn't *care*.

"Then there should be no problem letting me go see my friends," Gray said.

His internal time read just past 2130 hours shipboard time, about 1630 local. It hadn't taken him long to process through SupraQuito and take the high-velocity elevator straight down-cable to Quito. When the space elevator was first built in the early twenty-second century, that trip would have been a two-day journey; with grav thrusters the 36,000 kilometer drop from synchorbit only took a couple of hours now.

Quito had been much the same as he remembered it from his first trip up-cable after joining the Navy—big, sprawling, crowded, and impossibly busy, one of the three major port megalopoli, the Equatorial Jewels, the biggest and richest cities on Earth.

From Quito's elaborately decorated *Estación Grande Central de la Tierra* he'd taken a subsurface shuttle for the 4500-kilometer leg north to new New York, hurtling in silence through the vacuum gravtube that, at midpoint, passed nearly four hundred kilometers beneath what was left of the West Indies, a straight-line chord running point-to-point beneath the curving arc of the surface. Gray knew that titanic energies had been mustered to keep the deepest tubes stable as they passed through the Earth's upper mantle, and that the temperature of the mantle rocks surrounding the tube approached 900 degrees Celsius. He could see none of it directly, however, for the shuttle had no external monitors. His choices were watching a mindless romance on the simfeed, striking up a conversation with other shuttle passengers, or sleeping. Like military personnel the world over and since time immemorial, he'd chosen sleep.

The passage, in any case, only lasted forty-five minutes. He'd arrived in Morningside Heights at 1320 local, 1820 ship time. Three hours he'd been here, waiting in waiting areas, talking to bored bureaucrats and minor officials, being sent down brightly lit passageways to see *other* bored bureaucrats and minor officials. It was actually taking him longer to get from the Columbia Arcology to TriBeCa, just eleven kilometers away, than it had taken him to travel 36,000 kilometers down-cable from SupraQuito, and 4500 kilometers more from Quito to the New City.

"Look, Lieutenant," the Authority captain told him, shaking his head. "I'd like to help you. I really would. But I gotta put down a reason for your visit. Who the hell do you need to see in the *Ruins*, fer chrissake?"

A good question.

What, he wondered, *was* he looking for? Why had he come?

Oh, he knew why *Fifer* had wanted him to come. He needed to face his fears, needed to face directly the fact that, if he didn't belong in the Navy, he no longer belonged *here* either.

He decided to risk telling the man the truth.

"My family."

The man's eyes widened slightly, then he nodded. "Oh. Sorry." Gray couldn't tell if he was apologizing for forcing the admission, or showing sympathy at Gray's origins.

"Family . . . business . . ." the peaceforcer said, making an entry. "Palm me."

"Pardon?"

"Give me your hand."

He pressed the network of circuitry exposed against the heel of Gray's right palm against a data feed. Gray felt the inner flag go up that told him he'd just received new data.

"What was that?"

"Your pass. If a monitor or an Authority ship or anybody else pings you, that'll flash back your ID and my personal seal of approval on you bein' there. You won't be bothered."

"Then I can go?"

"You got transport?"

"I've already lined up a broom." There'd been a gravcycle rental shop outside the Authority Center.

"Then you can go."

"Thanks."

"Just one thing, though, Lieutenant."

"Yeah?"

"You'll be on your own in there. There's no Net-Cloud in there, so you won't be able to call for help. And things can get rough in the Ruins, know what I mean?"

"I lived there for most of my life, Captain. Remember?"

"Well, there've been some changes. They've been killing each other a lot more enthusiastically lately. Migrations. Political fighting. That sort of thing."

"I think I can handle myself, Captain."

"On your own head be it, then." The peaceforcer went back to his console, effectively dismissing Gray.

But as he walked out, he distinctly heard the man mutter, "Damned squatties."

Koenig's Office
TC/USNA CVS America
Mars Synchorbital, Sol System
2148 hours, TFT

Koenig came to what passed for attention in his office chair as the inner commconnect came through. He'd been working on a request for two new fighter squadrons—replacements for the fighters and pilots lost at Eta Boötis—when his personal AI had announced a call from the Senate Military Directorate.

He'd half been expecting it.

"Sir."

"Relax, Alex," Rear Admiral Karyn Mendelson said, her image appearing on a newly opened in-head display window. "It's just me."

"Well?"

"Well what?"

"Damn it, Karyn—"

She laughed. "Simmer down. The vote is in and you're okay."

" 'Okay.' You mean . . . ?"

" 'It has been determined by this Board of Inquiry that Rear Admiral Alexander Koenig has consistently and honorably served in the best traditions of the service,' " she quoted. "Or legal gobbledygook to that effect. You're free and clear."

"And still in command of the battlegroup?"

"Abso-damn-lutely."

Koenig felt himself begin to relax. He'd been sure the board would clear him. And yet . . .

"I figured you would be getting an earful from Quintanilla."

"That's why things ran this late," she told him. "Did you really throw him out of CIC?"

"Yes I did. You saw the command logs, didn't you?" Everything that happened on the bridge and the CIC was recorded, optical and audio. Normally those records were kept sealed by the AI that collected them, but they could be retrieved for boards of inquiry, promotion boards, courts martial, and other legal proceedings.

She grinned in his mind. "Yes, but it still was a little hard to believe." Her face grew more serious. "I'm afraid you've made some enemies in the Senate, Alex."

"Already had 'em. A few more won't hurt."

"We were right about Noranaga. He was the one dissenting vote, by the way. He's giving a deposition to a Senate probe tomorrow."

"What probe?"

"Command attenuation."

"I haven't heard about that one."

"It's new. There was some agitation for hearings along those lines when we got kicked out of Arcturus last year. Your . . . um . . . *independence* at Eta Boötis kind of brought things to a head."

While Koenig hadn't heard of a specific Senate probe into the topic, he knew well what command attenuation was. The basic theory was taught at the Academy and accepted as holy writ throughout the hierarchy of naval command. It stated, essentially, that the limitations imposed on communications by the speed of light severely restricted the ability of the highest command levels—the Senate in Columbus and the Supreme Military Command Staff on Mars—to manage both strategy and diplomacy through the Fleet. It took three weeks under Alcubierre Drive to reach Eta Boötis, another three weeks to return. There were special high-velocity courier ships that could make the voyage faster—a week or two, perhaps—but the fact remained that by the time the Senate had learned of a threat at Eta Boötis and dispatched a carrier battlegroup to deal with it, the 1MEF had been pinned down and was under siege. Armchair strategists on Earth or Mars had no chance of managing a battle light years distant, and word of defeats or victories by Earth forces could take weeks or months to get back home.

The Navy had accepted command attenuation as a fact of life, and trained its command officers to operate with a high degree of autonomy, making both military and political decisions that could easily have a strong effect on life and politics back in the solar system. The problem was that, by long tradition, the military was supposed to be subservient to the civilian government. If the military became too independent in its thinking and operation, civilian oversight and control would be lost. The farther away a fleet or battlegroup was operating, the less control the Senate Military Directorate had over it—command attenuation in action.

Political liaisons like John Quintanilla were the Senate's answer to the problem, an attempt to put someone into the fleet command structure who represented the political interests of the Senate. Deployed fleet commanders like Koenig despised the idea; political liaisons by their very nature complicated already complex missions, and that could translate as higher losses, quite possibly defeat. Political liaisons rarely had the military training that let them see a developing situation through the strategic and tactical training and experience of a command officer.

"You're telling me I haven't heard the last of this," Koenig said after a moment's thought.

"Good God! Of *course* you haven't! As long as we're saddled with PLs, there's going to be friction. The PL insisting on doing things his way so the civilians stay in charge, the CO insisting that doing it that way will lose the battle."

"So what's going to happen?"

"Nothing for a long time. That's the problem with political assemblies . . . or maybe it's a blessing. They take *forever* to decide something. And by the time they do, their decision may no longer have anything to do with the problem." She hesitated. "Quintanilla mentioned something in passing this afternoon. He said your deep-strike plan is being reviewed again. He's against it, of course . . . but he mentioned that if the Senate approved it, it was tantamount to cutting you off from any Senate oversight whatsoever."

"Operation Crown Arrow? It's back on the table?"

"Exactly."

Operation Crown Arrow had been conceived a year ago, shortly after the twin defeats at Arcturus Station and at Yong Yuan Dan, the Battle of Everdawn. The WHISPERS deep space listening posts on Pluto, Eris, Orca, and distant Sedna had tentatively identified a major Turusch base or supply depot at Alphekka, seventy-two light years from Earth, forty-two light years from Arcturus, forty-four from Eta Boötis.

Intelligence believed Alphekka—Alpha Corona Borealis—might be the Sh'daar/Turusch staging area for operations into human space. Humans had not been out that far, but it was thought that the Turusch homeworlds lay somewhere in that direction. Operation Crown Arrow—*Crown* was a reference to the constellation Corona Borealis, the "Northern Crown," lying just to the east of Boötis in Earth's night sky—had been a proposed long-range carrier strike against the presumed base.

The original idea for Crown Arrow had been Koenig's, first described in a proposal submitted to the Senate Military Directorate eight months ago. The *America* carrier battlegroup would have been the heart of the strike force, which Koenig thought should number at least three carriers and one hundred supporting vessels.

The Directorate, perhaps predictably, had balked. One hundred ships represented about 20 percent of the total Confederation naval force; half of those ships would be logistical and supply vessels, and sending them out beyond the edge of Humankind space would put a serious strain on the Navy's ability to keep the stay-at-home fleet elements and some hundreds of outposts and colonies supplied.

"So why are they reconsidering Crown Arrow *now*?" Koenig asked.

Mendelson shrugged. "Possibly because it makes sense. Even if Alphekka isn't an invasion staging point, WHISPERS has picked up enough traffic out in that region to suggest something is going on. Our most serious weakness right now is that we don't know our enemy. We know nothing about them, their homeworlds, the extent of their empires, or even what they want."

"We *know* what they want. We become a part of the empire of the 'Galactic Masters.' *Humankind va Sh'daar.* And we give up our right to continue making our own technological advances. They were pretty clear about that much, at least."

"A long-range strike like the one you propose might let us learn a lot more about their technological level, their deployment, their political structure, their plans. We're fighting them blindfolded if we don't. Anyway . . . there's a faction within the Directorate that wants to deploy a battle-group out into Alphekkan space. It won't be a hundred ships. It might just be *America*'s battlegroup. But it will be something. And if you're out there, the Senate's going to have a tough time calling you on the carpet to answer for Eta Boötis."

He grinned at her. "Are you *always* this sunshine-optimistic, Karyn?"

"I'm a realist, Alex. Sometimes things *do* break the right way."

"Not often enough. Excuse me a sec."

Koenig called up a file in a side window, studying it for a moment. WHISPERS—the unlikely acronym stood for weak heterodyned interstellar signal passband-emission radio search. Ten-kilometer radio telescope antennae orbiting several widely scattered trans-Neptunian dwarf planets far out in Sol's Kuiper Belt used very wide baseline interferometry to probe target stars at radio wavelengths. It wasn't as simple as dialing in on alien radio broadcasts; for a century after the advent of radio telescopy, scientists had fretted over the apparent absence of radio signals from other civilizations in space—evidence, it seemed, that Humankind was alone among the stars. By the mid-twenty-first century, it was understood that radio transmissions tended to fade out within a distance of two or three light years, becoming lost in the hash of random interstellar noise and background radiation. There was lots of radio and laser noise out there; it just required very large antenna and extremely fast computer processing to separate it from the background noise.

Large antennae and interferometry baselines of as much as several hundred AUs let sharp-eared AIs sift heterodyned signals out of the static. Alphekka had been a source of weak but numerous signals since the system had first come on-line, back in the mid-twenty-second century.

The fact that Alphekka was in the same general stretch of sky as Arcturus and Eta Boötis, just forty-some light years farther out, strongly suggested that the enemy had a presence there, most likely a military presence.

Disrupting that base with a long-range strike just might stop the enemy's steady advance into human-colonized space.

"Okay," he said. "I was checking to see if there was anything new on the Alphekkan transmissions. There isn't."

"There wouldn't be, of course. The signals we're reading on Pluto are seventy-two years old."

"I know. But there's been debate on whether what we're hearing out there is ship-to-ship stuff, like you might expect from a military force . . . or background chatter from a civilization. Looks like the jury's still out."

On the face of it, Alphekka was an unlikely place to find a civilization. The star consisted of a brilliant type A0 V blue-white star in a close binary embrace with a dimmer, yellow G5 V dwarf just 27 million kilometers away; these circled each other every 17.3 days. Together, the twin stars gave off forty-five times the light of Sol. There was also evidence of an extensive disk of debris and dust about the two stars, a possible solar system in the making . . . though xenoplanetologists still didn't understand how such a disk could have survived the gravitational perturbations caused by the binary system at its center.

But *something* strange was going on out there. The disk suggested that there were no planets in the system yet, or that any planets that *had* managed to form were still very young . . . a few hundred million years old at the most.

And that suggested that the radio traffic WHISPERS was eavesdropping on came from ships or star-orbiting bases—and Alphekka's location suggested that it was likely the Sh'daar or Turusch staging point for their operations at Arcturus and Eta Boötis, at least.

If only the Senate would authorize a mission to find out.

"It'll come, Alex," Mendelson told him. "The important thing is you're off the hook so far as Eta Boötis is concerned, a least for now. You'll be summoned to another virtual meeting with the Board of Inquiry tomorrow morning at 0900 for the official notification."

"Thanks, Karyn. I appreciate your telling me."

"Any time. So . . . you want to celebrate?"

"Celebrate? How?"

"I was thinking my quarters. Phobia Green-Alpha."

"It's pretty late."

"So? You'll be here when we have to report to the Directorate chambers in the morning."

Koenig and Mendelson had been lovers for a couple of years now, at least off and on. Deployments and reassignments tended to keep couples in the military apart—one reason that the military services tended to adopt the freewheeling polyamory of Earth's more mobile cultures. Such liaisons weren't exactly encouraged within the service, especially between people of different ranks, but so long as they didn't get in the way of routine or spark jealous rivalries, they were tolerated. Sexual relationships were definitely in the old "don't ask, don't tell" category that had once defined the homosexual liaisons of earlier centuries. Casual sex with Karyn would have been unthinkable when she'd been his commanding officer on the Lexington.

With them both rear admirals now, and working in different directorates, there was no reason whatsoever not to . . . "celebrate," as she'd put it.

"That sounds . . . very good," he said.

She smiled. "I'll expect you, then. You still have my pass code?"

"Yes. I'll be there in . . ." He checked his internal time. "Twenty minutes."

"I'll be waiting."

The logistics report, he decided, could wait.

Manhattan Ruins
North American Periphery
1850 hours, local time

Trevor Gray stood atop the ruined skyscraper, staring south into the mist-soaked evening. It was raining, a light sprinkling from a low cloud ceiling, with a chill wind bringing with it the smell of salt out of the south. His uniform kept his body dry and warm, but water dripped from his nose and ran down his cheeks, and he could feel within himself a hint of trembling, despite the smartsuit's warmth. This was the place from which he'd started in so many in-head replays of the events of five years ago, fifty meters above the hiss of the surf rolling in across East 32nd Street.

South, the gray water was dotted by hundreds of islands, most slumped into mounds, most covered over by vines and low-growing vegetation.

The Manhattan Ruins.

The vegetation-shrouded mounds were all that remained of thousands of buildings, separated from one another by narrow avenues of water, stretching for five and a half kilometers south southwest. A green forest of islands, interspersed with exposed beams and frameworks where concrete and glass had shattered and collapsed. The tallest were marked by flashing automated strobes, warning off low-flying aircraft and personal fliers.

He could just make out the green-shrouded mound of the TriBeCa Arcology, one large island among many, rising less than four kilometers to the south, shadowed and blurred behind the mist and in the fading evening light.

So what was he waiting for? The peaceforcers wouldn't stop him this time, even if travel to the Ruins was not something the Authority encouraged. So far as they were concerned, the squatties were illegals, squatters on what was still, technically, public property, men and women—social exiles by their own choosing—who either refused to fit in with the decent citizenry or people who were mentally ill and both unable to fit in and unwilling to apply for treatment.

He was still somewhat surprised that the peaceforcer captain he'd spoken with last had actually issued the pass. There was nothing standing in his way now from flying down to TriBeCa and looking up his old tribe.

But he found he didn't want to go. He'd traveled all this way, all the way from Mars for Void's sake . . . and now he didn't want to fly the last four kilometers.

Was he afraid of meeting Chiseler and Janine and Macro and the rest of his old tribe? Hell . . . they should be happy for him, right? He'd gotten his ticket punched for a one-way boost out of the Ruins. Plenty of creds, good food, free healthcare, high-tech perks like these water-shedding dress blacks, everything a squattie ever dreamed of.

Was he afraid because now *he* was the Authority?

Fuck that. He was decided now. Stooping, he picked up the gravcycle broom and switched it on, rolling into the saddle and kicking in a gentle boost.

On a wet day like this, Chiseler and the rest would be holed up inside TriBeCa Tower.

They would talk to him. They *had* to.

Squinting against the blast of spray against his face, he arrowed south through the mist-laden afternoon sky.

Chapter Eighteen

USNA Gallagher
Sol System Inner Kuiper Belt
0029 hours, TFT

Captain David Lederer let himself drift with the surging tide of incoming data. He'd received the first burst transmission at 2220 hours, just over two hours ago.

The destroyer *Gallagher* was on High Guard patrol, and had been fifteen and a half AUs from Neptune when the base on Triton had been destroyed. He'd immediately passed the warning in-system toward Mars and Earth, then ordered *Gallagher*'s grav drives fired up to five hundred gravities. For the past two hours now, the destroyer had been accelerating out into the Kuiper Belt. She'd covered .86 of an AU and was now moving at some 160 kilometers per second, and still accelerating.

He'd ordered a continuous-stream lock on Mars. The ship would continue broadcasting status reports, position and vector, and sensor updates for as long as she could.

Lederer had been with the Confederation contingent at Everdawn. He did not expect that he, his ship, or the four hundred men and women on board would survive the next few hours.

He'd also contacted four other High Guard ships within range, and they, too, were accelerating outward now—the

Chinese frigate *Jianghua*, the Indian States' *Godavari*, the Japanese *Hatakaze*, and the American *John Paul Jones*. Their chances for survival during the next few hours were no better than *Gallagher*'s.

The High Guard was one of the few truly international organizations operating out of Earth, a multinational task force designed primarily to monitor the outer reaches of the solar system, track asteroids and comets that might one day be a threat to Earth, and to watch for nudgers. The Earth Confederation had grown out of an economic partnership between the old United States and a number of other nations, most of them former members of the British Commonwealth—Canada, the Bahamas, Australia, and New Zealand. Several non-Commonwealth states had joined later on—Mexico, Brazil, Japan, and the Russian Federation.

The High Guard, however, included ships from the Chinese Hegemony, the Indian States, and the European Union as well, which perhaps made that organization more representative of the entire Earth than the Earth Confederation itself.

The Earth Confederation had become more than an economic alliance in 2132, toward the end of the Second Sino-Western War. In 2129, a Chinese warship, the *Xiang Yang Hong*, had used nuclear munitions to nudge three small asteroids in Main Belt orbits into new trajectories that, three years later, had entered circumlunar space, falling toward Earth.

The *Xiang Yang Hong* had almost certainly been operating independently; Beijing later claimed the captain had gone rogue when he learned of the destruction of his home city of Fuzhou, and had carried out what was essentially a terrorist operation. His plan had been to devastate both the United States and the European Union by dropping all three asteroids into the Atlantic Ocean, causing devastating tsunamis that would wipe out the coastal cities on two continents. U.S. and European fleet elements had destroyed two of the three incoming two-kilometer rocks in what became known as the Battle of Wormwood—a reference to a biblical prophecy in the Book of Revelation that sounded eerily like an asteroid hitting the ocean. One rock—a piece of it, actually, had gotten through, falling into the Atlantic halfway between West Africa and Brazil.

The devastation had been incalculable. The loss of life, fortunately, had been less than it might have been, since most of the world's coastline cities were already slowly being evacuated in the face of steadily rising sea levels. Even so, an estimated half billion people had died, from West Africa to Spain, France, and England, to the slowly submerging cities of the U.S. East Coast, to the vanishing islands of the Caribbean, to the coastlines of Brazil and Argentina. The ancient term *weapon of mass destruction* had, with that single deadly blow, taken on a radically new and expanded meaning. Coming hard on the heels of the deaths of 1.5 billion people in the Blood Death pandemic, Wormwood's fall into the Atlantic had come close to ending technic civilization across much of the Earth.

The partial success of the American-EU fleet, however, had spurred further cooperation, and the rapid expansion of the automated High Guard project that had been in place for the previous century. Every space-faring nation on the planet—even the recently defeated Chinese Hegemony—had contributed ships and personnel to the newly expanded High Guard, with the sacred charge that never again would mountains fall from the sky. The Guard's motto was "A Shield Against the Sky." Its headquarters was located in neutral Switzerland, at Geneva.

Two centuries later, with the Sh'daar Ultimatum, the High Guard offered the teeming worlds and colonies of the inner solar system their best first line of defense against this new and still mysterious enemy. Their charter had been expanded; besides watching for nudgers—the ships of nation-states or terrorists attempting to push asteroids or comets into new and Earth-threatening orbits—they were tasked with patrolling the outer perimeter of the solar system, identifying incoming ships and, if they were hostile, engaging them.

The High Guard's oath, a solemn and sacred promise sworn before the souls of those who had died at the Battle of Wormwood, both in space and in the thunderous doom of the incoming tsunamis, offered the lives of the High Guard's men and women as a literal shield against *any* threat from the solar system's depths.

It was an immense task . . . one far too vast to be practical. The High Guard currently numbered about two hundred warships, most of them aging Marshall-class destroyers like the *Gallagher*, or the even older Jackson-class frigates. At any given time, at least half of those vessels were in port for refit, maintenance, and resupply. Typically, they deployed for nine months at a time, patrolling out beyond the orbit of Neptune, serving as backup to the half million remote probes in the forty-AU shell.

That arbitrary shell around Sol gave scale to what was lightly called "the vastness of space." The surface area of a sphere with a radius of 40 astronomical units was over 20,000 square AUs . . . close to 450 *quintillion* square kilometers.

That worked out to one ship per four and a half quintillion square kilometers—an obvious impossibility. In fact, both patrols and remote sensors tended to be concentrated within about 30 degrees of the ecliptic, which cut down things a bit . . . but there was always the possibility that an enemy would sneak in from zenith or nadir, where tens of billions of kilometers separated one sentry from the next.

Thinly spread or not, in the thirty-seven years since the Sh'daar Ultimatum, not one alien vessel had approached Earth's solar system, and the general perception of the civilian population back home was that the war was far away, too far to be a threat.

According to the data flooding in through *Gallagher*'s sensors, that illusion of security had just been ripped away. At least thirty Turusch warships had materialized almost seven hours ago, some six light hours out from the sun and 25 degrees above the ecliptic . . . roughly in the same part of the sky as Arcturus and Eta Boötis. Exactly what they'd been doing since then was not clear; the ships weren't registering on long-range tracking, and no more data was coming through from Triton since that one, quick, burst transmission.

But Lederer could make a good guess. Confederation tactics called for launching a high-G fighter or near-c bombardment of the target immediately, so that local defenses were overwhelmed. It was possible that enemy near-c impactors were already approaching Earth.

The main fleet would accelerate toward the target behind the bombardment and fighters. Turusch ships, depending on their class, could accelerate at anywhere between three hundred and six hundred gravities. That meant that by now they could have traveled anywhere between one and two billion kilometers—say, between six and thirteen astronomical units.

Based on that data, and the assumption that the invaders would be heading for the inner system as quickly as possible, Lederer had given orders to attempt an intercept, calculating an IP—an intercept point—some five AUs ahead, just beyond the orbit of Neptune, and trailing that world by half a billion kilometers. Ideally, all five High Guard vessels would reach the IP within a few minutes of one another.

The operation was not unlike hitting one high-velocity bullet head-on simultaneously with four other bullets, with the marksmen all firing blindfolded. Still, *Gallagher* might be able to get close enough to send Earth an updated report . . . *if* the enemy fleet was behaving in a predictable manner.

And if there still was an Earth to report to.

"Nav, this is the captain," he said.

"Yeah, Skipper."

"If Triton went off the air, it probably means a strike there."

"Roger that, Skipper. Combat thinks it might have been near-c impacters."

"Right. But it's also possible that the Trash fleet showed up in person. They don't know anything about the layout of our solar system, no more than we know about theirs. The smart play might be to muster their fleet somewhere close to the first large outpost they pick up . . . and that would be Triton. From there, they could watch our response, scope out our defenses, maybe plan a long-range strike once they know where our orbital bases and inhabited worlds are."

"Makes sense, sir."

"I want you to prepare a series of course plots. Assume we don't find anything at the IP. I want you to give me a vector that will carry us into Neptune space. I also want a plot that will send one or two of our ships straight to Triton, bypassing the IP."

"Aye, aye, sir. Give me a moment here. . . ."

Five aging frigates and destroyers against at least thirty Turusch warships . . . probably more by now, probably a *lot* more.

The odds, he thought, were not at all good.

Manhattan Ruins
North American Periphery
2009 hours, local time

"Hello! Anyone here?"

Gray's voice echoed back at him from empty passageways and silent chambers. It seemed impossible that TriBeCa Arcology could be vacant . . . but he'd been searching through its halls for over an hour now, and he had yet to see any other humans.

He walked down the passageway leading to the suite of rooms he'd lived in with Angela, carrying the rented gravcycle over his shoulder. The broom was his ticket out of this place, and he knew that had he left it up on the roof where he'd landed, it would have been gone by the time he returned.

And *that* had been an odd point, too, now that he thought about it. His family had always maintained a watch up on the arc roof, but there'd been no one there when he'd landed. What in hell was going on?

"It's Trevor! Trevor Gray!" he yelled. He thought he heard a scuttling sound in the distance, the scrape of shoes on floor tiles. He wasn't certain. It *might* have been rats. "I'm looking for the TriBeCan Eagles! Is anyone here?"

The sun had set some time ago, and it was dark. Gray was wearing a small but powerful wristlight that illuminated the passageway ahead, but he was beginning to worry about getting lost in this maze.

He *thought* this was the way. . . .

Yes! That was the entrance to the rooms he'd shared with Angela!

Of course his old quarters had long since been occupied by someone else. Ragged curtains had been hung to divide large spaces into smaller, private areas. Mattresses and blankets lay on the floors. The remains of a cook fire, the ashes still warm to the touch, had blackened a patch on what once had been the floor of a sunken living room. None of this stuff was his, however. Others had moved in after he and Angela had gone.

Which was only to be expected. But . . . surely they would remember him? It had only been five years, after all.

"*Chiseler!*" he shouted, almost screaming the name.

He walked over to the living-room window, what once had been an actual wall-sized picture window and sliding door with a balcony outside. When he and Angela had lived here, the balcony had been long gone, crumbled away a century before, but the window had still been solid, a sheet of scratched and sun-clouded plasglas extending from floor to ceiling. The plasglas was gone now, the opening admitting a steady spray of cold mist from the ongoing drizzle outside.

Carefully, he put a hand out to one frame of the vanished door and looked down, four hundred meters to the water, the depths between island-buildings lost in the growing darkness below, though there was still pale light in the sky. Vines growing on the outside surface of the arcology were curling in through the missing window, and beginning to flourish on the inside.

So why hadn't the Authority reclaimed the Ruins? The largest buildings, like TriBeCa, were still sound. There'd been plans to rebuild the Old City out over the water using structures like the TriBeCa Arcology as pylons, he knew, for two centuries or more. It was technically feasible, at least.

There'd been no money for such projects after the Crash

in the late twenty-second century, when nanotech had overthrown the old economic models. But things were prosperous enough *now*. At least for the rest of the Confederation.

Maybe people just got used to things the way they were. So far as that peaceforcer up in Morningside Heights was concerned, the squatties had always been here, the Ruins always a place of danger and primitive discomfort.

It hadn't always been so, though. He and Angela had often stood on this spot, trying to imagine what life had been like when the Old City had been alive, vibrant with power and life, the first and greatest of the modern megalopoli. He'd seen old memory clips of the city before the first evacuations in the twenty-first century. Primitive . . . but astonishing, breathtaking, and miraculous in scope and in audacity, nonetheless.

He sensed, rather than heard, the movement at his back.

Gray spun, the gravcycle snapping down off his shoulder and into a port-arms position. The squattie was halfway across the sunken floor, short, black-haired, clad in stinking rags. He was holding a spear made from a lightweight metal rod with a kitchen knife taped to the end.

The man was rushing him, clearly intent on either stabbing Gray in the back or knocking him forward through the window, and into a four-hundred meter drop to the water below. Gray snapped out with the back end of the gravcycle, using it like a quarterstaff, blocking the man's lunge and sharply bending the light metal rod of his improvised spear.

"Stop!" Gray shouted. "I'm not your enemy!"

His attacker barked something in an unknown language, and Gray's eyes widened at a sudden realization. *His attacker was Asian.*

But that wasn't possible.

Tens of thousands of individual families had made up the fabric of squattie life and culture within the Manhattan Ruins, but above the family level—individual groups of twenty to fifty people—there'd been hierarchies of tribe and race—divisions along racial lines, for the most part, though there were plenty of tribal groupings based on nations of origin as well. Blacks. Whites. Latinos. Hindi. Paks. Thais. Viets. Chinese. Khmers. Russians. All of these were represented within the Ruins, and many, many more. Though families might raid and forage across most of the Ruins, from the Battery to the Bronx, they did so by trespassing on the turf of other tribes . . . and that was what made life in the Ruins so dangerous. Chinatown, just to the east of TriBeCa, remained an Asian enclave that stubbornly resisted the influx of other ethnic groups; when he and Angela had lived here, an agreement of sorts had existed between the TriBeCa families and Chinatown, to the effect that each stayed out of the other's turf, maintaining a wary truce. The islands beyond Broadway Canyon and south of the Canal were deadly to non-ethnic Chinese.

Gray couldn't decide if the man in front of him was North Chinese, Korean, or Japanese. The language had sounded more like Japanese—explosive and guttural—rather than like the more musical Mandarin or Cantonese. His rags included a fairly new-looking smartsuit jacket, presumably scavenged from the ruins of some clothing store, but the indicator light at the collar wasn't on, so it wasn't powered. Most smartsuits could maintain a comfortable temperature, interface with local Net-Clouds in order to pull down weather reports and other data, or serve as communications centers . . . but some used biofeedback to enhance significantly the wearer's speed and strength. If Gray had to face someone hand-to-hand, he didn't want them wearing one of *those* things.

"Take it easy!" Gray said, motioning with his hand. His mind was racing. If Asians were here in TriBeCa, it could only mean the old families, including Gray's family, the Eagles, had left, driven out, perhaps, when the truce had failed. "Do you understand me?"

The man barked something again, the words unintelligible, then lunged again with his bent spear. Gray sidestepped the thrust, snapped his broom up and around, knocking the man flat on his back.

Shit. The peaceforcer had said there'd been changes in the Ruins. And something about the inhabitants killing each other even more enthusiastically than usual.

If the truce had failed, if the Chinese had moved in on

TriBeCa, there was no telling where the rest of his family was now. Hell, it hadn't been that long since captured enemies had been skinned and suspended still living from building walls as no-trespass warnings to marauders, and there were still occasional stories, whispered and wildly embellished, of cannibalism and mass murder among the crumbling islands. Life in the Manhattan Ruins had never been easy, but at times it got downright *interesting*. Hellishly so.

His family might have migrated to another part of the Ruins, moving in with allies, possibly, or taking away some other group's hab space to replace the hab stolen from them. That was the way of life in the Ruins.

Or the Eagles might all have been butchered. That, too, was life—and death—in the Old City.

It was strange . . . and a bit unnerving. Just five years ago, Gray had been a squattie, a life he didn't particularly like, but which he accepted, and which he'd been convinced was better than life under the Authority.

But now . . .

The man on the floor groaned and stirred. There was no point in interrogating him; Gray doubted that he spoke English. Once the Authority had withdrawn from the Ruins, individual families and tribes had pretty much fallen back on the customs and languages of their individual ethnicities, and English was a second language, if it was even known at all.

He set his broom on the floor, stretched out on the seat and let the safety harness engage, then gave it a boost and rolled for the open window. Cold, wet air engulfed him as he fell . . . and then he was feeding in power and leveling off, flying toward the south.

He wasn't at all certain where he was going now.

Admiral Karyn Mendelson's Quarters
Mars Synchorbit, Sol System
0234 hours, TFT

Alex Koenig and Karyn Mendelson both snapped awake at the same instant, the Priority One alert sounding within both of their minds, yanking them from a deep, sex-induced slumber. They were still entangled with each other, holding each other, staring into each other's eyes from just a few centimeters apart.

"Lights!" Mendelson called, and the bedroom lights came up. Rolling out of opposite sides of the bed, they began reaching for articles of clothing scattered on the deck a few hours earlier.

"P-A!" Koenig called, summoning his Personal Assistant out of the Net-Cloud as he stepped into his underpants. "What the fuck is going on?"

"A Priority One defense alert has just been issued by the Military Directorate," his AI replied. "An announcement follows."

He and Mendelson exchanged glances as they continued getting dressed. She'd evidently gotten the same news from her AI.

"To all military personnel within range of this Net-Cloud. This is Admiral John C. Carruthers of the Confederation Joint Command Staff." Carruthers was the five-star admiral on the Joint Chiefs, the senior military officer, under the civilian secretary of defense, of the Confederation Navy. "At approximately seventeen hundred forty-five hours Fleet Time yesterday, a large Turusch battle fleet began dropping into normal space, forty-five astronomical units from Sol, roughly on a line between Earth and the constellation Boötis. The photon release of that emergence was detected by our automated systems roughly three hours later, and a warning broadcasted to our listening post on Triton. One hour after that, contact with Triton was lost. We must now assume that Turusch fleet elements have destroyed that base.

"High Guard elements are seeking to close with the intruders in order to gather more intelligence. We do not expect them to materially hamper the enemy's operations.

"The Senate president and the secretary of defense have authorized me to declare an immediate crimson alert, and to scramble *all*, repeat *all* available military and High Guard vessels for the defense of the Inner System. We do not at this time know how much time we have or whether the enemy has launched a high-velocity preemptive strike against Inner System targets. In light of this latter possibility, it is imperative that all ships launch in the shortest possible time.

"Repeating. To all military personnel . . ."

Having heard and acknowledged the alert, Koenig and Mendelson were able to switch it off. Koenig finished pulling on his uniform jacket as Mendelson shrugged into a military smartsuit. "Where are you going?" he asked.

"My duty station," she replied. "Phobia's CIC. I'm on Admiral Henderson's command staff. You're headed for the *America*." It wasn't a question.

"If I get there in time." He gave a wan grin. "Buchanan's still aboard. He'll be readying her for boost by now."

"Good luck, Alex."

"And you, Karyn. Stay . . ." He stopped. He'd been about to say "Stay safe," but that wasn't an option for naval personnel, who by long tradition went into harm's way. "Stay out of trouble," he finished lamely. "I'll see you when we get back."

He didn't add that there was a distinct possibility that the promised meeting would never happen.

Liberty Column
North American Periphery
2134 hours, local time

Trevor Gray sat alone atop the crown of the ancient Statue of Liberty.

Once, Lady Liberty had stood at a much lower elevation, the statue and its pedestal and foundation rising some 93 meters from an irregular, eleven-pointed star-shaped base. In the late twenty-first century, as rising sea levels had repeatedly threatened New York City and promised to completely drown little Liberty Island, the old pedestal had been replaced by a new, taller column. That column now thrust up out of the black waters submerging Liberty Island, supporting the 40-meter copper statue some 120 meters above the new sea level.

Technically, the Statue of Liberty still belonged to the old U.S. government, by way of the National Park Service and under the provisions of the Confederation Charter. She had fallen on hard times lately, however. Low-voltage electrical charges, generated by the interaction of salt water and corroding copper, were slowly loosening the Lady's rivets. The upper six meters of her arm had broken off and fallen into the sea long ago. Like plans to reclaim Manhattan, the ancient icon of liberty was being forgotten, the statue allowed to collapse into ruin.

You could see her from the southern and western windows of TriBeCa, though, at least when the weather was clear, and she'd always been a powerful and deeply moving symbol for Gray. Life in the Ruins, even when it was brutish and short, was supposed to be about *liberty*.

He sat on Lady Liberty's hairline immediately in front of the gaping windows lining the front of her crown, his legs dangling over the side. In the darkness off to his left, to the north, the Ruins loomed across New York Harbor, the hundreds of individual green-cloaked islands merging into shadows upon shadows. The tallest islands were marked by strobing navigational beacons, warning off low-flying aircraft or personal fliers. Beyond, the New City gave off a glow as intense as a false dawn, backlighting the darkened islands.

The rain had ended an hour ago, and the sky was clearing. To the south, out over the ocean, he could see the faint, in-line stars of SupraQuito twinkling some 50 degrees above the horizon.

Gray was feeling torn, torn between past and present, between what he'd been and what he'd become. Given time, he thought he could track down the Eagle family, if there were any left alive. Once daybreak illuminated the Ruins, he could fly in, spot a scavenger or, better, a hunting party, and question them.

Just so long as the Chinese hadn't taken over the entire mass of islands.

But that was impossible. Unless they'd gotten hold of a cache of military weaponry, they couldn't possibly take over the entire expanse of Manhattan. They simply didn't have the numbers.

He was still coming to grips with the fact that the place he'd thought of as *home* for all these years, including his years in the Navy, was gone. It left him feeling adrift in a way he'd never felt during his five years of military service.

It felt like he no longer had a home to come home to.

Worse, it felt like home was now shipboard. His berth aboard the *America*. The thought was unsettling, and left him depressed and bitter. What was left for him . . . going back to the Navy and serving out a twenty-year career? *Then* what?

He wondered if he dared fly back up to Morningside Heights and see if he could see Angela. She'd seemed pretty definite about not wanting to see him anymore, but she could have changed.

It was possible, at least. . . .

The shrill bleat of an in-head warning signal so startled him he nearly fell off of his precarious perch. *Damn* it! How was it possible? There was no Net-Cloud here, the peace-forcer had told him. The signal must be being punched through at extraordinarily high power from synchorbit itself, bypassing the local Net-Cloud nodes and transmitting directly to individual in-head units.

"To all military personnel within range of this Net-Cloud," a voice announced, sharp in his head. "This is Admiral John C. Carruthers of the Confederation Joint Command Staff. . . ."

And suddenly things were *very* much more serious indeed.

Chapter Nineteen

USNA Gallagher
Neptune Space, Sol System
0250 hours, TFT

The IP had come up empty.

The five High Guard vessels had rendezvoused in a high-velocity pass-through, but there'd been nothing there within range of their scanners. Captain Lederer had ordered the release of a dozen battlespace drones, set to disperse through local space and transmit anything they detected both to the *Gallagher* and to the Inner System. However, the good news for the moment was that the Turusch fleet was not in a hurry to reach Earth.

A careful scan of ambient space for the ionization trails left by near-c impactors or high-V fighters turned up nothing as well. Local space was thin—no more than a hydrogen atom or two per cubic centimeter, but the passage of anything traveling at a generous percentage of the speed of light swept up some of those atoms and ionized others, leaving a faint but detectable trail. The lack of such trails suggested that the enemy had not started bombarding the Inner System.

All *very* good news.

But that left the question of just where they were and what they were doing. That they *would* eventually head in-system was patently obvious. If they waited too long, the tactical advantage would pass to the Confederation.

So where in this hell of frozen emptiness were they?

Following the op plan drawn up by *Gallagher*'s navigational team, Lederer had ordered the tiny flotilla to apply side thrust, slightly changing their vector, until they were on a course taking them directly into the Neptune system. Neptune was ahead of the High Guard flotilla in its orbit and, at the moment, its moon Triton was located on the far side of the planet from the approaching ships. The alignment offered Lederer and the other High Guard captains a unique tactical advantage.

If the enemy fleet had gathered at Triton, perhaps the High Guard squadron could sneak up on them, using giant Neptune as a screen.

Lederer leaned forward in his recliner, studying the three-dimensional tactical display of local space. The other four High Guard ships, another destroyer and three frigates, trailed along behind the *Gallagher* in line-ahead. Ahead, less than half an AU now, lay the planet Neptune, shown in the display as an actual image, a tiny sea-blue sphere, rather than as an icon.

He was searching for some sign of the enemy fleet.

There were several ways of spotting other ships at a distance. Radar and lidar, of course, assuming the target wasn't cloaked in either a grav-field effect or adaptive surface nano that absorbed those wavelengths rather than reflecting them back. Fusion power plants gave off neutrinos—but most modern Confederation ships used quantum zero-point field emission plants now, and it was thought that Turusch ships were powered by vacuum energy as well. A ship under drive was projecting artificial gravitational singularities either ahead or astern, and those created ripples—gravity waves—in the fabric of space that could be detected at considerable distances.

Gravity waves were transmitted at the speed of light; they also vanished when a ship's singularity projectors were switched off. And even when plowing ahead at full speed, gravity waves tended to fuzz out and vanish in the background static of normal matter. The local star, planets, even asteroidal debris or large starships could damp out the space/time ripples from a projected singularity within a distance of a few astronomical units.

The best and most unambiguous way of detecting an enemy fleet was by the intense burst of photons released as it dropped below light speed. Under Alcubierre Drive and similar FTL systems, a starship essentially had no velocity at all in relation to the folded-up pocket of space within which it traveled. When the drive field was switched off, the ship was dumped into normal space with only a small residual velocity; the ship had carried a tremendous potential energy, however, much of which bled off into the local space/time background as an intense and expanding ring of radiation.

So far, thirty-three such flashes had been detected out in the Kuiper Belt, ranging from forty-five AUs from Sol out to more than eighty. The incoming Turusch had scattered badly. They needed a rendezvous point, and Neptune, it seemed, was the nearest convenient large object. In the past hours, however, the enemy fleet had vanished . . . save for the clue offered by the sudden silence of the base on Triton. The enemy could be anywhere, with its drives shut down and its shields up, effectively invisible.

But with shields up, it was difficult to impossible to detect ships outside your own little pocket universe; with shields up you were as cut off from the universe outside as you were under Alcubierre Drive. It was possible, even likely, that the enemy fleet had their shields full up in order to mask their presence.

Twelve minutes to go.

After four hours at five hundred gravities, *Gallagher* was coming in toward Neptune's horizon at 72,000 kilometers per second—nearly one quarter of the speed of light. Half an AU was fifteen minutes at that speed. He called up *Gallagher*'s ephemeris data, studying it.

Since icy little Pluto had been demoted from planet status in the early twenty-first century, Neptune had held the honor of being the solar system's outer planetary sentinel. Pure

chance that it had happened to be in the same part of the
sky where the Turusch had emerged from their equivalent
of Alcubierre Drive, of course; at thirty AUs from the sun,
Neptune took 165 years to complete one solar orbit. Because the atmospheres of both Neptune and of its near-twin
Uranus were slightly different from those of the larger gas
giants, Jupiter and Saturn, so much farther in toward the
sun's warmth and light, the two were officially known as
ice giants.

Neptune's large moon Triton was just visible beyond the
planet's limb, not perfectly masked by the planet from this
position, but close.

Current theory stated that Triton had started out as a trans-
Neptunian Kuiper object . . . a dwarf planet like Pluto or Eris.
Its retrograde orbit—unique for such a large moon—showed
that it had been captured by Neptune in eons past, probably in the early days of the solar system, when Neptune's
orbit migrated outward from between Saturn and Uranus to
its present position. Triton, in fact, was slightly larger than
Pluto; the surface composition of the two—frozen nitrogen,
water ice, and frozen carbon dioxide—was nearly identical.
Its surface temperature hovered at just 38 degrees Celsius
above absolute zero, a few degrees colder even than the
mean temperature on Pluto.

"We're coming up on the final course correction, Skipper,"
the Nav Officer told him, his voice edged with excitement.
Lieutenant Raymond Seborg was a washout from Oceana, a
would-be fighter-jock who'd ended up in the High Guard on
the fast track to line command. The bridge crew still teased
him about his predilection for handling a 220-meter-long
destroyer like a Starhawk fighter.

"Very well, Mr. Seborg." He opened his intercom link.
"All hands, this is the captain. We're about to drop into
MGF. So far, there's no sign that the enemy has seen us . . .
or even that the enemy is here at all. Stay alert, and record
everything that happens. When things start happening,
they're going to happen *fast*."

MGF was the acronym for microgravitic flight . . . a fancy
way of saying that the drive singularities would be shut down

and the *Gallagher* would be falling solely under the influences of nearby planetary bodies, and its current velocity.

"Mr. Carlyle," he added. "Shields to ninety percent, please."

"Shields at nine-zero percent, aye, aye, sir."

That would provide a reasonable level of protection, while allowing *Gallagher*'s sensors to continue to probe nearby space.

Astern, the other ships fell into the agreed-upon formation, a rough wedge with *Gallagher* at the leading point.

Getting the other four High Guard captains to follow his lead had been a real treat in and of itself. Balakrishnan on the *Godavari* was senior to Lederer by two years, and Zeng, of the *Jianghua*, had argued that the flotilla's strategic decisions should be put to a vote. The High Guard, rather than maintaining a strict hierarchy of command, had been established as a free participation among the space-faring nations of Earth, under the direction of a multinational board of command. It worked well enough for organizing and sending out routine patrols, but was somewhat lacking when faced with a distinct *military* threat.

Lederer had bulled through by saying the others could follow his lead or get the hell out and return to the Inner System.

He'd broken all the rules of diplomacy, protocol, and international propriety, but they'd followed.

On the forward display, Neptune was rapidly growing larger, swelling from a blue dot lost among the stars to a half-phase, faintly banded giant. The small flotilla was falling toward Neptune's south polar region; the planet was circled by fragmentary rings or ring arcs, which would make a high-velocity pass over the equatorial areas deadly.

The blue planet continued growing larger, and the distant red speck that was Triton dropped behind the horizon.

"Captain Lederer," the ship's AI said, "sensors are picking up numerous IR and radio wavelength anomalies within several million kilometers of Triton. The data are consistent with the presence of numerous large starships similar in configuration to those operated by the Turusch."

"Thank you, Galley," Lederer replied. The news was at once reassuring and frightening. It suggested that his guess had been right, that the alien fleet had closed in on Triton, then settled down to wait.

"Comm!" He added. "Are we transmitting?"

"Yes, sir. We're sending it off as soon as we get it. Time lag to Earth, two hundred thirty-eight minutes. Time lag to Mars two hundred forty-five minutes."

"Roger that."

One minute to go. Neptune filled the forward screen, rushing out to block out half of the entire surrounding sky. Seborg's last maneuver had nudged the *Gallagher* just enough to send the High Guard ship skimming within a thousand kilometers of Neptune's cloud deck, close enough that they'd be burning through the tenuous outer layers of the huge planet's atmosphere.

At a quarter of the speed of light, their passage through that tenuous atmosphere would be spectacular, but *extremely* brief.

It would also announce their arrival in rather definite terms, but the chances were good that the enemy had spotted them already. Even with their shields up, remote drones and sensors scattered throughout the area would be watching everything entering local space.

He wished there were a way for the little squadron to somehow strike at the enemy, but that was impossible. With no hard data on any targets near Triton, aiming would have been problematic. It was a moot point in any case. High Guard ships carried fusion bombs to nudge asteroids into new and non–Earth-threatening trajectories, but no ranged weapons. The destroyer's missile launchers and particle-beam projectors all had been stripped out long ago to make more room for consumables on extended deep-space patrols.

There was a flash, then darkness as *Gallagher*'s shields went up full, together with a savage shock as the spacecraft tunneled through several thousand kilometers of hydrogen gas in a fraction of a second. They emerged on the far side, their trajectory slightly reshaped by Neptune's gravity well.

They were now 350,000 kilometers from Triton—less

than the distance from Earth to Earth's moon. At their current velocity, they would cross that distance in slightly less than five seconds.

"*Enemy ships!*" Alys Newton, his scanner officer shouted. "*I've got—*"

Something struck the *Gallagher* amidships, a hammer-blow jolting the ship hard enough to snap internal struts and braces. Shields collapsed as power feeds were broken, and a large chunk of the ship's aft section ripped free, sending the rest of the destroyer into an out-of-control tumble.

In the tactical display, bright white, expanding spheres of light marked the deaths of the *Jianghua* and the *Hatakaze*. The icons representing both the *John Paul Johns* and the *Godavari* were flashing on and off rapidly, indicating serious damage. There wasn't even time to determine just what had hit them. Things were happening far too fast.

The scanners stayed on-line long enough for Lederer, pinned to his couch by sudden centripetal acceleration, to glimpse the odd mixed blue and pink hues of Triton as the moon flashed past less than five thousand kilometers away. Seborg's calculations had been uncannily precise.

Then the scanners went down, as did the last of the shields.

Lederer heard the roar of escaping atmosphere as the tumbling ship continued to come apart. "Comm! Are we still transmitting?"

"Yes, sir!" Her reply seemed muted in the fast-dropping pressure of the bridge.

"All hands, this is the captain! Abandon ship! Repeat, abandon ship!"

He already knew that most of them would never make it to the life pods. Even if they did, the chances of being picked up *this* far out, moving this fast, were next to nill.

But if their automated scanners had picked up the enemy's positions and orbits, and if that data had been transmitted to Earth, then *Gallagher* and her sister High Guard ships had successfully accomplished their mission.

It was, Lederer thought, a fitting epitaph for ships and crews alike.

CIC, TC/USNA CVS America
Mars Synchorbit, Sol System
0258 hours, TFT

Koenig had made it on board the *America* just in time. The
ship was already casting off its magnetic grapples, and only
a single passenger tube remained connecting the vessel's
spine with the dock facility. Koenig had boarded a gravtube
for the ten-minute trip to the dock, then elbowed his way
on board along with hundreds of other personnel returning
from liberty. An enlisted rating had volunteered to serve as
his personal shoehorn, pulling his way along the microgravity passageway bellowing "Gangway! Make a hole! Admiral
coming through!"

Pulling himself into the hub accessway, he made his
way hand-over-hand to the command deck, the bridge
and CIC tucked in along the spine close behind *America*'s
shield.

Quintanilla was waiting for him in CIC, reclining in his
seat, watching the painfully slow movement of ships in the
tactical display. "We have our orders from the Military Directorate," the man said. "The fleet is to take up a holding
position between Earth and Mars until we know what the
enemy plans to do."

"Get the *fuck* out of my seat," Koenig replied.

"I was just—"

"You were just about to get yourself ejected from my CIC
again," Koenig growled. Technically, he'd not yet had that
morning meeting with the Board of Inquiry, and wasn't supposed to know yet that he'd been cleared. He wondered if
Quintanilla knew.

Quintanilla looked as though he were about to argue, but
then evidently thought better of it. Koenig was tired, recently woken from too little sleep, and obviously was in no
mood for back talk.

"Welcome aboard, Admiral," Buchanan told him from the
bridge.

"Situation?" Koenig demanded.

"*America* is ready to cast off. We're just taking the last few liberty personnel back on board. Zero-point fields running and tuned, ready to deliver at one hundred percent."

"Very well. Commander Craig? Battlegroup status."

"The battlegroup is forming up and preparing for boost," Craig replied. "*Symmons, Puller, Doyle, Milton,* and *Kinkaid* have already cast off and are maneuvering clear of the dock area. *Ticonderoga* reports readiness to depart. *California, Andreyev, Arkansas,* and *Wyecoff* all report ready for release from dock. *Saskatchewan* reports they will be ready for release in five minutes. Battlegroup orders have been received and are awaiting your acknowledgement."

"Thank you."

Placing his palm over the through-put circuitry on the arm of his recliner, Koenig opened a window in his head and mindclicked the orders icon. There were two sets of orders, in fact, one from the Senate Military Directorate, and one from Admiral John C. Caruthers on the Joint Chiefs of Staff. As Quintanilla had told him, the Directorate was ordering all Confederation ships to rendezvous at a single point roughly midway between Earth and Mars, designated Solar One. At their current points in their orbits around the sun, Mars was roughly at the eleven-o'clock position, Earth at seven o'clock, Solar One at nine, and with Neptune in the direction of nine o'clock, thirty astronomical units out.

The orders from Caruthers, however, offered a little more leeway. "The body of the Confederation fleet is to rendezvous at Solar One," the recording said, "until we are certain of the enemy's attack path into the Inner System. When all fleet elements are assembled and at full combat readiness, they will proceed to move out-system in order to intercept the enemy as far from Sol as possible. Minor fleet elements will be deployed to forward positions to monitor and confirm the enemy's approach. . . ."

Koenig had his own ideas on the matter.

No one in the Confederation could be said to be a true expert on Turusch tactics or combat doctrine. Only two people even approached that description—Admiral Karyn Mendelson, who'd commanded the Confederation fleet at Arcturus last year . . .

. . . and Koenig himself, after the Battle of Eta Boötis.

Karyn had been reassigned to Henderson's command staff after Arcturus—not as punishment, exactly, but it certainly couldn't be called a reward. With the carrier *Hornet* crippled and nearly destroyed at Arcturus, she'd been yanked from her position as CO of Battlegroup Hornet and given the new assignment at Confederation Fleet Headquarters, jockeying virtual departments, AI simulations and data download archives.

His pillow talk with Karyn last night had been about Turusch tactics, comparing the battle at Arcturus with Eta Boötis, and especially discussing what Koenig felt might be a key weakness that Confederation forces could exploit.

They were conservative.

Not in a political sense, of course. But the Turusch, even when they possessed overwhelming superiority of numbers and fleet tonnage, as had been the case both at Arcturus and at Eta Boötis, tended move slowly and they tended to be careful not to overextend themselves. At Eta Boötis, the asteroid ship—likely the enemy's command vessel or flagship—had withdrawn as soon as it came under direct threat, even though the rest of the Turusch fleet seemed to be winning, and the rest of the fleet had retreated as well. Koenig hadn't understood what the Turusch had been doing at the time, but he thought he saw their reasoning now. They tended to take the long view, conserving forces, avoiding unnecessary damage, and where possible, outwaiting the enemy.

In fact, it was possible that the Sh'daar were actually running the show . . . and that implied an even greater conservatism. If it was true that the mysterious Sh'daar had been around for half a billion years, they, likely, would be even more loath to make a hasty move or a snap judgment. The fact that fifty-five years had passed between the first human contact with the Spiders and the Sh'daar Ultimatum seemed to confirm that guess. The Sh'daar were cautious, moving slowly, taking their time to decide the best course, and taking no chances.

The Senate Military Directorate was playing it cautious as well, it seemed. By holding the majority of the Confederation fleet at Solar One, they would be in a position to move to either Mars or Earth once the Turusch approach path was known with precision. Admiral Caruthers would be planning a defensive fight; the Senate would be urging him to keep the fleet close to Earth, and not to take chances.

The problem was that if the Sh'daar/Turusch warfleet had decided to attack the Sol System, they would be coming in "loaded for bear"—an extinct mammal, Koenig gathered, that had been massive, extremely fierce, and hard to kill. In fact . . .

Koenig's brow wrinkled as he took another look at the tactical updates. The display still showed thirty-three Turusch ships at an emergence point within the constellation Pisces. Neptune, currently, was in Taurus, some 30 degrees further east.

A number of things were not adding up.

The presumed initial destination of the enemy fleet, of course, was Neptune. The Confederation base on Triton had been destroyed five hours ago. By now, the High Guard ships that had helped pass the word of the initial attack would have reached Neptune; their report—if they survived to make one—would not reach Earth for another three and a half hours.

Until then, the presumption was that the enemy fleet was at Neptune . . . but it was a presumption that bothered Koenig.

For one thing, there were far too few ships out there. The Turusch had mustered more than fifty ships for the attack on Eta Boötis, and that was for the bombardment of a small and lightly defended base. They wouldn't have known going in that the Marines were there waiting for them, or that Battlegroup *America* would show up three weeks later.

Now they were, presumably, launching an assault on the human homeworld, a star system certain to possess numerous bases, colonies, and planetary defense systems.

And they only sent thirty-three ships?

Something was very seriously wrong with the tactical picture.

"Admiral?" Buchanan's voice asked, interrupting his thoughts. "All personnel are on board, except for a few who were taking liberty on Earth. We are ready to cast off."

"Do it," Koenig replied, distracted. He noted the time: 0308 hours.

"Aye, aye, sir. Helm! Maneuvering thrusters! Take us clear of the dock."

Koenig felt the faint shudder as magnetic grapples released. The microgravity of CIC was momentarily interrupted by a hard nudge—the maneuvering thrusters firing to ease the kilometer-long star carrier clear. The external view displayed across CIC's curving bulkheads showed the close-knit crisscross of struts and girders in the space dock gantry that now were receding at twenty meters per second.

Only thirty-three ships. That didn't make any sense whatsoever. When Koenig had been planning to launch an incursion to Alphekka, Crown Arrow, he'd been planning on one hundred ships, including four carriers. And Alphekka, young, raw, and hot, wasn't the home system of the Turusch or anybody else. At most it was only a logistics base or military staging area.

The Turusch would have to be insane as a species even to consider taking on the home system of Humankind with thirty-three ships.

But thirty-three ships would make a good diversion.

Neptune was in the constellation Taurus, at a right ascension of four hours. The Turusch had emerged from metaspace in Pisces—around right ascension one hour. But if the Turusch were coming straight to Sol from either Eta Boötis or Alphekka, they would arrive first almost halfway around the sky—somewhere in the constellations of Boötis or Corona Borealis . . . say, somewhere around a right ascension of fifteen hours.

Did the Sh'daar empire completely surround Sol and the handful of star systems explored and colonized so far by men? Or had they sent those thirty-three ships on a long, round-about flank march, to have them approach Sol from Pisces, that part of the sky almost directly opposite Boötis and Corona Borealis?

Of one thing Koenig was certain. The enemy would not do such a thing for no reason . . . and right now the best reason Koenig could think of was that the Turusch wanted to focus the Confederation Navy's attention on Taurus and Pisces right now.

Perhaps while the main fleet came in on a straight line from Eta Boötis or Alphekka. If they came fast enough, moved deep enough into the solar system before dropping out of metaspace, they might catch the majority of the Confederation fleet tens of AUs away from Earth . . . and accelerating in the wrong direction.

"God in heaven," Koenig said softly.

"Is there a problem, Admiral?" Quintanilla asked. He was floating near the admiral's couch.

"Yes, Mr. Quintanilla, there is. I think the Turusch are trying to pull a fast one on us."

"Indeed?"

"Neptune is a diversion," Koenig said. "They're coming from the opposite side of the solar system."

"And how do you figure that?"

"It's what I would have done."

"Admiral, the Joint Chiefs have given the matter considerable thought, and—"

"Comm!" Koenig barked, cutting Quintanilla off. "Put me through to Admiral Caruthers."

He needed to discuss this with someone higher up in the command hierarchy.

And there wouldn't be much time left.

Chapter Twenty

CIC, TC/USNA CVS America
Mars Synchorbit, Sol System
0311 hours, TFT

"I think, Admiral," Koenig said, "that Neptune is a trap."

He was simlinked with Caruthers, standing in a virtual meeting space representing a conference room in Phobia. A holographic display of Neptune glowed in the center of the room, with dozens of straight white lines marking the planned trajectories of Confederation fleet elements. Triton was a small green-and-gray globe far off to one side.

"And just what do you suggest, Koenig?" Caruthers replied. He was an older, harassed-looking man, white-haired, with a perpetually worried expression. Koenig honestly couldn't tell whether the icon he was interacting with represented the real Caruthers' current appearance, or if he always looked this way, even when all hell *wasn't* breaking loose.

Koenig manipulated the three dimensional map, pulling back to show the orbits of all eight planets. "Neptune and Triton," he said, and a red symbol winked on at nine o'clock. "The Turusch emergence at Point Pisces," and a second red light winked on at about ten o'clock. "And where the main enemy fleet will strike, *if* I'm right." A red light came on all the way around on the far side of the sun, at two o'clock.

"They may already have ships out there. We don't have anything looking for them out that way. I would like to take my battlegroup out to *this* area—call it Point Libra. We launch a fighter strike ahead of us. They could be thirty AUs out in four hours, objective."

"And how many ships in your battlegroup?"

"Twelve, sir. Not counting auxiliaries." But they would be leaving the auxiliaries behind in any case.

"That's twelve ships we're going to need to defend Earth. If you're wrong, Admiral, I'll be crippling my defense."

"Sir . . . we've detected thirty-three ships at Point Pisces. *Thirty-three ships.* You know what that means. Where are the rest of them?"

"I understand that. But why have the main fleet come in from *that* direction, just because it faces Boötis and Corona Borealis? Why come in on the solar ecliptic at all? Why not from the zenith, or the nadir?"

"Because they'll want to keep open lines of retreat that don't pass through our space." He was remembering the Turusch retreat back at Eta Boötis. They'd pulled off in the direction of Alphekka—further confirmation that that star was their staging area. "I agree they'll come in off-ecliptic. My guess is they'll emerge somewhere in southern Boötis or Serpens Caput, not down in Libra."

"We'd be better off keeping the entire fleet in close, waiting for them to come to us. From whatever direction."

"Sir, I must disagree. That would put us in exactly the same tactical situation as the Turusch at Eta Boötis. You've seen the after-action?"

"I've read your report, Admiral, yes. And that's the only reason I'm even listening to this."

"The enemy may already have launched near-c impactors. They would be foolish not to. That would give them the chance to inflict damage on our fleet and planetary defense facilities before the ship action even begins."

"If they'd launched impactors when they first emerged," Caruthers pointed out, "we would have been hit around midnight. Three hours ago."

"They're scoping us out, Admiral. Identifying planets,

population centers, military facilities, orbital manufactories, ship positions. And they need to watch all of those long enough to be able to predict orbits."

"Which is why we're moving our fleet elements, getting them out of the space docks." He sounded impatient, and Koenig could guess just how busy he was right now, marshalling as many ships as possible for the defense of Earth.

"Of course. But we can't change the orbits of Earth and Mars. Or move our major bases, like Phobia and SupraQuito."

"I know . . ." Caruthers was silent for a long moment. "There's been no warning from our High Guard automated probes out that way. Not since the original alert last night."

"Agreed." That was the one weak point in his reasoning, he knew. The probes had picked up Force Alpha. Why hadn't they detected the hypothetical Force Bravo? "But if the enemy was aware of our detector net, they might have found a way to nullify it."

"That's a long string of suppositions," Caruthers said. He hesitated again. "Admiral Koenig . . . I appreciate what you're saying. But there's just too much space to cover. I send you out to the area of Corona Borealis, and they pop in at Libra. Or, hell, Octans, or Ursa Minor. I'd be dividing my fleet in the face of the enemy, with a very good chance that you would never engage the enemy at all. And this time there's just too much at stake. Damn it, we could be looking at the destruction of human civilization."

"I understand, Admiral Caruthers. What I'm suggesting, though, is to launch four of *America*'s fighter squadrons. Divide them up into two-ship elements. We send one toward Boötis, one toward Libra, one toward Corona Borealis. Hell, one to Octans, if you insist . . . although I'm absolutely convinced they're going to be coming through more or less on a straight line from the direction of either Eta Boötis or Alphekka, probably Alphekka. It will take them four hours to get out to the thirty-AU shell.

"Now look at this." On the solar-system diagram, a straight red line drew itself from Neptune, at nine o'clock, across the solar system to Point Libra, at two. "Let's call the thirty-three ships at Neptune Force Alpha. The *real* strike force, over here at Point Libra, is Force Bravo. Okay?"

Caruthers' image nodded.

"Alpha has been gathering data on our Inner System for nine hours plus now, since they dropped out of metaspace at 1745 yesterday. My guess is that they started beaming that data from Pisces to Libra immediately. Force Alpha, or a part of it, then moved to Neptune-Triton, but they continued beaming updates to Libra. The Libra force is going to need the most recent data on our fleet deployment possible."

"Okay . . ."

"Look here." The image magnified, zooming in on the red line. At the chord's midpoint, the line skimmed close to another icon, a small yellow point.

"What's that?" Caruthers asked, even as he triggered the data block.

"A deep-space communications relay at 60558 Echeclus. Close to its aphelion right now, fifteen AUs from the sun. A Centaur . . ."

Centaurs were a type of asteroid or comet—they showed characteristics of both—first catalogued with the discovery of Chiron in 1977. Echeclus—pronounced "Eh-*kek*-les"—had been discovered more than two decades later, in 2000. In 2178 an automated communications relay had been built on it. Its thirty-five year orbit took it from just outside of Jupiter's orbit to several AUs inside the orbit of Uranus. There wasn't much to the thing—an 84-kilometer chunk of ice and rock. For a time, the High Guard had maintained a base there; the object's orbit was unstable, and it would have been a good candidate for a deliberate nudge that would have threatened an Inner System world.

Now, though, the base was purely automated.

"It's run by an AI named Echeclus," Koenig said. "He's smart and he's curious. He's also about six and a half light hours from Neptune. If Force Alpha started transmitting tight-beam updates to Point Libra as soon as they took over Neptune-Triton, he should be picking up the signal just about now. I would expect an AI of Echeclus's caliber to rebroadcast the signal to us. At fifteen AUs out . . . that's just two hours."

"We could expect to get the transmission at around 0515, then."

"Exactly. But it gets better. That transmission from Echeclus will be nondirectional, spreading through the solar system like an expanding bubble. Our fighter reconnaissance will be outbound one hour into their mission, assuming *America* launches at once, and they'll encounter that bubble before we do. They'll have comprehensive if-then orders: if they pick up the signal, it means I'm right and Force Bravo is out there, waiting for the signal from Neptune that *they* won't get for another three and a quarter hours or so. If Echeclus reports no signal, they decelerate immediately, then boost back for the Inner System."

"Damn, that's complicated," Caruthers complained.

"The joys of communications limited by *c*, Admiral. But it *will* work. It'll let us deploy out toward Point Libra *now*, and maybe get the jump on the Turusch before they're expecting us. If I'm wrong, if there's no signal, the fighters will turn around and be back in the Inner System three hours later. Think of them as a tactical reserve."

"And we have other squadrons," Caruthers said, thoughtful. "*Essex* and *Kennedy* are all at full strength. I'm inclined to say yes, Admiral. There's just one problem."

"What's that, sir?"

"The Senate. Specifically the Senate Military Directorate. I have a certain amount of freedom in how I deploy the fleet for the defense of Earth, but I know damned well they're not going to authorize sending four fighter squadrons out on what they'll be convinced is a wild goose chase. The request is going to get bounced back to Earth. That's a time lag of twelve minutes right now. And twelve minutes more for the reply."

"So we have twenty-four minutes before they say no. I suggest, sir, that you let me commence launching now."

"Admiral . . . you're still under something of a cloud with this Board of Inquiry. Technically, you shouldn't even be in command of that battlegroup while you're waiting for the Board's decision."

Koenig decided not to tell Caruthers that he already knew what the Board's decision was. He suspected, though, that Caruthers already knew the outcome as well.

"I'll take full responsibility for my decision, Admiral. Hell, tell them I boosted without orders, without consulting *you*. They can crucify me when I return."

"You're intending to take your battlegroup out toward Libra as well."

"Of course. We won't get there for sixteen hours, but my fighters will need to be recovered. If we start boosting behind *America*'s fighters immediately, we'll still be in a position to turn around and return if we don't hear from Echeclus in a reasonable time."

"I'm going to authorize this, Koenig," Caruthers said after a moment's thought. "God help your career if you're wrong."

"God help us all if I'm right *or* wrong," Koenig said.

He didn't add that twelve capital ships and a few fighter squadrons would not last long against Force Bravo. He didn't know how many ships the Turusch would be sending in their main force, but it would certainly be more than the thirty-three ships of Force Alpha. A *lot* more.

It was possible that the deployment of Battlegroup *America* would prove to be nothing more than a spoiling attack— a means of damaging and perhaps slowing down the enemy fleet before it reached Earth, but at the cost of *America* and her consorts.

"Either way, Admiral Koenig, good luck."

The connection was broken, and Koenig was again in CIC, strapped in his recliner. "Commander Craig!"

"Yes, sir!"

"New orders to all ships in the battlegroup. Prepare for acceleration. Course fifteen-plus-fifteen."

"Aye, aye, sir. New course fifteen hours right ascension, plus fifteen degrees declination." She blinked, looked puzzled. "Sir? . . ."

"You have your orders, Commander."

"Just a moment, Admiral," Quintanilla said. "Those coordinates . . . that's in almost the exact opposite direction from the enemy's emergence point!"

"Almost," Koenig replied easily.

"B-but . . . but you can't *do* that!"

"*Mister* Quintanilla, you would be surprised at what I can do when I put my mind to it. Now strap yourself down and stop floating around my CIC, or I'll have you ejected. Again. We are going to be doing some maneuvering in the next few moments, and I don't want you crashing into the instrumentation."

"All hands, prepare for maneuvering," the voice of *America*'s helm officer announced. "Two gravities in fifteen seconds."

The twelve vessels of the battlegroup would be jostling their way into formation now, using plasma thrusters to maneuver. The gantry of the Phobia dock facility continued dropping away, drifting now until it was off *America*'s stern quarter.

Quintanilla barely made it to a spare acceleration couch. When the ship was under grav acceleration, of course, CIC was in free fall, and couches were hardly a necessity. A two-G nudge from the main thrusters, though, could break bones if you weren't prepared. They provided an added safety precaution as well for officers and crew who were working in simlinks, and unaware of their actual surroundings. Having everyone strapped down while they were linked kept them from blindly drifting into one another, or into the ship's consoles or instrumentation.

The helm officer was speaking again. "And five . . . and four . . . and three . . . and two . . . plasma torch sequence initiated . . . fire!"

And Koenig, now, was committed to what might be his last deployment as a naval officer.

He opened another channel. "Commodore Dixon."

"Yes, Admiral," Captain Joseph Victor Dixon replied. Dixon was *America*'s CAG, the officer in command of all squadrons operating off of the carrier. The term was an ancient acronym, one standing for commander air group. The title had eventually been changed to commander air *wing*, and, still later, to commander *space* wing, but the original name had remained unchanged throughout four centuries, clearly preferable to suggested official alternatives such as CAW and COSPAW.

His naval rank was captain, but in formal conversation he was given the honorary title of commodore. There could be only one "captain" on board ship.

Dixon flew with *America*'s lead squadron, VFA-51, the Black Lightnings.

"What's our squadron status, CAG?"

"Three at full readiness, Admiral. One, the Rattlers, is light at nine spacecraft on the flight line. I took what was left of the Dragonfires and put two of them in with the Black Lightnings, the other two in with the Nighthawks." He hesitated. "One pilot hasn't reported back aboard, so the Nighthawks are down one fighter as well."

"Understood. How fast can you get them off the carrier?"

"The Nighthawks and the Impactors are on ready five, Admiral. Lightnings at ready ten. The rest . . . half an hour."

"Do it. Commander Craig will be sending down specific orders. Your people are going on deep recon."

"*All* of them?"

"As many as we can kick out there, CAG. And as quickly as we can do it." He began filling Dixon in on his conversation with Caruthers, and on the threat of a Turusch alpha strike from one side of the sun, with a diversion on the other.

"I see," Dixon said after Koenig had explained the situation. "If Force Bravo isn't there, we're late to the party. If it is, we show up early, with real shit for odds."

"That's about the size of it. The battlegroup will be following along behind you."

"To pick up the pieces?"

"Are you and your people up for this, CAG?"

"Of course we are. It'll be worth it, if we can spoil their strike. I'll pass the word."

"Good. We'll begin launching as soon as we begin gravitic acceleration. You may scramble your pilots."

"Aye, aye, sir."

When Koenig emerged from the simlink, Quintanilla was gone. The two-G acceleration had let up a moment before, and he must have left then.

"All hands, this is the captain. Stand by for gravitic acceleration, five hundred gravities, in five . . . four . . . three . . . two . . . one . . . *boost!*"

Space-bending energies flowed from *America*'s zero-point fields, projecting ahead of the ship's enormous shield cap, folding a tight little knot of spacetime in upon itself. The artificial singularity grew rapidly with the influx of energy. As the star carrier began falling toward it, the singularity vanished, to be reprojected again a few nanoseconds later.

Carefully balanced to avoid catching the ship in a destructive flux of tidal forces, the singularity continued winking on and off, on and off, creating the effect of a steady pull of five hundred gravities out ahead of *America*'s shield. Mars and the Phobos Synchorbital facility both dwindled away rapidly, vanishing in an instant as they dropped astern at five kilometers per second per second.

And the carrier fell outward into darkness.

Flight Deck
TC/USNA CVS America
Mars Space, Sol System
0315 hours, TFT

Joseph Dixon squeezed down into his Starhawk, letting the seat accept his weight and enfold him in its harness. Above him, his crew chief slapped the top of his helmet. "You're good t'go, CAG!"

"Keep the coffee hot, Chief. We'll be back."

"Roger that!"

The cockpit sealed around him, plunging him momentarily into darkness. The lights came up an instant later.

Around him, on the Alpha flight deck, other Black Lightning pilots were racing across the deck, lowering themselves into cockpits, settling into their seats. The alarm klaxon blared somewhere overhead, echoing through the cavernous chamber.

He turned his full attention to his instruments, both those glowing at him from his console and those now appearing in open windows in his mind as his neural hardware linked in. His fighter was sinking now through the viscous black liquid of the nanoseal covering the hatch beneath him. He felt the sudden shift of attitude as his nose pivoted down; he brought up his visual display, and found himself looking out through the carrier's open launch deck, at stars wheeling past as the hab modules continued to turn.

"This is Lightning One-zero-one," he announced over the comm. "I am clear of the hatch. Ship systems are hot. AI on-line. Weapons safed. Ready for drop."

"One-zero-one, PriFly. You're clear for drop, CAG."

"Copy. Release when clear."

"Hold for other fighters in your stick coming on-line. Ten seconds, CAG."

Dropping was slow. The launch tubes had the advantage of giving the fighter an extra burst of speed—a free six hundred kilometers per hour of velocity, but fighters could only launch two at a time that way, and it took special preparation to get all twelve spacecraft in a squadron up to the keel for sequential loading into the tubes. This time out, the Nighthawks were going out the bow—the luck of the draw, since they were next on the rotation and the fighters already loaded on the spinal flight deck.

Everyone else would be dropping out of one of the three rotating flight decks, outboard on the hab modules. The hab rotation gave them a free half-G kick outward, a lateral delta-V of five meters per second, easily compensated for later. The advantage was that six fighters could be launched at a time, with just thirty seconds between drops; an entire squadron could be spaceborne in half a minute.

"And *three*!" the voice of PriFly announced. "And *two*! And *one*! And *drop*!"

The steady pull of half a gravity vanished as he went into free fall, his fighter slipping through the launch deck opening and into space. To either side, the other five fighters of his stick fell in perfect unison. Peters. Aguilera. Hennessey. Michaels. And one of the replacements from the Dragonfires, Collins.

He had an uneasy feeling about that one. She'd come from a squadron that had suffered a paralyzing sixty-six percent casualties, including, he gathered from the psychtech's report, her lover. She might well be psychologically unstable, even after three weeks.

Still, she'd been cleared by psych, as had the other Dragonfire pilot transferred to the Lightnings. That was Allyn, the Dragonfires' former skipper, and she would be hurting, too, after losing most of her squadron. It was important to get them back into the thick of things as quickly as possible, let them start fitting in with the new unit before they had too much time to think of dead comrades.

The other two Dragonfire pilots, Tucker and Gray, had been assigned to the Nighthawks . . . except that Gray didn't have medical clearance yet. According to the records, Gray was absent in any case, left behind when *America* had pulled clear of the dock. *He* might have some explaining to do once this was all over.

The Starhawk's AI rotated the fighter and applied a gravitational boost of two Gs. The maneuver was perfectly orchestrated with the other five Lightnings in the stick. They continued to fall out from the *America* at five meters per second, but now they were accelerating alongside the mammoth vessel, clearing the rim of the shield cap, then pulling out ahead of the carrier. Dixon saw movement out of the corner of his eye and turned his head. Two of the Nighthawks had just exited *America*'s spinal launch tubes, hurtling into the distance at 167 meters per second.

Ahead, Dixon could see the familiar kite-shaped constellation of Boötis; alongside was a U-shaped curve of stars, like an upraised arm. That was Corona Borealis, and the provisional navigation point for him and three other pilots—Aguilera, Hennessy, and Collins.

Astern, the second stick of six fighters in the Black Lightnings dropped clear of *America*. Friedman, Walsh, Cutler, Huerta, Hernandez. And the former CO of VFA-44, Allyn.

Once clear of the *America*'s shield cap, they used maneuvering thrusters to adjust their Starhawks' attitudes and kill the sideways drift imparted by their drop, and configured their craft into high-G needles.

"*America* CIC, this is Deep Recon Red," Dixon said. "Handing off from PriFly. We are clear of the ship and formed up. Ready to initiate PL boost."

"Copy, Deep Recon Red. Primary Flight Control confirms handoff to *America* CIC. You are clear for high-grav boost."

"Acknowledge. Cleared for boost." Dixon switched to the formation frequency. "Okay, people. You heard the lady. Engage squadron taclink. Fifty-kay acceleration in three . . . two . . . one . . . *engage*!"

And the fighters vanished toward the unwinking stars at half a million meters per second.

Oceana Naval Station
North American Periphery
2245 hours, local time

It had taken almost an hour to get here.

Trevor Gray had dropped off the rented broom at the Columbia Arcology, then caught a suborbital hopper for the twenty-minute flight to Oceana.

Four centuries before, Naval Air Station Oceana had been the largest U.S. naval base on the East Coast, and the command center for all Atlantic strike fighter activities when they were not actually on deployment. The relentless rise of the warming oceans eventually had forced the evacuation of nearby Virginia Beach, Portsmouth, and vast swaths of tidewater Virginia.

The naval base had remained, however, first under a sealed dome, then building up as the water levels rose, creating the iconic flat-topped base on pylons, often derided as the world's largest and least maneuverable seagoing aircraft carrier.

The hopper had touched down on the upper landing deck in darkness at just past 2230 hours, local time, and Gray,

with the handful of the military passengers from Morningside Heights, had checked in at the base quarterdeck.

The place was crowded. The recall order had caught a lot
of naval and Marine personnel on Earth, and all of them
were trying to get back to their ships.

Gray slapped his hand on the reader pad as a bored rating
asked for his name and id. When Gray's data flashed up on
the man's screen, however, he appeared to become more interested. "Lieutenant Gray? Fighter pilot, VFA-44?"

"That's me." A bold enough statement, considering he
still wasn't sure *what* he wanted to be.

"Okay . . . according to this thing, sir," he jabbed a finger
at his console monitor, "your ship, the *America*, is boosting
out-system. She left Mars half an hour ago."

"Shit." All he could think was that Collins was going to
have a field day with this. "Where are they headed?"

"Classified . . . but I'd be willing to bet it has something to
do with all the commotion about the Tushies out at Neptune,
wouldn't you say?"

"Reasonable guess."

"I thought so. Anyway, a few hours ago, a request came
through from the *America* for replacements. Two brand-
new squadrons of Starhawks. With nugget pilots. We were
putting together a flight plan to get those squadrons out to
Mars."

"So you're sending them out there now?"

"The request was from your admiral, and it *was* flagged
'urgent,'" the rating said. "How would you like to skipper
them out to the ship?"

Gray thought about this. Technically, he was still off the
flight line, pending a final clearance from psych. Either the
enlisted rating hadn't noted that data line on his electronic
id . . . or he didn't care.

Skippering a bunch of kid-nuggets to *America*? Sure, he
could do that. Oceana was where Gray had begun his flight
training four years ago. There were several dozen squadrons
home-ported there, and some hundreds of fighters. Carriers
throughout the fleet used them as reserves, replacing indi-

vidual spacecraft—or entire squadrons—when they wore out, or when they were used up.

Hell, it wasn't like he had anything back in the Manhattan Ruins to go home to.

"Sounds like a plan," he told the rating. "Where do I sign on?"

"Billingsly!" the rating shouted, turning to look over his shoulder. "Get this man down to Flight Ops!"

It might be against his better judgment, but he was going back to the *America*.

Chapter Twenty-One

Oceana Naval Station
North American Periphery
2314 hours, local time

The fighters would be making the ferry passage fully armed.

Normally, this kind of shuttle flight would be made with the spacecraft unarmed, but these were special circumstances. Oceana was rife with rumor about the threat from Outside . . . rumors of Turusch ships bombarding Triton, of a battle with High Guard ships, of clashes with Confederation fleet elements in deep space.

There was no way to verify any of it. Even after Gray was back within reach of local Net-Clouds, information on any of the ships of the Confederation Navy had been blocked, and he didn't have the passwords to mindclick access to it.

As the rating at Oceana's quarterdeck had suggested, it almost certainly meant a Turusch incursion of some kind. The more certain he became of that, the more he felt a pounding need to get back to the carrier.

Back where he belonged.

"Starhawk Transit One, Oceana Control," the voice said in his mind, "you are cleared for launch."

"Roger that, Oceana Control."

The launch tunnel was wide, flat, and slanted upward at 45 degrees from deep within the Oceana base. It would be decidedly unhealthy to engage drive singularities inside the tunnel, where a miscalculation could eat the fighter going up in front of you. Instead, they would be accelerated up and out by a magnetic sling, and engage drives once out over the ocean.

"Railgun power in three . . . two . . . one . . . release."

Gray's fighter began moving—with only about two gravities of acceleration, moving up the long, slanting tunnel toward a patch of black night sky. Behind him, twenty-three other fighters followed in tight, four-ship groups. The Starhawks were configured in their atmospheric flight modes, black manta rays with down-curving wing tips. Gray snapped out of the tunnel and into open sky.

A green light in his mind showed that all of the Starhawks had emerged at once. Black ocean blurred beneath his keel.

"Fifty-gravity acceleration," he told the others. "Engage!"

He moved his hands through the control field, and his Starhawk began accelerating as his drive singularity became a white-hot star out ahead of his craft, devouring air molecules in his path and drawing behind him a white contrail of shocked water vapor. He brought his nose up, and in seconds he was thundering vertically though a low cloud deck, then punching past more rarified altitudes, the air growing thinner with each passing second.

The stars shone ahead, bright, cold, and hard.

"Oceana Control," Gray called. "Starhawk Transit One passing one-hundred-kilometer mark."

"Copy that, Starhawk Transit One. Oceana Control handing off to SupraQuito Control."

"Copy that."

One hundred kilometers was the traditional, if arbitrary, point at which space began as Earth's atmosphere thinned away to almost nothing. Behind and below the accelerating Starhawks, the night side of Earth spread out in a vast, black bulk blotting out half of the sky. Scattered city lights showed here and there, some as sharp pinpoints, some as broader masses of light, some as diffuse glows beneath layers of cloud.

A lightning storm pulsed and flickered silently within the clouds off to the south.

This was something from which Gray could never walk away. He knew that now. When he'd been considering resigning his commission and going down to the fleet to serve out his time, he'd thought that what he was clinging to was the privilege and prerogatives of a naval officer. But that, he now knew, wasn't it, not at all. He'd lived once scavenging garbage in the Ruins; he could live that way again, if forced to.

But the thought of giving up *flight*, free, unfettered *flight* among the stars . . .

"So . . . Lieutenant Gray," one of the pilots called to him from the pack—Anders, Transit One-five. "They say you've had experience. You seen any action?"

"Yeah. I've seen action. Keep it quiet, people. Form on my heading. Engage squadron taclink."

He gave the tactical display a last check, making certain that neither local traffic nor the ring arcs out in synchorbit lay anywhere near their outbound course. Slamming into one of SupraQuito's hab modules at a few million meters per second was an excellent way of ending your Navy career . . . and taking quite a few civilians with you.

His nav marker was set for the calculated position of the *America*, somewhere out near Mars, about twelve light minutes away.

"Fifty-kay acceleration," Gray announced, "in three . . . two . . . one . . . *go*!"

They went.

Red Bravo Flight
America *Deep Recon, Sol System*
0415 hours, TFT

Commander Marissa Allyn put her Starhawk into a high-velocity coast configuration, knowing that her shields would be dropping soon. She was seven AUs out from Sol, her outbound voyage one quarter over.

After launching from the *America*, she'd formed up with three other Lightning pilots—Lieutenants Cutler, Friedman, and Walsh. At the CAG's orders, they'd linked their ships and boosted at fifty thousand gravities, leaving Mars and the *America* far behind in an instant.

Ten minutes after engaging their drives, they were moving at just over 299,000 kilometers per second—a hair less than the speed of light—and had traveled almost 90 million kilometers. At that point, they'd shut down their drives, drifting now at near-*c*, cocooned within the gravitic shields that deflected the bits of dust and stray hydrogen atoms that could fry an unprotected pilot at those velocities.

To Allyn, it felt like only a few minutes had passed, but her AI informed her that she'd been drifting now for one hour. Since shutting down the gravitic drive, she'd coasted outward for more than a billion kilometers, traveling so quickly that her subjective time had been shortened to four and a half minutes.

"Reconfiguration complete," her AI informed her.

"Okay," she told it. "Drop shields."

Lowering shields at near-*c* was risky, and advisable only for short periods of time. The reconfiguration had moved a large percentage of her ship's nanomaterial mass forward, creating a cone-shaped shield forward containing her fighter's store of water, which was used as reaction mass for the plasma maneuvering thrusters. The Starhawk, in fact, was now imitating the *America* and other capital ships, creating a radiation shield forward to screen the pilot from high-energy particles. The defense wasn't perfect. Some heavy particles, when the fighter hit them at near-*c*, generated cascade radiation that filtered back through the shielding mass, with long-term problems for the pilot's health.

But her orders were clear. It was possible, she'd been told by the CAG, that a radio signal from an automated High Guard station on a Centaur asteroid up ahead would be passing her on its way to Earth and Mars. With shields up, with their gravitic twist in space surrounding her Starhawk shunting all radiation aside, her ship's comm systems wouldn't be able to pick up that signal. So she would coast for one minute, subjective, with shields down, as her AI attempted to sift a message out of the high-energy blast of static washing across her ship.

That one minute subjective was almost fourteen minutes objective, as the outside universe measured time; if that AI on Echeclus was transmitting, that should be time enough to pick it up.

To her ears, the incoming radio waves were noise—hissing static and faint traces of modulated signals. At this speed they were all blue-shifted, however, almost all the way up into the visible spectrum. No matter. Her AI would sort out the frequency shift.

"Signal detected," her AI announced. "Signal is from the AI on Echeclus, and includes a retransmission of an alien signal at optical laser frequencies."

Allyn felt her stomach knot. She'd half expected that they would pick up nothing, that they would have to decelerate, then boost back for the Inner System. But if they picked up the signal, they were to change course, not for the Inner System, but for one of several navigational waypoints in the general direction of Point Libra.

The likely emergence point of the enemy's Force Bravo.

"Hey, Commander! I'm getting the signal," Walsh's voice said, blasting through the static.

"Same here," Cutler added.

"Roger that," Friedman added. "Can't translate the imbedded part at all."

"Right, people," Allyn told them. "You know what that means. Our primary orders are in effect."

"Yeah," Cutler said. "There's no going back."

They knew the enemy fleet would be out there.

If the enemy hadn't already started boosting for the Inner System.

CIC, TC/USNA CVS America
Outbound, Sol System
0420 hours, TFT

"Well," Captain Buchanan said, "the fighter recon group ought to know by now, one way or the other."

"They're there," Koenig said, his voice, his thoughts distant. "By God, they're *there*."

"The Turusch? Force Bravo?"

"Yes."

It had been all he'd been thinking about since they'd left Mars orbit. Suppose he was wrong? Suppose there *was* no Force Bravo . . . or that they were coming in from zenith or nadir? So many possibilities.

"Admiral Koenig?" a voice spoke in his head. "This is Comm. Message coming through from Earth. Priority One. And it's red-coded for you, sir."

He sighed. He'd been waiting for this. "Put it through."

There was a pause, then a blast of static. After one hour at five hundred gravities, *America* was moving at a respectable eighteen thousand kilometers per second. That still was only 6 percent of *c*, but it was fast enough to leave a trail of ionized hydrogen in her wake. That and the fringe effect of her shields caused a lot of white noise.

But the signal from Earth had been tight-beamed and pumped up to make sure *America* received it. The software resident in Koenig's implants decrypted the mind-only code, translating it for him. A window opened in his mind, and he saw the face of Vice Admiral Michael Noranaga.

Noranaga was in his selkie form rather than the human electronic avatar Koenig has seen at the Board of Inquiry. Large, lidless and unblinking eyes stared at Koenig from the mental window. Gill slits worked convulsively in the rubbery gray skin of the neck. Noranaga was speaking in a room filled with air, not water, and breathing—and speech—were difficult for him.

"Admiral Koenig!" the changeling naval officer demanded. "I have a report here that you are taking the *America* battlegroup into deep space, toward right ascension fifteen hours.

This is in *direct* violation of the Senate Military Directorate's orders! You are to decelerate immediately, repeat, *immediately*, and rendezvous with the rest of the fleet between Earth and Mars!" The image shifted slightly, cutting back to the beginning of the message. "Admiral Koenig! . . ."

He closed the window. Noranaga would have looped the short message and sent it out on continuous repeat. *America* was now more than twenty light minutes from Earth, and anything like a real conversation, with questions or immediate responses, was impossible.

"Admiral?" the comm officer said. "There's an imbedded reply order in the signal."

"Ignore it, Comm," Koenig said. "We didn't hear the message. Too much static."

"Aye, aye, sir."

Koenig knew that his career was now literally on the line.

Selkies, he thought, tended to be unusually conservative, even within the overtly conservative hierarchies of the Navy. For two centuries now, genetic prostheses had allowed them to take on the selkie somaform, enabling them to work directly on one of the greatest projects of modern human technology—the reclamation of the oceans.

Earth's planetary ocean had come uncomfortably close to dying in the mass extinction of the twentieth and twenty-first centuries, overfished, overexploited, poisoned first by industrial pollution, then later by the effects of devouring the world's coastal cities. The selkies were working on the enormous oceanic converters, on the genetic restocking of the ocean's sealife populations, on rebuilding pylon cities over the ruins of sunken metropolises, and on brand-new submarine megalopoli on the submerged continental shelves.

The selkies, more than their dry-land cousins, felt a special attachment to Earth and to her healing; there was a sizeable selkie contingent within the Confederation government, Koenig knew, that advocated abandoning space entirely. Earth and Earth's oceans required Humankind's complete devotion and dedication until they were once again healthy. Only then should the species even consider moving outward again . . . and then with a sharpened awareness of how fragile a living planet and its ecosystems were.

The defense of Earth would be paramount in Noranaga's mind.

Well, it was paramount in Koenig's mind as well. If he was wrong, they could court martial him, *if* there was a Confederation Navy left to take on the job.

But he wasn't wrong. He stared at the starfield sprawled across the overhead dome of CIC. The Sun and Mars lay astern, the stars of Taurus and Pisces astern and to port; ahead, not yet distorted by their speed, he could see the familiar constellations of Boötis and adjoining Corona Borealis. The enemy was *there*.

And he would find them, find them and *hurt* them enough that the rest of Earth's fleet could deal with them.

Even if it meant his death and the destruction of his battlegroup.

Red Bravo Flight
America *Deep Recon*
30-AU Shell, Sol System
0702 hours, TFT

Marissa Allyn had become her Starhawk, her senses inextricably entwined with its sensor suite, to the flow and pulse and rhythm of incoming signals. Part of the problem, of course, was that this patch of space was so damnably *empty*, a vast abyssal gulf four light hours out from a dwindled sun.

This was just one of a dozen distinct navigational waypoints determined by Combat back on board the *America*—guesses, really, as to where the enemy fleet might be.

The four-hour coast out from Mars had, for her, passed in just seventeen minutes. Five objective minutes ago, she and the other three Starhawks in her flight had begun decelerating. Now they were coasting once more, still moving at nearly half the speed of light.

That velocity was a compromise. With such a huge area

within which the enemy's Force Bravo might have emerged, it was more than likely that they would be someplace else, that Allyn and her flight would have to change course and rendezvous elsewhere, perhaps as much as two light hours away. Zorching along at half-*c*, she was moving too fast to effectively engage the enemy if she found him.

On the other hand, if the bad guys *were* here in her personal corner of the Outer System, she'd be crazy to engage them with only four fighters.

"Anyone see anything yet?" she asked over the squadron frequency.

"Nothing, Skipper," Walsh replied. "Just a whole lot of nothing."

Allyn felt a small, inner warming at Walsh calling her "skipper." She was no longer the CO—the *skipper*—of a squadron, but her commander's rank did put her in charge of the little four-ship group. The others in the Black Lightnings had been a bit standoffish when she'd first joined them in their ready room a week ago. Technically, her rank would have made her the CAG's executive officer, the Assistant CAG, though that position was already filled by Commander Huerta.

By calling her "Skipper," Walsh was showing that she'd been accepted by the others.

Family. . . .

And Walsh was right. *A whole lot of nothing . . .*

The problem was that Force Bravo could not have emerged at a single point. Because starships under warp drive couldn't see outside of their tightly folded little pocket universe, they were completely reliant on the accuracy of their ships' AIs in determining when to break out of metaspace. Tiny discrepancies at the beginning of the boost translated into enormous distances at the end, with the result that ships emerged at different places and different times scattered over half of the sky. The enemy needed time to assemble his scattered forces—one very good reason for the delay, so far, in launching a strike on the Inner System.

"Hey, Skipper?" Friedman called. "Something funny here. I'm not getting Repeater Four-one."

Friedman's fighter was twenty thousand kilometers to high-starboard, and slightly ahead of Allyn's ship.

Repeater Four-one was one of several hundred long-range communications repeater units set in solar orbit at the thirty-AU shell. Four-one was one of the dozen or so stations following in Neptune's orbit, but others followed inclined orbits that let them cover the entirety of the thirty-AU shell.

"Well, well," she said. "*That* might explain some things."

The original warning of the enemy's presence, of course, had been transmitted by High Guard Watch Station 8734 and several of its sisters. Lacking the power to transmit a clear signal all the way to Earth or Mars when they'd picked up the photon flash of emerging Turusch warships out at 45 AU, they'd transmitted an alert to the base at Triton. But the base on Triton was within range of only a tiny fraction of the High Guard watch stations. The repeater stations were spread out over the entire thirty-AU shell, serving as relays for transmissions from any of the tiny automated probes.

The system wasn't perfect. There weren't enough watch stations or repeater stations to cover the entire 450 quintillion square kilometers of the forty-AU shell, and the constantly changing orbital positions of the repeater stations at the thirty-AU shell left occasional gaps in the signal coverage. It was possible that Force Bravo had emerged somewhere where coverage was scant or nonexistent.

But if they'd emerged here, they would have been detected, and Repeater Station Four-one would have transmitted the warning to Earth.

Unless . . .

"I've got a contact!" Lieutenant Friedman yelled. "Contact at one-seven-niner plus five one!" There was a harsh pause, then, "*Toad!* I've got a Toad fighter, confirmed, range kay forty-three!"

Allyn saw the contact at the same moment . . . a single fighter, outbound, 43,000 kilometers beyond Friedman's ship.

"Transmit log!" Allyn told her AI; the other fighters in her group would be doing the same. *Whatever* happened, Earth would have confirmation that Turusch warships were out here in another four hours. "All ships! *Get* the bastard!"

Shifting her projected drive singularity to starboard, she put her fighter into a sharp turn.

Turning a ship at high-G was always a risky proposition. Space fighters, especially, couldn't swoop or turn the way their atmospheric counterparts did, not without an atmosphere in which to bank, turn, and bleed off excess speed.

But they could come close. By projecting the singularity to the side or above or below, rather than straight ahead or astern, the fighter could travel along what technically was a straight line passing through gravitationally curved space . . . and the end result was a curved path. If the maneuver was performed correctly, the fighter could make the turn without acceleration effects—just as a spacecraft or hab module orbiting the Earth was following the curvature of space around the planet without feeling the effects of centripetal force.

But make the turn too tight, and the fighter could get caught by the singularity's tidal effects. Its nose could be whipped around, throwing the ship into a nightmare spin; closer still, and the fighter would be ripped to shreds . . . or devoured in a flash of fragments and hard radiation by its own artificial singularity.

She kept her turn on the gentle side, giving the focus of her turn a generous berth. As her prow fell into line with the distant, fleeing fighter, she kicked in the forward drive once more, accelerating now at 48,000 gravities.

"AI targeting!" she called. "Beams!"

At these velocities, human reflexes simply weren't fast enough—by several orders of magnitude—to track the target, lock on, and destroy it.

The Toad was also accelerating hard and fast, but the Starhawk was faster. The AI signaled target lock, a red cursor on the combat display capturing the target icon in its embrace and flashing quickly.

Before she could fire, the target vanished.

No matter. Her ship's sensors couldn't detect the Toad when it was completely shielded; it had been detected only because of its drive field. By shutting off its drive, the enemy fighter effectively became invisible . . . but it also could not change course or speed. Allyn's AI could easily calculate where the Toad would be when the PBP-2 beam caught it.

Allyn's AI triggered her Blue Lightning projector, three quick pulses invisible in the emptiness of space, but shown on her display as a bright, blue thread of light reaching toward the fleeing, invisible target, touching it. . . .

Friedman had fired almost at the same instant. Two charged-particle beams caught the Toad from behind, slashing at its shields. One of the impacts caused substantial damage to the Toad's aft shield projectors and part of the shield went down. The Toad was now nakedly exposed, fully visible, and still in her sights.

"Again!" she yelled, the adrenaline of the chase pounding through her system. "Fire!"

Her AI fired again, and the Toad vanished in a tiny nova of light.

"Good shot, Skipper!" Friedman called.

"Thank the wonders of technology," she replied. But she was pleased. That had been a shot at extremely long-range for a fighter, and her AI had performed flawlessly. "All ships! Go to CTT."

CCT—constant tactical transmission—meant that their AIs were beaming out steady reports on everything that was happening. Four hours from now, those transmissions would reach Earth, and headquarters would know that the enemy was, indeed, here as well as at Triton. Normally, CCT was left off during deep recon flights; there was no sense in letting the enemy know you were there. But Allyn had to assume that the Toad had flashed a warning to other Turusch ships out here as soon as it had detected the Confederation Starhawks. The enemy knew that four Starhawks were out here, and they would be reacting soon.

The CCT was beaming out in all directions, too, so the rest of the Black Lightnings would know, sooner or later, that Red Bravo One had run into bad guys, and they would be coming to help.

The question was whether they would be here in time.

There would be other cloaked Toads out here, probably a lot of them. Allyn guessed that the enemy had penetrated the High Guard warning net by slipping fighters through to the repeater station and destroying it . . . possibly by destroying a number of repeater stations. Those automated stations pinged their locations back to Earth and Mars, usually, twice a day, and it was possible that in all the excitement back there no one had yet noticed that one of the relays was off-line. A number of enemy fighters, brought in, perhaps, by a carrier that had deliberately emerged far out in Sol's Kuiper Belt, had cloaked themselves and slipped in to the thirty-AU shell unobserved, slipping close enough that they could destroy the repeater station without being spotted.

It was a necessary and obvious prelude to an all-out Inner System assault—punching a hole through the enemy's early-warning net to admit the attacking force unobserved.

And it was proof, positive, that the Turusch were sending a Force Bravo through the hole they'd opened. That was why no hasty, snap-launched impactor bombardment, or waves of high-velocity incoming fighters. The Turusch had had this operation *planned* down to the last detail, and would be descending on Earth with their full fleet, en masse.

Unless the Black Lightnings could launch a spoiler attack.

Unless the fleet back in the Inner System could be warned in time.

Unless *America*'s battlegroup could delay the enemy's assault.

There were so many variables. So little chance of complete success. . . .

"Target acquired ahead," her AI announced. "Range approximately two tenths of an AU, closing at point six *c*."

At that range, the target must be *enormous* . . . and it was traveling inbound at a tenth of the speed of light if the total rate of closure was sixth-tenths light. She studied the icon that had just winked on against her combat display.

Gods of the cosmos . . . what *was* that thing?

"Close in tight, people!" she ordered. "I think we have problems! . . ."

Chapter Twenty-Two

Tactician Emphatic Blossom at Dawn
Annihilator Regrets of Parting
30-AU Shell, Sol System
0713 hours, TFT

"Deep Tactician!" a communicator throbbed from the console-shelf overhead. "Four enemy fighters, range ninety *lurm'm* and closing quickly!"

Emphatic Blossom's forward tendrils curled with a distinctly Turusch emotion, part frustration, part surprise, part rigidly unyielding determination. The Turusch did not believe in *luck*, as such, since theirs was a harshly deterministic and mechanistic view of the universe, but the universe was known to be unpleasantly perverse at times. *Everything* had been riding on the premise that the Fleet of Raucous Driving would fully engage the enemy's attention, permitting the much larger and more powerful Fleet of Objective Silence to move, cloaked behind their shields, deep into their star system.

How had the enemy discovered the ruse? How, in all of the near-infinite possibilities of a probabilistically determined cosmos, had the enemy been able to divine precisely where the main fleet had emerged?

"Have they detected us yet?" its bonded other asked.

The Turusch tactician speaking to Emphatic Blossom was

Blossom's twin, the other half of its life-pair, and it was, technically speaking, the *combination* of the two that was named Radiant Blossom. Others addressed it as a single unit, and Radiant Blossom itself always knew which of its halves was speaking, so there was no confusion . . . at least for those familiar with Turusch psychology; in a very real sense, Radiant Blossom was always in two places at once.

It watched the icon representing the approaching enemy ships for a moment. "That seems almost certain," it replied. "Their course is directly toward us . . . an unlikely eventuality if this were random chance."

"Agreement. Their mass sensors may have detected the curvature of local space around us."

"Destroy them, then. Before they alert others to our presence."

"That may already have happened. We detected radiofrequency transmission from those ships several *url'i* ago. They will have warned other vessels in the area."

Emphatic Blossom considered this for a moment.

"Then gather what is available of the fleet so far. We will launch the attack at once."

"We have yet to reestablish contact with two and a half twelves of our vessels."

"They will join us eventually. As will the Fleet of Raucous Driving. When the time is right."

"The crew is ready. Our weapons are prepared."

"The threat is there. *Kill!*"

Red Bravo Flight
America *Deep Recon*
30-AU Shell, Sol System
0713 hours, TFT

"Fire missiles!" Allyn cried. "Dump everything!"

Thirty-two Krait missiles, two of them in the one-hundred-megaton range, streaked off her Starhawk's launch rails, accelerating at maximum. With their closing velocity, they would impact in seconds.

"Now hard one-eighty," she commanded as the last missile pair flashed from her rails. "And *zorch* it!"

There was no sense in holding back with the Kraits. The object bearing down on the four fighters was enormous—a dwarf planet some nine hundred kilometers in diameter and massing over nine times ten to the twenty kilograms—about 900 quadrillion tonnes. That put it roughly on a par with the dwarf planet Ceres, orbiting within Sol's Asteroid Belt.

The four fighters all were turning now as tightly as they dared, swinging around their flank-projected drive singularities. Allyn could feel the unequal tug between her head and her feet now, a sure sign that she was riding right on the deadly edge of high-G destruction.

Some thousands of kilometers away, a beam from the oncoming monster ship brushed Cutler's Starhawk . . . not enough to damage his shields, but explosive ablation kicked his fighter at the critical point of his turn.

"I'm hit! I'm hit!" Cutler cried . . . and then his Starhawk was in a helpless tumble, whipping in close around his drive singularity. The singularity winked out as his drive projectors failed, but his ship was already fragmenting.

The icon on the combat display flared and vanished.

"Stay with the turn, people!" Allyn called. "Stay with it! . . ."

And then the three remaining fighters had completed the 180-degree turn and were under full acceleration, fifty thousand gravities. She tensed, waiting for the first impact from astern . . .

And then the first Kraits were slamming home against the super-ship, nuclear fireballs blossoming silently in the night.

"I'm picking up other ships now, Skipper," Walsh told her. "They're powering up, starting to move . . ."

"I see them."

Her AI picked out some seventy other vessels . . . with more appearing all the time as they received new orders from their flagship and began to power up. Allyn felt a cold prickling at the base of her neck; there might be hundreds of vessels out there, masked by their shields or still too far out to register on her fighter's sensors. God in heaven, how were they supposed to fight *that*?

But the large asteroid-starship they'd just slammed with their missile barrage was half-molten now, its surface glowing white-hot in places, and it was trailing a faint, hazy stream of gas and debris. They'd clobbered the thing, all right, and hurt it, bad.

She hoped they would be seeing all of this back on Earth through the CCT.

She doubted that she'd be alive long enough to deliver the recordings in person.

Tactician Emphatic Blossom at Dawn
Annihilator Regrets of Parting
30-AU Shell, Sol System
0715 hours, TFT

The Turusch thought in terms of pairs, and of pairings, of joining two in such a way that they became one.

It was a biological imperative, with twinned individuals working closely together under the same name and designation, but the principle could be applied to ships and tactics as well. Emphatic Blossom at Dawn's ship, the *Radiant Severing*, had been nested inside the far larger Annihilator *Regrets of Parting*, becoming a part of the much larger vessel. Now, though, with portions of the *Parting*'s external crust molten, *Radiant Severing* would become a lifeboat.

Emphatic Blossom—one of them—gave an order, and the Radiant Severing blasted through weakening crust in a geyser of loose rock, nanolaminates, and hot gasses. It would have been good if others of *Parting*'s crew could have been pulled off the dying ship as well, but there was no time. Several thousand Turusch might perish with *Regrets of Parting*'s demise . . . but such was the harsh reality of interstellar war.

In fact, the inhabitants of *Regrets of Parting* might yet be saved. The mobile planet's power plants were down, its weapons melted into ruin, its drives useless, but the craft's sheer bulk was still intact. If the enemy threw nothing more at it, it would continue to hurtle through this star system at its current velocity, something more than one-twelfth of the speed of light. Once the local system had been crushed, rescue transports could rendezvous with the *Regrets of Parting* and take off its crew.

Radiant Severing, free of the dying giant's embrace, began accelerating starward now, taking up position with the other inbound ships. Some eight twelfths of the fleet had been gathered so far. The others, scattered across the outer reaches of this star system, would follow later as they got the orders *Severing* was broadcasting toward them now. On Blossom's display, fed through cables implanted in its brain case, the *Parting* rapidly smaller and smaller, rapidly falling away behind until it was lost among the stars.

"We should be prepared for the possibility of further attacks," Blossom's twin said.

"Agreement. I do not understand how those fighters found us, lost in so vast an emptiness. They either have technological resources of which we have been unaware, or there are numerous enemy fighters in this area, operating in small groups."

"Agreement. It seems unlikely that they could seriously hamper the Fleet of Objective Silence, however."

"Obviously, single strikes, hit-and-run assaults like the one just past, can destroy or cripple even our largest vessels."

"The high closing speed and short period of awareness worked against us. We could not deploy sand, or other defensive measures."

"As has been noted before, we must not underestimate these creatures. The Sh'daar Seed has warned us that they are extraordinarily adaptable, resourceful, and tenacious, that they *will* surprise us if we do not exercise extreme care."

"Agreement."

Another surprise was in store for the Turusch strike force.

But it would be some minutes yet before that surprise revealed itself.

CIC, TC/USNA CVS America
Outbound, Sol System
0721 hours, TFT

"Update coming through, Admiral!" the Comm Officer reported. "Sir . . . it's the transmission from Triton!"

"What the hell? . . ."

Koenig checked the time. Of course. The transmission from the High Guard ships was due in now. The message would have reached Earth a few minutes ago, and been rebroadcast to the accelerating battlegroup. He opened a window in his mind. . . .

He watched the five High Guard ships in their approach across the Neptunian pole. He watched the squadron of five ships, four *unarmed* ships, flash across the remaining distance to Triton, saw the enemy fleet orbiting the frigid moon.

The data acquired by the *Gallagher*, the *Hatakaze*, the *John Paul Johns*, the *Jianghua*, and the *Godavari* had been compiled, dissected, and analyzed by powerful AIs at Earth and Mars both before being redirected to the battlegroup. Koenig could look at the enemy fleet from any direction, at any level of detail, could separate out individual vessels and read pages of information concerning their mass, weaponry, maneuvering capabilities, and combat potency. There were thirty-six ships altogether, the largest a pair of small asteroids each several kilometers across, the rest designs Koenig had encountered before, or studied in training downloads.

Koenig watched the destruction of the tiny High Guard flotilla.

"Comm, this is Koenig."

"Yes, Admiral."

"Patch this through the fleet memories. Everyone should see this."

"Aye, aye, sir."

There was a theory prevalent in some of the upper hierarchies of the military, a bit of nonsense to the effect that it was better not to let the rank-and-file access to the truth about the enemy—like how strong he was, how dangerous, how ruthless. Information was disseminated strictly on a need-to-know basis. After all, robots didn't need to know the details . . . and the odds of not coming back.

Koenig was an officer of the old school, descended from the military traditions of the old United States. Soldiers, Marines, and sailors were not robots, and they fought better when they had a stake in the matter. Their morale was better, and they pulled together better as a unit. And sometimes bad news, even desperation, could rally them, boost them to greater levels of determination, courage, and will.

They needed to know what they were fighting for, and why.

He studied the images from Triton for several minutes more. Right now, the armchair strategists at the Directorate were going to be fixated on them. It would be up to Caruthers and a few others like him to keep them focused on the likelihood that Triton was a diversion, that a larger force would be coming in from another direction.

The prophesied message from Echeclus had come through at just past 0515 that morning, just a little more than two hours earlier. Assuming the outbound fighter squadrons off the *America* had, indeed, intercepted that message wave front, they would have continued out to the thirty-AU shell, and would be searching for the enemy there now, perhaps even engaging him.

The data stream intercepted by the communications relay was not translatable, of course. If it was possible—with less than satisfactory results—to understand Turusch speech when they were using Lingua Galactica, it was still impossible to understand their native language. Naval Intelligence hadn't even been able to take a guess at whether the data stream captured and retransmitted by Echeclus was a language or a code.

They couldn't even be certain if there was one message imbedded in the stream or two; information heterodyned on the carrier wave appeared to be in two separate, parallel tracks at slightly different frequencies. Whether that meant two separate messages, or was an artifact of the code, it was impossible to tell.

"Admiral Koenig?" Lieutenant Commander Cleary said, breaking into his thoughts. "Dr. Wilkerson wants to speak with you, from the lab."

"Put him through."

"Ah, Admiral. Thank you. I know you're busy right now. . . ."

"Actually no, Doctor. *Alea iacta est.* We've crossed the Rubicon, and there's not a lot for us to do now until tonight."

"Alea . . . what?"

"Never mind, Doctor. A minor reference from ancient military history. What's on your mind?"

"I thought you should know, Admiral. We have the breakthrough we've been looking for on the Turusch language."

The announcement sent a thrill through Koenig's body, like an electric jolt. "The Devil, you say."

"There's more than one level to their speech."

Wilkerson had his full attention. He'd just been thinking about the nested signals in the Turusch transmission between Triton and Point Libra.

"It was Dr. George who figured it out, actually. You see, the Turusch communicate by vibrating those tympani set into the bony shells behind their heads. And we've noticed that they always seem to speak in unison."

"Yes. Drove me crazy."

"Now, *all* audio speech, of course, is a series of vibrations moving through the atmosphere. Waves of various frequencies and amplitudes going out from the speaker, right?"

"I'm with you so far."

"If you have one tone, it's possible to play a second, differently modulated tone over the top of the first, with the result that you get resonances. Harmonics. Sympathetic frequencies. I'm . . . I'm not saying this well, I'm afraid. . . ."

"You're doing fine, Dr. Wilkerson. You're saying that when the two Turusch were speaking together . . ." Koenig's eyes widened as the realization hit. "Good God. You're saying there was a *third* line of dialogue from those things?"

"Exactly!" Wilkerson's icon said, nodding its head. "The Turusch must have absolutely incredible brains, incredible neural circuitry, to do it on the fly like that. The autopsies of their bodies bears that out. They appear to have *two* brains each, one above the other. Of course, in a sense the human brain is a stack of increasingly complex and more highly evolved brains . . . the brain stem, the cerebellum, the cerebral cortex—"

"What about the Turusch language, Doctor?"

"I'm getting to that, Admiral. We need to understand the Turusch neurological anatomy, however, and the way it contrasts with ours. In humans, the cerebral cortex is divided—left brain and right brain. Although this is an oversimplification, in very general terms the left side deals with analytical abilities, language, mathematics, and so on. The right side tends to deal with things like emotion and artistic expression, while the two halves communicate with one another through a nerve plexus called the *corpus collosum*—"

"And what's the point of all of this, Doctor?"

"Sir, the division of the Turusch brain is far more pronounced than in humans. We don't know for sure, yet, but we suspect that the Turusch may carry on a constant internal dialogue . . . as if there were two individuals sharing a single body. And that . . . that evolutionary development may have facilitated their social organization, to the point that two Turusch pair up as partners, as very *close* partners. A meta-Turusch, if you will."

"Like our friend Falling Droplets and his partner."

"It's . . . a little more complicated than that, sir. Here. Look at this. . . ."

Another window opened in Koenig's mind. Once again, he was in the carrier's research Center, watching the two brown and black tendriled slugs on the deck from the vantage point of the NTE robots suspended from the overhead.

"This one was Falling Droplet, of the Third Hierarchy," one of the aliens said, the words printed out across the bottom of the window.

"Speak we now with the Mind Here or the Mind Below?" said the other.

And beneath the two lines, a *third* sentence wrote itself: "Together I am Falling Droplet."

"They're both Falling Droplet?" Koenig asked. "I thought they just neglected to tell us the other one's name."

"The third sentence was there, Admiral, imbedded in the resonant frequencies created by the first two overlaying one another."

There was a slight jump in the image, where Wilkerson had edited out some of the conversation.

"Why do you work for the Sh'daar?" Koenig's voice asked.

"The Sh'daar reject your transcendence and accept you if it is only you," one Turusch said.

"The Seed encompasses and arises from the Mind Below. How would it be otherwise?" said the other.

"We work with them, our minds in harmony with theirs," the third line read. "They fear your rapid technological growth."

"What do you mean, they reject our transcendence?" Koenig's voice asked. "What is that?"

"Your species approaches the point of transcendence," one said.

"Transcendence is the ultimate evil that has been banished," said the other.

"Technic species evolve into higher forms. When they pass beyond, they leave behind . . . death."

"Are your needs being looked after?" Koenig's voice asked. "Are your nutritional needs being met?"

"We require the Seed," said one.

"We are the Seed," said the other.

The third line read, "We are dying alone."

"My God," Koenig said.

"Their meaning is still a bit opaque in places," Wilkerson said. "Their psychologies are *very* different."

"But they're making a hell of a lot more sense now than they did the other day." He shook his head. "It must have been terribly frustrating for them. They were holding what they thought was a perfectly normal conversation with us . . . and we didn't understand, didn't have a clue to what they were actually saying. 'We are dying alone'?"

"Yes. We think—this is still all speculation, understand—

we *think* that the internal dialogue predisposes them to working in groups. First with their twins . . . but then in successively higher and higher groupings. It's possible that the meta-Turusch I mentioned is a kind of group mind created by superimposing tens or hundreds or even thousands of separate conversations, all going on at once, and having new meaning arising from the background hash of separate voices."

"You said they had to have incredible brains to think on so many different levels at once. I think I'm beginning to understand."

"By comparison, we're *very* slow," Wilkerson agreed. "Just think about it. This concept of multiple layers in their conversation, even in their thinking, that's something they evolved over the course of millions of years, probably, as they evolved speech. But what Falling Droplet was doing was communicating on three levels—one from each individual Turusch and a third arising from the two at once— and *it was doing that in a language that was alien to it, in* Lingua Galactica."

Koenig blinked, confused for a moment by Wilkerson's use of the singular to refer to the two Turusch together . . . but it *did* make sense in an eldritch way. Turusch concepts of "them" and "me," of "others" and "self," must be quite different from the way humans thought of those concepts.

He wondered if there was a way the difference could be used against them.

Or if greater understanding would facilitate better communication . . . and an end to the war.

"I'll want you to put this together into a report, Doctor. Something we can broadcast to Earth and Mars. The Directorate needs to see this. So does Naval Intelligence. This could be what we need to put a stop to this war."

"I don't think I see how, Admiral."

"*Know your enemy*, Doctor. One of the oldest and most basic of military dictums. If we know the enemy, that's half of the battle. Half of the victory."

"Ah. And the other half?"

"Knowing ourselves."

Wilkerson cut the electronic connection, and Koenig was alone with his thoughts once more in the CIC. The others of the CIC watch manned their stations in the pit, but, as Koenig had said, there wasn't a lot for any of them to do now except to stay alert. The carrier battlegroup was now four hours into her 16.64-hour voyage out to the thirty-AU shell, approaching the orbit of Saturn and traveling now at a bit under 75,000 kilometers per second. At a quarter of the speed of light, there wasn't yet any visible aberration in the view of the stars ahead. Boötis and neighboring Corona Borealis maintained their familiar shapes—a kite to the right, with bright Arcturus at the base, and a broad *U* shape of stars, like an upraised arm, to the left.

What was it about transcendence that the Turusch—or, more likely, their Sh'daar masters—so feared? For that matter, what was transcendence, as *they* understood the term? That was the real problem here . . . knowing what completely alien cultures meant by the term.

Hell, Koenig wasn't certain *he* understood what the word meant. And beings with such different brains as the Turusch likely meant something very different, very *alien*.

What was it the Turusch had said, their third-line description of transcendence? "Technic species evolve into higher forms. When they pass beyond, they leave behind . . . death."

That was it. The first half of that statement was transparent enough. For centuries now, humankind had speculated about its relationship with its technology, and about where that technology might be taking it. Humans today, human technology today, would be comprehensible—barely—to humans of three or four hundred years ago. But the GRIN technologies, especially, were rapidly going a long way toward changing what it meant to be human.

Genetics. People like Michael Noranaga had engaged genetic prostheses to change their somatypes. Noranaga had done so in the line of duty, becoming a semi-aquatic selkie with more in common with marine mammals than with unaltered humans. But on Earth there were humans who changed their body shapes as a form of cultural or artistic

expression . . . shapeshifters, they called themselves. The
very idea of a human who looked like an elf or a mixture
of wolf and human challenged the very concept of what it
meant to be human.

Robotics. Robots had become ubiquitous throughout
human culture. The teleoperation of NTE robots let human
minds explore toxic and deadly environments like the surface of Venus or the nitrogen-ice plains of Triton . . . human
minds temporarily taking on bodies of plastic and nano-
laminate alloys. And non-sentient robotic intelligences were
everywhere, from smart clothes to smart buildings to smart
missiles.

Information Systems. Perhaps the biggest changes had occurred in that field. Through cerebral implants, any human
in any civilized location could have instant access to all
available information through the Net-Cloud. He could talk
to anyone anywhere, limited only by the speed of light, and
at great distances he could converse with another person's
AI-generated avatar. AIs, artificial intelligences of greater
than human capability, operated everywhere throughout
the myriad Net-Clouds, gathering and storing information,
transmitting it, reshaping it, editing it, artificial minds that
had already transcended the merely human.

And Nanotechnology. Ships that reshaped themselves in
flight, buildings that grew themselves from piles of debris,
those were the most visible applications of the technology.
Less visible but even more powerful were examples such
as the trillions of nanorobotic devices pumping through
Koenig's circulatory system, cleaning out arteries, maintaining key balances within his metabolic processes, even
repairing damaged chromosomes and guarding against can-
cers, disease, even the effects of aging. Alexander Koenig
could expect to live to see the age of five hundred, they told
him—theoretically, given ongoing nanomedical advances,
there was no way to even guess how long he might live—
assuming he survived the next day or so.

The more far-reaching effects, though, the most transforming ones, appeared when various technologies mingled—
the use of nanotechnology to grow the cerebral implants

that gave people their links with the Net-Cloud, and which allowed people to have their own personal AI software running on their internal hardware. The four technologies designated as GRIN interacted with one another, multiplied one another's effects and potencies.

And where, and *what*, were they all leading to?

Of greater concern right now, though, to Koenig's mind, was the second half of the Turusch statement: "When they pass beyond, they leave behind death."

How did transcendence equate with death?

Why would human transcendence be of concern to an alien species . . . in particular, an alien species like the Sh'daar, which might be half a billion years old?

Humans had just taken the first step in beginning to understand the Turusch; they didn't yet know what the Sh'daar looked like, much less understand how they thought.

Somehow, Koenig thought, humans were going to have to come to grips with those questions, to begin to understand who and what the Sh'daar were and how they thought.

And they would have to do so very swiftly indeed, if humankind was going to survive. . . .

Chapter Twenty-Three

Starhawk Transit
Fleet Rendezvous Point
1.3-AU Orbit, Sol System
0735 hours, TFT

Hurry up and wait.

Lieutenant Gray had heard that ancient military axiom often enough during the past five years. Likely it had been invoked by grizzled NCOs in the army of Sargon the Great forty-eight centuries before. But this was ludicrous.

Starhawk Transit had boosted from Oceana at 0414 hours. It had taken nine minutes to get up to whispering range of *c*, a coasting phase of just three minutes, and another nine minutes of deceleration to reach Rendezvous Point Defender, roughly halfway between the current positions of Earth and Mars. By 0445, Gray and the other twenty-three Starhawk pilots were drifting in an empty sector of space, waiting. There was no one else there.

Other naval vessels had begun arriving a few at a time. The destroyers *Trumbull* and *Nehman* and *Ishigara*. A heavy monitor out of Earth Synchorbit, the *Warden*. A Russian heavy cruiser, the *Groznyy*. One light fleet carrier from the European Federation, the *Jeanne d'Arc*. Others would be coming, but they were scattered across much of the Inner System—or they were still docked at synchorbital bases circling Earth or Mars, their crews still in the process of returning aboard, their power plants still off-line, some even with their weapons or drive systems partially disassembled for routine maintenance.

It took time to get a capital ship under way unless, like *America* and her consorts, the quantum taps were already running and the ship rigged for space.

Three fucking hours, Gray thought. *We could have been out there by now. . . .*

Just over an hour and a half earlier, at 0600 hours, he'd transmitted a request to the *America*, now outbound. At that time, the *America* battlegroup had been about one AU out from Mars, about two from the fleet rendezvous point, so they would have received the transmission at around 0615.

It had been over an hour now, and still no response. By now, the battlegroup, accelerating at 500 gravities, would be three and a half AUs from Mars, about four and a half from the fleet rendezvous point, and traveling at around 72,000 kps. Even with the thirty-six-minute time lag one-way, he should have gotten a reply—if one was coming—at *some* point in the last forty-five minutes.

"What the hell are they doing out there?" Gray said.

"Don't sweat it, Skipper," Lieutenant j.g. Alys McMasters told him. "They're probably arguing about it with Earth, and the time lag's a killer!"

Gray started, then bit off a curse. He'd not realized the channel was open, that he'd transmitted his exasperated comment over the fighter commnet.

"I'm seriously considering boosting anyway," Gray replied. "We're useless here."

"A great way to end a promising career, Boss," Lieutenant Frank Osterman said. "Last I heard, we go where we're told, when we're told. We don't make strategy."

"Roger that," Gray replied.

But that didn't make the wait easy.

During the past hours, information had been moving across the solar system like expanding ripples from stones chucked in a lake. Limited by the speed of light, representing only small portions of the total picture, that information only slowly reached all of the people involved, all of the decision makers, all of the ships. The picture was complicated by retransmission delays, and by decisions by various officers and politicians along the way to pass the data along only to certain command levels.

Which meant that units like the Starhawk transit squadron were operating in the dark. For all Gray and the newbie pilots in his command knew, the enemy fleet was zorching in at this moment, only a few minutes out . . . and no one had bothered to tell them. They knew that a Turusch signal beam had been intercepted some three hours earlier, confirming that there were at least two groups of enemy ships out at the thirty-AU shell, knew that the *America* battlegroup was headed for Point Libra, *away* from Triton.

But they knew precious little else.

"Incoming transmission," Gray's AI announced. "Source TCN *America*."

"Let's hear it!"

"Starhawk Transit Squadron, this is *America* CIC," a woman's voice said, static hissing and crackling behind the transmission as the Starhawk's communication suite up-shifted the frequency to compensate for the Doppler effect. "Your provisional op plan is approved. Initiate immediately. You are designated Green Squadron, and are now under *America* CIC control. Lieutenant Gray is confirmed as Green Squadron Leader. Please note attached transmission, and acknowledge receipt. Transmission ends."

Gray felt a surge of relief . . . mingled with adrenaline-sparked terror. *We're going!*

His "provisional op plan," as the CIC officer on *America* had put it, had been the rather strongly worded suggestion, made hours ago, that the twenty-four Starhawk fighters now orbiting at 1.3 AUs begin boosting immediately toward Point Libra. *America* had sent five squadrons toward Libra some four and a half hours ago—fifty-some fighters against a Turusch invasion fleet of unknown but certainly powerful composition.

Throwing twenty-four more fighters into the ongoing battle out there might, *might* make a difference.

He checked the attached transmission, an imbedded signal . . . and saw that it was an intercept picked up first at Earth, then transmitted under a classified security lock to the *America*, then retransmitted back to the rest of *America*'s battlegroup, including Green Squadron.

Opening the imbed, he and the others in his squadron watched the final seconds of the *Gallagher* and the other unarmed High Guard ships at Triton, watched until the final camera view spun crazily, then vanished in a burst of white noise.

"Jesus, Qwan-yin, and Buddha!" someone muttered.

"It's okay, people," Gray said. "We're going in the other direction—out to Point Libra."

"Yeah, where it'll be *worse*," Lieutenant j.g. Harper pointed out.

"Volunteers only," Gray said. "If you'd rather sit here feeling useless until the Tushies come to you, do so. *I'm* boosting out to meet the bastards."

"I'm with you, Lieutenant Gray," McMasters told him.

"Yeah, Skipper," Lieutenant Tolliver added. "Let's go kick Tushie tush!"

Gray was already feeding orders to his AI, his Starhawk rotating sharply, bringing its prow into line with an invisible point against the sky in the direction of the constellation Libra. One by one, the other pilots chimed in.

All twenty-three would follow him out toward Point Libra. He checked the time—0738 hours. "Kick it," he told his AI.

"Transit Squadron, this is the *Jeanne d'Arc*. Our CIC notes that you are leaving formation without proper authorization. Explain yourself."

The French light carrier had assumed the responsibility for control of local space traffic. The *Jeanne* carried three fighter squadrons—Franco-German KRG-17 Raschadler fighters, according to the fleet Warbook—and all of her bays were full. Gray had requested permission to dock when he and the newbies had arrived, and had had his request denied.

"*Jeanne d'Arc*, this is Green Squadron," he replied. "We have new orders."

"Negative, Green Squadron," came the reply. "Captain La-Salle says that you are under his jurisdiction now. We need confirmation before releasing you to another command."

"Stuff it, *Jeanne*," Gray replied. "We're going where the action is."

And, followed by the rest of the fighters, he accelerated to fifty thousand gravities.

Red Bravo Flight
America *Deep Recon*
Inbound, Sol System
0814 hours, TFT

Marissa Allyn's Starhawk was out of missiles, but she still had power for her PBP and rounds for the KK cannon. Pulling her fighter into a hard turn, feeling the heavy drag of tidal forces as she rounded the projected drive singularity, she brought her ship into line with another Turusch ship and fired, sending a particle beam slashing cross the vessel, knocking down defensive shields and boring into the hull metal beneath. White flame—metal flash-heated into vapor—exploded across her forward display, and in another instant she'd hurtled through the fireball, debris flaring off her own shields.

"Red Five!" Lieutenant Huerta called. "You have a Toad coming down on your six!"

"Thanks, Red Seven! I see him!"

No need to risk a turn. She spun her Starhawk end-for-end, the ship continuing in a straight online as she now faced back the way she'd come. A Toad, malevolent and chunky, burst though the expanding debris cloud of the destroyed Trash ship, and her AI immediately achieved a target lock, signaling her with a tone in her ear.

Switching to guns, she triggered a long burst of kinetic-kill projectiles, accelerating a stream of depleted uranium slugs toward the target at twelve per second. The Toad's shields had been up at around 90 percent to bring it through the debris field unhurt, shrouding the craft in a hazy blur, but as soon as it was clear of the evaporating fireball, this forward shields dropped to allow it to fire . . . and in that instant Allyn's volley struck home.

White flashes sparked and scintillated across the Toad's prow. Allyn kept firing, kept hammering at the oncoming Toad, which suddenly ripped open under the punishment in a spray of fragments and molten metal.

She spun her fighter through a full one-eighty once more and kicked in the acceleration. The sky around her was filled with ships, with drifting fragments, with flaring, silent explosions of light.

The lopsided battle had been continuing for over an hour now. Allyn and the other three Starhawks in her flight had been harassing the Turusch fleet, making high-velocity passes through the enemy formation, creating as much damage and havoc on each pass as possible. There'd been two casualties. Lieutenant Cutler in the first run . . . and Lieutenant Friedman had been skimming low across the outer hull of a Turusch Echo-class battleship when a pair of homing Golf-Mikes had closed with his Starhawk and detonated. The blast had actually damaged the Echo; Nancy Friedman's ship had been obliterated, half vaporized in the triggering detonation, half crumpled into the singularity in an instant.

As the minutes slipped past, however, other Confederation fighters had begun arriving. All of the other Black Lightnings were now in the fight, along with ten of the Impactors and four Nighthawks—a total of twenty Starhawks and four SG-55 War Eagles. Red Bravo had been constantly broadcasting a streaming update on the engagement; the CTT by now had reached every Confederation fighter within one light hour of the battle, and they were coming in now from farther and farther away.

A Turusch Sierra-class cruiser appeared on her combat display, five thousand kilometers ahead, and she adjusted her course to intercept, kicking in her grav drive to a full fifty thousand gravities, accelerating at 500 kilometers per second squared. She let her AI handle the weapons release. When she passed the enemy battleship four and a half seconds later, she was moving at over 2200 kilometers per second relative to the target; mere human reflexes were simply not quick enough to react at such velocities.

There was a flash of motion, a flicker of *something* huge as she hurtled past the target at a range of just over one hundred kilometers, and she felt her Starhawk pivot, felt its beam weapon trigger. Unfortunately, not even her AI could give her a damage assessment. The target was gone before whatever damage she'd inflicted could register on the fighter's scanners.

But all she could do, all *any* of them could do, was continue buzzing the ponderous enemy fleet, hitting individual ships when they could, where they could, as hard as they could.

The blue icon representing one of the Nighthawks flared and winked out, and she winced. The Nighthawks' older War Eagle fighters wouldn't last long in this kind of knife fight. They just weren't as maneuverable in a close-in fight as a Starhawk. Survival in this type of space combat depended on speed and maneuverability, on not being where the enemy expected you to be at any given instant.

And then another Black Lightning was hit—Hector Aguilera's ship—and she heard him scream as his Starhawk spun out of control, whipping around its own drive singularity with impossible speed before it ripped itself into white-hot fragments.

Twenty-three fighters left, of those that had arrived so far.

She wondered how long any of them would be able to keep pressing the attack.

Green Squadron
Outbound, Sol System
0848 hours, TFT

"Green Leader, to all Greens. Anything yet?"

The answers came back, distorted by high velocity and the tightly curving geometry of spacetime at near-c . . . all negative.

"Keep listening. Trust me. It won't be much longer."

They'd accelerated for ten minutes at fifty thousand gravities, crossing six tenths of an AU and reaching a velocity of 299,000 kps—99.7 percent of the speed of light. For the next hour, then, they'd flashed out into emptiness under free fall, traveling another seven AUs, past the orbit of Mars, past the orbits of the Main Belt asteroids and the orbit of Jupiter, and into the Abyss beyond.

Green Squadron—Gray kept wondering if *America*'s CIC had given them that designation because the nugget pilots were *green*—would reach the thirty-AU shell, the orbit of Neptune, by 1148 hours Fleet Time—another three hours, or a bit less. The total near-*c* coast time for the squadron, though, would *seem* to be only seventeen and a half minutes, subjective time versus objective, thanks to the effects of relativistic time dilation. From Gray's point of view, fewer than fifteen minutes had passed since he'd given the order to boost, including the acceleration period up to near-*c*.

To make matters *really* exciting, there was the distinct possibility—even the *probability*—that the Turusch fleet had begun accelerating for the Inner System at some point during the past four hours or so.

Gray stared at his navigational display, thinking about this.

He'd ordered the other fighters to deploy in a receiver rosette—a tactical flight formation designed to transform the entire fighter unit into a *very* large antenna array. Even at near-*c*, each fighter *could* receive incoming radio traffic, but unscrambling them could be a problem. Those messages tended to be garbled and static-blasted, as well as strongly blue-shifted from ahead, red-shifted from astern.

To counter this, ships traveling in formation sometimes assumed the rosette pattern while maintaining laser taclinks, allowing them to use wide-baseline interferometry to pick up and process weak or garbled signals. In effect, Green Squadron was now a single antenna over ten thousand kilometers across—the largest separation between any two of the twenty-four fighters in the formation.

He knew that when *America*'s squadrons engaged the

Turusch out at thirty-AU, they would have begun transmitting combat report updates back to the Inner System. Green Squadron was now a quarter of the way out-system between the *America* and the thirty-AU shell, and in the perfect position to pick up a transmission from *America*'s fighters first, well before they reached the *America*.

If that transmission came, *when* it came, Gray and the rest of Green Squadron would know exactly where the enemy fleet was, and be able to make the necessary course corrections that would let them meet the enemy, somewhere out there beyond the dark orbit of Saturn. Depending on what that transmission told him about the enemy's position and vector, he thought he might be able to make a solid tactical contribution to the battle. It was a long shot, certainly, but one of the time-hallowed bits of advice to anyone in combat had been playing through his brain for hours now.

Do *something! It may be wrong, but do* something!

Gray intended to do exactly that.

Red Bravo Flight
America *Deep Recon*
Inbound, Sol System
0930 hours, TFT

They were losing.

The enemy was becoming quicker, more adept, was learning how to anticipate the quick-pass maneuvers of the fighters and lay down heavy fields of fire—particle beams, clouds of kinetic impactors, gravitic missiles, blossoming thermonuclear warheads. During the past two hours, thirteen Confederation fighters had been destroyed and five incapacitated, their systems down as they hurtled on blind and unpowered trajectories into darkness.

The fighters were also having to route more and more of their power to their drives. The enemy had been accelerating now at about five hundred gravities for two hours, fifteen minutes, and were now traveling at 40,500 kps, after having crossed just over one AU. With their higher accelerations, the fighters could match that speed easily enough, but every kilometer per second per second applied toward matching the enemy's course toward the Inner System made that much less power available for maneuvering.

And maybe, Allyn thought to herself, *maybe we're just getting too damned tired to think straight.*

Lieutenant Theod Young's War Eagle tumbled helplessly out of control, impacting against the shields of a Turusch behemoth, a small and heavily armed powered planetoid.

We're losing, she thought again, *and there's nothing we can do to stop them.*

Green Squadron
Outbound, Sol System
1002 hours, TFT

A window opened in his mind, and Gray felt the inrushing cascade of raw data.

The antenna rosette maneuver had worked, plucking the speed-blasted signal from space as it passed the hurtling formation of Starhawks. The fighter AIs, working together across the laser taclink, had processed and enhanced the data, transforming it into something intelligible.

They wouldn't know about it for hours, yet, on the *America* or back on Earth and Mars, but *America*'s five squadrons had engaged the enemy fleet Bravo some three hours ago, at 0712 hours. Gray saw the attack led by his former squadron leader, Marissa Allyn, saw the destruction of the Turusch mobile dwarf planet, saw the death of Lieutenant Cutler.

Perhaps most important of all, thanks to Commander Allyn, he now had precise coordinates for the Turusch fleet. As minute followed objective minute, he saw more and more Turusch warships being plotted on Allyn's tactical display, saw them accelerating, ponderously, toward the Inner System.

Green Squadron had been traveling outbound on a heading toward 15 hours right ascension, declination minus 10 degrees, in the northern reaches of the constellation Libra, the "Point Libra" designated as a nav point for ships trying to intercept the alien fleet. Allyn had intercepted the Turusch ships at a different nav point, however . . . Right Ascension 15 hours, 34 minutes; Declination plus 26 degrees, 43 minutes.

This second point was located some 37 degrees across the sky from Point Libra—meaning that Green Squadron was 37 degrees off the proper heading. This was what Gray had been waiting for . . . an *exact* navigational heading. The new nav point was located, he noticed, within the constellation Corona Borealis—close beside the bright star Alphekka, in fact.

He wondered if there was any significance in that. His onboard sky charts listed Alphekka as an A0V/G5V double star seventy-two light years from Sol. The system was only about 300 million years old, though, and thick with protoplanetary dust and gas—too young for a planetary system to have fully formed.

Perhaps it was only coincidence that a bright, relatively nearby star lay close to that point. But possibly not. . . .

"Green Squadron, all ships," he called. "Set your nav beacons for Right Ascension fifteen hours, thirty-four minutes; Declination plus twenty-six degrees, forty-three minutes. On my mark, execute a thirty-seven-degree course change to the new heading. In three . . . two . . . one . . . *mark!*"

Still moving at close to light speed, the fighters threw out drive singularities, putting a steep gradient into space ahead, their straight-line courses bending through curved space and onto the new heading. Gray was holding his breath, waiting as fighter after fighter called in, acknowledging completion of the maneuver. At these speeds, the *slightest* miscalculation would mean disaster, a fighter literally vaporized by impossible tidal forces, or devoured by its own drive singularity.

Fortunately, the pilots might be green, but the AIs handling the details of the maneuver were, if not experienced, *very* highly skilled. Every ship came through perfectly, dropping onto the new outbound heading.

All of the stars of the surrounding sky were crowded by

the effects of relativistic travel into a narrow band of light now, some 30 degrees off his bow. The stars of Corona Borealis were among them, of course, but quite unrecognizable in the photic distortion. Gray told the AI to transmit the course change to Earth. They would learn of it shortly after they got the signal from Allyn's fighters.

"AI," he said. "I need a theoretical plot. Take the positions, course, and velocities of all of the Turusch ships in Allyn's transmission, and work up an extended targeting estimate."

"That estimate will, necessarily, be inaccurate," the ship's AI told him. "The enemy will be changing acceleration, if nothing else, while fighting Allyn's wing."

"Best guess," he told the system. "We're not God."

"This will take several minutes."

"Fast as you can." Several minutes subjective could be an hour objective, and they didn't have much more time than that.

Sooner than he'd feared, the AI announced, "Calculations complete."

"Transmit it to the other ships in the squadron," Gray said, "as targeting data."

"Which weapons?" the AI asked.

"Something that will make a mark at ten or fifteen AUs," Gray replied. "AMSOs."

They were going to throw sand at the oncoming Turusch ships.

Red Bravo Flight
America *Deep Recon*
Inbound, Sol System
1012 hours, TFT

All of the fighters launched from *America* had joined the engagement, a rapidly moving fur ball hurtling toward the Inner System now at 58,500 kps. Assuming the enemy pulled a mid-course flip and decelerated the rest of the way in, the total voyage was going to be on the order of fifteen more hours.

The handful of *America*'s fighters simply weren't going to last that much longer. Twenty fighters had been destroyed total so far . . . and seven sent spinning away into space, helplessly out of control. They'd started this op with fifty-six fighters. Thirty Confederation fighters were left . . . close to 50 percent casualties.

Not again! Allyn thought, desperate, stressed to the point of screaming. *I can't go through this again!*

"CAG," she called. "Lightning One-zero-one . . . this is Red Bravo Five. Private channel."

"Go ahead, Red Five," Captian Dixon's voice replied.

"CAG, we're down by half. We have to break off!"

"Commander, we are going to keep hammering at these bastards until they break and run, or until our expendables run dry and our PBPs are melted into slag. When that happens, we will begin *ramming* the sons of bitches if we have to! Is that understood?"

"Understood. Sir."

Allyn's mind was reeling. She was afraid . . . yes—it was impossible *not* to be afraid in such a position—but more pressing was the overwhelming feeling of frustration, of failure, of *helplessness* in the face of such an enemy. They'd been hammering at the Turusch fleet, to use Dixon's word, for a full three hours now. They'd lost half of their own fighters . . . and managed to destroy or badly damage perhaps twelve enemy capital ships and twenty-two Toad fighters. An excellent tactical trade-off, perhaps . . . but essentially useless when you realized that there were still nearly ninety Turusch ships out here, *not* counting the swarms of fighters. The vessels had been appearing out of the Outer System night for three hours now, catching up, rendezvousing with the main fleet, joining them in their stately procession toward the Inner System.

Thirty fighters, almost all out of Krait missiles, most running low on KK rounds, with nothing but their Blue Lightning particle beams to use as weapons. PBPs were sometimes called "infinite repeaters" since they couldn't run out of ammo so long as they were connected to a quantum power tap, but they did have a finite life. Allyn's beam projector was already giving her trouble, cutting out now and again as the system overheated. If the circuitry got hot enough to melt, even her nanorepair systems wouldn't be able to keep her in the fight.

And for all she knew, Dixon wasn't kidding with his threat to start ramming the enemy.

The plan, of course, was to cause enough damage to the Turusch fleet that they'd be vulnerable to attack by the main fleet elements waiting back in the Inner System.

Swinging around for yet another pass, she lined up on a Turusch mobile planetoid, triggering her charged particle beam from fifty thousand kilometers out, continuing to fire as she flashed past at a relative speed of nearly five thousand kilometers per second. The planetoid's surface was still partially shielded, though a number of shields had evidently collapsed. Neither she nor her AI could tell whether they'd managed to hit any of the exposed surface installations, or if her fire had been absorbed or deflected by the gravitic screens. The enemy's particle beams reached out toward her; her jinking pattern, random course shifts implemented by her AI, avoided the incoming fire, but something struck her aft shields and jolted her hard. A quick check of her system diagnostics—no damage, thank God.

But her PBP was overheated, a red warning light showing on her panel and in her mind.

"My God!" Hennessy cried out. "Look at that!"

On her display, the asteroid ship she'd just attacked was firing.

Not at her. The projectile appeared to be a KK missile, accelerating at high-G and likely carrying simple mass as a warhead, a *lot* of it. It wasn't aimed at any of the fighters attacking the Turusch fleet. Instead, it appeared to be accelerating hard for the Inner System, toward Earth or Mars or the Confederation warships waiting there.

"It's the bombardment!" Lieutenant Malvar of the Rattlers called out. "They've started bombarding Earth and Mars!"

Other Turusch warships were firing as well, hurling warheads toward the tiny, shrunken sun in unending streams, some massing as much as a ton, some as little as a kilogram.

"That's it," Collins said. "I'm fucking out of here. We've *lost. . . .*"

And the *America* deep-recon flight, what was left of it, began to fall apart.

Chapter Twenty-Four

Green Squadron
Outbound, Sol System
1015 hours, TFT

"It ain't gonna work, Lieutenant!" Lieutenant j.g. Mark Rafferty insisted. "Sand grains are *tiny*. They'll hit hydrogen atoms on the way . . . protons in the solar wind, that sort of thing. They'll all get zapped into plasma!"

"Sand grains are tiny," Gray agreed, "but they're a *lot* bigger than protons. Some might be ablated, turned to plasma . . . and so what? You can't destroy *mass*, and it's the mass traveling at near-c that does the damage. You ever hear of an A-7 strike package?"

"Yeah, but . . . that doesn't make . . . sense." It sounded as though he was thinking about it, trying to wrap his mind around the idea.

"First-year Academy physics, Rafferty. Matter and/or energy cannot be created or destroyed, except as allowed by the very special case of quantum power taps. Besides, even if all the sand at the leading edge of the cloud did get turned to plasma, it would just sweep out a tunnel for the rest of the sand following along behind. Like a lightning bolt burning a vacuum channel through the atmosphere. One way or the other, the sand *will* get there."

"There's another problem, sir," McMasters pointed out.

"At this range, it'll be like firing a shotgun. We might hit the Turusch ships, but we'll hit our own fighters as well."

"There's a chance of that, yes," Gray conceded. "But we're going to be broadcasting a warning ahead of our release. Our fighters are a lot more maneuverable than the Turusch, even their Toads. They'll have time to sidestep the volley."

"But if we did hit our own guys—"

"Enough, people. I'm in charge, the responsibility is mine." He checked his display a final time, an abstract representation of the enemy fleet seen bow-on . . . or how the enemy fleet was *probably* laid out, now some sixteen AUs ahead.

McMasters was right. This was like firing a shotgun at long range. Precision of aim, thank God, wasn't necessary.

"Okay," he told his AI. "Transmit the warning."

"Transmitting."

"And transmit a complete log to *America*. They need to be in the loop."

They may need it, he thought, with a sudden stab of gloom, for the court martial. Despite the transmitted warning, despite the maneuverability of Starhawk and War Eagle fighters, of *course* it was possible that some would be caught in the blast.

And the first rule of warfare was—friendly fire isn't.

"We will fire in volleys," Gray told the others. "By the numbers. Group one, ready . . . *fire!*"

And from each of six Starhawk fighters, two AMSO missiles dropped and streaked into blackness, accelerating at two thousand gravities. "*Fox Two!*"

The idea was hardly a new one. As Gray had mentioned, the A-7 strike package used for long-range planetary or fleet bombardment used the same concept. The twist was using AMSO defensive fire as an offensive weapon—a weapon of decidedly mass destruction.

"Group two, ready . . . *fire!*"

Twelve more AS-78 missiles slipped from Starhawk missile bays and engaged their drives, vanishing into the twisted strangeness of near-*c* space. "*Fox Two!*"

"Group three, ready . . . *fire*!"

The missiles had been reprogrammed. They would not automatically detonate, scattering their matter-compressed lead-grain warloads a few seconds after firing. Instead, they would detonate when their onboard radars picked up the first enemy ships ten light seconds ahead. The sand clouds should still be fairly tightly packed in that distance, still carry a staggering kinetic punch.

Gray knew there'd been experiments with using sand-casters as offensive weapons. The idea had been dropped years ago, primarily because it was such a blind, area-effect, deadly weapon; fire one of the things at near-*c* in the general direction of Earth, and you might find you'd accidentally scoured away the continent of Africa, and wrecked the planet's weather patterns for the next couple of centuries.

But in this particular tactical setup . . . why not? The only thing in that direction was the star Alphekka. Maybe a few grains of sand or hot plasma would sizzle into that star system seventy-five years or so from now, still traveling at 99.7 percent *c*, and maybe by then the interstellar medium would wear the individual grains down to nothing and absorb the plasma's kinetic energy.

"Group four, *fire*!"

He felt his own Starhawk lurch as his missiles slid off the launch rails. "Fox Two!" he called, adding his cry to the fox calls of the others.

In the meantime, seventy-two AMSO missiles packed with sand-sized lead BBs were going to burn their way through the oncoming Turusch fleet. Their shields would stop a lot of the attack . . . but this was a *lot* of mass traveling at relativistic velocities.

Handfuls of sand, turned into weapons of mass destruction.

Relativistic shotgun blasts.

Gray prayed that he hadn't just made a cataclysmic error in judgment.

Red Bravo Flight
America *Deep Recon*
Inbound, Sol System
1031 hours, TFT

Marissa Allyn was shaking. It was happening *again*, her entire unit, wiped out.

The surviving Confederation fighters were breaking away from the Turusch fleet now, individual ships spreading out in all directions. Their best efforts had worn away at the massive, inbound enemy force, but the remaining Turusch warships still outnumbered the fleet waiting for them in the Inner System, *vastly* outnumbered the handful of ships in the *America* battlegroup, and had just fired salvo after salvo of high-G impactor warheads. Accelerating at two thousand gravities, those kinetic-kill projectiles would reach near-*c* velocity in just over three hours, and the vicinity of Earth and Mars less than three hours later.

How *accurate* that hivel bombardment would be was anyone's guess. The Turusch had spent a lot of time out at the thirty-AU shell and beyond, and would have been gathering volumes of data on the orbital velocities of the planets, the locations and vectors of ships, even the precise positions and orbital details of factories, shipyards, military bases, deep-space habitats, and other large facilities, both those circling planets and those in solar orbit.

The infalling salvo could well devastate the technological infrastructure throughout the Inner System, could leave the cities of both Earth and Mars in smoldering ruins.

And the handful of *America*'s fighters hadn't been able to do a thing to stop it.

"Regroup!" Captain Dixon was yelling over the tactical channel. "All fighters, regroup!"

What the hell was the point? They, all of humankind, had *lost*. . . .

On her tactical display, she saw red pinpoints, clouds of them, sweeping out from the Turusch warfleet, Toad fighters in pursuit of the fleeing Confederation fighters.

Allyn struggled to stop the shaking. Those Toads were relentlessly hunting down individual fleeing Confederation fighters, trying to sweep them from the sky. There were only twenty-three fighters left now, twenty-three out of the initial fifty-seven.

A pair of Toads was dropping onto Dixon's six, dogging him, closing on him . . .

"I've got two on my tail!" Dixon called.

Allyn threw her Starhawk into a sharp one-eighty, as tight a turn as she could manage as the tidal forces generated by her drive singularity threatened to pull her and her ship to pieces. Then she was hurtling back the way she'd come, heading straight for the CAG and the Turusch fighter now five hundred kilometers behind him.

"Hold your vector, CAG!" she called. She didn't want him pulling a sudden maneuver and crashing into her. She lined up on the nearest Toad and triggered a long burst from her KK cannon, sending a stream of compressed, depleted uranium slugs slamming past Dixon's fighter and into the enemy ship. The Toad had dropped its forward shields to get a clear shot at the CAG, and the impact opened the enemy craft as if it had been unzipped.

And then her weapon ran dry, the last of her KK projectiles gone. She targeted the second Toad as she flashed past Dixon . . . but in the instant she fired, the Toad fired its particle beams at the CAG's ship.

She hurtled past the Toad at a relative velocity of some hundreds of kilometers per second, too fast to see if she'd hurt it. On her display, however, Captain Dixon's Starhawk flared up in a brilliant fireball, then faded out.

"CAG! CAG, do you copy?"

Maybe his transponder was out. Maybe . . . maybe . . .

"CAG, do you copy?" There was no reply.

And a new thought struck Allyn, struck her and shook her and left a hard, cold knot behind her breastbone. The CAG was dead . . . and so was Commander Jacelyn, the skipper of the Impactors and the wing's deputy CAG.

Commander Fremont, CO of the Death Rattlers . . . dead.

Commander Murcheson, skipper of the Star Tigers . . . dead.

Commander Burnham, CO of the Nighthawks . . . out of control, missing, presumed dead.

Marissa Allyn was the last squadron commander left, even if she no longer had a squadron . . . and her rank had just put her in command of the surviving fighters.

And somehow she was going to have to bring them out of this.

Between the Squadrons
Sol System
1032 hours, TFT

AS-78 Anti-Missile Shield Ordnance, or AMSO missiles, accelerated at two thousand gravities. Normally they popped—scattering their warload of compressed, depleted uranium micropellets—a few thousand meters ahead of the firing ship, dispersing the sand in a fast-moving and expanding cloud that could refract incoming lasers, absorb particle beams, and explode or ablate missiles, creating a cheap, simple, and reasonably effective defensive shield.

They had to be used selectively and with tactical precision, of course. If the firing ship changed course, the sand cloud kept moving on the original vector, vanishing uselessly into space. And explosions and particle-beam hits tended to disperse the cloud, or transform much of it into expanding plasma, so a few incoming shots rendered it ineffective.

By reprogramming the missile guidance, Gray had set them to proximity detonation—"proximity" in this case being a rather broad term that included ten light seconds, approximately three million kilometers. Radar signals transmitted when the warhead was twenty seconds from the target took only ten to make the trip back, since the warhead itself was also traveling at very close to the speed of light.

The missiles had been accelerating at two thousand gravities the entire time. Without Alcubierre capabilities, however, the extra acceleration nudged the projectiles a bit closer to the speed of light, but essentially only added to the warhead's relativistic mass.

Five and a quarter AUs out from Green Squadron, some sixty minutes after launch, the lead AS-78 salvo picked up a return within ten light seconds and detonated. What Gray had not allowed for was the possibility that the target itself would be traveling close to light speed, and was approaching the AMSO warheads just behind the reflected radar signals that triggered the sandcaster firing. Six missiles exploded. Five missed, the sand clouds still tightly packed as they streaked past the oncoming KK impactor rounds fired by the Turusch fleet.

One sand cloud caught one impactor, however, and the results were . . . spectacular. Grains of sand—perhaps as much as one gram out of the ten kilograms in the missile's warhead—traveling at close to c hit a one-ton projectile traveling in the opposite direction at close to c. The combined velocity of that impact, of course, was *not* twice the speed of light, not if Einstein knew what he was talking about, but it *did* release a nontrivial flash of energy.

A *lot* of energy.

The alignment of the two converging salvos of impactor warheads and sandcaster rounds was not perfect; all of the AS-78s detonated as they passed within three million kilometers of the Turusch impactors, but the fast-moving sand clouds were gone, hurtling on at .998 c, long before the blast front reached them. And the Turusch impactors, an hour after launch, were scattered enough that not all were caught in the sudden, supernova flare of released kinetic energy.

But many were.

And the flash of that one impact burned for long seconds in the darkness of the Outer System, the wave front spreading out in all directions at the speed of light.

Red Bravo Flight
America *Deep Recon*
Inbound, Sol System
1115 hours, TFT

"Incoming transmission," Allyn's AI told her. "Source, Green Squadron."

"What the hell is Green Squadron?" she asked . . . but just the possibility that reinforcements were on the way out from Earth made her immediately accept the signal.

Help *was* on the way . . . twenty-four more Starhawks straight from Oceana, and under the command of Lieutenant Trevor Gray. And they had launched . . . great God in heaven!

"All fighters!" she yelled over the tactical channel. "All fighters! We have near-*c* incoming! *Clear the battlespace!*"

And a moment later, a flash appeared, briefly outshining the sun.

The survivors of *America*'s five-squadron deployment had already begun clustering together, ahead of and several thousand kilometers off the line of the Turusch fleet's advance. By forming up together, they could better protect one another from attack runs by Turusch Toads; for some time now, however, the enemy had seemed content to leave the Confederation fighters alone, to watch them, to match their course with a group of Toads pacing them from a few thousand kilometers away.

Perhaps the Turusch had been hurt more badly than Allyn's wing had realized. Perhaps they were sick of the bloodletting as well.

Or perhaps the handful of remaining Confederation fighters simply didn't matter any longer.

"My God!" Collins said over the tac channel as the light flash grew brighter, grew larger. "What the hell is *that*?"

"At a guess . . . it's sandcaster rounds hitting the Trash impactors. Hivel kinetic release." Allyn didn't trust herself to even guess at how much energy was represented by that brilliant star. It had appeared on their inbound flight path, and was shining within a few degrees of the distant sun. It wasn't more than a star, a pinpoint of light, but it hurt to look at it with unshielded optics, and for a moment or two, Sol was blotted out by its glare.

Together, the fighters began accelerating away from the Turusch fleet. Gray's warning had been specific; near-*c* sand clouds were coming in close behind the warning itself, and any fighters close to the enemy fleet might be hit. Maybe none of the outbound AMSO rounds had made it past that first, far-off detonation. But if any *had*—

A Turusch Juliet-class cruiser near the enemy's van began *sparkling* . . . or the forward gravitic shields of the vessel did, at any rate. Each flash was dazzlingly bright but very tiny, a single flash by itself too small to cause major damage . . . but as flash followed flash the enemy's gravitic shields collapsed, and then a storm of strobing detonations began eating through the enemy warship's bow cap.

Allyn watched, transfixed, as the Turusch cruiser began coming apart, shields smashed down, hull devoured bite by bite, as internal structure began showing through the missing gaps in hullo plate and armor, as the ship's interior began glowing white-hot.

The same was happening to other ships in the Turusch fleet as well.

"I'm being hit!" Lieutenant Wellesly cried. His was one of the last of the Star Tigers' War Eagles, and he was struggling to bring up the rear of the retreating Confederation fighters. His grav shields were sparkling and flashing like those of the Turusch warships.

Then Lieutenant Cavanaugh's Starhawk was being hit . . . and Lieutenant Dolermann's ship, one by one, working from the back of the flight toward the front. Allyn was registering impacts on her fighter's shielding now, isolated, individual hits by pellets each massing less than a tenth of a gram, but traveling at a fraction less than the speed of light. Her shields shrugged off one hit . . . a second . . . a third . . . but the rate of impacts was increasing, and her shields threatened to fall.

More and more of the Turusch vessels were being hit. Five had been destroyed outright, beginning with the Juliet. Eight more . . . ten more . . . *fifteen* more were badly damaged, their shields down, gaping, white-hot craters glowing against their outer hulls. Many of the enemy warships vanished as their gravitic shields went up full . . . but the impacts continued until the shields failed, exposing the naked hulls of the huge vessels within.

Numerous projectiles were striking the tight-wrapped

knots of folded spacetime ahead of each Turusch vessel, the drive singularities pulling them onward at five hundred gravities. Since those singularities, by definition, had escape velocities greater than the speed of light, the incoming sand grains couldn't pass through, but were trapped . . . and by becoming trapped, they each yielded *very* large amounts of energy.

Some of the enemy vessels began releasing their dust balls, switching off their forward drives. Some switched off the forward drives and flipped them astern, decelerating. Others threw out drive singularities to port or starboard, up or down, attempting to turn, to get out of the way of that incoming shotgun cloud of destruction.

Like a shotgun blast, the individual grains had been scattered across a very large area of sky, but the cloud was still thickest in the vicinity of the Turusch fleet, while Allyn and her fighters were accelerating out and away through the cloud's ragged, outer fringes. Wellesly's War Eagle suddenly exploded as his shields fell, and the fighter's hull succumbed to that thin, deadly sleet of sand. Cavanaugh's shields were down . . . and Collins' shields as well . . . and Raynell's and Donovan's and Tucker's as well.

Without orders, several of the Confederation pilots began cutting their acceleration somewhat, dropping back in the pack to put their fighters between those pilots whose shields had failed, and the incoming sleet.

And then, hurtling outward at half the speed of light, the surviving fighters cleared the vast, cone-shaped cloud of high-velocity sand.

Or, perhaps, the storm of sand had simply passed. Once she was sure the impacts had stopped, Allyn ordered the remaining fighters to decelerate, to turn, to again close with the enemy fleet.

Half of the enemy fighters that had been pacing them had been destroyed. Most of the rest were drifting, battered hulks, their shields down, their armor all but stripped away. The Confederation pilots burned past the enemy craft, hitting them with PBPs and a few remaining KK rounds. Those Turusch fighters that could scattered, some engaging, some fleeing. The battle broke up after a few seconds; both sides appeared shocked into a kind of fugue by the devastation. It was hard to think, hard to act.

But for the moment, the Confederation pilots held the advantage.

The Turusch battlefleet was in complete disarray. A cruiser turning one way had collided with a battleship turning another, filling the sky with broken fragments. Some of those fragments, tumbling outward at high speed, had struck other enemy warships, adding to the devastation.

The Confederation fighters made one high-speed run through the Turusch fleet, burning and killing wherever they could find targets of opportunity. Clouds of white-hot plasma and jagged, tumbling fragments of wreckage continued to drift with the fleet, however, and Allyn ordered the attack to break off before she lost any more pilots.

Some of the Turusch vessels *were* firing back, were still deadly adversaries.

"All fighters," she called over the tactical channel. "Regroup and reform on my position. We're going to stay clear of the battlespace for a while."

There might be further sandcaster volleys on the way out from Green Squadron. At this point, it was more important to track the enemy, to see what he intended to do. . . .

. . . and to await reinforcements. Green Squadron would be here soon.

"I'm not sure, people," Allyn transmitted to the others, "but I *think* we may have just won the battle."

Tactician Emphatic Blossom at Dawn
Enforcer Radiant Severing
1117 hours, TFT

Emphatic Blossom at Dawn knew the Turusch warfleet had lost.

It had begun having doubts about the practicality of this operation some *g'nya* before, as the ferocity, the sheer determination, the astonishing dedication of the defenders' attacks had become apparent. The humans had continued to assault a vastly superior Turusch battlefleet, arriving in twos and threes from all over the sky, hurling themselves at warships like tiny *d'cha* swarming around a behemoth *grolludh*. Even a *grolludh*'s massive gasbag could be punctured if enough of the mites attacked for long enough, if they wanted nothing other than the *grolludh* floater's death, if they didn't care how many of their number died.

"We must withdraw," Blossom's twin said, "while yet we can."

"This defeat will be . . . difficult to explain to the Sh'daar Seed."

The two voices speaking together said something quite different: "The Masters will not be pleased."

But orders were given and, one by one, the remaining Turusch warships began turning away, a ponderous change of course through 180 degrees.

It was an extremely risky maneuver, especially carried out by a closely formed fleet comprised of numerous damaged ships, some with sensors scoured away from ravaged hulls, some with faltering drive projectors or failing power plants. It would have been safer by far to flip end-for-end and decelerate at five hundred gravities, then accelerate back out-system, but that maneuver would have carried the battered fleet many light-*g'nyuu'm* deeper into the enemy's star system. The hunterfleet's deep-range scanners were already picking up returns of what likely were more enemy fighters outbound. If the Turusch hunterfleet came under heavy and sustained attacks by human capital vessels, few, if any, Turusch warships would escape at all.

One vessel, the *Scintillating Gleam*, began turning. A second, larger, ship, the *Devious Observer*, was supposed to turn, but its grav drive failed and it continued drifting straight ahead, directly into the *Gleam*'s path.

The *Scintillating Gleam* exploded as her power plant ran out of control. The *Devious Observer* took more damage to her flank, but the larger vessel continued ahead, a drifting hulk.

The enemy fighters watched the maneuver from a safe distance.

"You have won this time," Blossom said. "We don't know how."

"Enjoy the victory," the twin said. "Hard fought, bitterly won."

Together, the harmonics spoke a third time. "We shall grasp the final sharp reckoning, a new hunt . . . and soon."

Green Squadron
Outbound, Sol System
1120 hours, TFT

"Right, people," Gray called. "Stay tight! Keep jinking! *Hit 'em!*"

In close formation, the twenty-four Starhawks flashed in from astern of the Turusch fleet, a fleet now in full and tumultuous retreat. Gray locked on to an immense Alpha-class battleship, a ten-kilometer-long asteroid, potato-shaped and crater-pocked. Its shields were down, the weapons turrets and domes scattered across its surface nakedly exposed.

Gray locked on at ten thousand kilometers and fired a pair of Krait missiles, and a thousand megatons flared against the night. His Starhawk angled in close behind the missiles, pivoting as it zorched across half-molten craters seething into hard vacuum and lancing the stricken giant with its particle weapon.

Elsewhere, a Kilo-class light cruiser exploded . . . a brightly painted Toad fighter tumbled out of control, slamming into a mobile planetoid . . . a Gamma-class battle-cruiser began coming apart under the relentless pounding of four Confederation fighters, hull plates spinning into space, weapons housings collapsing into white-hot, molten metal, atmosphere spewing into emptiness like random rocket exhausts.

The attack continued with relentless purpose for twenty minutes, the fresh Starhawks of Green Squadron supported by the handful of exhausted survivors of Star Carrier *America*'s squadrons.

"About time someone else got out here," Commander Allyn quipped over the tactical channel.

"We weren't going to let you have all the fun to yourselves," Gray shot back. "Looks like you guys have been busy."

"Busy," Allyn replied. "Is *that* what you call it. . . ."

Green Squadron broke off the attack at last, however. The Turusch warfleet was scattering, and the pursuing fighters were being drawn further and further into the Abyss. Two of his nugget pilots were killed in the fight, burned out of the sky when they got a little too eager in their close pursuit.

The Turusch fleet had been badly mauled in the engagement—at least forty capital ships destroyed, and most of the rest had at least some damage from the sandblasting attack. The survivors were in full retreat, streaming out-system in the general direction of the star Alphekka. Those with disabled gravitic shields might not be able to jump to FTL. Unable to travel faster than light, their crews exposed to the harsh radiation cascade of near-*c* travel without screens, they would count as kills as well. Lifeless hulks doomed to fall endlessly through the gulfs between the cold and unwinking stars.

Confederation losses had been astonishingly light, with only fighters engaged, and no losses among the defending capital ship fleet. Allyn's ragged command had lost thirty-eight ships . . . and if SAR teams and tugs got out here in time, some of the missing pilots might yet be saved. Green Squadron had lost two. A stunning, lopsided, upset victory for the Confederation—forty fighters lost in exchange for forty or more capital ships, perhaps a hundred enemy fighters destroyed, and the salvation of the solar system as the enemy's attack fleet was turned back.

Or it *would* have been a lopsided victory . . . if not for one of the bitter ironies of modern space combat.

Some of the rounds fired by the enemy fleet had not, in fact, yet reached their targets. . . .

Chapter Twenty-Five

Inner System, Sol System
1430 hours, TFT

The remainder of the battle was anticlimax . . . but as Deep Tactician Emphatic Blossom had suggested, it was *bitter* anticlimax.

Most of the impactors fired by the Turusch hunterfleet were caught in the sandblast, but not all. Hurtling across the Abyss between the thirty-AU shell and the Inner planets, the impactors, each with a warhead massing slightly less than one kilogram, had been aimed with considerable precision; the plasma shock wave of the hivel explosion midway between Green Squadron and the Turusch fleet had deflected most of them ever so slightly . . . a minute course change that was magnified into a miss by hundreds, even thousands of kilometers twenty-five AUs away.

Most of those impactors that survived the explosion missed their targets on Earth, Mars, and in the spaces in between, but there *were* exceptions.

A Turusch impactor, a twelve-kilogram projectile traveling at near-*c*, struck the Martian desert 2200 kilometers north of Aethiopis. Plunging through the atmosphere within a fraction of a second, the mass detonated within the Apsus Valley, liberating an immense flood of melted permafrost surging toward Elysium. The shock wave rippled through the planet's crust, encountered the deeply anchored cable of the Aethiopian space elevator, and sent a crack-the-whip surge of energy up the ribbon.

Not even the super-tough nanocarbon buckyweave of the elevator's ground-to-space tether was strong enough to contain and carry that much energy. The cable parted some six thousand kilometers above the surface. The upper part of the cable, anchored in space by a small asteroid, was suddenly released from the planet's hold. With the anchor moving much faster than the velocity required to keep it in orbit at that altitude, when the tether snapped it took a tangential path outbound, dragging with it some millions of tons of interconnected factories, habs, and shipyards located at the cable's 17,000-kilometer level. More than eight thousand people lived and worked in those facilities, mostly naval personnel or technicians with the Mars terraforming project.

A few were still alive when SAR craft caught up with the free-flying space elevator fragment days later.

The six thousand kilometers of buckyweave tether still connected to the Martian surface began to fall. Most burned up in the planet's atmosphere, which fortunately was much thicker now than it had been at the beginning of the terraforming project. What got through, however, added to the destruction on the surface, where some hundreds of domes had cracked or been smashed by the initial shock wave, where tens of thousands of workers were killed when their pressurized habs vented to space, where entire colony domes were overwhelmed by planetquake, by shock wave, by flood, and erased from the Martian surface.

The entire planet would shudder, quake, and in one scientist's description "ring like a bell" for years after the impact.

Another impactor skimmed past the sun, striking Earth on her morning side, coming down in the Atlantic Ocean thirty-five hundred kilometers off the coast of North America. The effects were less severe than on Mars, for the projectile's passage within a few million kilometers of the sun had tunneled through the star's photosphere, slowing it somewhat, vaporizing much of the in-falling one-kilo mass, heating the remnant to molten and deformed plasticity. Ten minutes later, the mass struck Earth's atmosphere and exploded.

The shock wave and the fragments that made it all the way through the atmosphere generated a savage tsunami, a wall of water rippling out across the ocean. Minutes later, the tidal wave surged into shallow water, rearing to a hundred meters in height as it was funneled up the narrow bottleneck of old New York Harbor.

Old Manhattan was all but demolished, the crumbling ruins of buildings smashed and battered, like sandcastles caught by an incoming surge across a beach. Only slightly weakened, the wave slammed north into the New City, toppling the kilometer-high tower of the Columbia Arcology. The strike killed perhaps seventy thousand people for whom, until that instant, the war with the Turusch had been a dim and far-off affair, something mentioned in news downloads and special reports from the Authority . . . reports that most citizens ignored or shrugged off as of no consequence.

Elsewhere, the wave caused unimaginable devastation all along the continent's eastern shoreline.

Exact casualty figures were never compiled, but the number of dead was certainly in the tens of millions. The same out-rushing ripple struck the coast of Africa, the Atlantic shore of Europe, the nearly submerged islands of the Caribbean, and the coastline of South America, and millions more perished.

Bad as the catastrophe was, casualties and damage might have been much worse. With exceptions such as new New York, most of the urban centers that had been built during the exodus from the world's ocean shorelines over the past few centuries had been well inland. Rising sea levels had created a kind of buffer zone around the perimeter of each continent, largely uninhabited stretches of marsh and swamp, of shallow water and estuary.

Even so, millions died.

Potentially worse than the tidal waves were the storms that followed the impactor's wake, as super-heated air in Earth's upper atmosphere blasted out in all directions at supersonic speed, triggering a vast swirl of low pressure that swiftly collapsed into a super-hurricane. Storm winds of hundreds of kilometers per hour whipped seas already set in motion by tidal waves into white froth; the storm approached the mainland over the shallows that once had been Florida and blasted its way inland, moving first north, then curving with the mountains and the planet's coriolis forces to the northeast, pounding and booming up the already battered coast. After inundating Maine and Nova Scotia, it curved back out to sea . . . but by that time had taken on a life of its own, a hurricane swirl of clouds as large as the North Atlantic, a semi-permanent storm like Jupiter's centuries-old Red Spot slowly circling from North America to western Europe to Western Africa to the Caribbean and back to North America once more.

The storm would persist for months, until lasers fired from orbit were used to heat the stratosphere and create high-pressure systems that contained, then gradually dissipated the storm.

News downloads referred to the hurricane as the Starstorm, and predicted that the cloud disk would reflect so much of the sun's infalling light and warmth that it would trigger a new ice age. Winters were cooler for the next five years, but with the Starstorm's end, the climate returned to what *currently* was normal for the planet.

Other strikes across the Inner System were smaller in scale, less devastating. An impactor massing several hundred kilograms struck a cluster of manufactories anchored at SupraKenya. Thousands were killed, and other structures anchored nearby suffered significant damage, but the elevator, as some feared, did not fall, and the calamity of Aethiopis was not repeated on Earth. The bulk of the impactor, fortunately, missed the Earth.

At Phobia, the Confederation destroyer *Emmons* had been in spacedock, preparing for boost to join the rest of the fleet, when an impactor struck the dock facility. The *Emmons*, the facility gantry, and perhaps eight hundred naval and civilian personnel were instantly vaporized, and thousands more were killed as fragments from the disaster slashed through the delicate web of habs and crew modules in Mars synch-orbit . . . including Mars Fleet CIC.

Among the dead were Admiral Henderson and one of his senior aides, Rear Admiral Karyn Mendelson, killed when the base command hub was torn open and its atmosphere vented into space.

The near-c impactors flashed across the Inner System over the course of some minutes, and then were gone, vanished into the outer depths. Hours and even days later, however, the Inner System was bombarded again by the in-falling debris of blasted and shattered spacecraft, both Turusch and human.

A robotic nitrogen freighter, on the long, curved, in-falling trajectory from Triton to Mars, was struck by what was probably a large piece of a Confederation fighter—ironically, later identified as Lieutenant Robert Hauser's ship from VFA-31, the Impactors. The fragment struck with a relative velocity of nearly 90 kilometers per second. The freighter and its cargo were a total loss.

Two emergency-rescue team members were killed at Schiaparelli, on Mars, when a five-kilogram fragment that might have been from a Turusch warship struck their crawler on the south rim of the crater. They'd been trying to get to a terraforming team trapped when the Aethiopis impactor strike had overturned their pressure dome.

The Tsiolkovsky Observatory was damaged and three astronomers killed when fragments scattered across the far side of Earth's moon. Three of the ships waiting at the muster point between Earth and Mars took damage from high-velocity meteors—likely fragments from the battle.

The dazed human defenders began taking stock. On the one side, the invaders had lost forty ships, a hundred fighters, perhaps several tens of thousands of their military personnel. On the other, the humans had lost a handful of fighters . . . and perhaps sixty million people—most killed by the tidal waves on Earth.

The defense of Earth, it seemed, had not been so one-sided after all.

Landing Bay One
TC/USNA CVS America
Outer System, Sol System
2105 hours, TFT

"Lieutenant Gray! Lieutenant Gray! Over here! Look over here, please!"

Gray stepped onto the deck, startled by the crowd. Close by were his squadron mates, pounding him and one another on the back, cheering, even singing. Farther out, though, there were civilians . . . news media personnel wearing the high-tech headgear that turned their heads into living high-definition cameras and recorders.

Where the hell had they come from? They must have been on the *America* when she boosted clear of Mars early that morning, before her seventeen-hour run to the edge of the system.

"Lieutenant Gray!" one of the reporters yelled, her voice shrill above the mob noise. "Your CO says you're a hero! What do you have to say about that?"

He turned his head slightly and caught the eye of Marissa Allyn. Presumably she was the "CO" in question. She just grinned at him, then gave him a jaunty thumbs-up.

Gray shrugged, and shook his head. "I'm not a hero," he said. "The heroes are the ones that fought it out toe to toe with the Turusch."

"The Turusch don't *have* toes, idiot," Lieutenant Tucker said, nudging him in the side.

"Lieutenant Gray!" another called. "Your records say you're from Old Manhattan. Are you aware Old Manhattan got washed away by a tidal wave?"

The news had only just reached the *America*. News reports were still filtering in. Apparently, things were pretty bad back on Earth, in the Inner System.

"Lieutenant Gray! What do you think about the news that the Confederation Senate is going to talk to the Turusch about peace? . . .

"Lieutenant Gray! . . ."

He was too tired to answer, too tired to care. The next thing he knew, though, was that a dozen of his squadron mates—the kids of Green Squadron—had scooped him up and hoisted him to their shoulders, were chanting as they carried him toward the elevator down to the crew hab.

"Lieutenant Gray! . . ."

Good. If he didn't have to listen to any more nonsense questions, *good.*

Manhattan washed away? There was a pang there . . . a lingering grief.

But it didn't seem to matter any longer.

Koenig's Office
TC/USNA CVS America
Outer System, Sol System
2150 hours, TFT

"Admiral? The last of the fighters are being brought on board."

"Thank you. Tell Intel to stay off their backs for a little while, will you? The debriefs can wait until tomorrow. Our people deserve some downtime."

After what they've been through . . .

"Aye, aye, Admiral."

"What's our SAR status?"

"Both SAR squadrons are still on deep-search patrol. We've recovered and towed in five Starhawks. The pilots of two of them were picked up alive, will probably be okay."

"Good."

Two out of . . . how many? It wasn't enough.

"We've also recovered three Trash fighters with their crews alive . . . and are trying to communicate with the crew of one of their battleship asteroids. We may have as many as several thousand prisoners after this."

"Keep me informed."

"Yes, sir."

Koenig looked again at his desk display screen as he cut the mental connection. He wasn't particularly interested in

Turusch prisoners at the moment. He'd just learned that one of their hivel rounds had hit Phobia CIC, or a dockyard facility right next door. Reports filtering out from the Inner System were still fragmentary and maddeningly vague . . . but it sounded like much of the Phobos command staff had been killed.

Karyn . . .

He felt so damned fucking *helpless* out here, four light hours from Karyn, from the chaos rippling across the Inner System. The awful, sick irony was that he'd expected the *America* battlegroup to engage the enemy after the fighter strike softened it up but, in fact, and except for the launch of the carrier's fighter squadrons, they hadn't fired a shot. Lieutenant Gray's rather unorthodox use of sandcaster AMSOs had proven to be the tactical innovation that had changed near-certain defeat into victory.

But it has turned out to be a terribly, terribly *expensive* victory. The Navy, the Confederation, hell, all of humankind, would be recovering from the effects of that victory for a long time to come.

For the moment, at least, the invaders were gone. Force Alpha, the ships that had hit Triton, had turned around and fled once news of the defeat of Force Bravo had reached them, out across on the far edge of the solar system. Almost contemptuously, they had demolished the surface of Triton, giving it a thick but short-lived atmosphere of gaseous nitrogen, and erasing all traces of the human presence on the frigid surface. The nitrogen would freeze out as snow soon enough; the question was why they had done it. A show of force? A fit of pique?

How did you interpret the emotions of an entity so alien as the Turusch?

A battlefleet was on its way out to Neptune now, partly to secure the region and make sure the enemy was gone, partly to dispatch SAR vessels to look for the five High Guard ships lost out there. There'd been weak radio signals picked up hours ago, signals that suggested that the *Gallagher* might have survived. That would be excellent, if true, and if the survivors could be rescued. Those men and women were as much heroes as anyone in *America*'s fighter wing. They'd pulled that close flyby of the enemy fleet unarmed, knowing that they probably wouldn't survive.

And they'd transmitted everything they'd seen, information vital to the final battle all the way across on the other side of the solar system.

"Admiral? Dr. Wilkerson wishes to speak with you."

Koenig sighed as he opened the mental window. He would have to deal with the Turusch POWs after all.

"Yes, Doctor?"

"Excuse the interruption, Admiral. I just wanted to know how many more Turusch you were sending us."

"Unknown, Doctor. We may have a few thousand of them sitting in that battleship hulk out there."

"We have eighteen on board now," Wilkerson told him. "That's pushing our capacity here in the research lab."

"Don't worry, Dr. Wilkerson. I have a request on its way to Earth. They should have a high-acceleration transport out here within the next day or so. The prisoners will probably end up in a special facility on Luna."

"Ah, good."

"How's the communication project going so far?"

"Surprisingly well, Admiral. Our . . . guests *are* talking, and we *are* understanding them. Or at least we think we are."

"I understand." With the Turusch, it was difficult to tell, sometimes, whether you were getting a straight answer to a question or not. Even now, with the AI interrogators pulling third-level LG messages out of twinned Turusch sentences, the aliens' communications tended to be somewhat enigmatic. The xenopsych people hadn't yet been able to determine whether that was because they were playing it coy and mysterious, or simply because their psychology *was* genuinely alien. "Just try to keep them alive this time."

"Ah. Yes. We don't think that will be a problem now, Admiral. We've been talking to them about it. Apparently they require a community."

"How big of a community?"

"It seems to vary. We think they develop a need for others

close by just because of the internal dialogue, the separate brains talking to one another."

"I'd think that would just mean they could never be alone."

"Maybe. But they tend to form close pair bonds, two individuals who identify with one another so closely they share the same name, the same job, identify with one another very strongly. They always have a crowd around them . . . to the point that their philosophy seems to be the more, the merrier. Those first two—Falling Droplet—they . . . it . . ." He shook his head in frustration. "*Whatever* the damned pronoun should be. The two organisms apparently died of loneliness."

"I thought they stabbed each other."

"Used their caudal probosci to inject one another with digestive juices, actually. But suicide, yes. Whether it was a mutual suicide by two individuals or a single suicide is a very interesting question. We don't understand their psychology yet, but we think we're seeing all the earmarks of profound depression brought on by separation anxiety."

"But that won't happen again?"

"Not with eighteen of them. Funny thing. When you talk to one, they all get to buzzing and humming in the background . . . and it's like the one you're talking to gets smarter and smarter, quicker, more reactive. They really do have a multiple mind, a gestalt, one that probably works on several levels."

"Well, keep me informed, Doctor." He thought of something else. "Oh. Any reaction when you're questioned them about Alphekka?"

"No, sir. The fact of it is . . . we don't share a common mapping system, a common set of coordinates. We don't know what they call Alphekka, and they wouldn't know what we meant by that name. We're hoping to teach them enough astronomy that we can find the right way to ask the question."

"Well, it was probably too much to expect an answer immediately. Like I said, keep me informed. And good luck with the project."

"Thank you, Admiral."

The window closed, and Koenig was alone with his thoughts.

He would be talking to the Military Directorate about Crown Arrow soon—as soon as the battlegroup returned to Mars. The one thing Koenig knew beyond any shadow of a doubt was that the Confederation had to strike back, and strike hard. If they didn't, the Turusch would be back, this time with an even larger force.

The only way to stop that from happening that Koenig could see was to assemble a large and powerful strike force and take the war to the enemy. Alphekka. That had to be the key.

And perhaps some of the prisoners would be able to add to the Confederation's understanding of the strategic picture. Who were the Sh'daar? What was it they feared about human technology, and why?

Why were they determined to keep humankind from following their current technological path?

Already, Koenig was mustering his arguments. His next battle, he knew, would not be one of starships and nuclear warheads. It would be the far harder war, the sort of battle he detested, a political war fought with members of his own species.

Battles with alien empires he could understand. It was his own people, and, most especially, the *politicians* that left him wondering if humanity could even hope to survive.

Pilots' Lounge
TC/USNA CVS America
Outer System, Sol System
2214 hours, TFT

"Hey, Collins," Gray said. "I'm glad you made it."

The woman looked through him, stared past him as though he wasn't even there, then coldly brushed past on her way out the compartment door. Gray shrugged at the snub. She blamed him still, somehow, for Spaas' death . . . or for his not being there when Spaas had been killed out at Eta Boötis. He understood that. With luck, the reorganization of the *America*'s strike fighter squadrons would end with him and Collins in different squadrons, and they wouldn't have to deal with each other at all. And that would suit Gray just fine.

Despite her bitterness, his prestige within the carrier fighter wing, he had to admit, had gone up considerably since the Defense of Earth, as the reporters were calling the battle now.

He was still a bit in shock by the reception down up in the landing bay, the reporters, the shouted questions. There was even talk of a formal interview later. So far, he'd been able to push that back into the background, to put it off for another day or two. Damn it, he was *tired* after the long trip out from Oceana, after the battle, after the recovery on board the *America*.

And as for his squadron mates . . .

Not a word about him being a Prim or a squattie, not a word about his not fitting in. And not a word, he was happy to realize, about his not being on flight-approved status.

Even more to the point . . . he now felt like he *belonged*.

He still wasn't entirely sure what he thought about that. If what they'd said about Old Manhattan was true, he would be grieving when the realization finally hit him. There were rumors, even, that new New York had been hurt as well, that Morningside Heights and the Columbia Arcology were gone, along with so much else.

Angela . . .

But Earth and the people he'd left behind now felt very far away, felt like a part of another life, one lived long ago, separated from the now by light years and by years.

His life now was centered on board the Star Carrier *America*.

Koenig's Quarters
TC/USNA CVS America
Outer System, Sol System
2255 hours, TFT

"Admiral Koenig?"

"It's late, damn it." His personal AI could pick the

damnedest times to break into his thoughts with incoming communications, data, or unimportant details. He'd only just left his office, come down to his low-G quarters where his bed awaited him.

"I know. But it's fourteen fifty-five in Mecca, and I thought you'd want to know."

"Know what?"

"You've officially been declared a Grand Hero of the Islamic Theocracy. For your rescue of those civilians from Eta Boötis."

"Ah. I would imagine that saving the Earth had something to do with that. I'm more pleased by the decision of the Directorate."

"You should know, Admiral, that the Fleet's political liaison, John Quintanilla, is still trying to have that blocked . . . at least to have the Military Board reconsider its decision."

"Quintanilla is an asshole."

The AI, designed to provide information rather than to hold conversations, remained silent. "He *is* an asshole with power and with friends," Koenig added. "We'll have to watch our backs. But . . . I think we can discuss Mr. Quintanilla's shortcomings in the morning, don't you think?"

He was exhausted. He'd not slept since the alert had sounded, and he'd left Karyn's side for the ship . . . had that *only* been early this morning?

The memory gnawed at him, sharp and biting.

He began undressing, getting ready for bed.

"We *will* be going out there, again," he told his AI after a moment. "Arcturus. Alphekka. And as deep into the Beyond as we need to go to keep the Turusch from doing this again. They got entirely too close today."

"Twenty-nine astronomical units from Earth," the AI said. "Approximately."

"We got lucky. That young pilot, Lieutenant Gray. His idea was brilliant . . . and it almost didn't work. The AMSO warheads were triggered early by the Turusch impactor salvo. The sand clouds were so scattered by the time they hit the enemy fleet, it's a miracle they did any damage at all."

"Enough sand grains impacted enemy targets to destroy

shields and cause ablative damage," the AI said. "There was sufficient damage to render the enemy fleet vulnerable to conventional attack."

"Like I said. We got lucky."

"I suggest," the AI told him, "that you get some sleep. You will have a heavy agenda in the morning, both with fleet affairs and with conferences with Military Directorate personnel."

"Yes, Mother. Lights."

He fell asleep thinking about Karyn, and the savage tragedy of war.

He *would* take this war to the enemy. And soon.

Epilogue

Liberty Column
North American Periphery
0915 hours, local time

Trevor Gray sat once again upon the head of Lady Liberty. Just how the ancient icon had managed to survive the tidal wave coming up the Narrows of New York Harbor was still something of a minor mystery. Witnesses had said the wave had engulfed the statue, submerging her completely, before it had rolled on to smash across the vine-choked ruins of Old Manhattan. Likely, the geometry of the Narrows to the south had deflected the wave somewhat. Most of the unimaginable force of that wave had swept north across Brooklyn, and the green islands of the Manhattan Ruins.

Some of those islands still stood, stripped of their vegetation, looking naked and broken in the morning sun.

There was talk that they would be refurbishing Lady Liberty. They'd found her arm somewhere at the bottom of the harbor; there were rumors that the arm would at last be raised, that a nanocladding technique would be used to restore her coppery skin, to strengthen her, to rebuild her.

And the same rumors said that they would be rebuilding Old Manhattan as well.

The Turusch impactor had been a hell of an urban redevelopment program. But Gray was glad that people were at least talking again about rebuilding. To ignore the Periphery was to ignore one's own advancing illness. It was time that the Authority acknowledged the rights and the talents of *all* of its citizens.

With *America* back in port at SupraQuito, Gray had grabbed a precious couple of days ashore, had come back to this spot to do his grieving. So many people he'd known—his family in the Ruins—gone.

And Angela, too. There was no word on her, nothing definite, so there was still, he supposed, hope . . .

But he knew she was dead.

In fact, she'd been dead to him since her stroke, since the medtechs had tinkered with her brain. He knew that now. And, slowly, he was coming to *feel* it as well. The psych office had cleared him a week ago, officially put him back on flight status. Marissa Allyn had been working him like a dog ever since the Defense of Earth, using him as her deputy CAG to hammer out a new strike wing organizational chart . . . and to break in the newbies coming in each day from Oceana.

But it wouldn't be lasting much longer. Rumors were swirling through the fleet at faster-than-light speeds. Something called Operation Crown Arrow . . . a deep strike into Turusch space.

Good. He was ready. Ready to strike back at the bastards, ready to hit them, hit them *hard* wherever among the stars they tried to run.

A tone sounded in his mind. "All hands, now hear this, now hear this. This is a ship deployment update. Star Carrier *America* will be leaving space dock at 0700 hours tomorrow, shipboard time. You should be back on board and ready for space no later than two hours prior to debarkation."

He'd be up the space elevator tether and back on board long before that deadline.

Back home.

IAN DOUGLAS'S
MONUMENTAL SAGA
OF INTERGALACTIC WAR
THE INHERITANCE TRILOGY

STAR STRIKE: BOOK ONE
978-0-06-123858-1

Planet by planet, galaxy by galaxy, the inhabited universe has fallen to the alien Xul. Now only one obstacle stands between them and total domination: the warriors of a resilient human race the world-devourers nearly annihilated centuries ago.

GALACTIC CORPS: BOOK TWO
978-0-06-123862-8

In the year 2886, intelligence has located the gargantuan hidden homeworld of humankind's dedicated foe, the brutal Xul. The time has come for the courageous men and women of the 1st Marine Interstellar Expeditionary Force to strike the killing blow.

SEMPER HUMAN: BOOK THREE
978-0-06-116090-5

True terror looms at the edges of known reality. Humankind's eternal enemy, the Xul, approach wielding a weapon monstrous beyond imagining. If the Star Marines fail to eliminate their relentless xenophobic foe once and for all, the Great Annihilator will obliterate every last trace of human existence.

Visit www.AuthorTracker.com for exclusive
information on your favorite HarperCollins authors.

Available wherever books are sold or please call 1-800-331-3761 to order.

IDI 0609